Johan
Oster
023

making french chocolate

A prequel love story

A novel by O'Shan Waters

Nom De Plume is O'Shan Waters

Publisher Premiadia eLaunch LLC

Custom Cover Design by Germancreative - Lesia

Edited by Driss - EdIdawwg

Edited by Blessed-Kessed

Formatting by Hamza Khan

Print version through Lulu.com

Made in United States of America

ISBN 979-888896014-1

Acknowledgments

To my magnificent sister-girlfriend circle of remarkable women.

Diva Dolls:

Lady Songstress, CFO Onika, Duchess Vernise,
ROD Montinique, Sista Martine, Da Real Lola Peach

Authors:

Shiree McCarver & Pepper Pace

Southern Sweethearts:

Arkansas's Songbird & Momma Sue K.

Thank you for your continuous encouragement to fulfilling my dreams of writing powerful engaging stories. Without your loving support, I would not have made the leap from personal journal to published author and continued my dream of writing.

Merci, Mon Amie!

This book is dedicated to my
beloved grandparents
and all who believe in true love.

Information Share

Making French Chocolate is the second novel in The Moments Collection written by African American Author O'Shan Waters.

It is a prequel set long before her debut novel Moments With You takes place. Although part of the series collection, it is in a style of its own.

There are instances of terms in other languages for authenticity. Most are followed by a translation or an implied meaning that has been woven into the content for the reader. Making French Chocolate will have modern-day references mentioned for the realism of this fictional story. Creative persons and groups are respectfully credited for their individual works at time of mention as it flows within the storytelling experience.

This is a adult contemporary story which contains references to historical facts in America that are not always pleasant. Content will describe racial disparity, loathing, cruelty, and violence. Although, not promoted by the author, these behaviors are common and therefore necessary in telling a story about an African American family in the South. In addition, this story will depict childhood trauma, abuse, mental anguish, cultural customs, spiritual beliefs, and intense language and situations that may evoke strong feelings or memories; be advised.

MFC Playlist

This is a list of music in which you can feel many moments within the pages of Making French Chocolate. Some are referenced and others were used for mood inspiration when writing this story. Enhance your experience with a pre-listen on www.oshanwaters.com. Enjoy!

1. Lauren Wood: Fallen
2. Sam Cooke: Summertime
3. James Brown: Say It Loud- I'm Black and I'm Proud
4. Sam Cooke: A Change Is Gonna Come
5. Gloria Lasso: Etrangère au Paradis
6. Stylistics: Stop Look Listen
7. The Staple Singers: Let's Do It Again
8. The Dazz Band: Joystick
9. BeeGees: You Should Be Dancing
10. Atlantic Starr: Let's Get Closer
11. Johnny Mathis: Chances Are
12. Julio Iglesias: Moonlight Lady
13. Ludwig van Beethoven: Für Elise
14. Michael Jackson: Get on the Floor
15. S'en aller feat. Angèle: Swing
16. Dr. Saxlove A tribute to Bill Withers: Use Me
17. Billie English: I Love You

www.oshanwaters.com

Table of Contents

French Chocolate is typically not as sweet.

It is dark, bold, and thick with a subtle bitterness that delicately stimulates the soft palate with an extravagant explosion of rich and luxurious flavor.

When opposing strangers stumble into an unconventional association, the two become enlightened by the new friendship experience.

But secrets cannot always remain hidden, resulting in a shattered reality, branded wounds, and tragic consequences.

In moments of truth, courage, love, wisdom, and faith are required to make French Chocolate.

1 Moments After Midnight

The time was 12:04 a.m. when the private princess suite concierge rang to deliver a special package of flowers, an envelope, and a shoebox size square locked box.

He handed them to her and left. She read the calligraphy written message on the pastel yellow stationary envelope with the words, "Ma chère, please call my hotel room after you read these."

She opened the envelope and a key fell out onto the bed. Opening the delivered gift box surprised her and she broke out in a random laugh. Inside were two carat cognac and yellow diamond pear-shaped pendant necklace and matching earrings, along with two clothlike scrolls. One was tied with a white lace and the other with brown silk ribbons. She read the one with the white lace first, and it said:

"Love is patient and kind. Love is not jealous, it does not brag, does not get puffed up, does not behave indecently, does not look for its own interest, does not become provoked. It does not keep an account of the injury. It does not rejoice over unrighteousness but rejoices with truth. It bears all things, believes all things, hopes all things, endures all things. Love never fails." –1 Corinthians 13:4-7; part 8

Thinking over the words, she held it to her chest and smiled. Next, she opened and read the one tied with brown silk, and it said:

"On this day we must agree to strive to be the very best figurative sun and moon and heaven and earth. Everlasting companions always in unison, committed to truth, honesty, and love outlined in that scripture. Vibrant and powerful as complements to create necessary heating and cooling energy, supporting life as we shine only for each other. Being with one constant purpose to nourish one another and grow in love throughout our new life together. I make this commitment to you; will you make this commitment to me?"

It took her additional minutes to read both scrolls again out loud. Then she called his suite at his hotel.

Before he could speak, she simply said. "Oui." (Yes.)

His voice was low and sultry when he replied with, "C'est le jour de notre mariage, mon amour." (Tis our wedding day, my love.) Êtes-vous nerveuse?"

Getting back under the duvet she whispered, "Non. L'êtes-vous?"

He replied with a moan of no. There was no reason for him to be nervous.

"What you wrote, Philippe', it was beautiful. Will you write me more?" She said softly adjusting her head scarf that was a little too snug.

"Biensûr (Of course), I will always write my heart's lyrics to you. Ma chère, enjoy your morning. Do the spa things to relax as already planned. Nothing extra, you are already perfect for me. You can have a little wine but try not to drink any champagne. You know what happens."

He chuckled and she gasped before snickering. Then he said, "Meet me at the north of the Salle Belle Époque in front of the terrace windows facing the ocean. I'll have on a white tuxedo. Remember, it's 4:30 p.m. and that is not CP time either."

She heard him chuckling in the receiver.

"Ha-ha. Very funny. I'm never late! I am not Lorelle."

"Oh, that's right. Well, good, I'm marrying the correct twin.

Reposez-vous bien, ma chère."

"And you rest well, my sweet prince."

They hung up and went to sleep, dreaming of the day to come.

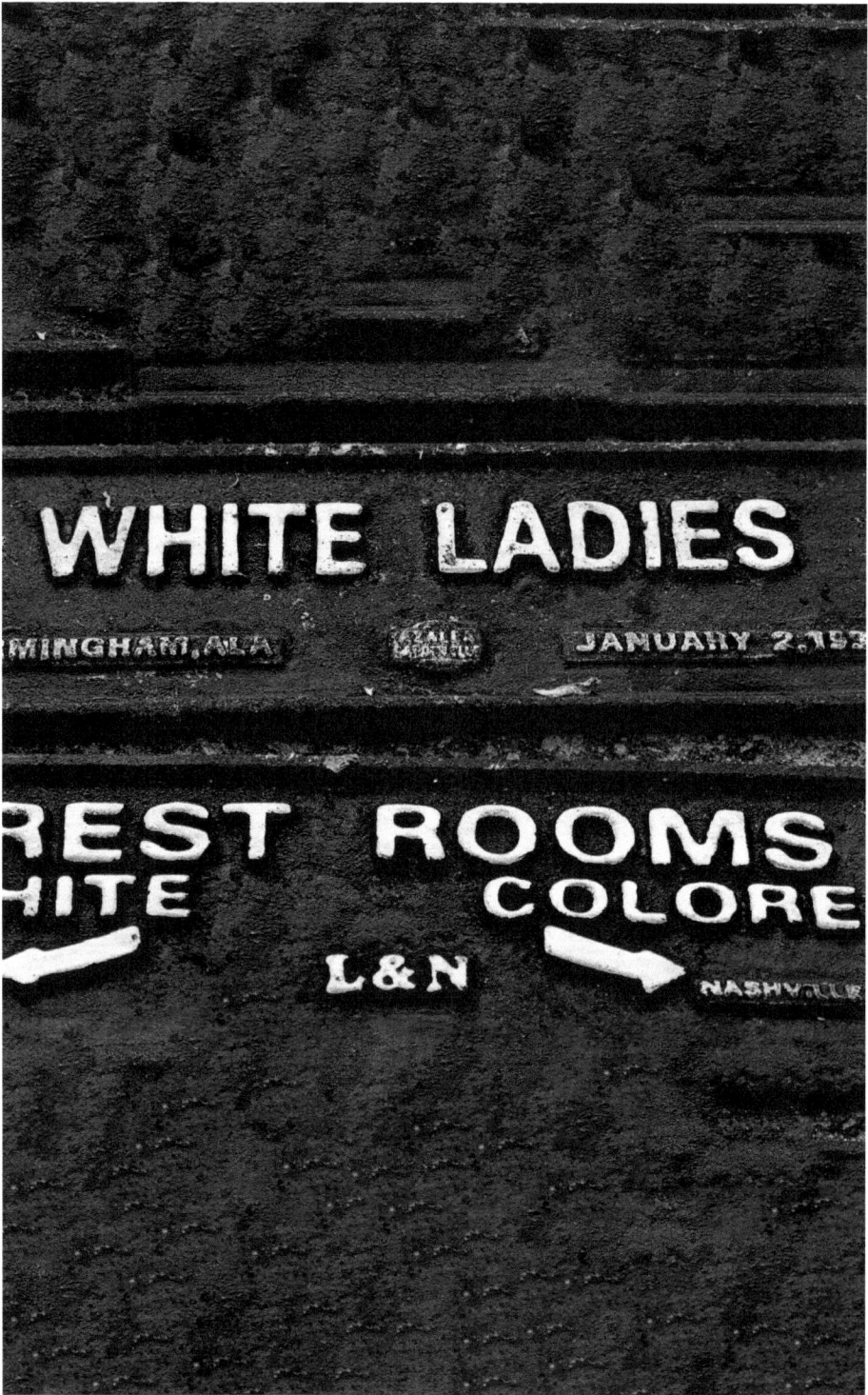

WHITE LADIES

MINGHAM, ALA.   JANUARY 2, 193

REST ROOMS
HITE   COLORE

L&N   NASHVILLE

2 Murry Family Tree

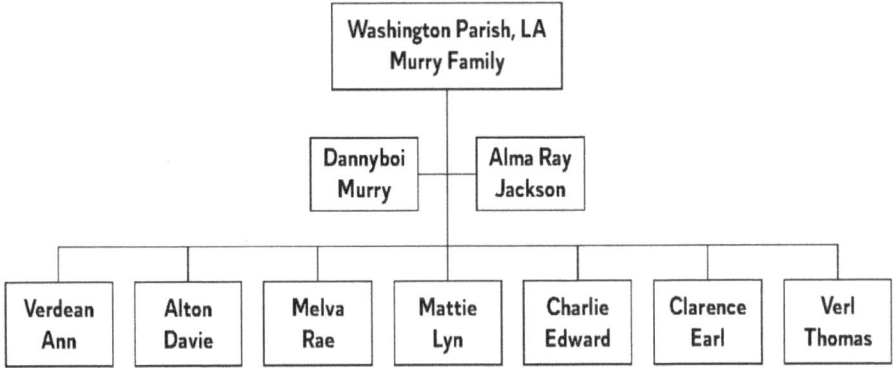

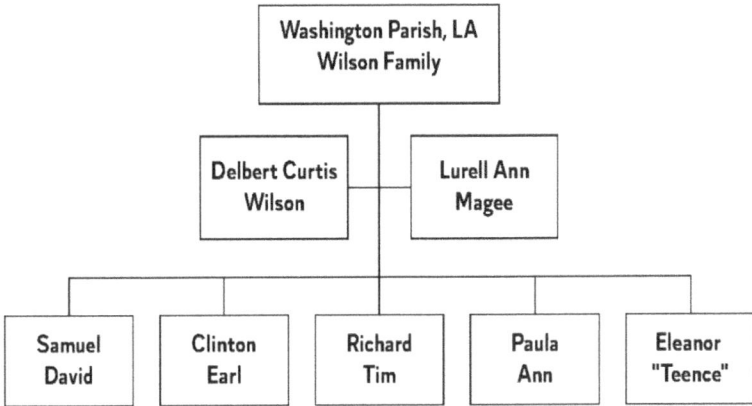

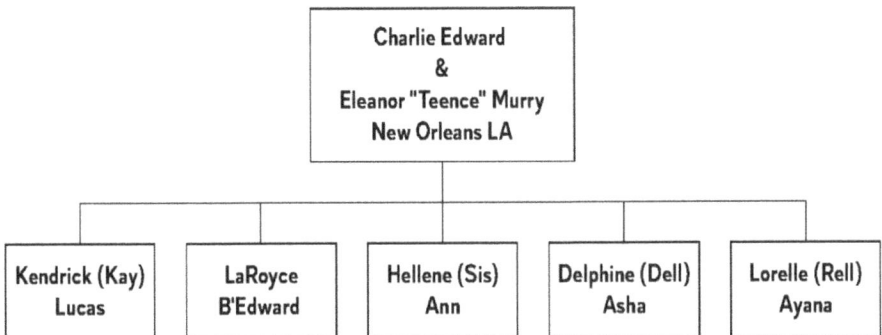

Washington Parish, LA Murry Family

- Dannyboi Murry
- Alma Ray Jackson

Children:
- Verdean Ann
- Alton Davie
- Melva Rae
- Mattie Lyn
- Charlie Edward
- Clarence Earl
- Verl Thomas

Washington Parish, LA Wilson Family

- Delbert Curtis Wilson
- Lurell Ann Magee

Children:
- Samuel David
- Clinton Earl
- Richard Tim
- Paula Ann
- Eleanor "Teence"

Charlie Edward & Eleanor "Teence" Murry New Orleans LA

Children:
- Kendrick (Kay) Lucas
- LaRoyce B'Edward
- Hellene (Sis) Ann
- Delphine (Dell) Asha
- Lorelle (Rell) Ayana

3 Trials of Being

Military veteran Charlie Edward Murry wanted to be a doctor or medical research scientist in hopes of developing new vaccines and treatment cures for his community. He was considered a kind of math and science genius in school and even later in the army. However, his future was uncertain due to living in Louisiana in the 1930's and 1940's when "Jim Crow" laws were in full swing.

From a very young age, he knew all too well the graphic lyrics from Billie Holiday's song "Strange Fruit". They were a daily reminder of life as a Black man, was to be one of constant fear. Still in school, he started thinking that serving his patriotic duty would help him escape some of the racism in Louisiana and open opportunities for medical education. It was an itch he had to scratch. So, Charlie, and his identical twin brother Clarence, lied about their age and joined up with their older cousins Felton Bickham, Clint Bell, and Wane Murry.

Before being shipped off to bootcamp, Charlie and his brother walked their schoolmate Paula Wilson home. His plan was to get her father's permission to marry. Paula and the Murry brothers were the same age and had known each other for several years. Although Paula Wilson was a stunning sixteen-year-old girl with the body of a movie star, the brothers had no romantic interest in their friend. It was common knowledge among the three that Clarence had an exclusive taste for exotic-looking girls in the French Quarter and Charlie was smitten with her younger sister Eleanor.

Once they got to the house, standing outside Charlie let his plan be known. Delbert Wilson was shocked. Walking back and forth across the porch, Delbert asked him three times if he was sure, it wasn't Paula he was asking for. Still in disbelief he finally called his youngest child outside.

"Teence, come out ch'here." Everybody called her "Teence" because that was her first word as a baby pointing to the sugar bowl.

Obeying her father, Eleanor came out wearing her sweater, long skirt, and flats, pulling on one of the two braids she had in her hair. "Yes, Diddy?"

"Charlie here come askin' ta marry ya. Wha-cha say 'bout dat?" He asked her while carving some wood with his pocketknife and watching closely to determine if he already had a bite of his fourteen-year-old little girl.

Eleanor started stomping her feet and made her feelings very clear. "Charlie Murry is ya crazy? I done told ya before. I'ma finish schoolin'. Why ya comin' round here askin' my Diddy now. Boy, I loves ya' but I say when I is done with my schoolin'."

"Aww honey. Look-a-here—"

She cut him off. "What I say, Charlie?!"

Charlie started sweating. Then he tried to explain he was leaving for the army, but she wasn't changing her mind. Delbert Wilson chuckled watching the begging and fussing between them. He sat back in his rocking chair much more relaxed figuring that based on her reaction; they had not been fooling around.

After about ten minutes, Delbert Wilson made a decision.

"She young ... But I tell ya what. If ya make it home, when she be ready, ya has my blessin'. Don't get cha self killed, Charlie Murry. Don't trust none dim crackers neither. No matter what, dim lyin' devils, a string ya up quick. Wat-cha self, ya hear."

He nodded with the permission given and the clear warning being understood. The reality that he was going to the army and leaving suddenly hit Eleanor and she stopped being angry. Saying goodbye to her beau was a tender moment and Delbert went inside the house to give them a minute alone.

Running into his arms with a sad face, she wrapped her arms around his thick waist and squeezed him. Then she started to cry looking up at his smooth round face the color of midnight.

"Charlie, I loves ya. Don't die. I can't be waitin' here and ya ass be dead. Please don't die."

Charlie kissed his sweetheart's forehead. "Ain't gone die, Teence. I'ma marry ya' soon as I gets home. Ya gonna wait?"

She nodded rapidly as his rough hands tenderly wiped her tears away.

After Charlie had been gone only a few weeks is when it happened. It was summertime and hot. Paula and Eleanor were on their way home from shopping a bit in town. When it started to rain, they cut through the woods and did the same with an open field to get home faster. The two were unaware that a small group of city boys had been sampling a batch of homemade hooch and secretly followed them. When she heard their far away howling and the truck kicking up dirt from the road, Paula instinctively helped her sister up a tree and then took off running in the opposite direction. She was in the nick of time hiding Eleanor because when she darted off into the open their truck was right on her tail trying to run her over. Hanging from the windows and yelling at her they kept charging faster into the field. She was quick jumping over a low fence of someone's plowed land.

Yelling for help, she zigged-zagged running across a mound of manure tossing the items from the store over her head. They never stopped racing behind her sprinting legs. She ran faster and faster even circling back trying to lose them. But they caught her after she fell.

Balancing herself on a large branch of the tree, her sister told her not to move or make a sound. Eleanor always obeyed her sister. She was her best friend and protected her no matter what. She couldn't hear anything but knew there was no one around to help them. All Eleanor could do was tearfully watch the three boys drag her sister to the back of their truck and take turns violating her.

Everyone knew Paula Wilson had big plans. She was going to attend school in California and become a social worker. She hated injustice and wanted equality for all people. She was going to be one of the first women in their family to go to college. Everyone was so proud of her. She was smart, kind, and beautiful. But on this day, under the shower of hot rain everything changed for Paula Ann Wilson and Eleanor.

It was a difficult delivery, but she did it. Paula Ann was exhausted but leaned up in her bed wanting her momma, Teence, or Mae Willa to hand her the baby, that moments earlier she felt was pulling her body apart.

"I wanna see him." She said barely able to take in enough air to speak.

Nobody moved to her request. Cleaning up the blood and things from the birth was the priority or the bedroom would smell something awful.

She called out again, "I wanna see him."

Her mother spoke, "He white as snow. Dis can't be no good … Dim white church folk take him. I'ma leave him at da door."

Covered in sweat, Paula exhaled heavily, sat up a bit and started yelling. "No! Don't ya dare. He my boy. No one cares for him but me… me and Teence. No! No, takin' him, no-where's! Ya hear me!"

Mae Willa, her older aunt, quickly rushed to her side and gave her water, saying, "Alright child, no one gonna take ya boy. Calm ya self. What cha gon name him?"

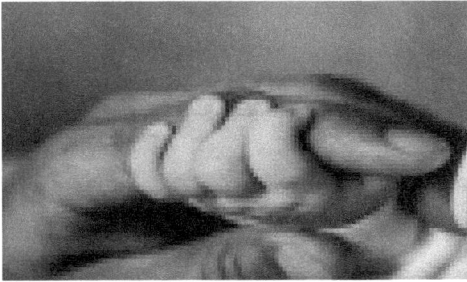

Teence picked up the wiggly crying little baby and made sure he was wrapped up tight. Then she brought him over to Paula as requested and said, "He cute. I loves him."

Paula smiled at her baby and then at her sister. "Kendrick … Kendrick Lucas. That be his name. Ya' right Teence. He be so cute. I loves him too. Dis be our baby, Teence. Ya' promise ya' help me raise 'em won't cha'?"

"For sho' tant nut-tin' to it!" She said with confidence in her grin.

Calming the cries from her newborn little one, she put him to her breast to suckle. In no time, he was content. Eleanor sat next to her sister as she fed her son. The two of them counted his fingers and toes then examined his long face and giggled while touching his small patch of light-brown hair. When the older women left the room, Paula held her sisters' hand and spoke.

"Ya member now, Kendrick Lucas be our baby. Don't ya never let momma alone with him. He ours. No matter what, ya swear right now for God, ta help me raise 'em. Ya swears it."

Fascinated by the now sleeping little bundle, Eleanor agreed without hesitating. "I swear. No worry. We be fine."

Later that night, while everyone was asleep, Paula left her baby securely folded in the arms of her little sister, saying, "Teence watch him fur me, I goin' ta da outhouse."

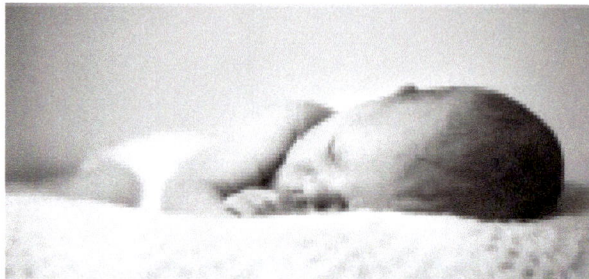

Just before sunrise, they found her lifeless body under a magnolia tree, with the bloody kitchen knife she had used in the grass.

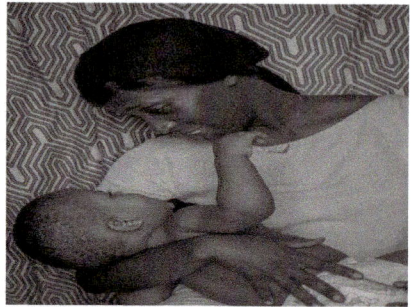

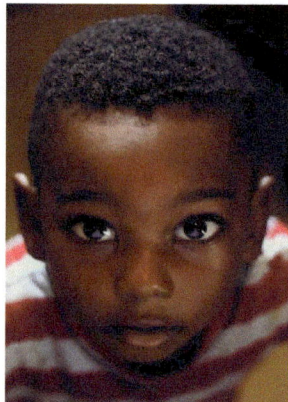

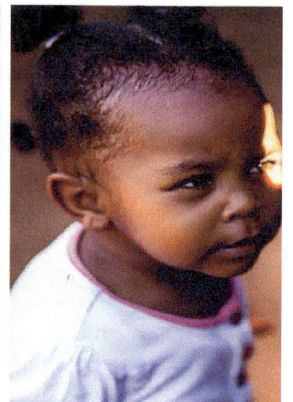

4 Hold on Tight

It had not been long after Charlie and Clarence Murry had come back from one war and were going to be sent off to another one. Before he left again, Charlie Murry married his sweetheart Eleanor Wilson in a small church in Franklinton, LA and in no time, she was pregnant with their first child, LaRoyce. The baby came while he was away in South Korea. Eleanor and their two boys Kendrick and LaRoyce were overjoyed with excitement when Charlie and Clarence returned home safely.

In a continued effort to leave behind the racial terror of the South, Clarence decided to move to California with his new wife Pearl, a bright skin Creole girl from Baton Rouge. However, Charlie stayed in Washington Parish with his beloved Eleanor, their adopted son Kendrick, and their son LaRoyce.

Initially Charlie thought he would get to use his superb math and science skills in the army but that was not what happened. When they weren't in active combat, the Murry brothers' job was to be janitors for the white officer clubs and training barracks. The closest Charlie got to something medical was when there was a need to clear out casualties from the mash unit to make room for incoming injured soldiers. Not only did the trauma of war leave a bitter scar on Charlie Murry, but the racial discrimination from whites had sometimes been crueler than being back at home. He felt no human kindness from anyone that wasn't Black. That included hearing racial slurs and being refused service in a country they were sent to help fight a war.

Then there was the constant reminder of what had happened to his friend Paula looking him in the face every day with his pale skin, light hair and green eyes calling him daddy. Although he had adopted Kendrick and treated him like his very own son, it was often just all too consuming. Charlie's hatred for White's, Korean's, Chinese, and Japanese, honestly anyone that was not Black or Native American seemed like a drop of acid on his skin. It grew with an unimaginable burning anger and pain that would always be felt.

It was the 1950s and just after the birth of their daughter Hellene Ann is when the Murry family moved to New Orleans. Charlie completed some additional education and worked in the new imaging service department of Covington Hospital. After years of working there in positions far below his very advanced skill level, he was promoted to supervisor, managing colored employees. This change aided in the family quickly moving out and far away from the Magnolia projects.

Seven years later in January, their twins Delphine and Lorelle were born. Charlie let Eleanor name them after her parents Delbert and Lurell who had died from pneumonia only four months before.

Having five children in the 1960s and 1970s proved to be more challenging than ever before. With the world going through rapid changes, being Black in America had its hardships. But there were civil rights movements taking things to another level of awareness for White America. This along with the bitter protests about the Vietnam War changed the hearts and minds of many people at the time. Racism was no longer in the dark and hidden by people under hooded sheets or badges. But it was vocal and, in your face, on national news and being protested by masses.

Not getting too caught up in the changing of the times, a determined hard-working Charlie Murry took the insults and unfair treat-ment year after year. Then one year a new boss from New York saw his exceptional work ethic and he was promoted into a newly created position called, junior director of the hospital imaging department.

While at the same time, Eleanor used her tenacity for reading and analytical research to begin her career working as an assistant in the New Orleans library.

The Murry family life was going well. But the basic rules never changed.

1. Don't trust anyone that doesn't look like you. Color lines are permanent.
2. Don't bring home any grades lower than the first letter of your middle name.
3. Don't tell family business.
4. Don't back down.
5. Keep your word.
6. Finish college, no exception.
7. Never do drugs.
8. Remember where you come from and the history of our people. Honor those before us with unity, strength, and excellence.

5 Storm Clouds

The Murry family was a strict and close one. But although he was loved as their oldest, Kendrick had an unpredictable and volatile temperament. It was thought that it was because he was distinctively different from everyone else, with no explanation caused him to be that way. All the Murry's had a dark coffee or ebony color complexion, and tight coils of full dark hair. Kendrick's lack of pigment, his light straight hair, and cold green-blue eyes made him a visual outsider. And that made him constantly depressed.

People in the community wouldn't dare speak about the rumors regarding his parentage; since the Murry brothers were boxers and it was well known, they protected each other. Not even in his family did anyone tell him the truth about his real mother, Paula Ann. Nor about what happened to her and how she died. Although he pestered them with questions, Eleanor would only insist he was her child that she had before she married Charlie.

Kendrick grew more distant, moved out of the home, and began to experiment with drugs. Weeks before turning twenty-six, he got the truth in a shocking revelation with the uncanny resemblance to the new attorney general, Budson 'Bud' Fuqua. Once he contacted his biological father, he learned a watered-down story of the truth. Bud could not deny the mirror image of his son. Although he did not officially bring Kendrick into his White family by giving him the name Fuqua, he privately accepted him. Because of Bud's position and legal connections, he also afforded him unsaid protection from his drug affiliation. These events further separated Kendrick from the Murry family and he began announcing to anyone who would listen that he was White.

In junior high school, Lorelle and Delphine proved to be very studious, respectful and goal oriented identical twins. Hellene had married Sam Dupree, a military man from St. Louis and had a cute chubby baby named little Sam. While Sam was away on an overseas military assignment, twenty-one-year-old Hellene and her baby lived at home with her parents and twin sisters. It was just easier that way.

With their parents working, Hellene had the daily chore to pick up her sisters from school and take care of the house. One Thursday afternoon, storm clouds were rolling in. As Hellene was leaving the house, little Sam had an explosion of diarrhea that oozed out of the plastic diaper pants and down his leg, up the back of his clothes and all over her arms, pants, and his car seat. "Damn!" She said, with her son simply laughing and reaching to play with the crap that was everywhere.

Lorelle and Delphine waited at the school for over thirty minutes for their sister, before deciding to walk to the bus stop to get home. As it started to drizzle, Lorelle recognized the dark green work truck of their older brother and waved him down. Delphine motioned to stop her since the strict rule was to only go with Hellene. The truck stopped at the corner.

"Rell, no we need to wait or catch the bus!"

"Come on it's raining." She said holding her backpack over her head and walking quickly to the curb.

Knowing they had been told numerous times to never be in company with their older brother, Kendrick, reluctantly, Delphine followed. Opening the door from the inside, Kendrick Murry chuckled at the sight of his sisters, while he swiped a large amount of Milky Way, Bounty, Maltesers, and Rolo candy wrappers from the brown vinyl seat. He said, "Y'all get in. What-cha doin' in da rain? Where be Sis? Ain't she suppose ta get y'all?"

Hopping in and out of the now pouring rainfall Lorelle expressed her gratitude.

"Hey now. We don't know where Hellene got to, but glad ya came this way. I can save my money." Lorelle said sliding over closer to him and helping Delphine inside. Tossing the backpacks to the floor and grabbing the magazines he had on the dashboard, they snuggled in as he pulled away.

"You ain't gonna speak girl?"

He glanced over at Delphine from under his baseball cap scrunching up his nose and poking out his thin lips from under his growing in mustache. His straight light brown hair was long on his neck and wiry. They had not seen him since last thanksgiving, when he came to dinner drunk with some light-skinned creole girl, he said it was his "lady friend". He had started some kind of ruckus and was escorted out the house. But now, his stocky 6'0 frame in his bell-bottom jeans and wide color casual shirt under his jean jacket, appeared to be in a good mood.

Delphine, giggled and smiled back before saying, "Thank ya, Kay."

He turned back to watch the road but smiled wide showing his bright white teeth that cost their parents a pretty penny to fix after his junior boxing career ended.

"I was gonna make ya walk if ya didn't speak."

Lorelle nudged him with her elbow and they both laughed as Delphine sucked air between her teeth and rolled her eyes.

"Y'all hungry? I can get ya sum-tin to eat at Chikin's place or somewhere." He said moving his head to see the road through the barely visible windshield of his truck. The sky was dark, and the rain was falling hard.

Delphine spoke up first. "No, I got homework— need to get home."

Lorelle followed up with, "I love Chikin's but yeah, we better get home."

The girls didn't notice that Kendrick had been driving in the opposite direction and pulled up to a corner store across from Liberty Park.

"I'll drop ya off but need ta make a stop. I'll get cha sum-tin, wait here." He said, swiftly turning off the engine and running into the store. The sky was dark from the storm clouds and the rain continued to pour down.

"Rell, we should've caught the bus. No tellin' what he be doin'. Ya know, Hellene gonna be mad."

"Bookworm, ya' homework ain't going nowhere. We be home soon."

Delphine grinned at Lorelle flipping through the summer issue of Jet-The Weekly Negro News magazine with Freda Payne in a multi-colored one-piece bathing suit on the cover.

Lorelle announced, "I wanna look like that when I get old." She tilted her hand to share the magazine. Delphine started laughing. "Ya' best stop eating all dim biscuits."

They laughed as Kendrick returned with two bottles of Coke, a bag of BBQ Cheese Curls and Voodoo Chips. He knew their favorites and handed them off with a grunted, "hmmp" getting back in the truck out of the rain.

"Thank ya'" and "merci," were expressed to him as he started up the truck and drove to the northern end of the park. Turning off the car, he took the keys and got out, saying, "Stay put ya' hear."

Munching they nodded not really listening. He locked them in and rushed out in the rain. It wasn't long before the windows were foggy from their constant chatter about the school day and the deliciousness of their favorite snacks. The rain outside was heavy and sounded like constant downpour of pebbles hitting the truck. Then a sound of pop …and then another pop. The girls weren't positive, but it didn't sound right.

"Dell, what was that?"

"Gunshot but maybe … maybe not."

Lorelle started to wipe the windshield with her hand to see if she could see Kendrick. Delphine did the same to the side windows but neither of them could see anything but constant water covering the windows.

Then a loud bang and the truck shook. The girls screamed from the sound and movement. Seconds later they saw figures outside of the driver side window. Shadows only but definite movement of two people maybe three. The driver side door opened; the girls jumped holding on to each other. It was Kendrick. He fell forward over the seat. His nose was bleeding and the tip of it was covered in what looked like the sugar from beignets.

Scared, they said nothing, when a large black man with dark shades and long coat opened the door wider. He lowered his shades and stared at them then said, "Ya' holdin', Kay?" He said it tilting his head and smirking, while another black man holding an umbrella over his head, peaked inside the truck to see.

"Nah, dis not fer ya' man. Deez ma' sistas."

Kendrick said rushing to sit up, while he brushed away the white powder and blood from his nose. He leaned back and closed the truck door. The two men spoke outside the truck loudly but what was said couldn't be understood. A few minutes later Kendrick got hit again by another man that seemed to come from out of nowhere.

In just minutes, Kendrick got back into the truck and started it up. He was soaking wet and breathing heavy. There was a reddish-purple bruise under his right eye, but he said nothing.

Immediately Delphine shouted out a demand, "Kay, ya' take us home right now!"

Followed by Lorelle saying, "Yeah. Who them men? Are y'all right?" She reached up to touch his face and he smacked her hand away.

It was noticeable that his eyes were now glossed over, and not clear and happy like before. He licked his lips frequently after grabbing the half bottle of Coke from Lorelle's hand and guzzled it. In silence he drove to a place unfamiliar to the girls. As the clouds grew darker and the rain kept falling, he pulled into a large building garage.

Turning off the truck, he started talking but didn't look at them. "Ya needs ta do as I say. Don't be scared now just do wha' I tell ya."

"Kendrick, we wanna go home." "Take us home, please."

"Nah yet. I gotta do sum-tin. Just do like I say. It'll be alright. Don't scream or run. Be just a little longer than I thought. Get out. Stay close ta me."

The girls slid across the seat getting out of the driver side after Kendrick stood next to the open door. Three men in black with big afros got out of the burgundy Cadillac followed by a lean Asian woman with long straight black hair in a gray fur coat and boots. The girls held hands following behind their older brother into the building elevator and then a large office with blue lights. It had an odor like something odd. The girls covered their noses as they bravely walked with these adults. Coming to a room, they were directed to sit on a small brown couch and be quiet.

Kendrick with two of the men and the woman went into another room with etched glass walls and closed the door. The other large black man sat across from the girls in a chair with his arms folded in silence. The girls looked at each other and started to pray quietly like they had done when they were much younger and about to get into trouble. The man in all black smiled at them then spoke, stopping their pleas to God.

"Your brother owes a lot a money. He holdin' out. All he gotta do is pay. We know he got it. He's been getting greedy. But it his debt. He needs to prove his loyalty or Lady Tran won't trust him. I won't let nuttin' happen to y'all."

Delphine and Lorelle released each other and slightly relaxed because of his words and soft smile. They sat quietly and waited. As images moved about like shadows beyond the glass, loud yet muffled voices came from inside the office.

Delphine took a chance and spoke to the man, "Please, let us go home. We shouldn't of got no ride but we just wanna go home. Our sister be worried."

Lorelle nodded at him as he leaned forward to reply, "I make sure he take ya'll home, after he settle–"

At that moment, the door of the office opened, and Kendrick came out flustered and sweaty. He snatched the girls by the hands and walked down a long dark hallway. Two men followed but not the woman. He was walking fast. Too fast. Their feet seem to stumble over with each step. He moved so quickly. Then stopped at a closed door with a number 3 on it. He let go of Lorelle's hand and placed her there. Filled with terror she looked at her sister with widened eyes. Lorelle started to cry.

Delphine shouted, "Wait! Lorelle! Wha' cha doin?! Kay, let go! Stop!"

Kendrick kept walking faster and snatching at Delphine's hand as she tried to stay with her twin sister.

"Dell … Delphine?!"

Was her last word before the big man that was so kind before picked her up and went into the room closing the door as she screamed her sister's name.

Delphine swung and bit Kendrick's arm trying to get back to her sister, but he slapped her into submission before flinging her into another dark room and closing the door behind them.

6 Never Tell

Lorelle and Delphine quietly walked into the back door of their home. It was still dark from the clouds and raining but not too late. They were met at the door by a frantic Hellene with little Sam in her arms.

"I'm sorry. Dis boy had pooped everywhere. It was late but went to—"

She stopped talking mid-sentence. She put her son in the play pen and helped them get out of their soaked clothes. The girls said nothing. They were totally drenched from the short two block walk, where they had been dropped off. They made no eye contact and Hellene could sense something else was wrong.

Standing in the kitchen and being slowly undressed by their older sister, Lorelle started to softly sob. The pulling away of the wet bell-bottoms and patchwork tops pressed against the tenderness on their shoulders and arms. Unlike when they had left for school neither had on those white bras or their brief cotton panties with little pink flowers. Hellene gasped and started to shake as she saw their lack of underwear.

She swallowed hard before taking them to the bathroom. With tears rolling down her face, she stood them in the shower and washed them as gently as possible. Then she ran the tub filled with Epson salt and hot water and made them sit. The girls only whimpered as she silently cried caring for them.

While they sat still in the hot water, she checked on her son who was now fast asleep and then she made them hot lemon water with honey and rum and made them drink it. Sitting next to them on the toilet, she cleared her throat and spoke.

"Dis … dis here be my fault. I shouldn't been late pickin' y'all up. It's my fault not y'all. I love y'all but it's my fault this happened to ya'. I'm sorry. I'm so sorry. Please forgive me for not pickin' ya up on time."

As she spoke to them, Hellene burst out in a wave of emotions. Tears fell from Lorelle's face as she nodded to her sister. Delphine only staired into the water emotionless. Hellene cleared her throat and gave instruction.

"After ya tell me … ya never tell it … not ever again. What's done is done. It ain't gonna break ya'. Ya'll go on and be grand beautiful strong women. This here was just sum-tin bad but it done make you bad. Ya good, always have been, ya still good girls. Ya' hear? No body gonna label ya 'cuz what somebody done to ya. Tell me now, from da beginning; leave nothin' out. After don't cha' never think on it. I mean what I say. No more thinkin'. Ya' hear?"

Trembling the girls nodded.

"Twins, we gonna get with uncle Verl, Shuga, lil Phil and LaRoyce, and learn us how to shoot and box. Nothin' like this gonna ever happen again … I swear it won't. Ya' hear?"

Again, they nodded in agreement.

Lorelle talked first and told the story. Shocked, Hellene got on the floor and held on to her sister as she cried reliving her terrifying one hundred and twenty minutes with Kendrick and his drug-dealing friends.

"He squeezed my arms so I would stop fightin' and screamin'. He made me take off my underwear but put my clothes back on. He kissed my cheek said don't cry. I was so scared, but he said he… he ain't gonna hurt me. He didn't. He just hold me in da room 'till someone knocked on da door."

Delphine started screaming. Hellene quieted her with soft kisses to her forehead.

"Tell me Dell, did that be what happen to ya too?" Hellene said stroking her wet hair along her temples.

Delphine gasped and shook her head as blood rushed into the water from between her legs. Lorelle got out of the tub wrapping herself in a towel. Th en she rushed to get some menstrual pads from under the sink. Hellene held Delphine's face and met her lost eyes.

"Dell, it alright, I promise it be alright. Tell me, please, twin, tell me. I'ma fix it. I will. Tell me."

Delphine only spoke of a few things Kendrick had said with broken words between cries. The retelling of that alone turned the stomach of her sisters and brought them all to tears. The reality of the horrific trauma they had both been through was enough. But finding out that Kendrick was so high on drugs that he called himself a privileged white man, told Delphine to pretend she was his slave, and had endangered them was too much for Hellene to keep to herself. Although Delphine never said anything more, Hellene felt an ache in her gut that Kendrick had done something unforgivable. She knew at that moment exactly what she would do to get her justice. Hellene finished cleaning up her sisters, especially Delphine who had started her monthly cycle early just sitting in the water. She made them eat something and then put them to bed. This way their parents would have no questions when they came home from work. Hellene made herself the only one they were to come to if they needed to talk but they never did.

The next day they got up and went to school like normal and Hellene was never again delayed when picking them up.

It had been just a week later when Hellene met with their older brother, LaRoyce hours after he had returned home from working in Cleveland. They were alone in his kitchen when she gave him every detail of what happened. It didn't take long for the blood to rush over the dark chocolate brown of his face, and he grit his teeth before speaking.

"Are … will they be alright? Don't lie to me."

"Rell is. Dell, she … Royce, she won't tell it. Not even to me. But he messed with her. I'm sure of it." She said it trembling with tears falling as she tried to sip her coffee.

"Is that all? I wanna know it all. Leave nuttin out." He said calmly moving to connect with her eyes.

"She said he kept tellin' her, he ain't their brother. He is white. His daddy is white, so, he can do anything he want. He called her his slave, his house slave, she said. He's back on that stuff Royce, no telling what he was thinkin'. Momma and Diddy can't know it. Twins be alright. But momma and diddy, they done been to hell and back with him and his drugs and demons he carries inside about his momma. I don't know why he went searchin' for the truth about that. We ain't told him and now he hates us."

"I'ma need to see the twins. Bring 'em here after school. I need to take care of some things right now. But I need to make sure they okay and they know I'ma fix it 'cus I love them and I'm their only brother. It's my job to fix it."

She agreed.

Later that afternoon, Hellene picked up Lorelle and Delphine from school like clockwork. She had a sitter for little Sam, and she took them to LaRoyce's house. They both were withdrawn and tried forgetting but fell into his arms when he opened the door. LaRoyce was always more affectionate and held them tightly for a long time before speaking sternly and calmly.

"Twins, I'm your only brother. I love y'all very much. I'ma fix it. Ain't no body white or colored ever hurt my twins and get away with it. I mean what I say. I'ma fix it. Don't you think 'bout it no more. It not ya fault. It his. Ya' hear? I ain't never lied to ya. I ain't startin' now. Y'all stick together do good in school. Make me proud. Get to da gym and learn from uncle Verl how to protect ya self. Never let no man touch ya, if you don't want him too. I love y'all. Once I fix it—it's over ya hear?"

They nodded as he kissed their cheeks. He held Delphine a little longer and as he kissed her forehead he whispered, "I'ma fix it for ya, sweet Dell."

LaRoyce handed Hellene a large envelope and the keys to his house. Then armed with his shotgun, he left the house in his truck.

Not long after he began his search, LaRoyce found him at the Lafitte's Blacksmith Shop Bar sitting on a bar stool talking to a white woman he didn't recognize. Calmly LaRoyce approached Kendrick from behind.

"Kay, I need ya to step outside with me right now."

Kendrick smiled then finished his third drink and agreed without a word. Walking ahead of him LaRoyce went to his truck and loaded his rifle resting on the seat. Kendrick adjusted his jacket and stopped a few feet in front of LaRoyce's truck when he saw him pull out the rifle. Holding up his hands mockingly, he started to yell.

"Wha chu 'bout to do, boy? Do ya know who my daddy be? Sure, you do. Ere' body know my daddy is state attorney general Fuqua. Ha ha. Ya know'd I be a Fuqua. I look just like him. I do. Outa all them boys on top my ma it was him—left his seed. Y'all lied. We ain't brothers. I'm white, just like my daddy. Ya can't do nuttin to me."

A rage filled LaRoyce with a heat that could not be extinguished as he aimed his rifle. People on the streets around started shouting. Kendrick stopped yelling and coughed a bit as he recognized the anger in his brother's eyes and his calm steady hands pointing the shotgun at him. Kendrick lowered his hands and spoke with more seriousness.

"What's dis 'bout Royce? Hey man, what's goin' on? What? What I do?"

"Da twins, Kay … Delphine."

Kendrick's eyes grew large, and his mouth opened wide knowing what was coming. "Uhm … it ain't wha' cha … R-R-Royce …" He tried to explain but LaRoyce spoke and silenced him.

"You ain't no damn good, Kay. No matter how much we loved and cared, ya rotten just like ya damn daddy. Ya no better than them white bastards that raped ya momma. Ya the devil Kendrick, and I'ma send you straight back to hell."

They stood facing each other motionless for a few silent moments in the street like in some old western standoff. LaRoyce had no thoughts of his high-paying engineer job in Ohio. Nothing about Michelle Lawson, that curvy soul sister in Cleveland that he was one day going to marry.

He didn't even have any flashes of past years filled with joy or the childhood love of brothers. The only thing he thought about was justified vengeance. It was in his eyes and on his heart. A slight smile came over Kendrick's face right before LaRoyce blew his head off.

7 Fixed Not Broke

The trial was a quick one. There was no testimony of conflicting facts, nor any reason given as to why he committed such a crime. LaRoyce never spoke to anyone not even his court appointed attorney. Since Kendrick's biological father was the Louisiana State Attorney General, even if he had a defense plan, it wouldn't have mattered. The plea was guilty and that was that.

On December 20, 1976, LaRoyce B'Edward Murry was sentence to life in prison for the murder of his older brother, Kendrick Lucas Murry.

The Murry family's unwavering disdain and loathing for "them white folks" constantly ran through their blood already ingrained from the stories of lynchings and crop burnouts to the gang rape of Paula Wilson. But now, it took stronger root in their eyes and the community in which they lived because whites were considered the cause of the growing influx of poverty and drug access in Louisiana. An evil blamed for uncontrollably feeding the demons inside a very troubled Kendrick Murry.

It was further fueled just weeks after LaRoyce went off to prison with the premiere airing of a groundbreaking television mini-series.

The 1977 drama "Roots" aided in building Black pride and the strong foundation of the family. But it also pointed out for the world to see in living color the horrible truth of slavery in American history. A reality Charlie and Eleanor saw as an unchanged wickedness in those people. For them never trusting them and staying close to your own people was for safety, unity, and survival of the Black family. This was a law carved in stone.

❧

Like many things in this American family, certain secrets were never questioned or discussed. As the years passed nothing had changed. Not even after LaRoyce was dying from stomach cancer in a prison infirmary. He privately told his parents the reason he had taken the life of Kendrick. He didn't ask for forgiveness but simply wanted them to know that it was his duty to give his sisters justice. Knowing that if he didn't, Charlie would have and that would not have been the best thing for the family. The news of what happened was a devastating emotional shock for Charlie and Eleanor but the two didn't talk about it after their meeting with LaRoyce. They never said one word to anyone. LaRoyce died twenty-four hours later at 11:48 p.m. on December 24, 1980.

The envelope he had handed Hellene were legal documents he had arranged before he left the house to "fix it." LaRoyce Murry had left his plot of land in Franklinton, given to him by his grandfather, Delbert Murry, his three-bedroom home in New Orleans, and his automobiles to his twin sisters, Lorelle and Delphine in care of his sister Hellene. The two girls were the only beneficiaries listed on both of his established life insurance policies that he maintained payment on through his POA while in prison. Because his death was not caused while committing a crime, Lorelle received thirty-five percent and Delphine received sixty-five percent of the total $300,000 insurance payouts.

By the time of LaRoyce's death, Hellene had moved to Lafayette and remained there after her divorce from Sam Dupree. But the twins maintained a very close relationship with her, and she continued to be their biggest supporter and closest confidant.

Over time, the two young girls evolved to survive the trauma from their youth.

8 Dark Chocolate

Throughout the years, Charlie and Eleanor grew to become proud supporters of the Black middle class in New Orleans. They regularly contributed to community projects that built up low- income areas of the city and helped those in need. Occasionally, they participated in New Orleans festivals and galas but that wasn't a favorite thing. They preferred to have socials with their close friends and family.

Since the Murry family were known in their circle to host "funtastic" themed parties, their house was the happening spot to go to every few months. Getting an invitation was something no one would pass up, knowing it was going to be the best Friday or Saturday night of the month. The legendary parties where everyone dressed as characters from a designated 70s movie like: "Blacula," "Cooley High," "Car Wash," "Shaft," "Carmen Jones," "The Wiz," "The Bingo Long Traveling All-Stars & Motor Kings," or "Cleopatra Jones," overflowed with good soul music, laughter, and lots of food. There was no such thing as a potluck at their house. Just leave your contribution in the money jar in the kitchen and enjoy. There was always a variety to choose from like fried chicken, boudin balls, crawfish bread, fried fish, gumbo, jambalaya, seafood boils, shrimp po'boys, mac and cheese, greens, fried okra, green beans, potatoes, biscuits, creole cornbread, banana pudding, cakes, and pies and so much more, except strangely, there never seemed to be any salad.

Having close family and friends constantly around was part of the strategy to help the twins put the past behind them. They grew up loving Soul and R & B music, singing, dancing, and skating parties, playing bid whist, golf, 10,000 and spades, eating, laughing, and having a list of trusted Black folks to call on whenever in need.

In school, the girls were pretty popular, but their clique circle was small. It formed in middle school after a small group of Creole girls tried to pick a fight with them and two others one day. Delphine and Lorelle usually didn't throw hands but on this spring day they had heard enough name-calling and shut down the bullying. The twins and two other girls Lolli and Claudine chased the five long hair light-skinned girls onto the junior high school track field and went to town, pulling out hair and busting lips. Forever sealing the bond of sisterhood and making best friends. Both Lolli and Claudine were also from middle-class working families, and everyone quickly became close, even becoming extensions of their families as play daughters.

Within their circle of Black middle-class friends, the Upton and Mitchell families were also frequent guests at the Murry's parties. This meant young Terry Upton and AJ Mitchell were also present. So not only did the girls see them at school but their parents were all friends.

Terry and mixed raced AJ had given the Murry sisters and their best friends a code name in middle school, "the untouchables". It possibly could've been because the two boys had witnessed them clobber those bullying Creole girls. But they never said why. Just at school if the boys saw all four together, they would shout "Here come da untouchables!" Then one of the four girls would playfully slug both and all six would laugh. It was their fun inside joke.

Moving into their high school years, the twins did more growing and maturing as Lorelle and Delphine's personalities took on other characteristics. Delphine had withdrawn from the lively adventurous young girl to a strict and pessimistic one, focused solely on her educational studies to become a doctor.

While Lorelle was also studious, she was more optimistic and sometimes became distracted by what felt good. Which in her case was social drinking, partying, and being a notorious flirt. Nevertheless, their closeness remained even more apparent which is often what happens with identical twins that grow to become opposites.

Lorelle wore her hair permed straight and short. She wore some make up to enhance her round face and high cheekbones and liked to wear the latest fashions often proudly sporting her curvy size 12 in her cheerleading outfit. While Delphine's longer pressed or natural hair was usually in cornrow braids or pulled back in a bun. She didn't wear make up as much and her thicker shapely size 18 was always hidden under her overly conservative style of dress.

When Lorelle was practicing her cheers or clarinet, Delphine was in the kitchen perfecting her family secret recipes with her mother. The two were different in other ways. Delphine was the bossy, reserved, and controlled older twin by three whole minutes. But Lorelle utilized her baby of the family card often to be loud and tease or loosen up her sister to do something risky. They complemented each other as a balanced pair.

Lolli DeReuen, a dark-skinned Creole girl was closer to Lorelle as they were cheerleaders and played in the band. But Claudine, aka 'Dene' Saint-Claire, a brown skin girl with a Native American mother was all about the books like Delphine.

All four girls were 4.0 GPA students that regularly studied and had planned their life together.

Unknown to them, the friendly inside joke calling the four "The untouchables" had a whole new meaning in High School, after a cou-ple football players changed it to secretly mean they were all "tough to crack." Even though Lolli and Lorelle partied and liked to date, they were very selective and usually already taken. Of course, Delphine and Claudine were the true 'untouchables' because they didn't really date, especially guys that liked to do more than kiss. Which was just about all of them.

These intelligent driven young women were focused and made strategic plans to attend Tulane University together after graduation. But when Lorelle found out she was pregnant by her track star boyfriend Cedric Ricard, she fell behind in her studies. Although she quickly married and had another child, Lorelle worked extra hard to stay on track to becoming a lawyer. However, with two kids and a husband, she couldn't join Lolli, Dene, and Delphine with a full-time class schedule at the start of junior year, at Tulane.

During the first week of their junior year, Professor Alphonso Allen from Claudine and Delphine's Advance French Studies class introduced something new, and it immediately caught their attention.

9 Delacroix Family Tree

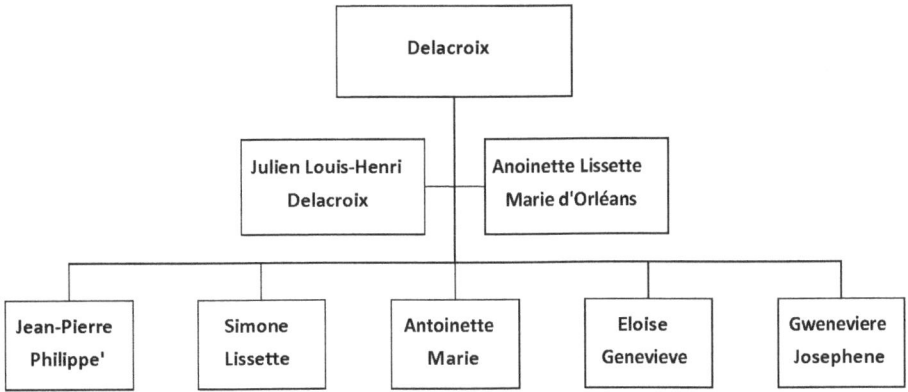

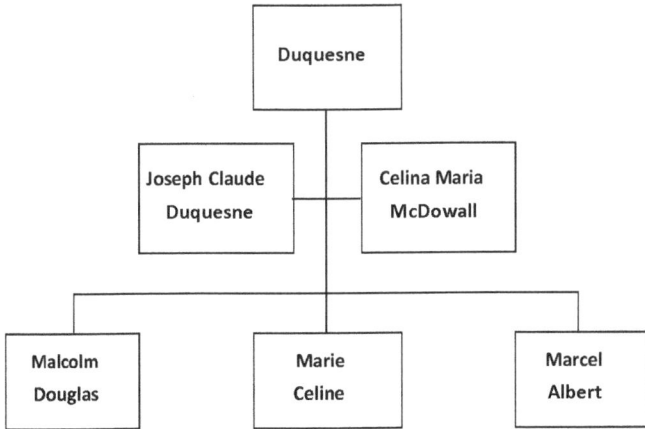

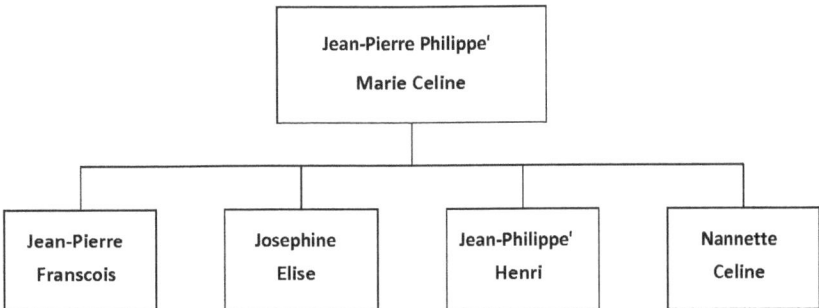

```
                    Delacroix

    Julien Louis-Henri        Anoinette Lissette
        Delacroix              Marie d'Orléans

Jean-Pierre    Simone    Antoinette    Eloise      Gweneviere
 Philippe'    Lissette      Marie     Genevieve    Josephene
```

```
                    Duquesne

    Joseph Claude            Celina Maria
      Duquesne                McDowall

    Malcolm          Marie           Marcel
    Douglas          Celine          Albert
```

```
              Jean-Pierre Philippe'
                  Marie Celine

Jean-Pierre   Josephine   Jean-Philippe'   Nannette
 Franscois      Elise         Henri         Celine
```

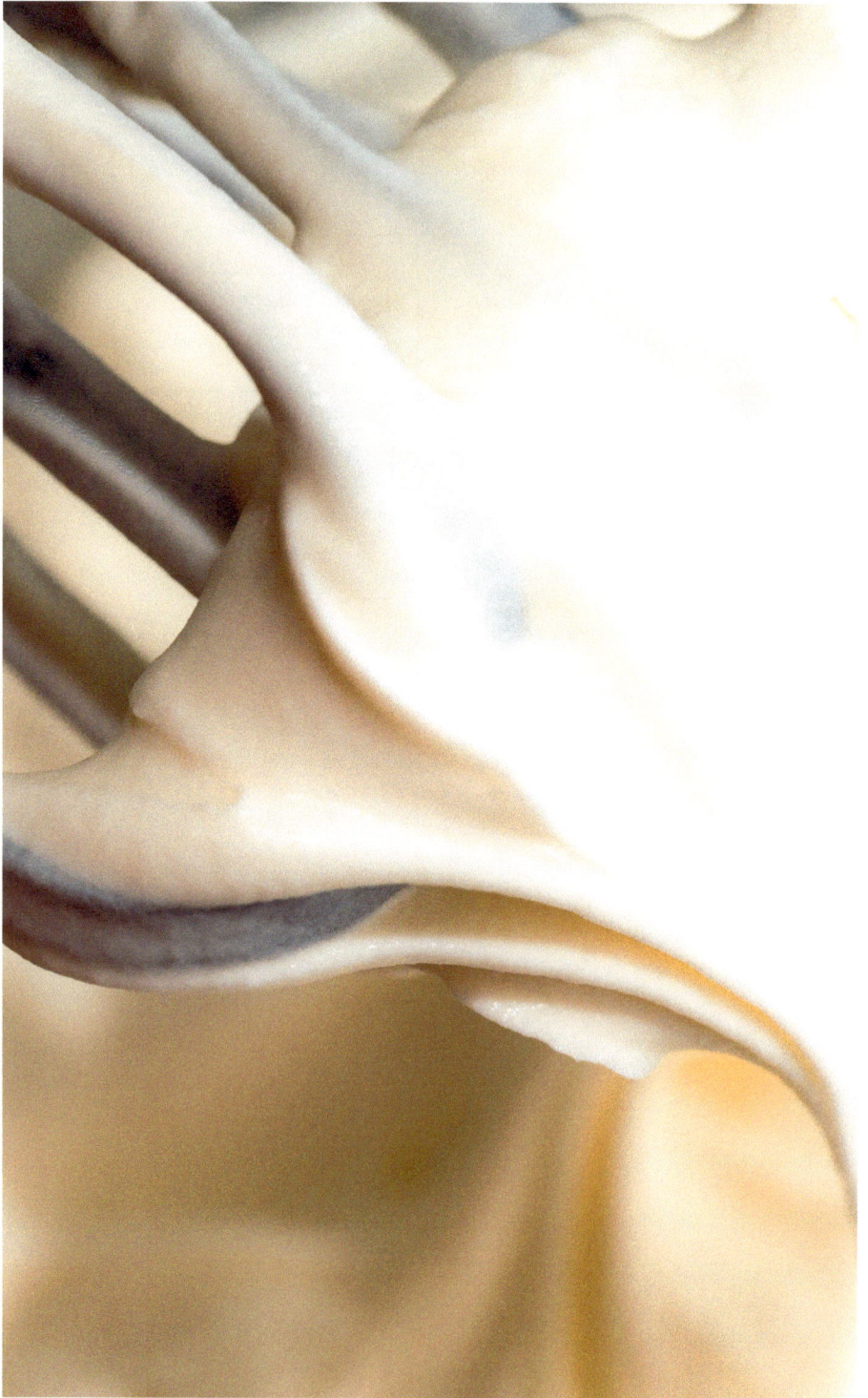

10 Sweet Crème

Professor Jean-Philippe' Henri Delacroix, who went by Philippe', was a distinguished, intellectual yet conservative member of French aristocracy. The almost 6'4 muscular man, was an active sportsman, saxophone player and poet. His baritone voice, chiseled features, light brown to blonde curly hair, full low beard and romantic charm made him deliciously irresistible.

He was not the first-born son, and therefore, Philippe' didn't have as many responsibilities to the family name, as his older brother Jean-Pierre François. However, being the grandson of Julien Louis-Henri, an influential wealthy government official and Duchess Antoinette Lissette Marie, a royal cousin from the House of d'Orleans, he did have noble expectations that historically he could not deviate. His profession was one. Early during his private school education, he was led to focus strictly on the only career options allowed, which were military officer, lawyer, or politician.

But Philippe' was a calculating young man. At the age of eleven, he reasoned with his grandfather Julien and father Jean that since his brother was the Delacroix heir and seven years older; already in the path of becoming a military officer, he proposed an alternative. Skillfully young Philippe' persuaded his very proper elders to make an exception, allowing him to pursue research and education as a career choice after military service. The men had no argument to decline the request as it had been proven thus far that Philippe' had a voracious appetite for history, arts, literature, philosophy and learning in general. Little did they know that the career alternative would give Philippe' much more freedom to travel and explore the world under the guise of a profession in higher education. Yes, he was that savvy even at that age.

Philippe' was also his grandmother, Celina Maria McDowall's favorite. It wasn't simply because he had her tall body frame, naturally blonde curls, and those striking deep blue eyes. Nor was it his fierce concentration on seeking to understand things with a meticulous eye for detail. But it was simply because he made her laugh. She would give him just about anything he asked. They had a special relationship, so much so that his charismatic grandmother was the only person that called him by his proper name of Jean (Zshjauon)-Philippe' and he didn't mind at all. Philippe' grew up hearing about wonderful stories from his mother's parents, Joseph Duquesne, a French Navy commander, and Celina, who was the daughter of a wealthy Scottish Lord and a debutante cousin to Josephine Buonaparte that owned land in several parts of the world. Learning about their travels and living in tropical places, adventures on the sea, delicious foods, and amazing animals had also affected young Philippe's determination to have a slightly different life with exploration and discovery that being a lawyer, a politician or a military officer could give him.

Philippe' and his younger sister Nannette were the shy and shadowing Delacroix children. The heir apparent Jean-Pierre François and his sister, Josephine Elise, just two years behind him had more eyes on them. It was his very good fortune that allowed the athletic and adventurous Philippe' to have brotherly bonds with childhood schoolmates, Andreas Moreau, a dark-haired inquisitive boy from a wealthy French political family; Tomas Durand, a flirtatious fair- skinned young man from a prominent French family; and Chevalier Ratliff, a jokester half-French and half-British boy with dark eyes and slight dimples, a caring demeanor, and handsome face that had a knack for getting women to take their clothes off. The young men did everything together, even during their military compulsory. They were truly all for one and one for all it seemed.

When one jumped, the others would either follow or wait on the sideline laughing. Most of the adventures and naughty behavior for the musketeers as they called themselves were not something they would ever tell anyone.

As all four spoke fluent British and American English and had completed extensive research studies on both cultures, they could navigate freely through many situations. Known to instantly analyze differences and similarities flawlessly, the four seamlessly adjusted to speaking with a group of foreigners without the slightest indication they were French. So, depending on any given situation, their throaty French accents could not even be detected unless they chose to relax their mouth and speak more naturally. These skills and many more came in handy growing up, since Philippe' was the researcher, Andreas was the first to try something dangerous, Tomas was the exit strategy planner, while Chevalier was the one to get the girls along with Philippe'.

Although cigarette smoking was a very common practice in France, they all tried it but decided it wasn't for them. Drinking on the other hand was their favorite thing to do. Well and sex, they did enjoy doing those two things at the same time.

At the age of fifteen when the four visited Tomas's relatives in Quebec, their favorite English word they used right away was a condom, or un préservatif in French. They were horny young men but not foolish. Andreas was the more experienced and liked to take risks. Whereas Philippe' was more cautious with a selective preference for lean and fair skin girls with long blonde hair and pouty lips. Tomas like foreign women more than French girls so this opened doors of opportunity for new discoveries for all. But Chevalier didn't dive in as often as the others. He was studying to be a physician and was very much aware of germs. Honestly, he had a creepy obsession with syphilis and shared the graphic details of what it did to the human body on a regular basis.

Philippe' and his musketeer brothers' young adult years were far below the radar of their traditional wealthy conservative families and their network of friends, which is probably why they are still living.

Old money as it is called, is always maintained, and circulated within the social constraints of other old money. It's a tradition to keep it that way so that property, privilege, and station remain at the highest level of retention. This meant that Philippe' would have an arranged marriage to someone with the same pedigree and level of financial security to sustain, secure or increase the value already established by the Delacroix family.

Her name was Angelique Dubois. She was the second daughter of a wealthy Belgian business tycoon and a French lady from a political family. The two had known this was the future planned for them, so when they met in school at age thirteen, they decided that they would do what was expected in their thirties. Agreeing to live life to the fullest, the two were often socially seen together to keep the spark alive for their families but neither had interest in fulfilling those obligations until it was absolutely necessary. He liked her and it was a delightful friendship with a person that equally wanted to explore life outside of the world to which they were born.

Right after their military service, the four men got more serious about their careers and it was necessary for Andreas, and Philippe' to part from Tomas and Chevalier for a time. The two were working and attending Sorbonne University as part of their educational doctorate program.

They had one year left and Philippe' had already completed cultural studies in England, Spain, Northern and Western Africa, and America but he had been laser focused on having more cultural diversity experience. Th is prompted him to apply for an exchange professorship in the United States as part of his Doctorate degree. He knew it would be an unforgettable opportunity to live and teach at a University in America. It could also expand his credentials for future teaching offers, give him additional research grants for literary projects he was outlining and make him one of the highest-ranking professors in the program. Now he had to convince Andreas to apply before the deadline of May 1, 1983.

"Andreas, they don't offer this often. We studied a lot in America but this time we will be working in French Studies along with completing our thesis, facilitating our own curriculum and the students will be reporting to us. I don't want to go alone. You need to do this with me." He said after taking a sip of his coffee.

Hesitating, Andreas moaned. Then he groaned before dipping a piece of his warm chocolate croissant into his creamy coffee and took a bite. Philippe' adjusted his seat outside the crowded café and lowered his reading glasses to get his attention. Then he said, "I will not let you marry my sister if you don't apply and do well on the interview to go with me."

"Merde! Why are you threatening me? Philippe' don't do that. Sweet Nannette is my dream. It's not even a university in places we have been. Not New York or California. It's Louisiana. I don't want to go there. Nobody goes there. We're not going to get laid when we're there! That's nine months, Philippe'. I know you can, but I can't, not nine months. No! ... And it's dirty in New Orleans. And Oh ... There are hurricanes and alligators!"

Philippe simply slid the application folder to him from across the table and continued to chuckle while he sipped his coffee. Andreas rolled his eyes at him but took the papers mumbling, "merde!"

11 Riptide - Tulane

At twenty-two years old, Delphine Asha Murry was a meticulous and organized student. She competed only with herself and strived to be at the top and win. Ranked in the top three percent of her class and ten percent of the university, Ms. Murry was known to regularly have overachievement goals and to push some professors past their limits with her questioning answers, theoretical counter moves, and complex theories. She had a conservative disposition and was very direct, almost too much in her communication style. Delphine lacked some of the common social pleasantries often displayed by young women in college.

Unlike her married identical twin sister, Lorelle, and their crazy girlfriend, Lolli, Delphine, and Claudine considered parties, men, and drinking to be distractions from their studies. Delphine didn't drink, unless it was a very special holiday meal, or she might have a small glass of sherry with her older sister Hellene. Delphine and her best friend Claudine never seriously dated, and hardly went out clubbin', except when the other two twisted their arms or badgered them to be their designated driver.

Although they didn't do everything together, the young women were as close as sardines in a can. Among them, it was common knowledge that Delphine was saving herself for marriage if she even decided to get married once she became a doctor. Lolli had a quick mind for complex mathematics. The sharp-tongued science major had the most dating experience, and she wasn't afraid to share her notes and give pointers. Claudine had dated some. Definitely more than Delphine who only liked to kiss but she was far from Lolli. But all three were painfully aware of Lorelle's example. Therefore, they were deliberately strategic to not follow in her footsteps.

Junior year started in the fall quarter of 1983 at Tulane University in New Orleans, home of the Riptide Pelican.

In the French Language courses something special was being offered this year. Two International Doctorate Fellow Program professors would aid in the education of culture, history, and literature. Professor Andreas Moreau was introduced to the French Language class and Professor Philippe' Delacroix was introduced to the Advanced French Studies (AFS) class.

In the AFS class, Professor Alphonso Allen explained, "These two professors are from Sorbonne Universite' completing their doctorate degrees. One will lead the advanced course and the other the non-advance. They will be facilitating the course learning in the fall, winter, and spring quarters. Also, the highest scoring students from the mid-term exam and assigned research paper would be given the opportunity to interview and be selected to learn first-hand French-Canadian dialects and culture on a six-day five-night trip."

Everyone was so excited to hear these plans. He continued, "At the end of the spring quarter, students from both courses scoring the highest on the final exam, the candidate interviews, and an early submitted culmination of their learning paper would be eligible to receive honored student awards and to attend school abroad. The awarded students would be able to apply to Sorbonne Université full-time for up to three quarters as an Advanced French studies exchange student."

Delphine's first impression of the two Professors was as expected. "Dang, why they couldn't get no Black professors? Okay, they are

White, and …" She said to Claudine in a low voice. Claudine laughed as Professor Allen provided more information about the AFS class they were sitting in and how Professor Delacroix would be adding his own educational strategies and activities to the course curriculum.

When Professor Delacroix took the podium and provided his background as a professor of French history, literature, language, and cultural studies with a master's in behavioral sciences, Delphine perked up to listen more attentively and really look at him. That was when she noticed he was very tall. He wore a stylish brown suit with a cream color shirt under his sweater vest. His shoes shined when he walked, and his hair was blonde with wavy curls. His beard was very low, and it seemed to be trimmed to perfection. His voice was deep, and when he occasionally spoke in English his accent almost disappeared.

As he continued speaking about students being set up for excellence with his diverse curriculum and his completing many years of extensive abroad research of history and cultural studies in several African Countries, Japan, and other states in America, she was impressed. Claudine was as well.

Delphine leaned in and said to her, "This is going to be more exciting than I thought." Claudine nodded just as Professor Delacroix said, "Excuse me, is there something you're saying that is more interesting? Please stand up and share with the class, Miss . . . Miss in the royal blue sweater." He was pointing at Delphine.

She proudly stood up in the class of over one-hundred students and looked at him dead in his face then said, "Ms. Murry. Professor, I was simply expressing to my friend that your resume is very impressive, and this course maybe even more exciting than anticipated. However, I'm sure even with all your credentials, you didn't get the understanding that in order to rise above a horrific four hundred years of history, and truly be successful, the need to stabilize your own community is necessary. Therefore, excellence is something developed and delivered from within not passed from one culture to another." She sat down but Philippe' motioned for her to stand up and she did.

Then he said, "Ms. Murry is your argument that you cannot learn excellence from me because I am French or because I'm White?" He paused for her to answer, as Professor Allen watched the intellectual showdown smirking behind his hand.

Delphine replied firmly, "Both."

Philippe' nodded poking out his lips as he moved next to the podium to lean on it facing her mid-way up in the crowd of eyes. Then he said, "Ms. Murry, it is unfortunate you think that way. In modern society, a segregated culture cannot advance beyond the restrictive limits of its own structural confines, and therefore would remain stagnant if not for perspectives, challenges, and innovation from others around them. I would like to pose a question to you, Ms. Murry. If you believe you can only learn excellence from within your own culture, why are you even taking this course?" He looked at her with an expression of seriousness. She exhaled heavily then spoke.

"Professor, learning about others is not the same as learning excellence. Being curious to expand one's understanding of other people from around the world that are not like oneself is a way to evolve and grow as a human being. For instance, the 1930s song protesting the genocide of Black people in America, "Strange Fruit" was written by Abel Meeropol, a Jewish man. However, the atrocities were not unknown to the community captured within its lyrics. Although the song became famous opening the eyes to many people, change did not begin to occur until a demand for it took place by the community being victimized. People can know about others, but awareness does not create excellence. Strength, unity, pride, power, courage, and actions are foundational elements for success and therefore, excellent people."

"Evolve and grow, you say. Yet in your argument, those things would not change a person to becoming excellent. Interesting. Let us see if you learn anything from this course, Ms. Murry. We can determine if your newly obtained knowledge has enhanced you enough to move you toward excellence or if the information is simply stored within an unused area of your brain. Then we will know for certain, which one of us is accurate." He gestured for her to sit down and continued with his original summary of information.

Delphine was instantly annoyed but maintained a calm exterior. However, Claudine could feel the angry heat coming off her body. She slipped Delphine a note that said:

"Girl, how ya gonna debate with the new professor on the first day? Dang."

She wrote back: "Just 'cuz he white and maybe smart, ya don't trust everythin' he say girl. Ya knows better. Besides he can't teach us how ta be proud, strong excellent Black people."

She wrote a reply: "Uh, Dell, it's French class. Leave your momma at home. By da way, ya lost da debate."

Delphine wrote a response: "Did I? I don't think it be over. We see what dis 'ere professor gonna teach me dat I can't read 'bout on my own. Hmp."

*Jambalaya Pasta...

...sage, Chicken, Shrimp, Tasso Ham...

...ons in a Creole Sauce with Fettuccine...

Crab and Shrimp Boil...$28

...und of Crab, Half Pound of Shrimp,

...oes, Corn, and Sausage in a Butter Sauce

Cioppino...$31

Fisherman's Stew of selected Seafood and

...matoes, Peppers and Spices over Linguini

Shrimp Scampi...$22

...imp sautéed with Fresh Herbs, Garlic,

...ts, Sun-Dried Tomatoes and Bell Pepper...

...th a creamy White Wine Sauce over Lin...

Linguini and Clams...$22

...pped Clams cooked in Garlic Butter

...reamy White Wine Sauce with Herl...

Louisiana Gumbo...$2...

From the Bayou...

Shrimp, Chicken, Tasso Ham a...

Andouille Sausage simmered...

Creole Spices, Onions and Pe...

Bouillabaisse...$2...

...Fresh Fish in a Light B...

...l Herbs se...

12 Sep - Dec

During the entire Fall quarter and most of the Winter, Delphine periodically questioned Professor Delacroix and a debate would result. Fortunately for her, his style was to allow space and grace for anyone to question, speak their truth or disagree with an alternative. She was not intending to be difficult, but she posed other perspectives to the case study or discussion points. This occasionally shed new light on the topic even for Professor Allen.

There was no doubt in Philippe's mind that she was very smart. He didn't feel as if she was challenging him, but he learned she was working out the complex angles of a data puzzle in her head when she asked a question. She had a look. Quickly, he realized she was a sponge for knowledge, similar to himself.

Since the French Professors were being hosted by a local wealthy Creole family in New Orleans, their tourist activities faded out after the first few weeks before the fall quarter began. A standard rule was to never socialize with students. Not your own or anyone else's. This was one the two didn't break. Fortunately, they had been learning about Louisiana's melting pot culture from the affluent Lermontaunt family, where they stayed. The two men had accepted several invitations to balls and parties connecting them to mingle with a variety of socialites and prominent people.

However, Andreas Moreau and Philippe' Delacroix, being comfortable interacting with the wealthy and the working class, enjoyed casual low-key things on their own. The two were made very aware of which Wards to stay far away from and they followed those rules to the letter.

New Orleans could be very dangerous, and they were not taking risks. Within those limitations, they did try out several recommended restaurants, and a few bars on their own or with other younger faculty staff. Philippe' often journaled about their good times meeting locals, the elite and enjoying the culture and food of the city.

One weekend they heard about a S.S. Skate party at a popular rink. Andreas convinced Philippe' to check it out. Both thought it would be ice skating, but upon arrival, they found out it wasn't. S.S. Skate meant Seventy's Soul Skate on roller-skates. After entering the adult party, they immediately noticed a lot of college students dressed in clothes from the 70s. In the sea of shades of brown, a few lighter people were spinning around the wood floor separated by carpeted barriers with a concession area and tables, a club deejay booth, mirrors, and disco lights.

Philippe' liked the song, "Zoom" by the Commodores that was playing when they entered but was a bit concerned it was too much of a college crowd. He said, "Andreas, who told you about this party? Everyone is dressed up."

Andreas moving his shoulders to the new song, The Spinners', "I'll Be Around," leaned closer to answer, "Professor Chambliss told me it was a big thing and it is! I didn't know it was like a disco. We look alright. We have on denim; we blend right in."

Philippe' looked at him with a side eye and said, "I am glad it is dark."

They decided to stay for a while. Grabbing snacks, they found a table close to a shoulder high barrier wall. Eating caramel popcorn and sipping a cold drink, the two people watched and enjoyed the music, as clusters of mostly brown bodies skate-danced around in a large circular direction in every kind of way. Backward, down low dipping, in groups doing choreographed moves, couples holding hands, and alone free style.

"Philippe', we should get skates. Hey, I know this song." Andreas shouted over the blasting music of Player's "Baby Come Back," then, he started singing. Philippe' smirked looking over at him chewing popcorn, he said, "I am not going out there. You can and get knocked down. Do you see how fast they are going? I am not holding your hand, either. No." He made it clear he wasn't risking it before he put more popcorn in his mouth. Andreas turned his body to face him, and said, "You don't want to couple skate with me, Philippe'?" He said playfully, batting his eyes at him. Philippe' tossed popcorn at him and the two laughed.

With the colored lights flashing and groovy soul music, the people watching for the late Saturday afternoon was pretty fun. As the slow songs continued with Switch's "I Call Your Name," in a flash, Philippe' thought he saw someone familiar, but he wasn't sure.

A few minutes into the next song, "Let's Do It Again" from The Staple Singers, Andreas was snapping his fingers, and said, "Oh, I like this music. Do it again. Yeah! We need to call those girls tonight." Philippe' tapping his foot and moving his head to the beat, nodded in the affirmative.

The music tempo sped up to "The Groove Line" from the group Heatwave and in a moment it happened again. Philippe' took a double take. He wasn't sure if he had seen a couple of women wearing black shiny pants and sparkling rainbow-colored tops skating by singing "Hoo, Hoo," that looked exactly alike ... *(Ms. Debate? No, can't be her. She is an uptight chick.)* He brushed it off.

When Andreas got up dancing to Kool and the Gang's "Lady's Night," on his way to the restroom, Philippe's eyes focused across the rink. That was when he noticed four women coming closer with their arms locked together. He watched their sexy hip bumps as they breezed by, but he didn't get a good look. Philippe' tried to navigate his eyes through the other skaters to see their faces, but he lost them in the crowd. Briefly, he wondered again but was interrupted by Andreas insisting on leaving to hang out with the blonde bombshells they had met at Senator Bland's party the week before. The two left to begin other types of fun.

<hr />

Old friends Terry and AJ had been in playful pursuit of two of the untouchables since they were all in school. Now popular college basketball players, Terrance (Terry) Upton, a 6'0 toffee brown, point guard and his buddy 6'5 power forward Alejandro (AJ) Mitchell with tan skin and pretty wavy black hair attended Xavier University. Attending a rival school and having different career paths didn't allow Terry and AJ to see their old classmates like they did growing up. Occasionally they had seen each other socially around New Orleans, but it usually had been just Lolli and Lorelle catching up with them.

However, at the S. S. Skate party Terry and AJ got a chance to really connect with the two they had always wanted as girlfriends. Delphine and Claudine even couple skated with them a few times. If ever they had seen one another, "See ya, when I see ya," was how their conversations ended.

Deciding to leave a little early, the four began removing their skates when the observation comments began from Lolli and Lorelle.

"Girl, I seen Terry tryin' ta hit on ya, wit his wingman talkin' ta Dene. He want ya Dell. He been sniffin' round ya forever. Why ya trippin'? Go out wit him."

"Stop it Lolli. He a player. I still see him pop lockin' like he ReRun, from What's Happening in Junior High. No, can do. We just friends."

"Dell he is cute, now. I loved his pretty smile ones them braces came off. I bet his kisses are bomb."

"Rell, shut up, or I'ma tell ya husband, what ya said. Ya know he never like them."

"Dene, why you so quiet? Ya gonna let the Black-Mexican get some tongue action? Or did ya already?"

"No! But he is fly." They all agreed, snickering, turning in their skates.

After leaving the S.S. Skate party, Lolli, Claudine, Lorelle and Delphine got to the restaurant close to around 8:30 p.m. They had been talking about getting Chickn's smothered pork chops dinner plate right after they left the rink. In a cozy booth eating, Lolli told her best girlfriends, "Dat was fun, we ain't gone skatin' in years."

They all nodded in agreement. Lorelle spoke up, "Since High School. Glad ya two come wit us this time, like we used ta do. Been like old times. Dell, I miss hangin' out wit cha. Lolli be messin' up da Murry dance moves." She began laughing as Lolli tossed a balled-up napkin across the table and hit her head. Delphine and Claudine chuckled. Delphine admitted, "Yeah, good ta get out but don't ask no more. Saturday be library day."

Lorelle frowned and tried to get support for more fun. "Dene, make her stop. Y'all come wit us one time a month. Okay?"

Claudine was eating and not trying to get in the middle of the tug of war that always happens between the wild party girls, Lolli and Lorelle, and the homebodies her, and Delphine. Shaking her head with her mouth full of food, she got most of it out of the way, and spoke, "Don't cha get me in dat. Ya know'd we study on Saturday. It be research. Be happy we come wit cha. Stop actin' greedy Rell. Damn. Ya got kids."

Lolli laughed as Lorelle began to plot. "Ya cows be makin' a sista be violent wit cha. Lolli we gonna have ta do sum-tin ta get 'em out da books ta come. Can ya feel it?" Lorelle looked over at her bestie, Lolli who continued laughing. The two plotters nodded and then gave each other high-fives over the table of food.

Delphine continued, "Look a here, we gotta get dem spots for da French Canada trip. So, don't be actin' up. We gotta study."

Delphine shared their end game goal reasons for the extra-long library visits and research study sessions. Lolli and Lorelle knew that was important to them and understood. The two looked at each other and in a nodding silent agreement, they made a mental note to get them out again in a few months.

Attending the 1983 Bayou Classic with a group of Tulane faculty, had really solidified the French Professors into the heartbeat of college life in New Orleans. Shouting and cheering with thousands of others, the two didn't care about who won. It was just fantastic to be there and watch. Both men played and loved European sports and liked American football among other things. Watching the rivalry football game at Caesars Superdome, hearing the music and the legendary battle of the bands performing wasn't something they could forget.

Later, while at the Napoleon House having a famous muffaletta sandwich and taking their first sip of the signature Pimm's Cup drink, Philippe' overheard what he thought was an argument. One voice sounded familiar. As he turned his head to quickly glance behind him, he recognized two of his students.

After weeks of being double teamed with nagging from Lolli and Lorelle, Claudine and Delphine finally went out with Terry and AJ. They connected Thanksgiving weekend at the Bayou classic game on November 26th. They had a friendly bet going and since the girls were cheering for Grambling State, who won, Terry and AJ were on the hook for the meal afterward.

As in the past, the four friends talked and had a good time together. But with the hype of the game, and finally being on a real date with Delphine, Terry was nervous. Dining in a crowded Napoleon House, Terry drank a little too much too fast. His frustration with Delphine's resisting his requests for more than friendship along with his alcohol consumption, unfortunately caused him to show his ass.

"Dell, why ya playin'? It been like five years asking, damn!" He said forcefully, while Claudine tried to swap his drink on the table for water. It didn't work.

"I don told ya, to stop askin'. Terry, we're here. Just enjoy this, okay?"

His voice got louder, and he started to point his finger at her. "Ya know how many girls wanna get with me. Dell ya freakin' smart but how you even gonna act so uppity. Ha-Ha. How ya be actin' all boojie when you a dark-skinned biggin'. I ain't never cared 'bout that but ya treatin' me like you too good, and I ain't shit!"

(Negro … Oh, no he didn't, say what I think he said.) Delphine took a few deep breaths. They had known each other since they were kids. She knew Terry was a little drunk but now she was angry. Claudine started squeezing AJ's hand as a signal to get control of his friend. But it was too late. The fire was lit. Claudine saw Delphine's face from across the table and knew it was coming. She thought, *(Oh, hell, we gonna get stuck with da check.)*

Releasing Claudine's hand under the table, AJ started mumbling in Spanish. Whatever he said Terry didn't get the clue because the next thing he said was wrong.

"Why am I sweatin' this girl. She don't know who I am. AJ, man, I told ya, I should've tried for Lorelle before Ced Ricard knocked her up and not her big snobby ass."

AJ interjected as Delphine slowly stood up with her neck twisting. "My man done had too much. Come on girl, calm down. Dell, we all friends."

Delphine put her hand on her hip, and said in a firm commanding tone, "You … Know … What …? Clearly, we're not friends. Since I'm such a big dark-skinned girl. Did you call me boojie? Is that what you said, Terry? You weren't thinkin' that when I secretly tutored you for two years in Honors English and Trig, so you could stay on the stupid basketball team and get them scholarships to Xavier, now did ya?"

AJ and Claudine looked up surprised. Claudine said, "You tutored him? Did you know that?" She looked at Delphine then focused on AJ, who shook his head no.

Still trying to defuse things, AJ said, "Dell, he's nervous bein' here with you. That's why he had so much to drink. Man, drink this damn water!"

After a few sips, and feeling the kicks from AJ under the table, Terry tried to back track. "Asha, I … I didn't mean it like that—"

She cut him off. "Oh, so, how did you mean it, Terry? Was it to uplift me as your strong African sista? Was it your intention to make me feel intelligent, a queen appreciated for your very existence? Joker, I know what you meant. Let me be clear, I don't need you or anybody else to validate my worth or my presence on this earth. I empower myself with knowledge and determination to seek and know the truth, be a success in Black excellence. Where's your Black excellence, Terry? Is it still your daddy's checkbook? Mine is in my head. Not between my legs. I refuse to be labeled. As the song say, I am young, gifted, and black, I'ma add beautiful in any shade, shape, or size. But you wouldn't know that 'cuz you been brainwashed by the white man. Too good ya say? Why yes, I am too damn good for the likes of you."

Claudine stood up as AJ shook his head no, pulling on the arm of her sweater to stay. Terry looked at Delphine. He was sweating and trying to gulp the water and take it all back. Holding up his hand for her to wait, he managed to get out the words, "Just a sec … Dell … We … Let me …"

Delphine kept right on talking. "Now I know who you've become, Terrance Astro Upton. Thanks for the date. I'll forget you as soon as I walk out of this restaurant because the Terry from back in the day, no longer exists! He was cool but you're a jackass. Perhaps destined to be one, since we all know your momma named you after the cartoon dog on the Jetsons. She was always so happy to tell us that funny story about her only son. Especially when she had one too many Tequila Sunrises. Your father couldn't stop her from telling it, over and over. Terry, do your parents know you a sellout? Bet ya makin' ya momma real proud, right about now. I'm sure you'll marry a white woman 'cause ya clearly ain't got what it takes ta have a real sista in your corner or on ya arm. Check ya later, A.J. I'm out!"

She turned walking through the crowd toward the exit. Terry tried to stand but flopped back down from dizziness. AJ still tugging on Claudine sweater, "Dene, baby, come on."

"AJ, I got ta go. Ya can call me later." she said, snatching her arm out of his grip, rolling her eyes at Terry, and following her best girlfriend to the door.

Making a conscious effort to hear the entire conversation behind him, Philippe' had random thoughts, *(Wow, it seems like Miss. Debate is that way all the time, not just in class. Ha-ha. He did not have a chance. Silenced by her tongue. Crashed and burned then she walked over his rubble, made dust. Why would you date her? Was it? No, they said school friend. Well, they were. Ha! He drank too much, first mistake. Never tell a woman about other women, who want you or you would choose over her, mistake number two. He needs lessons. Attacking her body type was very childish. Dumb. Of course, she would be angry. She didn't even yell. She is controlled. Not delicate. A tiger in the trees ready to pounce. Not a fun girl. They said she was mean. Smart but questions everything and everyone, not Black. Big walking attitude, chip on her shoulder looking to argue. A cartoon dog? Wow! She said forgetting him. She is cold-blooded.)*

He chuckled before chatting with his colleagues around the table.

13 Change in Dialect

Out of the one hundred and seventy-four AFS students, juniors Delphine Murry, Elroy Truman, Sandra Archer, Claudine Saint-Claire, Conan O'Conner, and Trevon Clarke had already secured the top spots of the Canada trip scheduled during the Christmas break in December.

Charlie and Eleanor Murry had no concerns with their daughter traveling to Canada on an educational adventure. There was never any worrying about Delphine, she was not the wilder one of the twins. Besides she would be with her professor and his wife, other students and of course her equally cautious and boring girlfriend Claudine.

Meeting the small group at the Louis Armstrong International Airport at 5:00 a.m. was the first hurdle. Delphine was not an early riser, but she was excited to go and made an extra effort to be ready when Claudine's father picked her up at her home. Sitting together on the plane, Claudine made notes and marked up the desired places to visit on a tourist Montreal City map while Delphine slept most of the flight. Traveling by rental cars, the girl's road with Professor Allen, his wife Tracey and Sandra Archer. While Trevon, Conan, and Elroy rode with Professor Delacroix.

They first stayed three days in Montreal and the students soaked up as much as possible with the history and food of the city. Next, they traveled to the Villa Boréale. It was a luxurious cottage surrounded by nature. Although it could accommodate twice as many people, the four-bedroom villa was just the right size for Delphine, Claudine, Sandra, and Professor Allen's wife Tracey. While the group of men shared the Villa Simone' a quarter of a mile away.

It was a beautiful scene. The snowy mountains and open air were just about two hours from the great educational experience of Montreal. The first day it snowed but there were plenty of things to see and adventures to be had. The group mostly explored together but occasionally went on some sightseeing excursions on their own. It was all about the experience and they got a great one.

Unknown to her, Philippe' Delacroix took note of her change from a cold demeanor to a friendly one with a bright smile. She had more of a whimsical behavior and mood, exploring the history of the city and conversing in French with the town's people. He could tell that she and Claudine were very close and often would be in private conversation that also appeared competitive and sometimes funny.

As her professor, Philippe' had been impressed with her on paper since her work was impeccable. But other than that, he hadn't paid her much attention before this trip. Although he was calculating and observant, he wasn't the type of man to look at female students beyond the learning. He didn't even find her attractive, so there was no temptation. Besides he was here to finish his doctorate and not to put his tongue in the flavors of New Orleans. But he liked seeing this side to her. She had been so serious all the time, he wondered if she even knew how to smile. On this trip he found out that she did.

Ms. Murry was a very smart and hard-working young woman, who wanted to be a pediatric specialist and volunteer in African countries. He got that from her candidate interview. Her dark-brown complexion was rich in color. She didn't seem to really wear makeup and her skin was flawless from what he could tell. It reminded him of someone be he couldn't remember who. She was about 5'7 with a plump body but it was hard to find the actual curves under all her layered clothing. He honestly thought she packed the exact same thing for every day of the entire trip because she only seemed to wear long dark twill skirts—way past her knees, black or brown boots, and a solid color turtleneck and a front button or sweater vest. The kind he had seen in the movie "Potiche" and on that character, Laverne DeFazio from the American television show "Laverne and Shirley."

On the day before Christmas everyone went on their own to town to enjoy the holiday spirit. There was a heavy snow and Delphine elected to stay in the villa she had been sharing with the women. She didn't celebrate anyway and didn't want to be around all the hoopla. It had been about two hours when Professor Delacroix returned from town to check on her. He didn't like that she would be staying alone on the hillside.

"Are you alright?" He said dusting off the fresh snow from his boots entering the villa that was not his own.

"Of course, I am. What did you think was going to happen? That I'd be carried off by wolves?" She said in a low sarcastic tone grabbing a wood log for the fireplace.

He darted over to her taking it out of her hand. "Uh, let me do that."

She snatched it back. "Professor I am fully capable, and I don't need your help." He backed away slowly holding up his hands. As she opened the fireplace to toss the log inside, a large black spider crawled onto her hand. "Crap!" She dropped it onto the floor flinging her hands around. "Kill it! Kill it!"

Philippe' chuckled, picking up the log and tossing it into the fireplace. Then grabbing a piece of newspaper, he scooped up the crawling creature next to her feet and carried it safely to the sliding glass door. "Now, now. We don't kill spiders unless they are poisonous. They are part of the ecosystem, Ms. Murry. Oh, wait you don't need my help, right?" He laughed, holding the paper back at her to dispose of the spider herself. She grunted, squinting her eyes then he tossed it outside.

Philippe' made himself comfortable preparing a snack retrieving a bottle of wine, bread, and a few different cheeses out of the fridge.

Watching his smug face, she thought, *(He is so French. Damn, it's only 11:45 a.m., wino!)*

"Would you like to join me?" He offered but she gracefully declined. "No thanks. I don't drink really and it's not even noon, professor."

He shrugged with a low, "Again, it's Philippe'. You are the only one on this trip that calls me professor. Why?"

"A habit I suppose. You are a professor, so you earned the right to be called one. Wouldn't you agree?"

Munching, he held his glass up and waited for her to pick up the empty one and cheers. Clink, clink was the sound that it made before he took a sip. "You're not as mean as you pretend to be, Ms. Murry. I have seen you smile at least twice on this trip. In France, it is considered impolite to eat and drink alone in the presence of someone else. Have a little snack with me."

She snarled at him then slowly nodded to join. He poured about an ounce in her glass and slid the plate of brie and bread over to partake. She turned down the old school mix tape of O'Jay songs, she had been playing.

It had only been because of the two glasses of sweet white wine and her sitting curled on the floor close to the warm blazing fire that Delphine relaxed and opened up to share about herself. Sitting across from her in an armed chair, he took note with analytical observation the tough as nails hard exterior of Delphine Murry cracked with each discussed topic and every other sip from her glass.

At first the conversation started with age, birthday, favorite color, food, movies, pets— the usual. Shortly thereafter, he learned she was a twin. Although they are identical, she added a few differences between her sister and herself. She shared about her closeness with her older married sister Hellene, who lives in Lafayette. Her strong desire to help mothers and children in Africa, her strict religious upbringing and her love of French culture and food. The more they talked the more relaxed they both felt.

Philippe' talked about being the second to the youngest, his admiration for his older brother serving his country in the military and his sisters but still being closer to his youngest sibling Nannette. He told her why he loved learning and how he had always wanted to be a higher learning educator. Even though his family wanted him to go into politics. Philippe' opened up about some of his travels to India, Iceland, Russia, Greece, and Japan, sparking curious excitement in her wide eyes.

"Your family is religious, but you don't celebrate Christmas. Is it Kwanza then?" He asked innocently, referencing his knowledge of other traditional customs some Black people in America celebrate. She paused a moment before answering. "We are but no, not that either. My older brother LaRoyce died a few years ago around the time people start decorating and whatnot. He suffered a lot from the stomach cancer that took him away. After that happened, we just stopped pretending it was a happy time and didn't bother anymore. It's all very commercial anyway, not really about Christ. People need to research and read more; he wasn't even born in December. It say clear as day in da Bible—da sheep was roaming 'round, couldn't been da winter. Would've so froze ta death bein' born in an open barn."

He grinned to her verbal annoyance to the conflict with commonly confused facts and her periodically speaking more informally with a natural Louisiana twang. Delphine looked into the vibrant flames of the fire while taking a few more sips from her glass. Analyzing her body language, Philippe' perceived she might just be a deep feeling person in addition to being smart, competitive, and ornery. Thinking, *(Perhaps she might be a little vulnerable underneath that bossy lioness persona. It is real but...)*

He broke the silence. "I'm sorry about your loss. Forgive me for calling that back to your mind."

She smiled at him and quickly changed the subject.

"So, this heiress you are supposed to marry, is she even your type? I mean do you even know what she looks like. That is so weird that people do that kind of thing."

They had talked about so many things; he had forgotten he had even mentioned the arranged marriage.

"Yes, we have been friends for a long time. At one time we had gone to school together. It's not like she is someone I don't know. But we both agreed marriage is for much later in life." He let out a soft chuckle to her smashed facial expression.

"What about you? Do you want to get married and have children one day?"He watched her look off into space a couple of seconds before she looked in his direction and answered his question.

"I never thought about it really. He would have to be a very established and strong Black man with his own successful career to even get me to have interest for consideration. I'm focused on other important things, right now. I adore when Hellene comes to visit and brings little Sam and her new daughter, Tamera. And Lorelle has two little ones I get to babysit and play with. That's enough." He made a low sound acknowledging her statements and discerning from the unsaid that she may not be much like her sister in other ways. Then there was silence. He gazed at her taking a few sips of his wine. Delphine sensed he was watching her and made sure not to look at him. Before she could speak to break the awkwardness, the villa door opened with loud caroling, chatter and laughing from the group returning from town.

Delphine rose to her feet to help Claudine with her bags. Claudine looked at the surroundings and gave her the What You Doin' big eye roll while Delphine turned up her nose and shook her head. Philippe' saw the exchange and licked his lips to cover up his smirking.

Making and enjoying the Italian pasta dinner that night with the group was different than the previous meals. Delphine felt as though Philippe' occasionally watched her now.

Their eyes often met as she periodically glanced over at him with a soft smile. (He was nice,) she thought. She liked the fact that they had spent several hours that afternoon talking and being friendly. Philippe' felt the same about getting to know her.

At the Montréal–Trudeau International Airport, the entire group waited to fly home, but Philippe' Delacroix would be staying one extra night before flying back to his home in Lyon. Due to the snow and a canceled flight, two out of the group were bummed from their seats and placed on later alternate flights.

Trevon and Delphine were left with Philippe' as the others left for New Orleans. The later scheduled flight was also cancelled due to weather but there was one seat available on a rerouted flight with changes of planes in New York and Dulles Airport before arriving in New Orleans at 1:30 a.m. However, it was snowing in both places and there was a strong possibility that one of them would be stuck there. Trevon volunteered to take the risk. Philippe' and Trevon agreed it was safer for her to be confirmed on something more direct. Delphine waited for the next flight only to be notified it would be canceled due to the snowstorm and the airport was shutting down.

"This is ridiculous." A frustrated Delphine couldn't get home. The airport was overrun with now stranded travelers. She found out that there was no compensation or accommodation provided when delays or cancelations were due to the weather. Calmly, Philippe' reassured her he would take care of everything.

"Ms. Murry retrieve your bags. My flight is tomorrow, and I have a hotel room. You can stay in my suite at the Ritz-Carlton-Montreal. I'll get another room and make sure you are back for your morning flight home."

Surprised she thought, *(Dang, Cha-Ching.)* Then she gave the appropriate response. "Oh, no, professor. I can stay here it's alright really."

She didn't do very well trying to convince him she was fine staying in a crowded airport alone until the morning. She snorted and covered her mouth embarrassed when he looked at her with raised eyebrows and pressed fish lips.

The roads were icy, and it took longer to get to the hotel. By the time they arrived the bad news came that there were no more rooms. Since Philippe' had a suite with a king-size bed and a sofa bed, they agreed to share. After ordering room service and consuming delicious French-inspired dishes from Maison Boulud, they settled in the accommodations for the night. In the gray sweats she wore to bed, Delphine couldn't sleep. She had never been overnight in a hotel in such close proximity with a man she wasn't kin to. Rustling with the flat pillows on a very uncomfortable sofa bed, Philippe's long legs hung over the side as he tossed and turned.

Getting up and opening the bedroom door, she peaked to see him try to make the best of it, but it was clear that he was miserable. Not thinking it all through carefully, she offered an option.

"That looks terribly uncomfortable. We can share the bed." Philippe' looked up at her, thinking, *(Is she serious?)*

She continued, "I mean, we have on sweats, and you should know, I can box."

They both chuckled as he rolled off the hard sofa bed rubbing the back of his neck. "Are you sure?" He asked before making a single move closer to her. She nodded with a smile, and he collected the blankets before following her.

Delphine tucked herself under and he remained on top of the bed covers. Being positioned with their backs to each other seemed the best solution for the situation. There was silence for a while but neither of them could sleep.

"Merci, Ms. Murry." He said inhaling a sweet fragrance from her side of the bed. He couldn't put his finger on the exactness of the scent. Her body wiggled but didn't turn around. "Merci de m'avoir fait confiance pour être un gentleman." (Thank you for trusting me to be a gentleman.)

"De rien. Je peux aussi te casser le nez." (You're welcome. I also can break your nose.) His deep laugh echoed in the room and a breathy giggle escaped from her lips. She randomly picked up from their earlier debate. "I disagree. Movies I like and listed are considered well-known classics. "Auntie Mame" "South Pacific" "The Sound of Music" "My Fair Lady" "Sabrina" "West Side Story" "Imitation of Life" but I'll agree to "The Godfather" "Rocky" and "Grease" from your list but for sure not "Flash Gordon" "Flashdance" "Ten" or "The Blue Lagoon" no way. Nope. Not classics. No matter who you ask."

He moaned with a little chuckle from her comments while thinking, *(Always debating. She's funny.)*

Both were exhausted. Inhaling deeply, it took only a short time before they had both fallen asleep. They were both amused but exhausted. Inhaling once deeply it took only a short time and they fell asleep.

14 Optimistic

Returning to her AFS class that first Monday after the break, Professor Allen took charge because Philippe' was still in France for another week. The following week, Delphine felt a little anxious for Professor Delacroix's return from his home. It had been two weeks since they parted after discussing great writings, literature, and classic compositions over breakfast before they took separate flights to their destinations.

She located him standing behind the professor desk to the left of the podium wearing pressed khaki trousers with a long green and tan sweater over a crisp white shirt that only showed the collar. She took more notice to the natural light brown and blonde curls of his hair and his beard being trimmed very low and neat. She kept walking up the auditorium stairs but looked back at him a few times as he focused on his notes and never glanced up.Instead of going to her normal seat on the right side she took one in the middle halfway up.The unexpected change forced Claudine to gather her things and move.

"Girl, what you doin'? We never sit here. What's up? A quiz or something?" She asked flopping down next to her.

"Just wanted to do something different that's all." Smiling at her best girlfriend, she put her bags down and pulled out her supplies for class.

The lecture had been an outline for Wednesday's class presentation from the Canadian dialect and culture trip winners. Although she was already prepared, Delphine wasn't sure why she was nervous about the presentation.

There was no need to be, her turn came and went receiving high marks from both professors as she captured several elements others didn't. Delphine had a relaxed feeling with her French professor, and it made her smile a bit inside.

But something happened the week before Mardi Gras festivities were to begin in New Orleans. It came as an unexpected ruffle to her feathers. Professor Delacroix teamed her with Chase BoDeen, a thick and chocolatey wide receiver on the Tulane football team, for a research project. The year before he had a crush on her. Fortunately, she had turned his attentions elsewhere when Lolli made it known he was a tree she wanted to climb and swing from. Lolli dated him for about four months and then she told all the business.

Delphine made a point not to look at him after that because she would burst out laughing. Knowing he tearfully whimpers getting to his peak, and then at his climax he releases a sneeze was too comical. Although it would be very awkward to work with him, she could get past that part but there was more. Chase wasn't a dumb jock by any means, but he was in no way close to her same intellectual league. The assignment was very detailed and complex, counting as part of the final grade. She was pissed by the pairing. Because if she didn't rank in the top four, she could kiss the Sorbonne exchange program opportunity goodbye.

She thought that they were cool after Canada but now she had questions that flashed in her mind. *(Why would he do this to me? Does he want me to fail?)* No, failure was not an option for Delphine Murry. After class she waited to speak to him about it and even suggest that she do it alone. But both professors rushed out as soon as class ended. It bothered her all day long, but she would soon get it straight.

On Friday, she arrived early to class and confronted him about his selection pairing. "Professor Delacroix, I would like to have another partner. Better yet, I would like to do the assignment on my own.

Nothing against Chase BoDeen but I need to get this right and he isn't really someone I can depend on to do the research needed."

Philippe' stared at her from behind the desk. Her breathing stopped momentarily when his beautiful blue eyes connected to her brown ones.

"You can not have a different partner because everyone is already assigned. Ms. Murry since you are one of the more gifted students you should look at this as an opportunity to help someone else learn some of your techniques and strategies for doing well in this course."

"What the hell?!" She didn't realize she had actually said it out loud until he leaned back, crossed his legs, and raised his eyebrow peering at her.

"Didn't you say you wanted to help those under privileged? Perhaps, you should consider this a dry run."

Her eyes filled with heat, and she began to tap her foot and grind her teeth. Philippe' took a moment then spoke again. "Ms. Murry, I tell you what. If you want to complete the assignment on your own, you must get it to me no later than next Friday. This is a week earlier than it is due. But that doesn't get you off the hook with Mr. BoDeen. You still are his partner and if his paper scores less than an eighty then you will take the same score regardless of your stand-alone paper."

She put her hands on her hips really annoyed with him for making her do this extra work. "Why are you making me do all this and still hold me accountable for him? That isn't fair professor. Especially when I will score higher on my own. Why are you discriminating against me being smart."

He swung around in his chair and said, "You can do this easily on your own, but others can't. If you took the time to look beyond yourself, you would have noticed that all the high-ranking students were paired with lower-ranking ones. The world does not just revolve around you, Ms. Murry."

(No, he didn't just say that!) She thought as her blood pressure rose from anger.

Students began to arrive, and he stood up from his desk to greet them. She rolled her eyes mumbling, "Bastard," walking away and making her way to her regular seat on the right side.

The following Friday evening, Hellene was visiting for the week-end. The family finally got to see her new baby Tamera who was a few months old. She was now in a much better mental state than she was right after the divorce. No one knew who Tamera's father was and she didn't say but the little Hershey kiss was too cute to care. Lorelle brought over LaRoyce and baby Lorelle-Latrice to play. Somehow Delphine was left to babysit for a few hours, and it had slipped her mind that her assignment hadn't been submitted.

Finally able to leave the house it was 10:00 p.m. and she rushed to the Lermontaunt's estate. They were the wealthy Creole family who had been hosting the French Professors. When Anna Lermontaunt answered the door dressed in a glittery evening gown, she turned her nose up at Delphine, thinking she was her date. Reluctantly, Anna advised her that the professors were both staying at The Roosevelt - New Orleans for the weekend due to the Governor's formal party, to which she was late.

Driving to the luxury hotel, she recognized many popular citizens dressed in tuxedos and formal gowns for the catered evening. At first Delphine was going to leave her portfolio with the concierge but when she saw Professor Delacroix come around the corner with two glamorous blonde women in sequin gowns on his arms, she decided to hand it to him.

"Professor …"

Startled the group of three paused and one woman snickered because with her gray and pink Puma tracksuit and K Swiss tennis shoes, Delphine was clearly not dressed or invited to the party. Professor Andreas Moreau came up from behind them and asked, "Why are we stopping?" He smiled assuming it was work related and said, "Ladies allow me, please." Extending his elbow for them to latch on, he escorted them across the way and down to the event ballroom.

Philippe' glanced at his wristwatch and said, "Cutting it a bit close wouldn't you say, Ms. Murry?"

She huffed and handed him the leather portfolio binder with her paper. He didn't take it but motioned to her to follow him to the elevator. Without a word she did. Opening his suite door, he offered her a drink. She moaned a no as he eased the leather binder from under her arm. At which time she began to explain.

"I'm sorry. I got tied up and lost track of the time. I didn't know you were here until I went to deliver this to the Leromtaunt's home."

"It's alright, I was expecting to see you before midnight. Take a seat let me read this now."

"Now?" She inhaled quickly.

"Of course. If I don't then it's not submitted and therefore, late. Remember?" He said returning his attention to the typed paper in the binder.

"Are you sure you don't want anything?" He asked, grabbing his glasses to read her paper.

"Mmm maybe, water." She said easing to the plush couch in the lounge.

"Help yourself." He said motioning to the bar across the room and removing his tuxedo jacket placing it on a chair.

Returning with a glass of water she took several gulps and then sat the glass down. It was quiet but she heard him mumbling as he read her paper. Periodically he would ask her to explain her thoughts about Napoleon Bonaparte's political strategies and undocumented successes, the cause of his mental illness and its impact on his actions, the perspectives on his complex love affairs with Josephine and Marie Louise, and to analyze the context of a poem by Lord Byron, she referenced.

After that, it was quiet again and she reclined back to relax. Her eyes slowly closed, and she was asleep.

Sitting up straight she woke gasping from slumber-shock. She was covered with a soft blanket and the bedroom pillow dropped to the floor when she sat up. Instinctively she checked her Swatch watch and realized it was 1:45 in the morning.

Panicking, she quickly scanned the room and saw Professor Delacroix reclined in a large chair asleep. His glasses were on top of his head and there were several opened books, a note pad, and her portfolio on the glass coffee table between them. Taking a closer look, she recognized her paper on the table with a red pen score of ninety-nine point five. Delphine slid her legs off the couch to quietly check her paper and find out why the half point was deducted. Moving to grab it an inch a second, she exhaled low when she snatched it without waking him.

Flipping through the multiple pages there were no red marks. Feeling a sense of irritation growing from not having a perfect score, she then got to the last page and saw his note. Being instantly upset before reading it she exhaled before tilting the paper to better see the words written from the lights coming from the suite bedroom. Pressing her lips inward to prevent herself from laughing out loud, she read each word slowly that Professor Delacroix had written in red pen ink.

"After checking your facts, understanding your theories, and verifying your excellent French grammar this paper technically is a score of 100. But I am taking a half point away because I was constantly distracted by the small bear cub sounds coming from your throat and then there was the time you wiped your drool on my sleeve thinking it was a pillow, when covering you with a blanket. Oh, and because you called me a bastard last week." – PD

Without waking him, she gathered her things, slipped on her shoes, and very quietly snuck out. When she got home and snuggled herself into bed, she was still giggling about the note he had written on her paper.

15 Spring Quarter

As the people of Louisiana were preparing for the World Fair to open in New Orleans in a few weeks, Delphine seemed to be more preoccupied than ever. She was spending less time at home and more in the French group led by Professor Delacroix and Professor Moreau, three times a week. Even though she had met and seen Professor Moreau, he had been assigned to lead learning with Professor Chambliss's non-advance students at Tulane U. She liked learning from them both as they had different perspectives and gave her more insight to the things, she was excited to learn about French history, culture, innovation, and its changing government system.

The group was small, and Claudine was also with her soaking up the golden nuggets one could never get in a class or lecture. Like some experiences the two shared about their school age adventures with their close friends Chevalier and Tomas. Social injustices and disparities throughout French history, and a few stories from the four men being together during the required military service were also discussed. Delphine was able to really see a bit more of the boyish charm and close friendship the two men had each time they met with the group of twenty students to chat in the sessions.

Delphine often had to deflect from her mother's constant snooping and questioning her about her fascination with France and going to school there.

"Ya go right ch'ere! No need ta waist money. What ya brah-dah left ya ain't ta be squandered on no foolishness, gal."

Seeking refuge from her father always helped. "Teence, let da twin be now. She done well. Made us proud, she can do both schoolin' for doctorin' and France-in'. Haa haa. Leave her be."

The few sentences from her father silenced her mother quickly for at least a week or two. So, she always gave her father a sly wink after he spoke and extra helpings of her bourbon peach cobbler, walnut ball cookies, coconut cake or chocolate souffle' when her mother wasn't looking.

In April the birds were out, and the air was warm which meant people were going to be coming to New Orleans. Delphine was excelling at every class as usual but hadn't been spending much time with Lorelle. Her sister was itching to get out of the house, on one Saturday evening.

"Lorelle, I don't wanna go out dancing with you, stop asking."

"Dell come on now. Cedric lettin' me out and I need a purse holder. Come on. I'll get Lolli ta come, okay?"

"No!" Delphine tried to run up the stairs and quickly close her bedroom door, but Lorelle followed right behind and barged in. Sitting on the full-size four-poster white canopy bed covered in white lace and pink roses, Delphine shouted at her twin. "Get out. I said no!"

Lorelle closed the door and sat on the bed close to her sister and whispered, "If ya don't go with me, I'ma tell Momma and Diddy 'bout ya lil crush."

Turning up her nose, Delphine looked at her sister confused. "What chu talkin' 'bout? I ain't got –"

Lorelle cut her off holding up her French Studies book and poking out her lips.

Delphine snatched the book out of her hand and whispered back, "Ya crazy. Don't have no crush."

Smirking, Lorelle laid her head across her sister's lap and looked up at her. "Ya fancy da tall blonde French professor. Dell don't say ya don't. It's alright. I no tell on ya'… if ya go."

The room was still and quiet as they played the stare down game to see who would move for the door first. Five … Four … Three … Two … One —both darted off the bed and Lorelle beat Delphine to the door and down the stairs through the kitchen to the living room. Where their parents were just settling down to watch their regular television shows, T.J. Hooker at 8:00, The Love Boat at 9:00, and sometimes Fantasy Island after, if they stayed up that late.

"Diddy, Momma, I need to tell ya some-tin about ya daughter…" snickering Lorelle yelled out to get their parents attention from sipping their glasses of sweet tea and reaching for the buttered popcorn on the wood TV tray placed between the two large recliners they sat in.

"Rell! Stop!" Delphine shouted just inches behind her tried to grab her blouse to pull her back from telling an untruth and getting her in trouble.

"Wha" Charlie turned to the racing young women bolting into the room from the kitchen.

Both stopped and gathered their composure and Lorelle looked at her sister smacking her lips waiting for her to say something.

Eleanor chomping on popcorn motioned for someone to speak because the show theme music was playing. "Well?" She said without swallowing.

Delphine silently sighed and spoke up. "I'ma go out with Rell don't wait up."

Lorelle folded her arms and giggled while Eleanor grunted "Bye" and Charlie waved with a mumbled, "Be safe, now." Then the two directed their attention back to the family's new 25' inch Zenith Smart floor model television.

Delphine rolled her eyes at her sister and went back into the kitchen mouthing the words, "You make me sick!"

Lorelle blew her a kiss then grabbed her by the arm and said, "Come on wear sum-tin cute."

16 Say What

At her family friend's local restaurant, Ruth's Chris Steak House on Broad Street, Creole beauty Anna Lermontaunt and her friend Sally LaFear were having laughs and drinks over dinner with the handsome French professors Andreas Moreau and Philippe' Delacroix. This had been the third "double date" they had together since the Frenchmen had been in New Orleans. Anna's parents had been key promoters and rather insistent to host the handsome dark-haired Andreas and the drop-dead gorgeous Philippe' when approached by Professor Allen about the exchange program, the year prior. Skillfully the Lermontaunt's had been strategic about linking their daughter to one of the wealthy men coming to New Orleans. It was well known to both professors that they were actively seeking to obtain a wealthy husband for their baby girl. Although she could have a list of men at her door to take on that responsibility, Anna was treated as a princess and just any man would not due. She was not only the latest runner up for the coveted crown of Ms. Louisiana, but she also had a lucrative contract with the Ford Modeling agency in New York. Her small mouth, big round hazel eyes, long straight dark brown hair, and toffee skin had ranked her as exotic to those not accustomed to the variety mixtures of Creoles in Louisiana. Her best friend Sally was one in the centerfold category. A statuesque Native American, Portuguese, and Black woman, who looked a great deal like a black-haired version of a young Marilyn Monroe. Sally oozed sexiness without even trying.

As they nibbled on the evening desserts, the ladies went to the restroom together. Andreas leaned over to his childhood friend, and said, "Why do females do that? It must be a class they take to learn how to hold each other up while squatting to pee."

Philippe' chuckled, taking another bite of cherries jubilee cheese-cake. Both men knew they were being set up and they were not falling for it. But the two felt it was entertaining to have some activities outside of work, research, and tourism things.

Andreas had suggested a sampling of the two beautiful women long before the date began. Now that dinner was coming to an end, he looked at Philippe' for his opinion.

Since this would be one of the only times they could chat, Philippe' whispered to his friend in French. "Il ne sera pas facile de se détacher après. Nous pouvons relancer les autres pour ces besoins. C'est beaucoup trop risqué." (It won't be easy to detach after. We can repeat the others for those needs. This is much too risky.)

Andreas agreed with a strong nod. Then he said, "Are we going to see them there later?"

Philippe' turned up his nose and answered, "I'm not in the mood."

Andreas was disappointed, "Philippe' we have only gone twice. I would like at least one more delicious taste of New Orleans before we go back to Paris."

Philippe' sighed and said, "You are becoming a bit addicted my friend. None for me. I have sampled enough."

Minutes later the ladies had returned.

"We should go dancing." Anna bounced back to the table with the suggestion. Sally grinned sliding her index finger over Andreas' suit jacket shoulder and batting her eyes. Andreas jumped quickly up shouting, "Yes, Let's!" Philippe' chuckled under his breath and went along with the plan after he kicked Andreas under the table with his leather loafers.

Exiting the restaurant, Anna led the way to a lively club called The Stardom but after being inside twenty minutes the crowd wasn't hot enough for the ladies. Philippe' recommended retiring for the evening but it was the much more urban Voodoo Mamma club that won the vote.

Entering the dark venue there were lively beats from the Rhythm & Blues music the deejay was spinning. Immediately Anna and Sally moved to the dance floor and asked for the fellas to get a spot and drinks. Andreas and Philippe' went searching and found an empty center booth that viewed the dance floor. Ordering two rum and cokes for the ladies, Philippe' sighed not wanting to be there ordered a beer. Andreas ordered a whiskey sour.

"Live eels in a barrel." Philippe' said making fun of the packed dance floor with gyrating male and female dancers. Taking a big swallow of his beer he looked over at Andreas frowning at him.

"Relax my friend, relax." Andreas said bobbing his head to Midnight Star's "Freak-A-Zoid" song and taking in the view of all the different colors, shapes, and sizes of the women in the club.

Andreas continued saying his thoughts out loud, "Jellybeans can be admired for their differences, non (no)? There can be enjoyment when you squeeze them to see what's inside."

The two laughed loudly. Philippe' shook his head at his horny buddy. Then he told him, "You are as bad as Tomas. Have you not learned that everything that looks delicious can taste like crap. Just because it's there doesn't mean you need to try it. You might catch something you can't toss back. If that happens, I won't let you marry Nannette."

"You Are in My System" by The System started playing while Andreas looked back at him and put up his fists up playfully, and said, "Don't threaten me, Philippe'. I am marrying my sweet Nannette as soon as we get back. Don't try to ruin my fun or my life plans."

Anna and Sally came into view as they danced with each other in front of the booth, beckoning Philippe' and Andreas to join them on the floor. He looked at Andreas and gave him a nod to go and enjoy.

He jumped up from the table as Philippe' was left to protect the spot and the drinks.

Taking in slow sips of his beer, he casually glanced over the dark room with moving body parts sparkling from glittery clothes and colorful lights. At mid-left turn he noticed her, or wait was it her sister? Philippe' wasn't always sure. He didn't approach the Murry sisters outside of class, if he had ever seen one of them. He either would ignore them or let Delphine come to him. It made him seem a little arrogant, but he didn't want to get it wrong. Especially knowing they were identical; one was married, and he had never seen them together.

It took him just a couple of minutes to get the answer in his head. Delphine Murry and her sister reminded him of someone he had seen in an old movie, and he couldn't figure out who. Then it came to him, "Carmen Jones." He said out loud to himself. That was the movie, and it was the actress Pearl Bailey's figure, round face, defined nose with a little wideness, those strong high cheekbones, full lined coffee color lips, jet black hair, and deep dark smooth complexion was most like the Murry twins.

"Finally." He mumbled grinning as it had been months since being in Canada and wondering about it.

He sat back scanning over the crowd as a few brief flashes came to his mind; Her excitement in Montreal, the fire side chat, sharing a bed, their debates, her research paper, her eagerness to know more during the study sessions. Then Philippe' remembered she always had this lovely scent to her, and he didn't know what it was. The fragrance was sweet with a hint of nuttiness. He chuckled to himself recalling that detail so vividly that he could almost smell it in front of him. But then it happened …

Delphine Murry was standing in front of his booth with her back turned to him. He inhaled that sweetness, and it was gradually intoxicating him. *(Snap out of it.)* Philippe' told himself. Seconds later without thinking he got her attention.

"Ms. Delphine Murry?"

She turned around and smiled. Secretly he congratulated himself.

(Yes! I got it right!)

"Professor Delacroix? Bonjour. Nice to see you enjoying yourself." She said softly. He motioned for her to come into the seating area, to repeat what she said. He had heard her but wanted her to get closer.

She moved in closer next to him but didn't sit down. "I said Hello and it's nice to see you enjoying yourself." Philippe' inhaled deeply as she leaned in to say it again. He almost closed his eyes and moaned but caught himself.

"You too, Ms. Murry. Are you here alone?" He scrunched his face slightly, immediately feeling protective.

She smiled. "No, my sister got out the house and needed a purse holder, so tag, I'm it." She motioned to her sister Lorelle on the dance floor shaking her groove thang to O'Bryan's "I'm Freaky" a few bodies away from Anna, Sally, and Andreas.

Philippe' made a mental note. *(They look different. Delphine is larger than her sister and her hair is longer.)*

Delphine was moving a little to the beat. He watched her keep her eye on her sister, who was getting down but periodically located and pointed at her from the dance floor. Delphine was shaking her head no but moments later Lorelle noticed him sitting in the booth where Delphine was standing. She quickly danced over to introduce herself.

"Hey now. I'm Lorelle, and you are?" She was acting very playfully flirty and clearly irritating Delphine. Philippe' cleared his throat and answered. "Philippe' Delacroix, Ms. Murry. Oh, no. You must be Mrs. Ricard."

The two chuckled but Delphine rolled her eyes. "Oui (yes). Can you not see we are not identical? I'm much more fun." She started laughing and snatched the water Delphine was carrying around in her hand for her then gulped some.

Philippe responded, "Sometime fun can be highly overrated." Delphine snorted then chuckled. Lorelle laughed loudly holding up her hands then pulling Delphine out of the way, so she could check out this foreign white man that she believed was eyeing her sister.

Leaning over Lorelle peered at him and said, "So, you're that French professor, Dell likes to talk about." She grunted looking him up and down making nonverbal judgements on his classic cut leisure suit that fit him very well. He raised his eyebrows simultaneously in surprise at Delphine. Quickly she raised her hand to her mouth as if to say, she had too much to drink. Philippe' smirked, trying to hold in his amusement not really believing there wasn't some truth to what she said.

Lorelle pointed at him and said, "We should talk." Then she jumped up singing the new song playing. The Dazz Band's "JoyStick" was one of the Murry twins' favorite jams they would never sing in public. Delphine so wanted to dance but thought he might watch her. She decided to remain in place attempting to be a stone. It was difficult, watching her sister have all the fun dancing and mocking her by pointing and singing versus like "of the stick, of the stick … take control and use me" while making slow hip circles. It was killing Delphine not to dance but Lorelle was purposefully being extra nasty.

Philippe' finished his beer and tried not to stare but he couldn't help being amused watching the interactions between them. Thenhe listened more carefully to the words and asked, "What is this song about?"

She turned and said, "Uh, a video game…" then pointed up when she heard them say those words in the song. Philippe' had never heard the song before, but it was obvious by Lorelle's playful teasing it could also mean something very different. Nodding to her in agreement, Philippe' felt it was all very comical.

As soon as a new beat started Lorelle screamed and shouted at her sister, "Delphine!"

Out of know where, she spoke to him. "Do you wanna dance?"

Shocked, he blinked and didn't say anything, just stood up. As he followed her to the floor, Sally, Anna, and Andreas were breathing heavily returning to the table for their drinks.

"Outstanding" by the Gap Band was one of her favorite songs and unknown to Philippe' there were two versions. He happened to be caught up in the extended one playing.

She sang snapping her fingers in the air but walking to the middle of the crowded dance floor. He thought, (*Why is she going so deep into the crowd? Maybe she doesn't think I know how to dance.*)

When she stopped walking and turned around, her eyes were closed. Then Delphine seemed to turn into someone he had not expected to see. She swayed slow to the rhythm and then changed it up to rotating her wide hips when the beat dropped in the song. "Damn." He was impressed and a bit intimidated. After about two minutes, she opened her eyes and realized he was standing there. Nervously she blinked a few times then stopped swinging her hands over her head. Now in control, she noticed he was moving on the beat. Her mind flashed with a thought, (*No way!*)

Recognizing her shocked facial expression, Philippe' announced, "Yes, I can dance." Then he broke out to prove it. He bit his bottom lip and started pointing, pausing, and moving like John Travolta in "Saturday Night Fever" dancing to the BeeGee's "Should Be Dancing." Delphine's mouth and eyes got big. "Oh my god. No, stop! It's not a disco, professor!" She grabbed his arms in the middle of his water wave hands and hip thrusting movements.

"What?" he said, trying not to laugh at her bugged-out eyes.

"Hmmkay, you can dance but try to be in this decade." She said moving to the beat. They both laughed and Philippe' eased up as they danced to one of her favorite songs.

The two continued dancing since she didn't stop moving when "Encore" from Cheryl Lynn and then later Evelyn 'Champagne' King's "Shame" were mixed in. She knew all the words and let loose singing. (*She has some interesting layers deep below the surface.*) Philippe' changed up his dance moves with the shifting rhythms to the urban rock steady and then a little robot moves to the beat. Delphine periodically turned around trying not to let him see her laughing. While turning once, he grabbed her hand and started doing the bump. Lorelle left Lolli dancing with her boyfriend and slid over, shouting, "Oreo!" getting on the other side of Philippe'. It was only a few seconds later that the three began double bumping, laughing, and taking turns dropping to bump down low and having a great time.

But then it happened right when the deejay blended in Michael Jackson's "Get on the floor" with a longer intro to the song, Lorelle and Delphine screamed, "Hey!"

Philippe' squinted and began sucking his teeth, a little unsure of what was going on. He slowed his movements to a side-to-side rocking as they let loose and shook that thang for real. A slow rotation of a fist in the air simultaneous with her hips was something he tried not to watch. But her plump round behind in those wide leg black suspender pants and satin red and black shirt made it difficult. He kept it cool noticing the suspenders were positioned around her large breasts, which seemed to be perfectly round. While the two women danced feeling the music, he thought it reminded him of moves from a Congolese dance called Ndombolo, which he remembered from his study of some African cultures. Philippe' had a momentary curiosity about Ms. Delphine Murry. But he refocused and smiled, moving and snapping his fingers to the dance tune.

As the song changed to "White Horse" by Laid Back, the three made their way back to his booth where the sisters quickly hustled to collect their things. Andreas and Sally were pretending to be in a conversation after watching him dance and ordering drinks from the waitress. Anna wasn't in view. Philippe' assisted the Murry sisters and offered for them to join their party. They gracefully declined but thanked him for the fun dance.

Standing watching them leave, Anna came up behind Philippe' placing her hand in his with an attempt to lure him to dance. He pulled her hand away and kissed it before politely telling her he would rather watch her. She smiled while he slid past her and sat down reaching for the new beer Andreas ordered for him. Sally joined Anna on the floor to dance. The men smiled as the ladies gave them a sultry dance show. When the song changed, they continued to dance with people around them.

Philippe' looked to his left sipping his beer. It was a sea of blackness grooving to Stevie Wonder's "Master Blaster (Jammin')." The beat was heavy, the lyrics being chanted, power fists were up, and hips were swinging to the reggae rhythm.

He witnessed Delphine and Lorelle on the floor frequently closing their eyes singing every verse. The two mirrored moves, bouncing their chests and rolling their bodies in unison like some ancient African tribal mating dance calling the men home to get some loving.

He switched his glance back and forth from the Murry twins to Anna and Sally without moving his head. Philippe' liked watching Delphine dance, she seemed to feel the music and let herself relax. He liked that. Biting his bottom lip he thought, *(She moves … Stop!)* He turned his head and Andreas was watching him grinning.

"What?" He said with raised eyebrows. Andreas smirked, and said, "Nothing."

Philippe' put his beer down and said it again. "What? Andreas, what?"

Andreas rubbed his nose, still smirking. Then he said, "I know that look. But that is not you. It is not even Tomas. Are you wanting to sample some of that?"

Philippe' grabbed his beer and said, "Absolutely not. I have no interest in anything of that nature. You know I like to see things others don't. Smart girl but not as rough as they say." He took a swig of his beer and directed his attention to Anna and Sally now dancing to Michael Jackson's "Billie Jean", while peeking to his left to see Delphine and her sister singing and dancing.

Andreas sat back sipping his whiskey and was quiet for a few minutes. Then he said, "Does this mean, after we drop them at home, we still are not going?"

Philippe' still watching the ladies said without looking his way, "No, I have changed my mind. We are definitely going."

Both men chuckled, while drinking and watching the dance floor.

In May, the World of Rivers-Fresh Waters 1984 World Fair held in New Orleans was to bring a lot of business opportunities and attention to Louisiana. Based on other places the exposition was held, it was supposed to offer jobs and boost the State's economy. Yeah, that didn't happen. Perhaps it was due to the Olympic Games in Los Angeles at about the same time, in any case it was a bust. Louisianians were upset and vocal about the turn of tide. Charlie and Eleanor often brought home the complaints they heard from the work week and discussed them over dinner. Th is made Delphine avoid eating at home and spending a little more time at Lorelle, Lolli or Claudine's house. Th e itch to get away from New Orleans was something Delphine needed to scratch, and the exchange program was her ticket out. She buckled down and pushed herself more to ensure she would get a spot to go in the fall.

❦

The last time she saw the French professors was a week before the quarter ended. They had to return earlier due to a mix-up with their visa. Delphine was shocked and felt unexplained emotions bubbling up to show on her face when Professor Delacroix announced he would be leaving after his lecture that day. She didn't hear anything else he said. She stared blankly at the podium for several minutes then exited to the restroom.

Philippe' watched her get her things and leave but continued with his lecture. He expected her to return but she never did. He was disappointed that he didn't get to say goodbye but wished her well with a quick note given to her friend Claudine.

"Ms. Murry, you unexpectedly left class today. I hope you are not ill. Thank you for your kindness in Canada and the joy of debate this year. May you find strength in your adventures ahead and explore new things to further your growth in excellence. I have no doubt you will become an amazing physician. It has been my honor and pleasure to have known you. Take Care". -PD

"Dell, ya good? Did ya start your monthly?" Claudine's voice was concerned, meeting her just outside a restroom in the Richardson building.

Moving to sit in an area of the lounge that wasn't crowded with students, she reassured her.

"No, I'm okay. I don't know why I got nauseous and dizzy. But no,

I'm good. Thanks."

Claudine adjusted herself on the couch and gawked at her best girlfriend.

"What?" Delphine huffed back at her as she moved her turned up lips before saying what she was thinking. "Dell, ya know why. I'm sad to. Best class ever! We learned so much. I hate they leavin'. We knew it was comin', douw."

With a low moan and slight nod, Delphine acknowledged their shared feelings. Claudine and Delphine's expanded French education opened their minds to so much more.

And for Delphine, it surprised her exactly how much. She liked other non-black professors before, but this was a different feeling. Perhaps because she was older, but this felt personal.

Claudine knew Delphine was upset. Adjusting quickly, she strategically continued expressing her thoughts, so that her best friend would freely share hers.

"Dell, it's not just dem stories 'bout French traditions, but stuff 'bout dem to. It was funny learnin' 'bout them sneakin' out da barracks ta meet girls, get drunk, and skinny dip."

Delphine started snickering and nodding in agreement before she added, "And fencing duels, pig wrestlin' none that can be tall tales. But tellin' they favorite things. Askin' what we thought 'bout different people and da world, not for lecture. Who does that? Da musketeer thing be like us kinda. Maybe that's why it feels like I got punched in da gut when he say today be his last lecture. I ain't have no plan yet worked out in my head to stop learnin' what he teachin'. I must be crazy. I'm crazy."

While handing her the note, Claudine gave her some truth. "Dell, I ain't friends' wit folks ain't got sense. Ya liked him. E'vry body can't tell it but we can. I knew ya did when ya stopped callin' him, "French-men" "Blonde Professor" "Whitieness" and "Cracker" and dat been way before we went ta Canada."

Delphine's face distorted from embarrassment and shock. She hadn't realized a change. "I ... I did?"

Claudine nodded with a smile, "Here, read da note girl. He wanna tell ya good-bye, he say."

After reading his note a second time, Delphine realized he had won their first debate. Admittedly, she felt a little bit excellent having had the experiences inside and outside of the classroom. She smiled standing to get moving across the quad to Gibson Hall.

A thought came to her of what she would have said to him if she had gotten the chance. *(Merci, Professor Philippe' Delacroix. Well played.)*

17 Nouvelle Expérience

Months later in late August, Delphine and Claudine began their studies at Sorbonne Université in Paris, France. A sophomore named Rex Chapmen was the other classmate from Tulane University, but they had not met him until after receiving their award letters and recognition from the Deans of Academic Innovation and Liberal Arts Student Services, and Professor Allen. Speaking fluent French made the transition as an exchange student easier for the three of them since they were not limited to taking only English classes but could enjoy the full educational experience offered.

Before arriving, Claudine and Delphine had submitted a request to be roommates in the dorm, and it was quickly approved. Like in America, they found that having a GPA of 4.0 year after year opened doors to special privileges not offered to others. At Sorbonne, there were a list of exclusive English and French honor and literary groups, history conferences, artifact exhibits, complementary metro, and meal passes, invitations for gallery openings, professional lectures, and much more. Delphine could drink it all in without her mother or family distracting her. She was away from Louisiana in a whole new world and was going to enjoy every minute she could during the nine months in France.

Since they arrived two weeks before the fall quarter began, meeting men and women from around the world started off very exciting. Joining an English social group helped the two connect early on with Meagan Autrey from Connecticut, Phillis Davison from New York, and brothers Victor and Floyd Turner from Vancouver. Although it was the first year for everyone, they bonded quickly doing things as a small group to explore the city before beginning their hectic schedules.

However, as the next week got underway their social group activities faded away as Delphine, Claudine and Phillis Davison blended into advance study groups with French professors and students from some of their classes, which left not much extra time.

Pursuing multiple degrees, Delphine had a medical educational path and Claudine a social humanity one. Therefore, they didn't have every class together for multidisciplinary bachelor's degrees, but they did have French Language and Culture Studies-510, and Psycology-550 at the same time. This made studying and rooming together even more fun. Claudine had been spending some extra time with a mixed French man that the girls had met in the school library one afternoon. His name was Gaston Nbamda. He was a junior at Sorbonne studying to be an engineer. It wasn't serious but she did like him and every once and a while she would go out with him leaving Delphine alone, which she didn't mind.

During the fourth week at Sorbonne, in Claudine's international humanities class, she was introduced to a professional man named Pierre Clement, a thirty-year-old, 5'11 dark-skin, lean Parisian man with Nigerian parents. He was a legal consultant. Pierre was one of four panel speakers whose companies supported local or international programs that developed housing and non-profit community resources. After class, she got a date. She asked for an appointment at his company to find out more of what they did, and Pierre asked her out for dinner instead.

"I need to bring my girlfriend Delphine." She said not declining but grinning with this condition. In his sultry French accent he said, "If she is as lovely as you, I can't be greedy, but I can bring my cousin. This way I can keep my eyes strictly on you, beautiful lady."

Numbers were quickly exchanged, and a dinner date was confirmed for Friday night. Now Claudine just needed to twist Delphine's arm to double with a blind date. Surprisingly, it wasn't hard. She wanted to get out and the way Claudine described Pierre, she was curious to see what his cousin looked like.

Arriving at Les Papilles dressed in stylish black dresses and heels, Claudine opted for a red leather jacket with her outfit and Delphine draped herself under a soft black shawl. The men were already seated when they arrived. Pierre was wearing dark taupe trousers and jacket, with a gold shirt opened at the neck and his cousin, Lucian wore a nice gray suit with a black turtleneck. Delphine didn't care what he had on once she saw his face. When he stood up to meet her as they walked toward them, she almost said damn out loud. Lucian, who preferred to be called Luc was a thirty-three- year-old, 6'2 lean deep chocolate man that was a dead ringer for the character PFC Petersen from the movie they had just seen called "A Soldier's Story". Leaning to Claudine as they walked toward the gentlemen's smiling faces, she mumbled, "Why does he look like fine ass Denzel Washington in that movie girl." Claudine could do nothing but grunt as the two had approached the table and were being introduced.

Claudine and Pierre were in their own private conversation most of the evening, leaving Delphine to only talk to his cousin. Fortunately, Luc Clement had a fun and casual personality that made Delphine relax, so it didn't seem like a real blind date. He was charming and handsome with a strong French accent when he spoke in English, that she found hypnotizing. So, she kept asking him questions in English just so he would reply that way. When he sipped his wine, he would occasionally look at her with his dark round eyes slowly fanning his long lashes and she could feel the liquid forming on her skin under her black queen-size stockings.

As she started to feel clammy from his intense gaze, she stopped drinking wine and stuck with water after the second course.

Luc Clement had an exciting career as a business intelligence analyst. As he explained at dinner, he worked for the government finding bad people laundering money.

"Would you say it's like the CIA or FBI in America?" Delphine asked nibbling on her crepes with crème and fruit. He smiled leaning forward and said, "More like the show Miami Vice but not as cool." She let out a louder laugh than she intended which made his beautiful smile and pretty teeth appear from her outburst.

The evening went very well, so much so that before they had left the car to return to their dorm, Pierre and Luc asked to see the ladies again. They agreed without hesitation. Slowly the two walked the short distance to their building sharing a few hip swings while the men watched and waited until they were safely inside. Once the door closed and locked behind them, Delphine and Claudine began sniggling and giggling about the date long into the late hours of the night.

18 Les Possibilités

O ver the next couple of weeks, the four had lunch dates a few times and then some serious discussions about the George Lucas films. This prompted a Saturday afternoon viewing "Star Wars", "The Empire Strikes Back" and then "Return of the Jedi" to continue the debate on the theme of the films and who were the real good guys over dinner. There were a lot of laughs, delicious food, and a great deal of fun.

One Sunday, Pierre, and Luc took them to breakfast at Ladurée where Delphine had the most amazing brioche French toast she had ever had. She kept humming and tapping her feet with each bite until Luc noticed her and she tried to play it cool.

"You look adorable when you eat." He said licking his dark full lips slowly with the tip of his wide tongue.

Delphine cleared her throat and said, "The breads and pastries here are so delicious ... so good, oh and the butter and cheese. But I need to slow it down, or I won't be able to fit anything by winter." She chuckled.

Luc sipped his coffee and said, lowly, "Perhaps by that time you won't need to wear any clothes." Delphine started choking and grabbed her water.

After breakfast Delphine realized, Luc was a man that wanted to have something serious. He basically told her so holding her hand tenderly as they walked under the Eiffel Tower watching the tourists.

"Delphine, I am very interested in getting to know you better. I would like to take you out alone." He said, turning her around and looking into her eyes. She felt a little put on the spot and didn't know how to really answer him. Delphine enjoyed spending time with him as a double date but alone would mean something more, and she wasn't really interested in dating like Claudine. She took a minute then looked up at him and before she could tell him how she was feeling, he leaned down giving her a sweet tender kiss on her lips. She closed her eyes and felt his overcoat surround her body as he wrapped his arms around her back for a seven second kiss. Pulling back, he whispered, "Why don't you think about it. I must travel to London for a few weeks and when I get back, I will ask again."

Delphine just nodded and smiled, still swirling from the unexpected kiss.

Living in Paris had brought many new experiences for the young women from New Orleans. Within the first ten weeks abroad, Claudine, the 5'5 top heavy, size 14 was ranking high in her classes and had a man friend and a boyfriend on the side. Claudine juggled both and her class load masterfully.

Although she felt no pressure to participate in the exciting fun Claudine was having, Delphine observed the wild craziness and often covered for her girlfriend when wires crossed with her dating two men, which wasn't very often.

Delphine was rejoicing with her life away from her family and everything French. She was one of the top students of her class, and had a good-looking professional Black Frenchman interested in her. Hours after their last double date, Delphine had decided when he returned from London in November, she would take him up on dating exclusively.

After being gone only a week, Luc had a large vase overflowing with fifty long stem red roses delivered to her dorm with a card that said, "can't stop thinking of you." Experiencing the thrill of his romantic gesture made Delphine giddy for several days. But she later told Claudine that she didn't want to get too serious; her education was first.

While Claudine continued to see Pierre more regularly, he asked, "Is Delphine feeling Luc? He is really into her."

Claudine simply said, "I believe so, but she's all about her studies. He better go slow. She is serious about saving herself for her husband. If he goes too fast, Dell will shut him down with the quickness."

Pierre relayed the important inside information to his cousin.

Luc got the message and decided to slow way down.

After about another week, he sent Delphine a letter saying he missed her and when he returned, they would pick up where they left off but, in the meantime, he wanted her to focus on her French education and culture experience while he was away. She liked that he said that, and Delphine didn't think any more about Lucian Clement.

19 Fantastique

As the weather turned wetter and colder, it seemed doing research in the library and study group discussions were not doing enough for them. So, they started to find lectures, exhibits, and a few social clubs to pass the down time.

On October the 17th, they went to an exclusive symposium and wine reception with literary and history professors from Sorbonne that were not their instructors and one from the Bibliothèque nationale de France. It was all so stimulating to experience the readings and research historical references. They took lots of notes filling their brains with these details and expanded topics of information.

Then it happened …

When Professor Philippe' Delacroix from the National Library of France was introduced, Delphine squeaked and almost wet her pants. Fortunately, there were almost one hundred and seventeen people in the auditorium, and no one heard her, except for Claudine. She slipped her a note that said, "Hmm, maybe now you can have two boyfriends like me, copycat."

She delivered a quick kick to her shin, but Claudine softly laughed like an asthmatic hyena while rubbing her leg.

Dressed in a deep blue classic single-breasted suit, crisp white dress shirt and dark blue leather oxfords, everything he wore accentu-ated his long lines and broad shoulders. Delphine thought, *(He looks like a model.)*

His hair was cut shorter but still long enough to see his blonde highlighted curls, his full beard was low and trimmed neatly around his chiseled face. His eyes couldn't be seen from where she sat but she knew they were those deep pools of beautiful blue ocean water.

At the after-hour reception, Claudine gave her a pep talk before she navigated her way through the crowd toward him.

"Dell, if you get his attention which you will because he likes you, we can get some serious hook-ups. He knows everybody. Don't be nervous, it's just da professor. You know he's a chill book nerd like us. No wait. Not me, more like you 'cuz I got two boyfriends. I'm so Lolli now! Ha-ha."

They laughed before she left her to go mingle.

Chatting with several people his back was to her as she approached. Waiting a few seconds, she took a deep breath and spoke in English.

"Good evening, Professor. I enjoyed your lecture and would love to hear more."

He was talking but politely turned to the voice behind him to give his appreciation. Philippe' reached out held her shoulders and kissed her cheeks. She stiffened but relaxed remembering it's the way French greet family and friends.

"Delphine Murry! I am so happy to see you. You made it to Sorbonne. I had no doubt."

She nodded and couldn't stop grinning. He continued speaking to her and forgot about others around. "I should have known it was you. You're wearing the same type of clothes you did in Canada."

Confused she said, "Huh, what?"

He quickly changed the subject. "So, you want to hear more about what exactly? The spies of the revolution, the secrets inside Notre Dame or maybe we should discuss Le Testament by François Villon or The Drunken boat by Arthur Rimbaud. No. How about the works of Victor Hugo? Wait, I recall you prefer Jane Austin, don't you? When and where, Ms. Murry, I will make it so."

She started snickering by his playful and discreet way he was asking to spend time with her, maybe even show her other sides of Paris.

That was the beginning of many rendezvous to discuss poetry and literature, art, and history. It didn't take long for Philippe' to take her to explore foods and places all over Paris. Outside of her class schedule and his work one, they spent just about two days a week and every other weekend together.

Philippe' became the official underground tour guide for Delphine and sometimes Claudine. They explored Paris from the views of a citizen not a tourist or student. It was fantastic. Delphine couldn't get enough and for the next several weeks, Philippe' and Delphine talked over coffee about art, and poetry. They shared more about their future aspirations, while listening to stories about her Southern Black American culture and him sharing aspects of his. Philippe' found learning about her family and their history fascinating. They had a common hunger for learning, and they were comfortable with one another. Occasionally, they would even finish each other's sentences during casual conversations about life and debates over films, novels, art and science, human behavior, and racial differences and similarities.

To Philippe', Delphine Murry had slowly let down some of her guarded walls to her conservative demanding demeanor and allowed him a peek inside. She was more relaxed around him, inquisitive, playful, and competitive. Often speaking her mind but valued his opinion and assessment of things she did not always understand. She was wonderful to talk to and he was deeply interested in her thoughts on the world and things they discussed in her studies. They were friends and he genuinely enjoyed being with her.

To Delphine, Philippe's nature was as he had always been,

a gentleman. Respectfully soft-spoken, opening doors, picking up the check, ensuring her safety back to her dorm. She had grown comfortable being around him and she felt safe. He was a few years older and possibly smarter about many things, but he didn't have an arrogant side. In debates, mostly literary ones, he regularly let her come to her own conclusion that he was right without saying a word. This made it easy for her to accept his views on things. She liked him. She liked him a lot.

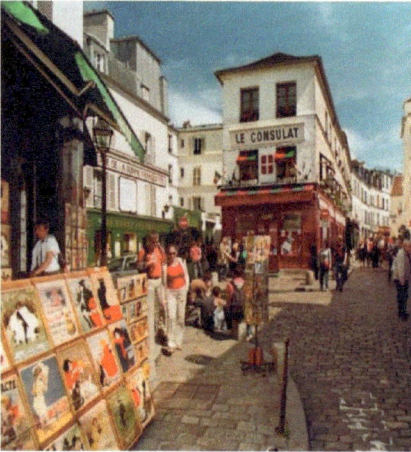

20 Café ou Crème

By late November, when Luc returned to Paris, it had been several weeks with no contact, and he wanted to rekindle what he left burning. Luc reached out to take Delphine out for coffee.

At a local café, they had a conversation about her studies and some of his business in England. They were friendly but it was not the same. It felt as if things were starting over from scratch. Luc just asked, "Delphine, are you seeing someone else?"

Delphine ate a bit of her vanilla macron before answering. "It has been a while since we've even spoken Luc but no I'm not dating anyone. Claudine and I reconnected with a professor we had at Tulane, and he has shared some historical research things with us, a few lectures, we went to a couple of museums, and art exhibits. It was more about learning outside of the classroom. That and the study groups are really all I have been doing outside of school. Why would you ask me that?"

He leaned to catch her eyes, and said, "I don't know, this feels different. You don't seem like you are as relaxed with me like before."

She smiled. "Luc we are friends. This is the first time you and I have been somewhere just the two of us, maybe that's it."

Luc nodded but was still analyzing her body language. He knew right away his stopping contact was a mistake and quickly needed to bounce back from being away so long.

The quick meet up ended with a soft kiss on the cheeks with a plan to follow up for dinner four days later. Unfortunately, Delphine had to cancel the day before after she came down with a cold.

Luc delivered soup and flowers to the dorm for her, which she appreciated but she made Claudine get it because she didn't want him to see her looking like death.

Following her recovery, they had their dinner date. Luc took her to Epicure an elegant dining experience in the city. Delphine knew he was taking her to some place nice, so she wore a black leather skirt and black lace top with a black silk jacket. She put her long braids up in a bun twist and had Claudine do her make up. When he picked her up and opened her car door, he was just about to drool but managed to keep it together. However, all during dinner he couldn't stop staring at her and touching her hand. "Delphine, I would like us to spend more time together. How do you feel about that?"

"I think that could be something we might be able to do." She said feeling a little on the spot. For some reason she started to feel nervous all of a sudden.

"You are a beautiful woman and very intelligent. I realize now it was a mistake not to write to you when I was in England. Claudine told Pierre I should take it slow because you are very determined to have the best educational experience. I took that to mean to back up, but I feel like that was the wrong move. Tell me what you need to be my lady."

.He moved his head to find her eyes that she was purposefully directing on her cup. Stirring her after dinner coffee for what felt like the seventy-fifth time, she tried not to look at him. She didn't know what to say. She liked Luc. He was nice, handsome but she wasn't looking for a spark. She was in Paris for school and was leaving when the year was over. This was not in her plan. Perhaps if she had met him later but she just got there, and in her mind, men were a distraction. She had the example of her twin sister, Lorelle.

Sighing after stopping the spoon from moving about her cup, she smiled and finally said it, "Luc you are a nice man. And… and I do like you, but I think you are looking for something that I don't have right now. My senior year here is for me to take in as much as I can because I won't get another chance. This was like a once in a lifetime thing for me and that is really where my head is. When you kissed me before you left, I honestly thought I maybe could be like Claudine, you know date and juggle things but while you were gone, I had to be honest with myself. I'm at the top of my class because my studies. I mean my education is number one. You don't seem like the type of man that would like to be third or fourth in a woman's list of priorities."

He grunted and smirked as he took a few sips of wine. She continued, "If I was at the end of my school year and we met, I might be telling you something very different, but I'm about to finish the fall quarter. I have two more to go and by the time I graduate, I must be one of the top seniors to obtain some of the very few awarded scholarships for international students. No exception. Thank you for inviting me to dinner, I had a very nice time. I can pay for my own meal. This way you're not out anything." She looked at him waiting for him to say or do something.

He just gave a slight grin before saying, "I have enjoyed the time with you as well. Dinner is on me, beautiful lady. Consider it a gift from a friend. I may check on you later after you complete your final exams. Would that be alright?"

She giggled, "You should, Luc. You should."

Lucian "Luc" Clement brought Delphine Murry back to her dorm. He walked her to the door and kissed her cheeks then whispered, "Late Springtime" as he winked at her. She smiled at him with a friendly nod and went inside.

Three weeks later, at a bistro enjoying lunch and waiting for Claudine to go to a research documentary about the founders of France, Philippe' had only picked at his Croque Madame. Commenting about his disappointment under his breath he said, "It is not at all as good as my mother's."

He seemed preoccupied. She could tell because his forehead creased, and he often rubbed his beard along his chin when he was thinking.

During the winter break, Philippe' wanted to ask her to join him in Lyon to show her the beauty of his hometown but he hesitated. It was obvious to her he had something on his mind.

Giving him an opening, she said, "Alright, what is it?"

He looked away at first but seconds later, said "Since you said you were not going home, I don't want you to be alone for the break. Not in your dorm that is terribly depressing. I wanted to invite you both to my home in Lyon. However, my entire family will be there and … well it is Christmas. I didn't want you to feel uncomfortable about that."

Delphine didn't delay in responding, "Really? Oh, oh, I'd love to come." In her excitement, she laid her hand on top of his on the table.

That had never happened before, and he felt strange about it. Philippe' quickly moved his hand away and leaned back away from her. Then he told her, "I will ask Andreas's former student Mr. Chapmen, as well. I am sure he would like to see his French professor, married to my sister and expecting a child soon."

She smiled but in the back of her mind, she was confused by his reaction to her touching his hand.

21 Lyon in Winter

Before leaving a couple of days ahead of them, Philippe' explained the five-night excursion planned activities. He casually mentioned that the Delacroix home had been built centuries earlier and in his family line for generations. Delphine, Claudine, and Rex arrived at his family home in Lyon, France just four days later, on Christmas Eve in the early afternoon.

Delphine had figured he must have had some money based on that hotel stay in Canada. Then there was his extended generosity when they had spent time together in Paris, and now this all- expense paid trip to Lyon. Not to mention she had picked up on his stylish yet conservative wardrobe, always having neatly trimmed hair and beard, loving to eat and drink expensive things, those clean manicured hands, polished shoes, and bright straight teeth. There was also the fact that he often smelled like soft new leather with a hint of evergreen or sometimes vanilla.

She thought she knew. Claudine thought maybe but it was not understood until they were riding on a road with no homes in sight just trees, hills and open fields covered with snow. It was a French chateau. She thought…*(Oh my god, it's a damn castle.)*

There weren't any knights in armor at the secure gate with large walls of cream stone enclosing the acres of the property. No draw bridge, or moat and it wasn't shaped like something out of a fairytale, but it was a massive multi-level home, that momentarily took their breath away. Inside it was immaculate and filled with art everywhere. Initially it felt very similar to being inside the Louvre or some other Musée in France but with a warm homie undertone. Claudine and Delphine agreed with eye rolls and blinking at each other to be cool and not act ghetto or American. It was difficult but they managed not to gasp, point, or scream.

Before getting settled, Philippe' introduced his parents, Jean-Pierre, and Marie as soon as they stepped inside. At first impression, his father seemed friendlier than his mother. Jean-Pierre made an unexpected joke that lightened the slight awkwardness.

"It is a pleasure to make your acquaintance. Welcome to our home. Marie and I find it delightfully enchanting when meeting new people from around the world. Since I am much older, I remember all the people I have lost over the years. Perhaps I should not have had a career as a tour guide after all."

Philippe' and his mother sighed and looked away for a moment. Rex, Claudine, and Delphine chuckled but more at the fact that Jean-Pierre had burst out laughing at his own joke before they did.

Mrs. Marie Delacroix was very proper and introduced them to the ladies of the Gauthier family before directing one, named Gert to assist them and Philippe' to aid Rex with getting settled.

Rex was to be in a room called "earth" and the girls were in a room called "pink". Delphine and Claudine smirked after they heard the rooms had names.

"Is this like a hotel?" Delphine mumbled to Claudine, while they gathered their bags for the lift. Claudine whispered, "It's big enough. Girl at least they didn't give us a room called black. You know we the only negros up in here."

Gert snickered and the two felt instantly relaxed to talk to her more and find out about things only servants knew about as they followed her lead. Gert Gauthier was a twenty-two-year-old fair skinned stocky woman that was studying at Le Cordon Bleu. She told them her entire French-German family were the Delacroix's ground and home overseers. The Gauthier family consisted of Gert, her sisters Heidi age 25, and Elke age 30; her brothers Wolfgang age 27, and Han's age 33; and their middle-aged parents Alexandre and Ava.

On the short ride to the third floor, Claudine asked, "Your English is very good. Did you study abroad?" She nodded with a smile, then she said, "London."

Not paying attention to the conversation, Delphine took note of the fantastic art sculptures, tapestries, and paintings along the hallway walls.

During the time they were getting settled in the pink room, Gert was joined by her sister, Heidi. Both of them shared more details about their family and the Delacroix household. Some of which were very interesting to Delphine. Like how all of them had been formally educated in the art of estate and luxury hospitality with some members having experience working in a few of the finest resorts in Europe.

Delphine innocently asked, "It's odd that your whole family … I mean, uh, how long has your family worked here?"

"We, Gauthier's have been with the Delacroix estate for over a hundred years. We're an extension rather than workers." Heidi said with a twinge of snootiness, while Gert guided them to the connecting bathroom and toiletries specifically for their stay usage. Delphine gasped when she took a looksee at their bathroom seeing the shiny marble and gold fixtures. But it was the huge white clawfoot tub that made her suck air through her teeth. Most French people are thin so the dorm showers she had been using were a little tight for her plus size figure. Delphine instantly knew she would be in that tub and stretched out in comfort. She raised her eyebrows at Claudine, who nodded knowing her girlfriend was going to have her big bossy behind in that bathtub first.

Taking a slow observation of the very large bedroom with two twin beds covered in a décor of pastel and bright shades of pink, Claudine said, "Wow it's really all pink." before Heidi corrected her. "Actually, the proper terms are blossom, blush, punch, bubble gum, rose, ballet slipper, and flamingo."

Delphine and Gert let out a loud laugh when Claudine replied with, "Like I said it's pink." Heidi was not amused.

Gert was very relaxed and continued to chat, which helped them feel less formal. While unpacking their suitcases and handing garment items to Heidi and Gert, for storage over the five-night guest holiday stay, Delphine recalled the comment earlier about the family connection and posed a question.

"Your family has been working here since like World War I, is that what you said?"

Heidi answered with a tone of pride in her voice. "Oui. Our mother's family escaped Belgium right before the Great War. They couldn't safely remain together, and our young grandmother and her brother sought refuge here from the Delacroix family. To save them from being imprisoned or taken off to war, the Delacroix family used their political influence to protect them and another sibling that eventually came here for safety. Our grandmother, Gerta and her brother Allas worked as grounds keepers and pretended to be a disabled married couple carrying for their younger sibling as their child. It saved their lives. They married French citizens but stayed working here on the estate. All through the years they made sure we were safe and cared for us, even when our family had to be in hiding. If it had not been for the history of deliberate kindness to strangers, none of us would be here right now. We are not treated as workers but as members of their family in many ways. My father was part of the underground resistance. It was very dangerous for him to marry our mother, but it was arrière grand-père Loui-Henri that made it possible. My education for another thing was paid without me even asking … all of ours was."

Claudine spoke without thinking, "So your family is indebted to them, a type of servitude."

Heidi's voice got higher, "No! They don't own us! We are not like American slaves!" Delphine punched Claudine, who had a surprised look that Heidi interpreted the word to mean that.

Gert grabbed her sisters' hand. That seemed to calm her down enough to keep explaining. "We are free to live our own lives. We do. But why go away if all we need is right here. Love, support, freedom to travel, to learn, and work for friends in this beautiful place. Why? Our brother Hans met someone and when he goes back to Ontario to get married, he can return with his new wife, Tess or live wherever he wants."

Claudine still felt the need to extend an olive branch. Walking over to Heidi, who was still holding Gert's hand, she reached up putting her hand on her chest to demonstrate her sincerity. Thenshe spoke. "Maybe the word I used wasn't the right one, but I apologize if I offended you."

Heidi smiled and everything was pleasant again. Gert quickly changed the subject to let us know the time arrangements for the evening, what to expect for dining and how to reach them if Delphine or Claudine needed anything. Then the two were alone.

Delphine folded her arms and said, "Look at you bein' all diplomatic and making friends, Claudine Mia Saint-Claire. Lorelle and Lolli wouldn't have even apologized. I'm proud of you, girlfriend."

Claudine peeked out the door to make sure they were gone before saying, "Girl, I don't want her putting crap in my food or waking up with a horse head in my bed."

Laughing from her "Godfather" movie scene reference, Delphine flopped on the bed and said, "Dene, you stupid. That's Italian mob not German. And what makes you think there are any horses? We ain't seen none."

Claudine turned up her nose at her and said, "Whatever. As big as this place is, looking like we at a giant park with a golf course and mystical forest. I bet they got some damn horses. Girl, after you get your ass in that bathtub, what you gonna wear tonight?"

Delphine thought a moment. Then replied, "Something black."

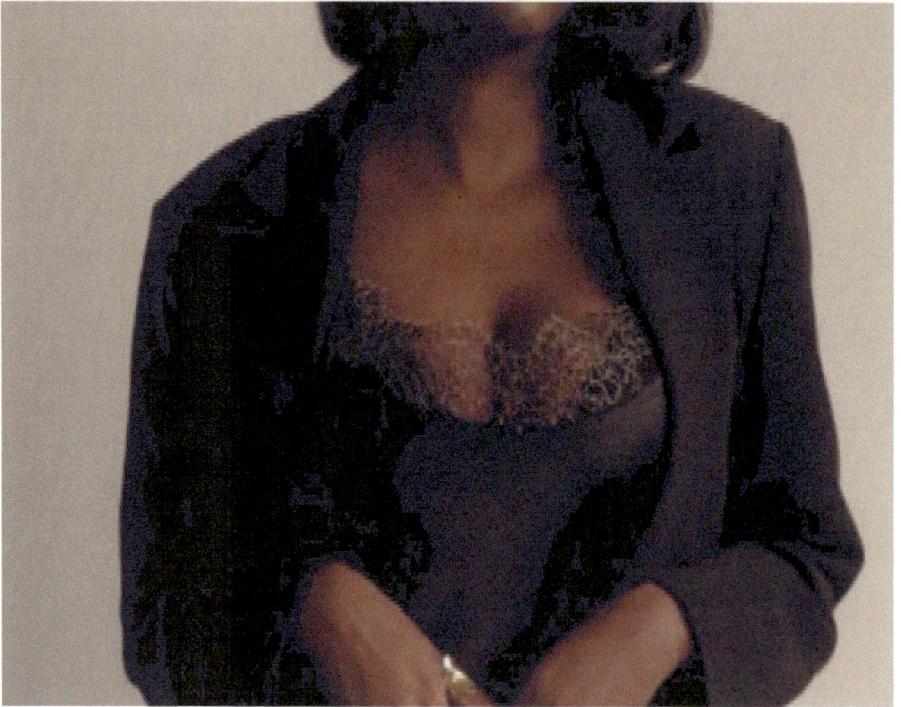

22 Gentleman's Holiday

Being raised in a Southern Baptist faith, joining his family for night mass at a grand, century old cathedral was a little uncomfortable for Delphine and Claudine. However, the two considered it as part of their French culture experience and soaked it all in. Philippe' and his best chum and brother-in-law Andreas made sure the three students were huddled around like chicks under a hen when the Delacroix family were on the move.

After returning from church services in a long procession of cars, was when the Le Réveillon, meaning awakening feast began. The festive time was meant to continue until the early morning. With the formal dining room set in fine white and gold, lit candelabras sparkling through gigantic windows draped with hand-stitched tapestries and sounds echoing due to the over twenty-foot-high ceilings; the mesmerized young women felt as if they were dining like royalty. They would frequently tap or pinch each other inconspicuously under the table rather than gawk at something magnificent they would discover while dining.

The multi-course meal had an array of delectable dishes delivered by gloved staff dressed in waist-high white jackets and black trousers or skirts. It started with caviar and terrine de saumon on blinis, oysters on the half shell, boudin blanc, foie gras, escargot with herbs, and coquilles saint Jacques. Then came the roasted turkey with chestnut stuffing, apples, magret à l'orange, boeuf en croute, buttery potatoes, creamed spinach, glazed carrots, and grilled asparagus. During the long hours of consumption, the table was constantly replenished with fresh baked breads and lots and lots of wine. Much later came the thirteen desserts consisting of cheeses, yule logs, olive oil bread, dried nuts, chocolates, fresh fruits, and candied jelly. The Delacroix traditional dinner was a scrumptious surprise. Over the long hours of playful teasing, and childhood stories of growing up in this immaculate 17th century chateau, the student guests from Louisiana learned a great deal about their hosts and laughed almost nonstop. Attending large family gatherings was a normal thing for Delphine but for Claudine and Rex it was a first.

Throughout the evening, Mr. and Mrs. Delacroix were hospitable and pleasant. Not once focusing on the foreigners present but treating everyone as if they were part of the family. The oldest sibling and Delacroix heir was a military officer named Jean-Pierre François. He and his petite wife Carmen seemed more observant than talkative after putting their seven-year-old son, François-Philippe' to bed.

Philippe's five-year older sister was unconventional, spontaneous and a little wacky. The girls had more interactions with Josephine Elise Delacroix because of her witty and comical comments trying to figure out why Philippe' chose to bring strangers—two Black women and one White man from the United States to Christmas dinner. She didn't start her periodic inquiries until her six-year-old son, Tomas and his three-year-old half-brother Kristoff had been taken away to bed. Kristoff's father, Josephine's fiancé Hassan Lazar had been unexpectedly called away and therefore unable to attend this year. Being told early on that he was a wealthy Moroccan businessman from Casablanca was nice to know but subconsciously Delphine wished he had been there to meet him. She curiously wanted to know what he looked like because their son Kristoff had an olive complexion, dark straight hair, deep dimples, and icy blue eyes.

Professor Andreas Moreau was less wild and playful than he had been at Tulane. He talked mostly to Rex about legal careers and politics, which was his field of study. And he was extra attentive to his very pregnant and soft-spoken wife Nannette, the last of the Delacroix children.

Delphine was very happy that she had been part of Philippe's and Andreas's special spring study sessions back at Tulane. Because after meeting the other musketeers, Aviator Tomas Durand and Doctor Chevalier Ratliff, she was internally amused recalling some stories of their mischief the professors shared. This year, Chevalier brought along his younger sister Elizabeth, who had been visiting from England and Tomas always came with his widowed mother, Constance Durand, Mrs. Delacroix's best friend.

All through dinner, Rex and Elizabeth had an obvious attraction and couldn't keep their eyes off each other. They also seemed to be having a naughty chat with their eyes and food. It was a comical interaction Claudine noticed right away. She nudged her bestie to check out the eye undressing and dirty food conversation they were having from across the table. Delphine was equally tickled once she saw them. Then she leaned over to her friend and whispered, "It's like that scene in "Flashdance" with the lobster."

Seeing them giggling, Josephine made her move to getting some answers and began her questions to Delphine and Claudine. "Tell us Ms. Saint-Claire and Ms. Murry how well did Philippe' and Andreas teach you in Louisiana? Was it a long and hard experience?"

Both men's heads snapped up and they peered at her. Several at the table were well aware what she was implying with the inappropriate framing of her question. Philippe' was about to say something harsh but Tomas motioned for him to wait because his parents were at the other end of the table and didn't hear her. Josephine smirked at her younger brother and sipped her recently refilled glass of wine waiting for an answer.

"We worked closely with Professor Delacroix because we were in Professor Allen's advance French studies course. He was tough but it was worth it. Dell and I got to hear stories about both professors' young adventures as musketeers, military life, and travels during our study sessions outside of class. Those were fun to learn about and it really gave us a different perspective of French culture." Claudine said before eating another piece of yule log dessert.

It was silent and she reached under the table to tap Delphine who was not really paying attention.

Delphine cleared her throat and added, "Oui, he did get a bit challenging sometimes but it was so we would work harder, and we did. It paid off because we are the one's attending Sorbonne and others are not."

Philippe' chuckled, catching Delphine's eyes before she looked back down at her plate grinning.

Tomas spoke up, "Philippe', did you tell these young impressionable students about being a musketeer?"

Delphine snorted and Claudine closed her eyes briefly attempting to hold in the urge to laugh out loud.

Chevalier blurted out, "Mon dieu! That is private. No, sacred.

How could you! Andreas, you ... you didn't stop him?!"

Nannette tapped her husband to answer, since he was talking to her belly. "Uh, well brothers, it was just a couple of stories, no real good ones. We wanted to be the super cool professors. You understand."

Everyone laughed for a few minutes. But Tomas stated loudly, "The two of you are the least cool of the four of us. The both of you must answer for this betrayal ... at noon."

Philippe' nodded in agreement as he gulped more wine. However, Andreas began to plead for mercy. "Brothers, I have a son coming. Let Philippe' duel for both of us. He fences more than I do anyway these days."

Chevalier shouted pointing at him from across the table. "Scoundrel! You will do your penance!"

Andreas lowered his head and loudly spoke directly to Nannette's bulging belly. "Oh, my son ... my son. Remember these two horribly mean uncles. Your father will do his best to win but I already know. I will not."

While everyone laughed, Josephine and her parents were carefully witnessing the chemistry across the table when Philippe' periodically began to playfully glance over and smile at Delphine.

23 Moment of Truth

A short time later, he volunteered to get more wine. Philippe' stood giving an inconspicuous finger tapping that was code for her to excuse herself after he stepped away. Delphine whispered for Claudine to join but she didn't want to move or stop eating the delicious dessert.

Breaking from the table, and meeting in a side hall, he took her to a dimly lit place to show her something. Once the two were inside, and Delphine curiously walked ahead of him, he said, "You know what I want." Smirking, he closed the door of the enormous wine cellar. They were now all alone.

Shaking her head in amazement with the seemingly endless rows of bottles and barrels, she turned giggling and replied, "You want more wine? I don't think there is enough here, monsieur."

Still chuckling, she took a few steps further and stood in front of a waist high selection table with baskets for transporting several bottles at a time. A few unopened bottles of champagne, cognac and wine had previously been placed there. She began reading the labels while her back was to him and the door. She felt his presence close behind her and thought, *(He's very relaxed and flirty. It's cute.)*

Seconds later, he held her hips and whispered into her ear, "I don't want wine." He pressed his body onto hers and he finally confessed, "I want to do many things to you."

Like everyone else, Philippe' had a lot of wine, but he wasn't drunk. Not even close. But Philippe' Delacroix had been in constant denial about wanting Delphine Murry. At first, she was his student. Not only that but she was an over-weight dark-skinned Black woman from America. Physically, those were not things he desired or found attractive even. But it was after what happened in Canada, he began to see her. Really see her. He had become fascinated by the complex inner workings that she hid from others. His curiosity reignited when he saw her after his lecture. The more time he spent with her, he grew to appreciate her loveliness inside and out. Then when she touched him, hearing the invitation to his home, he couldn't stop imagining what it would feel like to be with her. He often wondered if she was really a very hot sensual lover under all those layers of hard protective cover she displayed. The slow building fire burned out of control tonight as he watched her from across the table. Philippe' had to have her.

But Delphine was taken completely off guard. She gasped then froze as he licked her neck and cupped her from behind while stating, "Mmmh, J'ai faim de toi (I'm hungry for you). I want to tear your culotte away with my teeth." His breathing got heavier when he firmly squeezed her. Then without warning, he spun her body around to face him and never stopped sucking areas of her neck. Standing motionless, she heard the low growls from his lustful desire, and she shut her eyes. Leaning her further back onto the table he pressed his long body into hers and said, "I must have you right now!" Holding her head in place and biting her chin, he slyly moved up toward her mouth and found her eyes were tightly sealed shut. He paused inches away from her lips and chuckled saying, "You don't like dirty talk? I bet you do. Vixen, open your eyes." Her lips started to quiver when she slowly opened them.

Philippe' didn't recognize passion when he looked in her eyes. But what he saw made him immediately stop touching her. Her eyes screamed of fear.

"Delphine, you … you've been with a man, haven't you?"

She bit her lip shaking her head slightly no.

Stunned, his jaw dropped, and a high pitch creek escaped his throat, while he took several steps away from her. His large palm smashed over his long narrow nose, then covered his gaping mouth. When he spoke unfortunately, he said the first things that shot into his mind.

"Never?! For Christ's sake, why not?! Are you not about twenty-four? You … You were dating someone in Paris. Your sister is even—"

It had just come out that way. Loud, bitter, and unkind. What he had said, his fast-blinking eyes and the few seconds of his running his fingers through his blonde curls, triggered Delphine's feelings of hurt and embarrassment. She turned away from his eyes of judgement and started to walk toward the cellar door behind him.

Although he was still shuffling through the list of proper words to say, Philippe' snapped out of his confusion and blocked her exit. This kind of situation wasn't something he had encountered, since before entering military service. He had wrongfully assumed that she had been with someone before. Not because he stereotyped her as being promiscuous, but his research indicated that women in his generation had sex long before turning twenty-one. In addition, Claudine let it slip that Delphine had ended something with a man named Lucian about a month before to focus on her studies.

She excited him and he wanted her. But this new information about her virginity confirmed that it wasn't going to be something he could just do. Philippe' felt the pressure mounting from his knowledge of the complex emotions a woman has after her first time. Knowing she was a virgin, if he had sex with her, it would be complicated for her later when she returned home and there was no more contact between them. Philippe' knew he couldn't be that kind of scoundrel no matter how much he desired to have her. His growing attachment to her made him rethink what was important. He cared for Delphine, and he knew he didn't want to hurt her.

"I'm going back now." She said, looking only at the door.

Her words cleared his brain fog, and he placed his hands lightly over her shoulders. Delphine tensed her body; he could feel it as he touched her. So, he began to pat her shoulders to remove some of the awkwardness from the moment. Slowly she lifted her head to face him. Philippe' bent down a little and locked onto her eyes. It was then he realized she had an increase of unfallen water inside them which caused him to instinctively lick his lips and force a slight grin.

"Forgive me." he said softly. Then he displayed a sincere tender smile and continued, "I should not … Tonight, I would not have said or … If … If I had known … I … I apologize. Please forgive me for my impertinence, Delphine."

She pressed her thick and glossy lips inside her mouth briefly looking away. Philippe's hand simultaneously squeezed her shoulders to coax her to smile. She spoke instead.

"I'm not my sister."

"No, no you're not. I only meant to say she is married, nothing more." He paused, searching beyond the hurt in her eyes. She exhaled and continued to share her feelings.

"And … Lucian well … He is Pierre's cousin and I only double dated with Claudine. There wasn't any more. Philippe' you might think I'm strange or maybe old-fashioned, but sex is not something I ever wanted to do before I married. I've had a couple of boyfriends. I do like to kiss when I feel safe with the person, but I don't go further. I'm sure you are used to … I mean … We are friends, Philippe'; and I like being with you very much. But men need to have physical things that I won't do. Well, if this is where our friendship ends, let me tell you again, I have loved all the things you've shared with me. You know the stories about your home and Paris, fine literature, art, history, your travels, wine, food …" She smiled at him before giving him the out. "Merci beaucoup, gentil monsieur. I will never forget your genuine kindness to me."

Delphine reached for the door to leave but something unexpected happened.

Philippe' took his hand and stroked her right cheek tenderly. He leaned his body more forward and he reconnected his gaze locking their eyes once more. The crisp blueness of his eyes called her name, and she stopped moving to leave.

Then he said in that deep baritone voice, "Ma chère, a rare jewel you are, Delphine Murry. It is not necessary for me. I care for you without because you are that special. I promise I will continue being a gentleman. In doing so, it will not change our friendship or how I feel. Trust me to be a man of my word. Will you trust me?"

She let his sweet words take permanent residence in her mental rolodex and nodded with a moan of yes. Taking hold of her right hand, he brushed his long thumb over her knuckles before lifting her hand and sweetly kissing it. The slight moistness of his lips and warm air released from his nose hit her skin sending a signal of sensation to her brain. She exhaled, slowly clearing away the non-existing knot in her throat. As he rose slowly a few curls fell forward covering his left eye. When he paused, he caught sight of her watching him. With eyes connected in their stare of mutual affection, he gently pulled her hand to his cashmere sweater covered chest. Without a word she floated toward him, and he whispered, "May I kiss you, Delphine?"

She nodded. Leaning upward and slightly to the left she met his lowered head that tilted to the right. Her eyelids fluttered and closed quickly. The silkiness of his beard touched her skin just before his closed lips melted over hers. The romantic kiss held both suspended in the silent moments of time. Her hand held by him was secured to his chest. His closed pink lips engulfing her plump ebony ones were what entangled them. Sealed to her he released a long exhaling moan taking in more of that distinctive fragrance from her skin. Delphine delighted him by opening her mouth. Lovingly his tongue explored the opening and beyond. A delicate dance of tasting one another ensued. She had no thoughts because he tasted like buttery layers of a freshly baked croissant, something she loved about France. The affectionate exchange remained constant until he forced himself to ease away from the deliciousness of her mouth. His parting at the speed of rising dough allowed him to witness her delicate smile before she gradually opened her eyes.

Philippe' and Delphine's first kiss was a timeless moment of euphoria.

24 Après

O ver the next few days, Rex, Delphine, and Claudine received history lessons of the Delacroix land by Philippe' and his father during guided tours of the home and discussions of some family paintings, sculptures, war relics, and priceless memorabilia throughout their chateau. The men took such pride in their family legacy, Delphine felt as if she was on one of the many museum tours and gallery exhibits Philippe' had taken her on.

It was amazing to her that they had detailed knowledge of their family tracing back generations with historical documents to prove what happened and who they were as a family. Claudine shared how it was like following a history book. Although they didn't say it to others, alone the two women recalled how Alex Hailey was able to accomplish such a remarkable task with his family going back to Kunta Kinta in Africa.

"Girl, if we could it would be so amazing to know what tribes we come from." Delphine said soaking in the bathtub while Claudine was brushing her teeth.

"Yeah, it would be, but you know that ain't possible. We don lost their history. Alex Hailey was lucky. Most Black folks don't talk anyway so there are no stories to get past the grandparents. You for sure ain't getting no info, I can't even get your momma to give me her coconut cake recipe." Claudine said finishing up. They both snickered with the truth of her statement.

Sitting on the plush cushion chair after handing Delphine her Avon bottle of Skin So Soft to pour a little in her hot water, she then said, "I'm glad we ain't stuck in the dorm and …. Now tell me the truth, what you doing with da professor? I've seen the two of you look at each other like ya wanna play tag with cha' body parts."

Relaxing back in the water, she answered not looking into her beady dark eyes. "Dene, you know better. I don't do nothing."

"You a lie, Delphine Asha. Girl, you kissed Lance Fredricks at junior prom, I was there, cow don't deny it. Oh, you let Harvey Coute' slip his tongue in your mouth after graduation. He was so excited and didn't mind that you slapped the crap out of him. Let's not forget, sophomore year at Tulane, Simon-Nathan, if he had just been satisfied with the weeks of private kisses. But the dog wanted a lot more and got it from Lisa Petre. So don't say you do nothing. I know you. You will kiss someone. He likes you. He don't take other students around to shows, poetry readings, art exhibits and museums. So don't try to say he don't. I sensed it when we were in Canada. You were too comfortable on the floor having wine chatting with him. You didn't even drink. The man got your ass to have a drink! Yeah, he got some man charms alright. Okay, so, tell it. Did you? What was it like? He's White! But he nice lookin'. Got them dreamy eyes, like Paul Newman or maybe James Dean. He has a nice body too… wait what was I saying? Oh yea, what's up?" She knew there was something to tell, so she moved to the floor next to the tub to get the scoop.

Chuckling, Delphine nodded then added more information. "It was nice. He did kiss me on Christmas when we went to get wine from the cellar—"

She cut her off with a barrage of questions. "Ooh, does he smell like wet dog up close? That's what my mother and grandma used to say about White men growing up on the Tunica-Biloxi Reservation. Oh girl, is it like they say? Dell, ya got ta, tell me. Is it?" She sat up excited to learn the truth.

"Claudine! I said kiss I don't know nothing about what his johnson look like. Come on, who ya talkin' too? I am not Lisa Petre, Lolli or Lorelle!"

"Ya right, ya right." She said calmly waiving her hands as she sat back down to hear the rest.

"Oh, and ya momma, auntie Soyala was so wrong. At least she is 'bout him. Philippe' smells yummy, like vanilla and soft leather. His hair is soft, and them blonde curls just wrap around my fingers like a seahorse tail. He is very gentlemanly, and I like him. Philippe' makes me feel alive and free to explore all sorts of wonderful things. He is reserved but so smart. When we talk it feels like my whole mind is opening to an adventure from a perspective I never knew existed. He knows so much about different people, philosophy, psychology, the arts, cultures, great writers, the earth, the galaxy, food, and wine, so many things. He pushes me and I like that. He also really wants to know what I think about things, research he does for the national library or for the university. He even likes for me to red pen his lecture notes. He is the right kind of fun. This will probably be the best year of my entire life." Delphine stared off into space and Claudine was still for a moment. Then they looked at each other and started snickering.

Claudine tapped Delphine's wet hand resting on the side of the tub and said, "I could tell you were enjoying yourself with him. You are not like Lorelle, you don't show it. You always been a deeper person, requiring substance in a guy. Always talking circles around them boys at school. But when the professors came and had them analytical debates and study sessions focused on the views of everyone not just them it was really a jolt to the brain. We were hooked. But he's white. I mean, you of all people letting him kiss you. That wouldn't have ever happened back home for sure but here… here you're different Dell. Well, I am too. I got two boyfriends and with one I do a lot more than kiss."

She started laughing as Delphine flung some bath bubbles on to her nightgown. "You so nasty, Dene. Okay now, you gonna be hot to trot like Lolli. Don't mess around get married with two kids and it be extra hard trying ta finish school like Lorelle."

Claudine stood up putting her hands on her hips. "Don't be putting no curse on me. Better tell yourself that. These French men are freaky, and the professor is older than us. He may want to dip his twig in some young dark tree sap before we go home. Best watch ya self."

Their cackling squeals echoed in the bathroom for several minutes before they got themselves ready to get dressed for the day's adventures.

25 Confiance

During the days after the feast, Rex had spent a lot of time with the men, while Delphine and Claudine socialized with the lady's doing girlie activities. Delphine helped mostly in the tasks of daily cooking with Ava, Gert, Heidi, and Nannette. She enjoyed talking and learning new techniques and specialty dishes they made for the winter holiday. Learning some of their stories about being a lady of the house and their lives in France kept her interested in all the women she spent her afternoons with.

Claudine had more time spent with Mrs. Delacroix, Carmen, Josephine, and Mrs. Durand when she came to visit. Walks around the estate, learning about the land and family from a women's historical point of view fascinated her. But these French ladies were slick as they took their strolls learning more about her and Delphine, their families and being Black in America than Claudine probably would have shared knowingly.

At a formal tea was the time everyone came together to enjoy sharing feelings of gratefulness and a bit of their day with each other. It was also when, Philippe' got to see her smile and she could feel a warmth rush to her cheeks as he periodically glanced at her.

During the second round of tea service, Delphine requested Philippe' to explain some of the history of a few art pieces and share a childhood memory in an area of the home she had not explored. He agreed with a smile and helped her up as they broke away from the tea party. Not seeing the side eyes rolling or hearing a few grunts and low snickers, the two traveled first to the grand ballroom.

The detailed summery of the original architect and artist of the huge room with blue walls and twenty-two-foot cathedral ceilings painted like clouds in the heavens and the years of remodeling had been delivered like most other tours— as a formal historical lecture.

Delphine was more preoccupied with the beauty of the massive hanging crystal chandeliers wondering why some had candles, but others had lights, inspecting the pristine white grand piano, and a wood floor where she could see shadows of her reflection. As he spoke, he simply watched her eyes appear to dance with excitement as she scanned over some intricate details of the room.

When she heard the tone of his deep baritone voice change to slightly higher, she curiously glanced over at him. The brightness of his face appeared as if he was remembering something comical.

Philippe' then began telling her a story. "The musketeers and I learned to dance in this room. We were about eleven and Andreas being shorter, was always paired with Nannette. He didn't like it and constantly tried to switch with one of us, but we wouldn't change. Forcing him to partner with her for an hour four times a week became like a fun game, Tomas, Chevalier, and I were playing. We laughed watching him squirm. But after a while he just stopped asking to switch. I believe he has loved her since we were sixteen."

Moving to an open area on a wall, he tapped a few buttons, and an introduction of sound began. As he moved to the middle of the room a soft accented voice began to speak. He held out his hand and postured himself to lead a waltz. He asked, "Delphine, would you like to dance with me?"

Smiling with all her teeth showing, she moved into the space he had created for her and let him guide her around the room. Giggling, she had no idea what she was doing and stumbled over her own feet several times. Delphine tried to follow his feet, but he would tell her, "Look up," while never slowing. Occasionally, he'd lift her off her feet and spin her around to the music. From the tilt of his head, the glide of his stride and the twinkle of his stare had her feeling like a feather being gently blown into the air. He smiled softly humming Julio Iglesias's "Moonlight Lady" that filled the air surrounding them as they danced around the ballroom.

Delivering a wink and bow at the end of the song, Delphine gave him a fumbled curtsy she recalled seeing on "The Carol Burnett Show" which had been a family favorite growing up. Philippe' turned off the music and led her still chuckling to one of his favorite rooms in his family home.

Philippe' next took her to see their massive two-story library filled with literature from floor to ceiling, even with an attached ladder to access some of them. It was overwhelming to her eyes, but she couldn't stop grinning.

"So many books. I love it! How many have you read?" She was so excited she didn't hear his answer as she rushed to check out the art. She breezed by asking questions about each of the six large realistic and impressionistic paintings of lands and homes covering one wall. Philippe' explained they were historical pieces from his family lands, but one was only for decoration to even out the decor. Then she made it to the large staircase and began to climb to the second level of books lined neatly in shelves.

"Be careful, Delphine." He said waiting below, watching her plump round derrière wiggle in her denim jeans. A vision he wasn't expecting to get earlier, since she was covered in a buttoned to the neck white shirt and under a black and white striped double-breasted jacket with linebacker shoulders. But his decision to remain at the bottom of the stairs gave him the thrill. He smirked but inconspicuously covered his mouth knowing she didn't realize he was staring at her behind as she climbed the stairs.

"Delphine is there something specific you are looking for?"

Philippe' asked as he stepped back to see her above. She was tapping the white and black braided headpiece over her forehead thinking. Then she shouted, "One of your favorites. Musketeer … No. The Count … The Count of Monte Cristo … I know it must be here. I want to see if it has your little boy fingerprints all over the pages." She snickered covering her mouth with her hand.

Chuckling he slowly motioned with his long fingers for her to come back down to the main level.

Guiding her to a shelf closer to the atlas and floor globe of the world, he pulled out his tattered childhood copy of Alexandre Dumas's classic "Le Comte de Monte-Cristo" and placed it into her hands as she giggled. He grinned watching her opening it slowly like it would fall apart if she moved too fast. As Delphine inspected the old book, Philippe' leaned slightly to take in her fragrance and then he whispered, "I want to kiss you, Ms. Murry. May I?"

She paused still holding the book open and lifted her head to find him just inches away. Mesmerized by the current of his eyes luring her up to meet his lips, she moaned a slow yes.

His stepping forward just a bit forced her to take a half step backward, his long body towered over her as he rested his arm onto the wall and lowered his head. She closed her eyes inching upward to fill the breeze of his beard over her nose and then, contact. His liquid lips drizzled over her waiting mouth seemingly at the speed of a rising tide. Philippe' was deliberately tender. She melted inside when his lips covered hers. It was a romantic kiss. Nothing more. His mouth was the only thing touching her, but a volcanic heat was building. A charge of lightning passed through the air bringing forth a force of thunder growing deep inside her, while his tongue entered and delicately explored. She was being swept away by the waves of his passion, and it was difficult to release from his invisible hold.

With her eyes closed and still holding onto the book, now flat against her chest, Philippe' backed away licking his bottom lip with smug satisfaction. He moved quietly to a nearby desk chair and sat the several feet away and waited. Slowly her eyelids crept open, and she came back to the reality of the room. Without words, their eyes found each other. Her lungs silently released the whisper of paused air trapped inside. Philippe' smiled and waited for her to speak. What came out of her mouth took him completely by surprise.

"Are you a sex freak, professor?" His neck jerked back. "What?"

She cleared her throat and asked her question differently. "Is it true that the French are overly sexual? Especially French men just like to have it all the time, with anyone around. Is it true that you are taught and practice very risqué things?"

He wiped the corner of his mouth with the back of his hand, then said, "Stereotyping. That is not like you, Ms. Murry." He looked at her expecting her to comment but he got nothing. So, he said, "No, it isn't true of all perhaps some. Sex is meant to be an exchange of physical and emotional energy for optimum pleasure. An act of service to one's partner. Having a lot, in no way means a person does it well or that they come close to obtaining the pinnacle level of achievement. We French take pride in our love making. There is an art to it—yes, many forms. It is a craft. Anyone can bake a baguette but only a chef de partie-pâtissier is the master of the baked pastry."

She watched him without reacting. After taking a breath he added, "As for a choice in partner that is a personal preference. There are no rules specifically around that. However, I have always been a heterosexual male enjoying the exploration of women. I have never engaged in any way with a male or animal, in the ways I do with a female. When it comes a time for me to connaître a lady, how I 'know' her is between the two of us."

He cleared his throat then asked, "Delphine, why these sudden questions about intimacy?" He began smirking, feeling perhaps the conversation may lead to more than the kiss.

As she placed the book back on the bookshelf, she said in a tone very matter of fact. "Well, Claudine and I recently finished reading, "L'Amant" by Marguerite Duras required for psychology. And the other day, we were told your father took you to a brothel when you were very young maybe ten. So, I was curious if the hypersexuality of French people, rather true or imagined, was in fact a male domination inference as a way to deflect from certain inadequacies revered in other cultures or something actually trained from a young age to distract from or even diminish ideals of social injustices within the culture of French people."

Locking eyes with him, she had an expression he knew all too well. It was the same concentrated stare with the wrinkled brows that meant she was working out a data puzzle in her head. Philippe's brief thought of having more than a kiss instantly vaporized from his mind. He sniffled then though*t, (She is adorable.)* Then as usual, he gave a professional reply, "Those are possible theories and a different perception of French people and intimate behavior of humans. I don't think it would be fair to debate this without proper research. Let's schedule a time to do so when I am back at the library, alright?" She nodded with a smile while adjusting her dangling gold leaf earrings. Philippe' continued, "Now about the other, I was fourteen not ten years old. My father and grandfather initiated that. Who even told … Oh, I know. I will be having a talk with Ms. big mouth." He inhaled deep before rubbing his beard and his eyes in disgust. "What else did she say? Josephine tends to make things up for shock value. Don't believe everything she says."

Delphine started snickering, then confessed, "Uh, to be honest, we were discussing social and cultural similarities. Josephine told us that young French boys being taken to brothels by older men, usually their father, is a social tradition for education. This type of practice is much more frequent in aristocratic circles than others, she said. Then I said, it must be like a rite of passage similar to markings on the body, a walkabout, or circumcision that are common in many cultures as a transformation from childhood to manhood. Your sister didn't actually say you did at all. I just well. . . So, fourteen really. Hmmp."

Philippe' bit his bottom lip, not sure if he wanted to jump from the chair, grab her and kiss her or yell very loudly. She was just so enchanting. He decided to roll his tongue over his teeth and blink quickly before changing the subject.

"It's about time we see the Lyon murals and the Amphitheatre des Trois Gaules." She nodded with excitement, and they left to collect her coat and Claudine.

The following day consisted of a tour of Old Lyon and the family trip to Place Bellecour for a winter concert, shopping, and dining. It was the very first time Delphine and her girlfriend had been ice skating. The instructor guidance Philippe' gave to Delphine required her to hold onto him for dear life as he moved slowly around the rink laughing at her. Tomas assisted Claudine in her skating activities while he kept grabbing her firm behind in his efforts to catch her before falling. Of course, Rex and Elizabeth were couple skating like professionals.

"You need practice to balance. Don't pout. I won't let you fall again. Delphine come on get up." He tried to say it holding in his chuckles, but her expression sitting on the ice was priceless.

"This isn't something Black people are supposed to do Philippe'… and you're laughing." She was irritated. It was the second time she fell on her butt, and she was getting wet. It was cold and she didn't want to pretend to try anymore.

"Delphine, look at Claudine she is doing it. I won't believe Tomas is a better teacher. Get up." Holding out his long arms covered in his winter layers, he squatted down and pulled her up. Then said, "You can do this. It's just getting used to being on the blade not think of them as roller-skates. I'm going to skate backward, and you hold on to me going forward don't look down. Look at me, Delphine. Just look at me."

As he coaxed her to try again, she huffed but did what he said. The deep blueness from the seductive tranquility of his piercing eyes latched onto her ebony brown ones. There seemed to be an unseen force constantly pulling her toward him. The two took in air, exhaled, and moved in sync. He was right, she didn't fall again. Twenty minutes later, her skating instructor eased to the side and sat her down to rest.

"Bien joué. It is like the waltz; everything will be all right if you trust me."

Proud of her accomplishment, she glanced up at him with a wide smile and grateful nod.

Since they didn't gamble, later the two enjoyed a sort of double date at a café-theatre with Nannette and Andreas, while everyone else went to the casino or returned home for the evening. Delphine had less feelings of awkwardness with his affectionate touching her hand and winking with soft smirks in the presents of his younger sister and his best friend.

The two never mentioned it or looked shocked with what was happening right in front of their eyes. It was as if they already knew. Nannette and Andreas's periodic private whispers and giggles could not have been because of the comedy on stage or the movement of their unborn son but it seemed the two had a bit of delight in pretending not to notice.

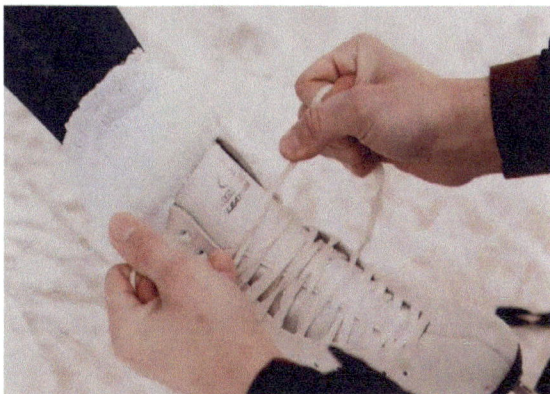

26 UNYE

Mr. and Mrs. Delacroix enjoyed these guests being in their home. They wanted it to continue and extended an invitation to their guests to remain for their annual New Year's Eve celebration in Lyon. However, Philippe' had previously shared with Delphine that New Year's in Paris was not to be missed and he had plans for them. Since Pierre Clement was out of town, Claudine didn't have plans, so she and Rex agreed to stay for the festivities. While Philippe' and Delphine flew back to Paris.

"Where are we going?" She said as the private car drove in a direction she didn't recognize as the way to her dorm. Sitting next to her with his legs crossed and hands on his lap, he smiled and spoke very calmly, "You will stay with me."

Instantly her eyelids reached for the stars and her jaw fell to the earth. Before she could utter a word, he placed his large, gloved hand over hers and said, "Remember, trust me." She swallowed as he tapped the top of her hand to ease her anxiety. Then he told her, "It won't be the first time we have slept together." He winked at her, and she slowly began to breathe with a relaxed giggle as they traveled to his home in Paris.

Philippe's home in Paris 13th- Tolbiac was stunning. The four-bedroom three-bathroom penthouse located on the top two floors of a freestone residence with an extended terrace and a library was modern luxury. His home had a very spacious and simplistic masculine vibe upon entering. Unlike his family estate in Lyon that overflowed with classic artwork and historical pieces, Philippe's place was more for a working professional that enjoyed elegant things.

A white grand piano had a little sparkle as the light from the 6'0 windows hit its polish. The dark hard wood floors, corner bar and fireplace, long burgundy leather couches and plush area rugs in complementary colors fit his conservative personality. However, his kitchen and a bedroom had bright yellow and blue décors that matched his friendliness, while two bathrooms and his dining room had colorful hints of lavender fields, grassy hills, and snowcapped mountains. He guided Delphine to an upstairs guestroom that he decorated and kept open for his sisters. The pastel-colored walls of peach, green and buttercream allowed for a light feminine feeling without being overly so.

"There is a guestroom downstairs but it's Andreas's. I would not want to have you in there and take the risk that he might come over drunk and want to crash. The other I use as my research office. This room is best." He said placing her bags down for her to unpack what she needed.

"It's lovely, thank you, Philippe'. Umm, where is your room?"

His head darted up to read her facial expression. Then he quickly answered. "Down the hall. Are you curious to know if I am an untidy person or do you want to know how firm my bed might be, Ms. Murry?"

He seductively gave her a grin while she smashed her lips together holding in her urge to laugh.

"I was only interested in knowing the colors scheme of the room since there are many different ones in your home, Mr. Delacroix. I do know how to box remember." She snickered kicking off her shoes and easing into the fluffy slippers from her smaller overnight bag.

Laughing and motioning for her to follow, Philippe' led her down a loft like hallway with one side of large windows and the other overlooking the living and dining rooms below. From the design to the décor, Delphine took note of everything passing her eyes and made internal comments of acceptance or disapproval.

Entering his bedroom and walking ahead of him, she rubbed her nose to cover the nibbling of the corner of her bottom lip. It was not what she was expecting to see, and it definitely made her giggle inside. She thought, *(He's still that boy pretending to be the Count of Monte-Cristo.)*

At the head of the large king-size bed and underneath a ruffled white canopy drapes around a gold and crystal chandelier hanging from the ceiling, there was a hand painted mural wall of large palm leaves and bamboo culms. His high square bed made of dark polished wood had four gigantic round posters that almost touched the ceiling. Each poster base on the floor was in the carved shape of an elephant foot halfway up it transitioned into an elephant tusk to a point that curved outward. Everything on the bed was white and pressed so straight it might cut someone if not careful. There were other doors, bookshelves, plants, and mirrors but as she turned around to survey the room, the glass wall to the visible bathtub and shower at the far end caught her attention.

"Uh, you don't like privacy?" She said pointing to the view from the middle of the room into the visible bathroom. He laughed then countered. "Why would I need privacy from myself?" She walked into the silver and white marble and glass bathroom, passed the basin, and opened a side door to find the bidet and toilet. Then said, "Oh, glad to see that you are behind closed doors to handle the other business."

He laughed holding his bearded chin and stepped back watching her inspection of his personal space.

Sauntering passed him to the other side of the room she opened the door of a large walk-in wardrobe and dressing room. In the corner of his room, she noticed two large rectangular black hard cases, which she assumed contained his saxophones. Then she walked across to his large carved desk that seemed to match the same dark rich wood of his bed and other bedroom furniture.

Placing the tip of her index finger on each one of his pens, the small clock, desk calendar, and then she tapped on a smooth burgundy leather portfolio trimmed in gold. She quickly flipped it open, and discovered cream lined stationary paper with burgundy monogrammed letters JPD at the bottom right corner. She pretended not to be impressed, releasing a snarky "hmp" sound, as she began to open the small drawers of the desk. With his eyes constantly following her every move, he smirked shaking his head before saying, "Is there anything else that your fi ngers would like to examine, Delphine?"

She stopped touching his personal things—gave a nervous smile and said, "You have a nice room. No. Uh, I am a little tired. I'd like to take a nap. But what time are we going? Oh, and what am I supposed to wear? Is it formal?"

He followed her back down the hallway to her room and put her at ease about his secret plans.

"Rest. We have plenty of time. I won't disturb you I have some things to do and will be downstairs in the library if you need anything. I'd say you should be in something warm but comfortable. But absolutely no twill skirt though."

She giggled and closed the door to take a long nap.

Delphine woke to the sound of soft classical piano music. Curious she slipped from under the throw blanket, slowly opened the door and crept halfway down the open hall. Inhaling quickly like a low gasp, she relaxed to smile watching Philippe' playing his beautiful white piano down below. Th e way his body moved with each keystroke reminded her of gentle waves rolling onto a sandy beach. With her hand over her chest her skin felt as if it was lightly vibrating like it does when he kisses her. She thought, *(He's simply brilliant! Oh, he makes me wanna kiss him. Huh? What am I thinking?)*

Delphine fought to keep her thoughts in check. *(We're friends, Delphine! He … He is the one that asks to kiss me. I do not initiate kissing him! Nope. You just like the fact that he really is a gentleman. He is smarter than you and teaches you all sorts of amazing things. You trust him. It's okay to be friends. Yeah, and he's adventurous, uh and so calm and respectful. Oh, and … and now he plays the piano! I wanna kiss him right now! No. I am not trippin' … Am I?)*

Delphine stood on the second floor of his penthouse gawking in silence. She was completely mesmerized by the sights and sounds around her and confused by her thoughts.

Philippe' had played Johann Sebastian Bach's – "Air" from his 3rd Orchestral Suite and Ludwig van Beethoven's "Für Elise" before glancing up and seeing her standing in the hallway looking down at him.

Immediately the music stopped, and he rose saying, "Why didn't you come downstairs?"

She snapped out of her torpor, and answered, "I was enjoying your concert. You play magnificently, Philippe'. So, I guess it's not just for show after all." She giggled after her last sentence.

Philippe' smiled while moving closer into the living room and still talking, "Would you like something before we get ready? We need to leave at 8:00 p.m. Right now, it is 6:30 p.m. but I can make you something, tea?"

Waving her hands gesturing no, she said, "I'm fine. You said warm and comfortable right?"

"Oui. But no twill skirt, remember!" He started snickering.

"Ha-ha. I'm going to wear a sweater and black pants smarty!" She announced, playfully rolling her eyes.

Philippe' let out a laugh and clapped his hands together shouting, "Excellent! I will do the same. We can be twins!"

Laughing, she gave him a thumbs up.

At 8:00 p.m., they were dressed in boots, dark slacks, warm long sweaters, and under overcoats and gloves. The two ventured off to dine on the luxury Bateaux Parisiens glass enclosed riverboat that slowly floated along the Seine, soaking in the lights and romantic ambiance.

Sitting in the front section of the boat to have the best view, listening to live music, and sipping expensive champagne before dinner was an experience they would not forget.

"This is beautiful." she said with a twinkle in her eyes gazing at him from across the table. Not that she minded but she was curious, so she asked, "Philippe', why are we the only ones sitting at the front?"

She had noticed boarding that no one followed them to the front of the boat. Around them were several other tables along the glass sides of the boat but they were empty.

"You see, I wanted to be alone with you, so I purchased all the tables to make it possible." He replied with a sly grin and a wink.

Tonight, his deep voice seemed to send waves of tantalizing surges throughout her body. The hair on her skin started to stand up from an unusual feeling of electricity as he spoke those words. Within seconds goosebumps rose slowly covering her skin underneath her black and white checkerboard sweater. She thought, *(Oh my goodness. Why am I so hot and have goosebumps?)* while taking a few more sips from her second glass of chilled sweet champagne.

As they discussed the music entertainment, the goals of the coming year and indulged in the second course of the six-course extravagant meal, something memorable occurred. Delphine grabbed her mouth and shut her eyes. Abruptly, Philippe' stopped speaking with his fork midway to his mouth. He froze with creased eyebrows and pressed lips. The sound didn't echo as loud or as fast as the stench hit the air from her unexpected gas release out of both ends during mid-conversation. Ultimately embarrassed, she rushed to the restroom while the rapid fire of simultaneous burping and farting continued uncontrollably.

It had been fifteen minutes, and she hadn't returned to the table. Philippe' had the maître d' hotêl hold serving additional courses and checked on Delphine.

"Ms. Murry, are you alright? What was it exactly? I have alerted the maître d' hotêl that something is wrong. Can you tell me what you think it might be?" He said after tapping on the door with the back of his bent fingers. It made a louder sound than he was intending due to having his family crest insignia diamond ring on his middle finger, one that he only wore on New Year's Eve. There was no sound, so he knocked again but this time with his fist.

"Delphine, answer me, please?"

Moments later, the door cracked open. Eager to make sure she was alright he leaned in before she could fully open it. "Ma chére, are you alright? Do you need a doctor?"

Not looking into his face but only at the floor, she answered, "I'm fine. I'm fine."

With an exhale of relief, he escorted her back to their candle-lit table. They sat quietly for a few minutes as she sipped her water. He continued to watch her carefully before asking again.

"Are you sure you are alright? Do you think you may be allergic to something you ate?" His eyes were burning with deep concern for her wellbeing. It took a few more sips of water and glances out at the darkness and festive lights along the Seine before she turned to see his face. Still embarrassed with flush warm cheeks she confessed, "I

… I think it's the champagne."

He leaned forward. "What do you mean?"

Nervously, she cleared her throat and swallowed before revealing her secret again. "It's the champagne. I … I've never had it before … umm it gave me horrible gas."

His reaction was a loud gregarious laugh followed by him hitting the table with his fist. "Oh, Delphine, you make me laugh! I thought you were sick … perhaps it was the escargot … never … never would have guessed the champagne!"

He continued to laugh as she tried to pinch his bicep but all she got was the black material from his cashmere turtleneck sweater.

"It's not funny. Do you know how embarrassed I am right now? Don't laugh, Philippe'. Please, please don't laugh." She had this pitiful look of embarrassment, horror, and sadness on her face. He sniffled and calmed his amusement quickly.

"Alright. I won't laugh anymore."

He adjusted in his seat and motioned for the servers to bring the next course. Then he said, "This wasn't what I had in mind for tonight. It is much better. Relax. I was the only one here. Imagine if the entire front of the ship was filled with dinner guests."

He raised his eyebrows and grinned. She gasped, "Oh lord!"

Philippe' winked at her then held her hand resting on the table before sharing calming words. "Relax. Now we will have wine or maybe you should just have water. Perhaps tea?"

"Tea, yes that's good."

Quickly the champagne was removed from the table, and Philippe' had a red wine, and several options of tea were brought for Delphine to choose.

When the plated entree came and the staff left them alone to enjoy, the table was quiet as they began eating the third course. Periodically glancing over they smiled at each other in full agreement that it was delicious. After sipping his wine, Philippe' could tell she was no longer embarrassed and decided to ask her something important.

"Delphine?"

Lifting her head sliding the fork from her mouth, she moaned. "I need to ask you something."

Quickly chewing the lobster, she had just placed in her mouth. She answered, "Yes."

"I think it's important that I know to prepare myself. Will there be more gas later?"

A gasp and snort came from her direction as she began leaning to punch his right bicep while giggling. He laughed as he attempted to lean away from her playful slugs to his upper arm. She shouted, "Oh, you make me sick!"

After dinner, he held her tightly as if he were a blanket swaddling her in secure comfort, while they watched the Paris fireworks show. It was an amazing and spectacular sight to see and a moment the two would always remember.

"Your eyes sparkle, reflecting the fireworks in the sky. Lovely. May I kiss you, Ms. Delphine Asha Murry?" He whispered holding her chin up by two soft black leather glove covered fingers.

Their eyes were bound in stillness, like high-security locks on a bank vault. She started to feel her skin melting, while plunging deep into the blue waters of his eyes. "Oui" was her answer.

Delphine held her breath a few seconds before the silkiness of his creamy lips oozed onto hers. She leaned in further. Inch by inch, pressing forward and the pressure deepened. She was mesmerized by each truth show by the man inside Professor Delacroix. He opened doors she didn't know existed and it was freeing and exciting to experience such wonders.

Her mind raced with thoughts… *(He is strong but very tender. Humble yet very accomplished. Genuinely kind, controlled, funny, curious, and very gallant. I like that he challenges me with his intelligence, searches for my thoughts and connects the dots even when we disagree. He is my friend, and he is a magnificent person.)*

In her presence, Philippe' felt her hidden magnetic energy all around him and it was intoxicating to his mind. Something about her dragged him into a place of emotions and desires he had never felt before. It was fascinating to explore and discover her. She was strong, almost fearless, determined, mature and enchanting. It scared him. But he could not help himself, he yearned for her. His mind flashed with words of reason, *(What am I doing? I must stop. We are friends. I have to…to stop!)*

It was an unforgettable New Year's Eve. As their lips gradually parted from their one sweet kiss at midnight, they clasped hands and silently gazed up at the sky to welcome the year 1985.

27 *What's Next*

Over the next several weeks, work for Philippe' and school for Delphine kept them busy and not as free to spend time together. They regularly talked on the phone. An occasional movie or play was about all they could squeeze in because of their conflicting schedules. Philippe' didn't even get to take her out on her birthday but he made a point to plan something special when he was back in town.

Delphine and Nannette spent girl time together, since she and Andreas also lived in Paris. Both had a lot in common and the friendship grew quickly. Delphine and Nannette shopped, even collaborat-ed to decorate the coming baby's room. They had long conversations about being a wife, a new mother, growing up as an American woman from New Orleans and a French woman from Lyon.

Delphine had been writing and receiving monthly correspondence from her parents, sisters, and a few cousins. She had been fairly caught up on her own family happenings, but she had decided to go home to visit. She made plans to do so during the coming break. When the weather started to warm, it seemed their calendar and routines quickly modified and Philippe' and Delphine were back to socializing together more. There were the regular afternoon teas at amazing places like Ladurée, Mariage Frères, and

La Galerie. Quick lunches and poetry readings at corner café's, local market excursions, attending art openings, and weekend dinners at his home.

Frequently, they took turns cooking for each other. Since Claudine was always off with her only boyfriend Pierre, Delphine spent her free weekends staying in the girl room at Philippe's house unless he went out of town or had a work function.

On a weekend stay, after they had been on the terrace sipping wine and talking about things he learned in Africa, abruptly, Philippe' stopped talking. He took the wine and a plate of cheese and bread into the kitchen. Delphine was unsure why he changed the mood slowly followed him inside.

"Philippe' are you alright?" she asked curiously standing next to the marble counter across from him. He gazed at her reaching up to cup her face in his left hand. He gave her a partial smile before he began to slowly bend down and conquer her lips. With a taste from his delicate searching tongue mixed with the sweetness of the fermented vine grapes, they both released brief moans of delight. Slowing the long moments of affection, Philippe' paused and withdrew inches away from her face. He silently waited for her to open her eyes. When she did, he locked onto the dark brown spheres of a glossy marble and whispered, "If I asked to touch your body while kissing you, would you allow it?" Philippe' was so close, her body shuttered underneath her top. Staring up into the dream depths of his deep blue eyes, she slowly moaned a yes. Philippe' raised his eyebrows while easing his hands around her onto the counter, said, "You would? Tell me why?"

"Huh?" She said softly, a little stunned by his question. Philippe' nodded for her to answer it. Delphine looked away for a second then back to him, then answered truthfully, "I trust you. And I know you would only do what you have asked."

Philippe' smirked slightly, then whispered, "Awww. I promised, so I won't. But now, I know you like me just as much as I like you. Ha ha ha." She gasped. Immediately, he grabbed her into a smothering bear hug, chuckling. Delphine huffed with her face pressed against his chest covered by his cotton rugby shirt playfully slugging his firm abdomen. She thought, *(He makes me sick. Ha! I feel so happy knowing him. How did he do that?)*

While she held him around his waist returning the friendship hug like a momma bear, Philippe' opened a side drawer in his kitchen pulling out a small, gift-wrapped box. He placed it on the counter for her to see. "Here is something for you." He said, releasing her and motioning to the box.

"What … What is this?" She held the box in her hand, looking back at him with a surprised yet curious smile.

"I know you said you didn't want anything, but I did get you something for your birthday in January. I know it is very late, but I wanted to give it to you now. Open it." He said, motioning for her to open her gift.

Delphine sucked on her bottom lip as she opened the small square box wrapped in purple paper and tied neatly with a white bow. Completely stunned, her eyes grew seemingly as large as saucers. She gasped pulling out the 24k gold peridot and amethyst drop earrings. "Philippe', didn't have . . . oh, they're beautiful." She said rushing to pull out her gold hoops to put them on. He grinned watching her tell her left ear hole off for not cooperating. After she got them in, she kissed him quickly, saying, "I got ta see." She rushed to the nearest bathroom next to Andreas's guestroom. "Oh, so pretty! Merci!" She shouted from the bathroom. Returning to the kitchen, she hugged him again. "Thank you so much. I wasn't expecting a gift, but I love them. Purple is one of my favorite colors. Wait, I told you that."

He kissed her forehead. "Happy belated birthday to you, Delphine Murry."

"Now what to give you for yours?" She said pretending to be thinking. He chuckled and said, "Just a kiss, please."

"Deal! Here it comes early." Delphine said, reaching up grabbing his cheeks and pulling his face down to hers for a sweet lip kiss.

Grinning, Philippe' slowly parted from her and reached over to the phone. He was going to call Andreas and Nannette to see if they wanted to come over for dinner.

When Nannette was feeling up to it, she and Andreas would join for Murry dinners at Philippe's home, where they got a real taste of Louisiana cooking.

A regular request from all three of them when it was Delphine's turn to cook was for her to make chicken and sausage gumbo, 7-up pound cake, banana pudding, salmon cakes, shrimp and grits, coconut cake, bourbon peach cobbler,and sweet potato biscuits.

The last time they all enjoyed her menu was a week before Nannette was unable to walk on her own.Her relief came when she finally gave birth to their son, Henri-François on March 21,1985.

Philippe's parents came up from Lyon and he insisted that they stay with him to visit their new grandson. They stayed a few weeks, and it was the first time Delphine hadn't visited or talked to Philippe' for more than a few days. It felt odd but she reasoned he needed to be with his family.

During this time apart, she did a little exploring on her own outside of her heavy class schedule and study routine. She did some social activities with Claudine and a few girls from Switzerland, Britain, Kenya, and Nigeria.

Since arriving in Paris, dorm mates Hazel, Amrah, Chelsea, Nadia, Lani, Claudine, and Delphine occasionally hung out together, since there is safety in numbers in any country. Although the club scene was very different in Europe than in America it was also lots of fun.

On the Friday evening before spring break, after a long day of classes, papers and lectures, a need to let off some steam was needed for the girls in Sorbonne dorm A456/Flr2. It was planned to be a night of fun before going back home.

Dressed in a stylish black pants suit, black lace shirt and pumps, she had dramatic red lips, soft gold eye shadow and her hair was in cornrows pinned in a large back right-side bun accented with a tilted black beret. Even though she felt a little too sexy, like always Delphine was the most modestly dressed of the group.

Hitting the popular night club venue that used to be an old bus station, the music was loud, the crowd was packed, the air was smoky, and everyone was having a good time. As usual Claudine and Delphine danced together, which was a common practice back in Louisiana and on the rare occasion the two ventured out into the night life of Paris. The rule is come together leave together no exception and everyone knew the rule.

A few hours, drinks, and lots of dancing later, Delphine was tired and wanted to go home. She planned to get some sleep before her morning flight back to New Orleans but most of the ladies wanted to make another club stop first. They packed in cabs and went to the club known as the secret playground of the city. A different type of crowd but just as packed and lively.

A few dances in and some numbers collected from cute men in this place, the ladies agreed they were ready to go. Delphine pushed her way to the entrance to step outside first as the others she thought were making their way to the door. But Delphine was outside in the dark alone for several minutes when two men approached her to take a ride. Positioning herself to fight and protect herself from these strangers, they spoke more aggressively.

One man grabbed her arm, and she broke his nose with one hard punch. As he yelled bleeding and holding his nose, the other snatched her by her hair bun yanking her backward. She swung to hit him, but he slapped her face instead. Unfazed by the strike, she jabbed with a connection to his jaw. He landed a hard punch to her face and then one to her gut. Before falling she used the last of her strength to shove her patent leather pump up his groin. Delphine fell to the ground. The ladies arrived and without pausing they continued to beat up the two men. One was on the ground in severe pain groaning, the other tried to run with his head back to stop his bleeding. He didn't get far.

Once the bouncers came out and held the men until the Police Nationale arrived. Statements were taken, and Delphine insisted that she didn't need a hospital but just a shower and her bed.

Waking from her night out, the left side of her face hurt. She had a black eye and a swollen bruise on her cheek. Exhausted and dragging, she and Claudine left for the airport and flew home. Only in the air and after more over the counter painkiller and sleep did she realize that she had not talked to Philippe' at all. She thought to leave a message but from where could she call him. Not from her house. Maybe Lorelle's. Then she thought, (*What will I tell my parents about my face? Shoot!*) Dozing back off to sleep she would figure out something before they landed.

Saturday was a Murry family dinner welcoming Delphine home. Both Hellene and Lorelle's families excitedly came early to help with the southern cooking and then they ate just like old times growing up. The Murry home was full of family and sleeping over was a must since there was late night cooking, cleaning, card playing, dancing, and storytelling. Although, her parents heard she collided with a dorm shower because they were not made for her size; privately Delphine told her sisters the truth about her bruised healing face.

In semi-annual tradition, that Sunday the four Murry women along with Claudine, her mother Soyala and aunt Naita, Lolli, her mother Patrice and sister Loni, Murry aunts Melva, Mattie and Barbara Jean, and cousins Sylvia, Sheryl, Gloria, Alvia, and Dorthie-ray dressed up and enjoyed a formal dinner. Then later the group had wine and hors d'oeuvres attending the Spring Elegance Ebony Fashion Show at Macy's. After the show, during a brief time alone, Delphine and Lorelle were shopping for the latest makeup. It was discussed and Lorelle agreed to deliver the message to Philippe' that she was in New Orleans for the week. With that now arranged, Delphine felt she could truly relax and continue to enjoy her time with her family.

The smell of magnolias wasn't something Delphine thought she would have missed but when she stepped outside onto Hampton Street, she closed her eyes and inhaled with a smile saying, "Some-things are just home."

Going to Café du Monde for early morning coffee and beignet was another favorite past time. Having the opportunity on Monday morning with Hellene and her parents to make that trip really made her recall the pleasant memories of being home. She hugged her parents and sister a lot during this quick visit, realizing she had really missed them.

Although, she was sad when Hellene returned to her home in Lafayette on Wednesday, everything about the week-long trip was going great. That was until the unexpected phone call from Lorelle on Thursday afternoon.

"Dell, I need ya ta come wit me somewhere's. I'ma pick ya up right now."

"Why? Where is we going? I'm supposed to—"

Lorelle cut her off. "It's important. I ain't coming in, meet me outside."

Seven minutes later, Delphine was in the front seat of her sister's blue Ford Sierra on her way somewhere she didn't know.

"Why ya actin' all nervous and sweatin'? Where we … Wait, is you pregnant, again? Damn, how ya' ever gone be a lawyer, now? Ya ain't never gonna finish school! Where we goin?"

Lorelle said nothing only drove. Delphine's voice rose to that tone of commanding authority. "No! Stop da car. Girl, no, I ain't goin' wit cha to da Geechee queen! No. Ya shouldn't be goin' neither. It's dangerous, Rell! Ya could die! Turn 'round, take me home, right now, damn it!"

Shaking her head, Lorelle answered her, "No, no, it ain't that. But uh … but listen." She pulled over and put the car in park.

"Look see, I called da French professor like ya asked but he didn't answer. I left a message. I said just what ya told me ta say. He called back but Cedric answered. It started a bunch a mess. He thought I was cheatin'. He was yellin', grabbin' da kids, packin' bags. Bein' all dramatic. Anyways, after I got all that straight, I was a lil upset, but I talked ta da professor. Cedric say he gotta be on da other line ta see if I'm lyin'. So, I told him what ya said … Well, I … Uh … and I told him 'bout ya face, what ya say happen in Paris."

"Huh? Why? No matter, it just 'bout healed now. No big deal." Biting her lip and fidgeting, she told more of the details. "Uhm, see Dell … Da professor was asking lots of questions. He worried 'bout ya getting hurt. Ceddy figure it true; he be ya friend—not mine."

"Lorelle, that's fine. I mean I could've told Cedric myself but long as he not tryin' ta leave ya or nothin' crazy. It's fine."

She took a deep breath then kept talking, "Delphine, that been on Tuesday." Delphine looked at her sister confused with the significance of the date. Then she found out.

"He here. He here."

"What! What chu mean he here? Philippe'? Why? Why didn't you tell him I was alright?"

"I did. I did but he called again today. I was takin' care of da kids. I hear Cedric given Momma and Diddy address. But I didn't know who he was talkin' to. When he hung up, he say da man don flew here today ta make sure ya is for himself. I was yellin' at Cedric. But Dell, ya know my husband don't know nothin' 'bout him bein' a French White professor. He thought he some Creole with a funny accent. Girl, he on his way ta da house right now. I had ta get ya out of there."

"LORELLE!" Panicked, Delphine didn't know what to do.

⚬⚬⚬

"Good evening, my name is Professor Philippe' Delacroix and I work at Sorbonne University. I am looking for Ms. Delphine Murry. Is this her home?"

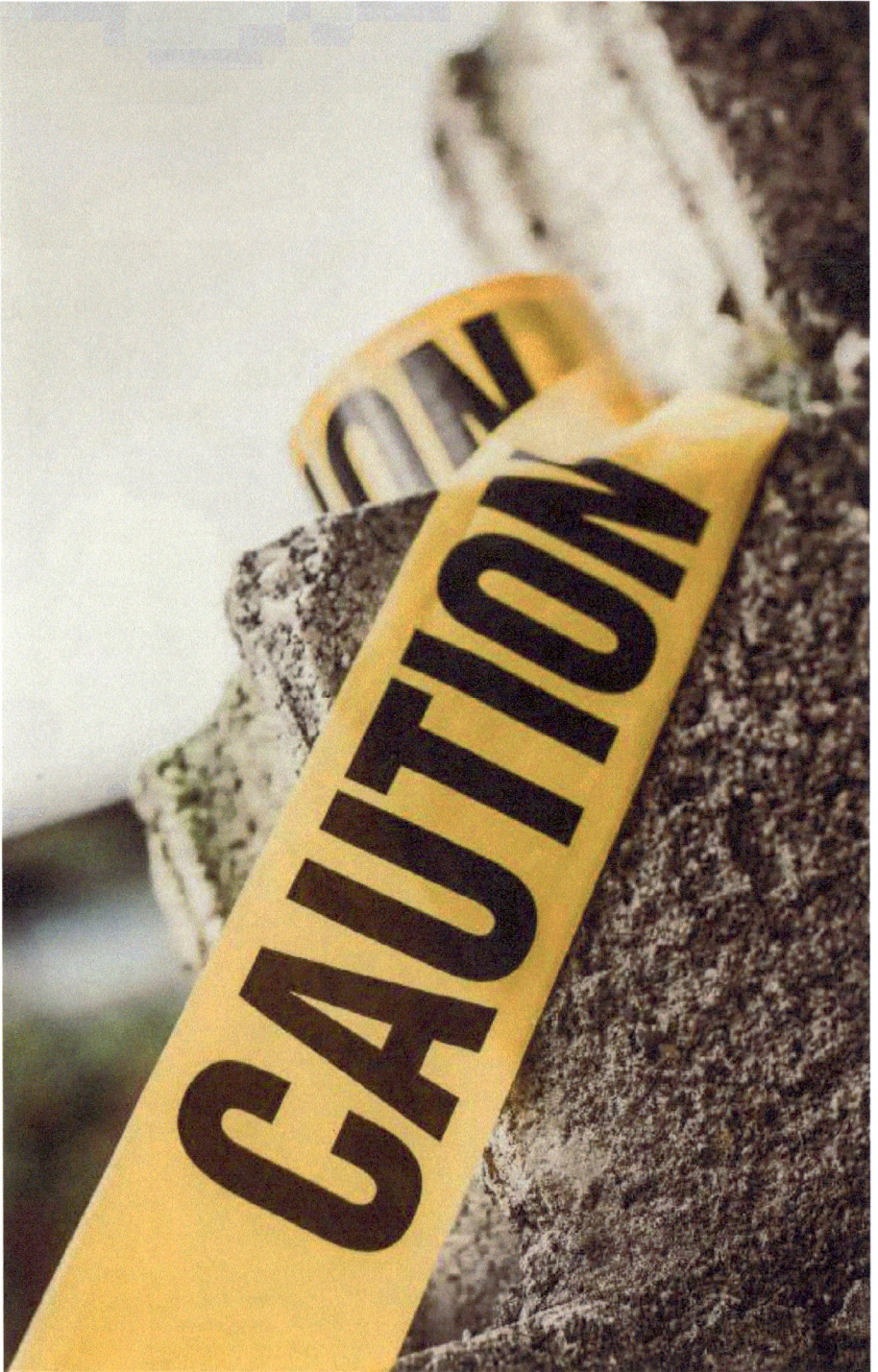

28 Undertow

It had been an hour when Lorelle drove Delphine back home. They both held hands and prayed like they did when they were younger right before they got into trouble. When they pulled up, they didn't see any unknown cars in the driveway. Delphine took the chance that only her parents were home, and she went inside alone.

Charlie and Eleanor Murry were in their usual places in front of the television watching the end of "The Cosby Show" when she came into the front door.

"Where ya been Dell?" Her father spoke as she closed the door behind her.

"Oh, with Lorelle ta help with her anniversary comin'."

She immediately noticed her mother not looking her way and felt something had happened in her absence. Moving to the kitchen to get to the stairs, she wasn't fast enough.

"Dell, ya know sum White professor name of Delacroix?"

She froze and closed her eyes before turning around slowly. "Yes'um. He from France."

"How he knows ya so well ta be comin' up ta da house, gal." Her mother spoke up in a sarcastic tone.

"Teence, stop. It be our Dell. He come here lookin for ya. Say he and his misses 'spose ta meet ya today. Ya' know his wife too do ya'?"

"Uh, no diddy, I don't know his wife. I musta forgot."

"Hmm, Delphine Murry ya keeps ya word, now. Don't let nuttin', mess up ya schoolin'. Th ere be a note in da kitchen. Stayin' at da Waldorf."

"Alright, I'll get it. Goodnight." She said taking two steps closer to the kitchen. But then she heard, "Da man seem real sad ya not here. Go on call now. There be da phone."

He said leisurely pointing to the telephone on the end table next to the television. Her mother turned down the "Family Ties" shows opening theme music and the two sat there waiting.

Dialing under the suspicious eyes of her parents, the hotel connected her call to his suite.

"Bonjour Professor, this is Delphine Murry. I apologize, I … I haven't been home for a while, and I was off with my sister. I will meet you both tomorrow if that works." Nodding with slight moans to what was in her ear and not acknowledging the peering four eyes from across the room, she stayed calm and made it brief.

"C'est bien convenu, bonne nuit." She agreed and wished him a good night.

Quickly she kissed her parents' good night, made her way to the kitchen, snatched the note left earlier by Philippe' and went upstairs to her bedroom reading the French note.

Nous sommes à la Nouvelle-Orléans mais nous ne nous souve-nons pas des endroits où vous nous avez dit d'aller. Pouvez- vous nous rencontrer dans le hall du Roosevelt demain à 8 heures Merci. -PD

(We are in New Orleans but can't remember the places you said to go. Can you meet us at The Roosevelt lobby tomorrow at 8. Thank you.)

The next morning, Delphine stayed in her room until her parents had gone off to work. Then she took a cab to The Roosevelt-Waldorf Astoria hotel. Going to the concierge she rang Philippe' suite and he gave her access through the concierge. When he opened the door, he looked so handsome in his dark blue jeans, a light jean jacket over a light blue and white striped long sleeve shirt cuffed over his jacket sleeves. Delphine thought, *(Dreamy … I've missed him.)* His curls waved back and lifted higher on the top of his head, while his round wire glasses indicated he had been reading. He delivered a half smile before pulling her into his suite and began bombarding her with questions before she could even speak.

"Are you alright? Why didn't you tell me what had happened? Why didn't you tell me you were returning home for Spring break? I have been in Virginia but would have come sooner if I knew you were here. I caused some problems for your sister. I'm sorry about that. But the message I had received from her by my service caused me to worry. Then there was all the commotion when I called. Who

… Who were these bastards? What did police say? What am I saying? Let me see your face. Does it hurt? Oh, Delphine." He said inspecting the crescent shaped dark spot under her eye and bruise marking still on her cheek.

Reaching her body up she kissed his creamy soft skin right above his bearded cheek, then she moved to sit on the couch. Reclining, she whispered, "I'm fine Philippe', truly. Don't worry. We haven't talked since Nannette had the baby; I didn't know you were in the U.S. My flight back is tomorrow. I didn't think you would come here. I'm fine. Everything is fine. Lorelle worked it out. Cedric doesn't believe you're her boyfriend anymore."

After saying the last sentence, she started laughing which relaxed him to smile. He offered her coffee, but she accepted water and held his hand, while his other caressed the side of her face that wasn't slightly discolored.

"I met with Lorelle and your brother-in-law late last night and cleared things up. We had a long talk. Your nephew, LaRoyce, is it? He said I sound like Inspector Clouseau from "The Curse of the Pink Panther" and your niece just stared up at me like I was a giant tree. I had already gone to your parent's home looking for you. They said it could have been something bad, but I let them know it wasn't. Your parents didn't act like I was one of the despised forever hated enemy of all Black people at all. Actually, although they were surprised, they treated me very hospitable. Did you make those family stories up about your family hating white people just to keep our association a secret?"

She shook her head and said, "I never said they were rude, silly. But they would never understand us being close … you know friends. Philippe', in their minds it would be egregious. Something vulgar created by your cunning plot to get into my pants. Well, telling them you had a wife took the pressure off me when I got home. That is from my father anyway— my mother, she is much more distrusting."

"Aww, that's right. It was your mother's family that you said suffered terrible cruelties when she was growing up. Now I know that was why she was kind of peering at me. Honestly, I thought she was checking me out, you know because it has been said I am somewhat attractive to the ladies." He laughed as she punched his arm while making a smack sound by sucking her tongue down from the roof of her mouth.

He brushed his large hand down onto the fluffiness of her medium length black hair curled and styled back away from her face saying, "I haven't seen you in a month, I just want to look at you." His hand moved to her mouth, and he began rolling his thumb over the curve of her bottom lip.

Catching his eyes upon their return from his slow analysis of her lips moistened with a smooth layer of magenta lipstick, she said, "Professor Delacroix, ya wanna kiss me, don't ya?"

She gave him a smug facial expression. An airy "Aww … Oui," oozed from his lips before delicately connecting with hers. Deep moans of exhalation followed with dancing tongues and folding arms over yearning bodies. Philippe' quickly removed his jacket without separating from the sweet deliciousness of her mouth. He wanted and needed to be closer. Wrapping his arms around her waist between the light cardigan red sweater and her black leotard body suit that tucked inside her black stirrup pants, he pulled her toward him. As their lips parted and pressed again, Delphine gripped the fullness of his hair and lay back further on the couch. Feeling his muscular body pressing onto her felt like a warm weighted blanket. It was a comfort she had missed over the month apart. Philippe' eased his long body on top of hers and then it happened …

They fell on the floor.

Loudly, "Merde," "Oh," and "Ouch," came before their hysterical laughter. Still over her, he began to lift himself up, but she started to roll her fingers through his wave like curls causing him to pause. He smiled at her, but she had no expression when she pulled his head back down and opened her mouth. Holding himself up by his arms he continued slowly kissing the woman he just couldn't seem to get enough of.

There had been only a few minutes of mouths merging before he tore his lips away and darted over to nibble on her earlobe. Then down to the smooth skin of her neck, leaving a trail of light wet kisses as his breathing grew more intense. Easing his body onto hers, he rested his knee between her legs with his upper body resting on his left elbow on the lush carpet.

Drifting off into a passion dream, Delphine loved the way he kissed her. She could hypothetically do this for hours but in the back of her mind she knew he probably couldn't. She decided to stop. Attempting to turn her head away, his mouth followed hers with tender movements of his tongue's caress. With each deeper plunge into carnal desire, they moaned lowly while somewhat entangled on the floor of his luxury suite.

Abruptly, he tore himself away from the buxom Delphine who remained still underneath him on the floor. Philippe' rested his head between her shoulder and neck as the force from his exhales hit her skin like gusts from a windstorm. Panting he whispered her name, "Delphine." Delirious from his lustful yearning he said the words he had been thinking, "Oh, I want …"

He caught himself, cleared his throat and stopped speaking. Before she could react, he sprung to his feet and changed the mood.

"We should go somewhere before my flight at 2:15 p.m. Where do you think?" He said sitting back onto the couch and guzzling her unfinished water on the side table.

Sitting up on her elbows, she looked at him a moment before saying the right thing instead of what she wanted to say. "You … you're leaving?"

He nodded. "Oui, I came to make sure you were alright. I must get back to Washington and Lee University and deliver my history presentation this evening. I'm on the agenda at eight."

Philippe' helped her up off the floor and onto the couch. But he didn't sit next to her. He moved to sit in the large armchair grabbing his jean jacket before crossing his long leg over the other in a shape of the number four.

Mentally noting the distance that he was now purposefully creating between them, she continued seeking information about his travels. "What kind of presentation? Is it the revolutionary research one you were working on before?"

"Not exactly. It is more of a selection process for new faculty. Come on let's go to the 24/7 breakfast place Andreas and I liked to eat at in the French Quarter."

After wiping the lipstick from his lips, he stood up putting on his jacket. But she didn't move closer, when she said, "Faculty? You … You're leaving the national library? Sorbonne? Wait … What's going on?" Her voice rose an octave higher with each question and her face had a look of confusion.

Philippe' reached out and held her hand pulling her up to rise. "It is for a future contract. There are two positions, and I am only one of six they are actively recruiting. The board reached out to me, another professor from Tokyo that I know, and one from London. The others are American so we shall see what happens. Allez! I'm starving."

He smiled while rushing her out the door.

29 Complexité

Upon returning to Paris, Delphine and Claudine had more luggage than before going home. They stocked up on beauty, hair, and clothing unavailable in France and of course delicious homemade care packages from loving mothers. Now the two were ready for the fast-paced routine of school and all set with some familiar things from home.

After spending several days in Lexington, Philippe' traveled to Los Angeles to attend a week-long conference for top ranked international colleagues. Then,he flew to Japan for another week working on several collaborative research and exhibition projects with the Kyoto and Tokyo National Museum.

By the time Philippe' arranged for Delphine to have lunch with him at his home, they had not seen each other again for almost a month. Since it was a Saturday, Delphine wanted to go out but Philippe' insisted he would cook for her, and maybe go to the movies. The two were in a very different entertainment mood. He picked, "The Breakfast Club," and her choice was "Trois Hommes Et Un Couffin." They could not agree and just saw both.

Before the movies, they did agree to grant each other a wish when they returned to Philippe's home. In the early evening and after a quick salad for dinner, Philippe' made his wish request known.

"Delphine, we agreed. You cannot say no." "Philippe' it's weird. Pick something else." "No. I want to watch."

She huffed and under her breath she said, "freaky Frenchman," then she stood in the living room and waited for him to turn the song on.

"Uh, you know I heard you." He said chuckling and getting comfortable on a couch aiming the remote at his multi-compact disc changer to play.

The song began and she started dancing like Charo as April Lopez on "The Love Boat." Laughing Philippe' said, "No. No. Do it correctly!"

Delphine exhaled, letting Michael Jackson's "Get on the Floor" take her away to the memories of her teenage bedroom. She forgot he was even there, which was exactly what he wanted. Singing every word, her eyes closed, her hips began swinging, her arms rose high, and she took off like a sexy rocket. Philippe' licked his lips smiling while watching her be free, beautiful. He had the song play repeatedly. In the middle of hearing it a second time, she began to lure him to dance with her. By the beginning of the third, he had gotten up to dance. Laughter and music filled his penthouse as they grooved doing old dance moves to the club jam. When the song faded to repeat again, he held her close brushing his lips over her neck feeling her chest rise and fall as she was catching her breath. Slowly he lifted her head licking his lips and smothered her opened mouth for a few seconds. She wrapped her arms around his waist as he bent down to deepen the kiss.

Suddenly, she leaned back breaking the lip lock, saying, "My turn. I get my wish now!" Philippe' released her grunting from the interruption of kissing.

While he turned off the music, Delphine backed up slyly to the staircase, saying, "My wish is that you do something with your mouth for me."

Laughing, she ran up the main stairs and down the hall to his bedroom, and he followed with a burst of enthusiasm.

She stood pointing to his saxophone cases, saying, "I believe it's just here to impress the ladies. I've never seen you play it."

Philippe' chuckled, taking off his jacket and getting one out. As he assembled the mouthpiece he said, "Is this really your wish? Wow."

Delphine nodded and flopped on his bed with her legs crossed waiting.

"Dell …" He lowly growled covering his mouth with his hand before breathing out heavily. She giggled knowing he was dying that she was sitting on his bed messing up the neat creases. He was so meticulous about his things and Delphine got so much enjoyment teasing him this way.

Philippe' sniffled and turned on his sound system to play a melody track. He closed his eyes and began to play The Temptations' 1971 song, "Just My Imagination" and she started to hum. Delphine was tingling all over and couldn't stop grinning. Philippe' moved his body and tapped his foot but never opened his eyes. When the melody faded and he ended with a long soft note, she clapped. He opened his eyes and another beat started playing. Her eyes widened when he began playing again. She placed her thumb nail between her teeth as her body lightly swayed to his sultry rendition of Bill Wither's "Use Me" from 1972. Philippe' came close to her and very softly played the notes to the song. He opened his eyes to see her crumbling like a sandcastle and he winked at her. "Ooh" came out of her throat as she bit down hard on her bottom lip and quickly sucked it before swallowing hard. He moved back away from the bed with a little bounce in is stride.

Clapping harder she shouted, "Please, one more!"

He stretched up his left eyebrow and licked his lips before changing the background music. Then he sat down at his desk chair across from her and started playing with his eyes closed. Her smile slowly faded. Delphine just watched him intensely blowing the horn as if he were speaking to her softly. Her heart was in her throat. She parted her lips slightly to release the hot air in her body. She tilted her head to the right and her eyes felt heavy as she was being seduced by every sound, he made from his large shiny brass instrument. Philippe' had no idea that Marvin Gaye's "I Want You" was a mellow song she used to like but hadn't heard since the late 70s. Playing with his eyes mostly closed, he also didn't know she was melting all over his bed, but he could feel she was watching him until the very end.

She didn't clap but stared at him with eyes of admiration. "It's beautiful, the way you play. Like it comes from your heart, Philippe'. Merci." She said feeling a bit tingly all over. He kissed her forehead, then began putting his saxophone away.

She slid off the bed and asked a question, while he was preoccupied. "Will you … Uhm … read to me?"

"Aww, now that is the real wish, right there." He said as she grinned.

Philippe' opened some wine and then read to her on the terrace until it got chilly. Moving inside and on top of her bed, Philippe' continued his readings of Walt Whitman poems as she lay on his chest feeling the gentle vibration from his thunderous voice and the rhythm of his heartbeat on her face. Over time, the two bottles of wine were consumed as late night came upon them.

Philippe' had no intention of sleeping in her room but when he stopped reading and moved to leave, she would wake up and nudge him to continue. Eventually, the two comfortably fell asleep holding one another.

Something about the night triggered a memory. Delphine was trapped in a flashback nightmare. Although completely asleep, she felt Philippe's body next to her and his hair lightly touching her skin. She exhaled a few desperate moans and mumbled from her growing fear. Within just a few minutes her body began to sweat and her head jerked from side to side. She could not escape her nightmare. Moments later her body thrashed uncontrollably on the bed, and she screamed out in terror, "No! No! I don't want to!"

Awakened startled, Philippe' sat up and held her shoulders trying to wake her. "Delphine, look at me. It's me, Philippe' wake up. It's alright. You're dreaming."

Shocked to awake, she opened her eyes. She sat straight up aggressively pushing his arms away. "Get off me! Don't touch me!" She shouted trembling.

He turned on the lights. Delphine looked around and realized where she was, in Philippe's guest room. They were both fully dressed on top of the duvet with only a throw blanket covering her legs. She covered her mouth holding in her emotions and exhaled deeply to prevent herself from crying. He moved next to her, "What were you dreaming about? What scared you? Tell me."

Turning her eyes to meet his, she felt calm. But she didn't want to tell him.

Timidly, she answered with a lie, "I ... I was falling."

"Falling? You said you didn't want to. Was someone pushing you to do something?" he asked, holding her hand gazing at her with curious yet tender eyes.

Delphine took a few seconds to gather her thoughts before speaking. Since she knew Philippe' had studied and frequently researched human behavior and psychology, she added more to the lie, and said, "Yes, out of an airplane."

He kissed her forehead and hugged her. "It's alright. I will never make you sky dive; I promise."

They chuckled briefly before he left to make her some tea. Delphine had not thought about what happened in over ten years. Rubbing her head from confusion, she wasn't sure what or why she had a flashback of Kendrick and the drug dealers, but it scared her.

Bringing her a large pot of chocolate tea, he watched her drink some and reassure him that she was alright before Philippe' retired to his bedroom.

Delphine laid back down and drifted off to sleep without any more recalling of the past.

30 Vantage Point

Claudine and Delphine were in the top five of their class and allowed to attend a special summer session until the end of July. The extension of her stay was exciting not only for her education but for her personal life as well.

Philippe' took her back to Lyon for a three-night stay with Andreas, Nannette and their little one. This visit Delphine got to spend more time with Mrs. Delacroix, Gert, and Nannette without all the formalities of a holiday season and the presence of the entire family.

Now, Marie Delacroix was less formal and much more curious about Delphine's future after Sorbonne. "That is delightful you want to be a physician. Much like our young Chevalier, a noble profession indeed. The care of infants and children you want to master, you have a kind heart, Ms. Murry, and you are to be commended." She said before taking a bite of her savory dessert while they were sitting in the shade outside for ladies' afternoon teatime.

Trying not to stuff the entire warm sweet buttery Kouign-Amann, another one of her favorites into her mouth, Delphine smiled and sipped her tea. Gert giggled watching Delphine attempt to pace herself, but she had already told Gert earlier that she was putting a few of them in her purse for later.

The table was full of many of the most fantastic things Delphine loved to eat. Éclairs, tropical exotic fruits, and several savories, of course but there was Profiterole. Those chocolate-covered puff pastries filled with vanilla ice cream, and there was Chouquette, injected with custard crème and assembled into a cone-shaped tower, glued together with caramel and sugar-coated almonds.

She was in fat girl heaven as her toes performed a tap dance show under the table every time, she put something in her mouth. There was no way for her to pretend well enough for Marie, Nannette, Gert, and her mother Ava not to notice her ultimate joy in eating the mouthwatering French pastries.

While Nannette took her son inside for a nap, Gert and Ava cleared away the table and went to make the second round of tea. This left Marie alone with Delphine. The friendly conversation about the beautiful spring flowers blooming around the estate continued as if the others were still sitting around. That is until Marie Delacroix said something new.

"My son is very fond of you, Ms. Murry. This is the second time he has brought you to our home. As my husband said to you the first time, we are both happy to know you and appreciate meeting delightful people from any country. But I must ask you, what is your expectation here? Or should I say, what are your specific desires regarding my son, Philippe'?"

She thought, *(Oh, no she didn't.)*

Delphine put down her teacup and made direct eye contact with the designer dressed fair skin petite woman with bright green eyes and seemingly long light brown hair neatly pinned in a bun.

"Madame Delacroix, thank you again for your hospitality. I am very fond of your son as well. He has shown me a great deal of kindness supporting my education beyond what I could have learned from books. I am grateful for his friendship. However, I am going to be a doctor. That is my main priority and focus."

Marie smiled with a gentle nod as she raised her tea glass to her lips. Then Delphine kept talking as her anger grew.

"Madame, I am not like any American you may have met before. I am not particularly impressed with the wealth your family possesses, your connections, nor your status in society. I am impressed with the honesty and goodness of all people. Your son in his wisdom chose to extend himself to me without anything in return. To be clear, I have not had sex with Philippe' nor do I intend to do so. I will give myself to my husband, who will in fact be a Black man. To that I am certain. With that said, you can rest your mind to any ideas of impropriety by myself or your well-bred gentlemanly son."

Delphine was now becoming enraged, and her hands started to tremble on the table. She sat as still as possible watching Marie Dela-croix continue to sip the last of her tea without any acknowledgment of what she had just said.

Thoughts came to Delphine's mind. *(Condescending? … You … know … what …)*

When Delphine exhaled sharply and began to rise from her seat is when she spoke. "Merci Ms. Murry for your honest directness to a difficult conversation a mother must have when a young woman is brought home by her son."

She motioned for Delphine to sit, and she did.

Then she continued. "Philippe' is required to fulfill his obligation to marry Angelique Dubois as has been arranged between our families when they were very young. I am no fool, Ms. Murry. My very handsome son is no angel. I am aware of his love of women and that he has had many over the years. But other than Angelique, and now you, none of them have been guests in our home. So, I hope you can understand my inquiry."

"Oui, Madame, I understand." Delphine was less angry with the conversation and more annoyed that Philippe' put her in the awkward situation without warning her beforehand. Gert and Ava had returned with fresh pots of tea and the ladies discussed and agreed on a shopping outing thereafter.

During dinner, Delphine was avoiding Philippe's eyes from across the table, and he felt something was wrong. She didn't eat much but stayed engaged in conversation throughout the evening. However, when the family withdrew to the library for a Delacroix game, she excused herself complaining of a headache. Once she took a long hot bath in the pink room again, Gert came to check on her with some tea, lavender macrons, and a warmed Kouign-Amann.

"Delphine, what's wrong? Even when we were shopping you were very quiet. Was it all the sweets you ate? I can take this away." Gert said sitting on the bed and reaching to take the tray of goodies and tea away from over her lap.

Delphine playfully smacked her hand saying, "Don't you dare." They chuckled.

"Nothing, I really do have a headache." She lied.

Gert nibbled at a macron on her tray and said, "Hmm. Did Madame Delacroix say something to you about her son?"

Delphine's eyes shut quickly. "Oh, lord, are there microphones and cameras in the trees outside?"

Gert tapped her knee to reassure her, and she opened her eyes. Then Gert confessed, "No. I know Madame was talking to mama about it when we were baking earlier this morning while you were learning how to play croquet."

"Tell me, honestly Gert, it's because I'm Black isn't it. I know that is why. Philippe' being White would be why in my family. Tell the truth, that's it, isn't it."

"I don't think so. As long as I have been alive the Delacroix's have welcomed all sorts of people into their home for parties and events. Even Carmen Delacroix is from Spain. I don't know any other Black Americans but you and Claudine. He is supposed to marry the second daughter of the Dubois family. I believe that is why."

Delphine listened attentively to every word she said while she sampled the snacks.

Unknown to them, Philippe' had come up to check on her. When he had gotten to the cracked door, he heard the beginning of the conversation and stood outside of the door quietly listening.

Gert volunteered more explanation, "Before my older sister, Elke was married, she had a crush on him. I think he liked her a bit too. They were caught in the wine cellar with her knickers down around her knees. I don't think it was their first time either. Elke is a year older than him. She was seventeen, I believe. Yes, she was. I remember because right after that Elke was sent away to school in England. She didn't come back until she was twenty-six and married to Kurt. It was just a crush, she told me. She said growing up together you develop feelings that you really shouldn't when you are so close as family. That is what she said, and I believed her. But I also believe that because of who he is, there was never a chance of her being anything more than a girl he had his way with, in the wine cellar."

"Well, of course, the wine cellar. How funny." Delphine said thinking about what had happened during her first visit.

"Why is it funny?" Gert asked. Quickly, she responded, "Oh, nothing. Do you really think his mother asking me what I expected was only because he's supposed to marry someone else? Really? I think there is more to it. Gert, I am Black, and he is White. Those are opposites in any country. But we are friends, Philippe' and I are friends. After I leave Paris, I know I won't ever see or speak to him again. I didn't think anything more of our friendship. Not ever. It made me angry and embarrassed that she thought I wanted something else. Like I don't have my own goals in life or my own responsibilities to be and do something for my family to be proud of. No, she thought me simple, common, and cheap. She thought that all I would want in life is to have her damn son have sex with me and get money. Like some insignificant gold-digging groupie tramp running behind a famous singer. As if my worth is nothing more than that. I'm offended by what she was implying. But I'm angrier that he put me in this situation for his mother to even think that about me. Why did he even bring me here? Why would he, knowing they were going to think that about me? Does he not care how that would make me feel? What is wrong with him? He knew they would think I …"

She started to cry. Gert rubbed her shoulders to comfort her. Philippe' had moved to the other side of the doorway to clearly see as well as hear.

(Damn ...) He thought. He wanted to interrupt, but his feet seemed to be glued to the floor and he couldn't move. *(What would I say?)*

Gert wiped her few dripping tears, and said, "I believe you are misunderstanding something, Delphine. Monsieur Philippe' is a respected and honorable professor and not a young foolish boy anymore. He must care for you deeply to invite you to his home, share his family and history with you while you explore Lyon. I think that Madame Delacroix only wanted to ensure you did not misinterpret his gestures in a more personal way. The Delacroix's do not throw people out just because they are different, they are very kind. Remember what Heidi told you about our family. Delphine, I honestly don't think she believes you are a black nymph from America."

"Nymph?" Delphine looked up at Gert and they both started laughing.

Rubbing his beard Philippe' left the pink room doorway and went back down the hall with a great deal on his mind.

Since Gert had stayed that night with Delphine and the two spent all night talking about other things, Delphine decided to forget about the entire incident and enjoy her stay. She did. Over the rest of the weekend stay, there were no awkward conversations or avoidance to their normal friendly interactions. Her French history education adventures continued as they visited more of the 2,000 year-old historical landmarks, like secret tunnels of Les Traboules, and Bartholdi Fountain. They enjoyed a playful family bike trip along a popular scenic river and ate mouth-watering dishes at restaurants, Un Deux Trois, La Pailleron and Chez Grand-Mere.

The weekend was fantastic, and like always Delphine captured all her memorable moments in her personal journals. She held on tightly to the belief that this was the best year of her life and she wanted to remember everything, seen, said, heard, tasted, and felt while she was in France.

31 Be That as It May

Philippe' and Delphine had a few more special times together before her time in France was to end. Philippe' took her away for a basket lunch filled with wines, cheeses, breads, smoked meats, and fruits, in a secluded part of the city along a grassy meadow. The two held hands as she read to him while he relaxed in the grass watching the clouds.

Knowing she loves the color of purple, another time he took her away for a day trip to see the most beautiful lavender fields in France called, Plateau de Valensole.

"This is a magnificent and beautiful place. Thank you so much for this adventure, my friend. I adore you!" She said hugging him with a bright smile.

"Dell, your eyes sparkle when you are happy and that gives me a peaceful feeling. I am glad I could share this with you." He said holding her from behind as they watched the glow of the sun begin to set over the valley shimmering with purple.

Delphine made a point of spending time visiting Nannette a couple of times. But after that her time left in Paris was extremely busy. Luc had even contacted her a few times to take her out, but she wasn't ever free.

The end of July came quickly. Attending the special summer session was an additional boost to Delphine's graduating with honors and receiving awards, and scholarships. She was excited to be entering medical school in the fall at Tulane.

Philippe', Nannette, Andreas, Pierre, and Luc all attended Claudine and Delphine's graduation. Introductions took place before the ceremony as Philippe' handed the ladies wrist corsages made of colorful roses.

Afterward, Pierre and Luc gave Claudine and Delphine each a large bouquet of African violets and daisies wrapped in vibrant colored Kente cloth. Although Luc wanted to take Delphine out to celebrate, Pierre had told him about a party their former professor had planned. Philippe' had arranged to celebrate their achievement with a lavish dinner in a private room at Le Cinq restaurant in the Four Seasons George V. Andreas and Nannette, Pierre, and Philippe' were part of the planned occasion and Luc was added to the guest list at the graduation ceremony.

Lots of photos were taken to capture the happiness of the occasion. Andreas, and Philippe' delivered formal professional toasts to the two former students, praising them for doing so well and wishing success in endeavors toward their future careers.

Followed by brief personal toasts from Pierre and Luc focusing on each woman's beauty. At the end of their toasting, the two men presented Claudine and Delphine with congratulation gifts. In that very second Philippe' decided not to give her what he had wrapped for her at his home. Especially after he observed her elated reaction to the gold butterfly bracelet Luc had given her for graduation.

Philippe' smiled and simply marveled at the joy in Delphine's face all throughout the entire evening. Philippe' was very proud of her, he knew it was difficult to achieve multiple degrees in biology and French studies with several nursing classes also under belt. Delphine was always calculating a plan for her path and a backup. Philippe' had been constantly mesmerized by the way her mind worked. He was proud of Claudine too with her degrees in social science, and foreign language. He felt both were pretty amazing women.

Tonight, his heart pounded just a little harder every time he saw Delphine's smile and heard her laugh. He felt such glee accompanied with sadness, knowing the very special connection he had with this magnificent woman was about to end. He nervously checked his watch to count how many more minutes he had left to soak in the essence he had grown accustomed to enjoying, that was Ms. Delphine Murry.

After the festivities, outside the hotel as valet brought up their cars, Philippe' oddly suggested that Luc escort her home. Then he abruptly, yet delicately kissed her cheeks, and said, "It has been a great joy in knowing you, Delphine Murry."

He didn't even wait for her eyes to connect to his when he said it, as he had turned away. Surprised with much to say, she was unable to utter a single word because he briskly walked to his car and without looking back, he drove away.

At that very moment the world had gone silent.

Delphine instantly felt a slight chill come over her skin. Her breathing began to quicken, while she was left standing motionless, watching the back lights of his sleek silver Peugeot get smaller and smaller as each half-second passed. She opened her mouth to speak but lodged in her throat were the words, *(… wait, Philippe' … wait.)* No sounds could be heard while she felt this pain as if a small part of her was being ripped out of her chest. She gasped and held her breath. Simultaneously, a few tears rolled down her round cheeks. Delphine partially smiled the moment his car disappeared in the night. She had such genuine care for the professor that taught her so much, not only France culture and history but about affection. Something she had not really allowed herself to feel before her senior year at Sorbonne. Philippe' Delacroix was a gust of wind that helped her see the sky and soar, and she knew she would always remember him.

Delphine was startled out of her daze when Nannette hugged her again before going with Andreas to their vehicle. When she turned her head to see Luc watching her, she smiled at him. He opened his car door for her with a soft grin.

The next day after completing her packing to leave, Luc Clement brought Delphine to his home in Paris for a wonderful meal. His intention was to give her a Nigerian experience with music and homemade traditional dishes passed down from his family. She was a little nervous but bravely tried his fufu and egusi soup, jollof rice and porridge yams and it was delicious. She even had seconds.

Finishing her last bite she told him, "I love this warm feeling of Africa. Luc it has been so amazing. Thank you."

"You are very welcome. I don't want you to leave, Delphine. I feel like we are missing a great love we can have." He said, taking hold of her hand.

Delphine looked into his round brown eyes and saw his genuine searching into hers. His smooth dark chocolate skin was so beautiful against hers as he caressed her hand lovingly. She was feeling like taking a leap now that her guard was down and open to have affection in her life. She swallowed before answering. "My flight home is tomorrow. I can't stay. I have a short turnaround to get ready for medical school at Tulane. But I want to try but how can we if you are here and I am there?" She reached to place her hand over his.

He smiled, "Maybe apply to Sorbonne, you don't have to attend medical school in the U. S. A., do you?"

She chuckled, "Luc I can't practice medicine without license in the U.S. I can attend medical school anywhere but the scholarships I received for Sorbonne Université - Faculté de Médecine just cover about one-year because I'm an international student not a French citizen."

"Well, I want you to seriously think about spending the year here with me."

She froze. "Huh, you mean live here with you?" Delphine started to feel pressure and uncomfortable but didn't show it.

He started chuckling and said, "That would be very nice, but I was thinking you could live with my sister and her family."

Delphine giggled and relaxed inside. "Sister? You're cute. Alright, I will do some research, but you can write me, and we can meet somewhere if I can't get back soon, can't we?"

He nodded but changed the mood. "Yes, we can. I would like that. Delphine, tell me truthfully, was something going on with you and that professor?"

She stiffened. "Excuse me?"

He exhaled and was very casual in his inquiry but clarified. "I saw the way he looked at you and how you watched him leave last night. It felt . . . Let me say it this way, I won't be second to any man."

Instantly irritated by his implication, Delphine stood up from the table tossing her linen napkin. "Wait a minute. Philippe' is white that is first! Second, we were friends Luc. Just friends and I have known him a whole hell of a lot longer than I have known you, but I have only thought about being in a relationship with you. But perhaps I should rethink that."

He sat quietly listening to her words but analyzed her reaction.

"Don't sit here and try to make me think that you just waited for me to finish school. I know you dated, you are a man, a fine French Black one, I might add. So don't play some jealousy game with me. I told you what my priorities were…are! That did not include what you are thinking. He taught me things about French culture and language that made it possible for me to stay at the top of my class. Being at the top, let me achieve things international students usually don't. No matter how much we have in common, in no way did the word friend mean I paid for his instruction on my back or with my legs up in the air. You know what . . . Take me home."

She walked off to grab her coat. He watched her and exhaled deeply before walking over to her. Holding her shoulders firmly, Luc spoke calmly.

"Delphine, you even pout like a French woman." He smirked then kept speaking. "You have strong emotions about what I said. Perhaps he got to spend the time I desired to have with you. Let me ask you this— if he were a Black man would your answer be the same?"

Without pausing she answered, "Luc, he isn't Black. So having a hypothetical discussion is irrelevant. We were friends and now we are not. I am going home and that is the end of it. I'm not going to let you tarnish the best year of my life with disgusting inuendo about me and a Caucasian professor from France. Take me home."

She tried to move from his holding, but his grip tightened, and she stood facing him. He smiled at her leaning forward to catch her eyes. Then he said with bass in his voice. "I will be the only man you think about from now on." She turned up the side of her lip and rolled her eyes. His mouth smashed over hers for a firm kiss. He forced her mouth open with his tongue and conquered hers without much resistance. *(Don't move.)* She let him kiss her as fiercely as he wanted.

Luc grabbed the back of her head pushing her into him and he folded his other arm around her body tightly. As he took control of her, she allowed him the few minutes of fondling her body over her clothes. Delphine instinctively knew she was being tested. She needed to prove her point, which required her to endure his aggressiveness for him to believe what she said about Philippe'.

Twelve minutes later, Luc was satisfied that Delphine had no thoughts of that professor. Before taking her back, he drove to his sister Awnika's house and introduced her. The three discussed possible hosting plans for her future return.

Leaving her at her dorm door with a gentle kiss, and the words, "You'll be all mine from now on. I will not let you slip away from me, beautiful lady. We will make this work."

She gave him a warm smile and went inside.

Twelve hours later, Delphine flew home to New Orleans, Louisiana. In doing so she left both men in Paris. But on the plane, she had already decided that one man she would remember affectionately and the other she would easily forget.

32 Surrender

Days after Delphine flew home, she received a letter sent to her sister, Lorelle's house from Philippe'. It was a funny graduation card with a note inside that congratulated her on the achievements and wished her success in medical school. He had included about twelve photos taken from her graduation ceremony and dinner party.

Within about a week, he had received a one-page letter from Delphine. In it she thanked him for her amazing party and listed several things she had learned from him. She expressed her gratitude for his guidance and friendship.

Hours after reading her letter, Philippe' sent a card featuring a Paris café they had visited together, extending himself to provide any support she may ever need and two more photographs she had never seen before. One taken when they were laughing after her gas explosion on New Year's Eve and the other, he secretly took of her taking a nap peacefully on top of the covers in his guestroom.

After that, there was nothing more exchanged.

In late August, it had been four weeks after he had said goodbye to her and got on with his life. Philippe' went on the pre-scheduled summer getaway trip with Chevalier, Andreas, and Tomas. The much older but still handsome, rich, and occasionally mischievous musketeer brothers enjoyed great food, fishing, spa treatments, wine, and relaxation in Saint-Tropez. Some had the pleasure of female company but not everyone.

On a hot day in the French Riviera, the men were on a sixty-five-foot luxury yacht, fishing, drinking and relaxing, when Tomas asked, "Philippe' are you going to take the position with that American university in Virginia?" He waited for the answer while adjusting his fishing rod in the water securing it to the yacht.

Philippe' answered after swallowing a gulp of his beer. "It is beautiful there; I could build a house but I'm not sure I want to live in America. There is a lot of time to decide. The two positions are not available until the fall of '87. It's a creation of new courses for international culture studies to enhance the business degree program. At first there were the two professor positions, but they said one of us would be offered a new department head position that will be open in 1989. I know my Japanese friend Haru Yamada from Kyoto University; got the same letter I did. It said, the department head, confirmed he would be retiring and wanted one of the four of us to be selected for his replacement. We are already working at other universities or national libraries, and we all need to continue to develop history and cultural studies curriculum until notified. It really could be anybody."

Leaning back tanning on the deck, Chevalier blurted out, "I thought that was on your mind. Philippe', you didn't even do it with Federica when the girls came to the rental last night. You've always spent time with her. I think she was a little hurt, that all you did was talk. Ha-ha." The men laughed and drank more.

Before he replied, Philippe' moved his rod to grab some sunscreen and applied it over his uncovered skin that glistened under the mid-day sun. Then he confirmed, "She was not hurt. Federica was just fine with talking. It was difficult to hear our conversation with all that loud grunting, banging and screams."

Two of the musketeers laughed and gave each other cheers with their cold beers. "I don't know why Donetta always yells so loud. It's fun though." Chevalier said removing his tee-shirt.

"Hand me another beer, you animal!" Andreas said to Tomas. Tossing him one, Tomas looked confused before stating, "Me? I didn't do anything unusual. When I come to visit, Simone and I always play cat with yarn before, we change to the burglar and the detective." He began snickering remembering the wild activities.

"I should have come after you met with them. I didn't want to hear all that last night!" Andreas said, rolling his eyes while taking a chug of beer.

"You're only saying that because you are married and can't fool around. Ha-ha!" Tomas shouted back. They chuckled, while Andreas covered his face with a cool wet towel and let out a disgusted groan.

"I can't believe you just talked, Philippe' what's wrong with you? Are you feeling old? You are going to be thirty-one next year. Is that it?" Tomas asked as Chevalier looked at him waiting for a reply. Andreas didn't move from under his towel, he knew the answer already.

"There is nothing wrong." He answered in his normal tone and moved to adjust his fishing rod and look out at the open sea.

Tomas and Chevalier noticed Andreas was still under the towel and not acting curious, moving, or making any sound. They knew something was hidden. They darted into the inside area of the rented yacht grabbing several firm round cushions. Then began throwing them like a rugby ball at Andreas's head to get his attention.

Andreas sat up after the first few hits, blocking the rest and shouting as he tried to keep the secret. "He … he said it was nothing! Why are you hitting me?!"

Tomas holding another firm cushion ready to hit him with it, demanded an answer, "Andreas, what is it?! Tell us!"

Philippe' cut his eyes at Andreas but the signal was witnessed by Chevalier, and he shouted, "I saw that! There is something! What! Tell us?! Ooh, is… is Angelique pregnant?!"

"What?! I should toss you overboard for even thinking that!" Philippe's voice sounded irritated as he glared at him.

Chevalier held up his hands and lowered his head a bit, while saying, "Forgive me. Forgive me. What is it, Philippe'? But… Tell us."

Philippe' still gazed out at the sun beaming on the ripples of the blue green ocean water, let out a heavy sigh. The two relaxed and sat down knowing that meant he was going to talk and waited while sipping their beer in silence.

Philippe' shared his feelings with his musketeer brothers by saying just six words. "I can't stop thinking about her."

Tomas moved closer and said, "Who?"

There was silence. The two men looked at the other too waiting for one of them to speak up but got nothing.

"Holy hell, will one of you just tell us!" The suspense was making Chevalier crazy.

Andreas said what he was thinking, "It's the young woman that came for Christmas dinner."

"Elizabeth? You … You want my sister?" Chevalier was very confused but only thought of his sister as the one he would be talking about.

Andreas hit him with one of the cushions this time, shouting, "No idiot!"

"The bigger African girl from America isn't it. The one you were ice skating with. It has to be, because if you liked the other one you definitely wouldn't have let me feel on her ass." Tomas said, finishing his beer and grabbing another along with some chips.

"What?!" Chevalier was in disbelief. "Philippe', is he kidding? Was she that good? I find that hard to believe but I could be wrong. I'm sure you will get a chance to bend her over again. Is it true what they say about Black Americans? I heard they have a dormant violent quality. It's like a sort of volcanic fire, deep within. . .Very intense and can erupt during intercourse, which makes being intimate with them unlike with any other culture—it's probably because they were damn slaves. Ha, ha!"

He said jokingly but immediately dropped his beer when Philippe' unexpectedly charged over to punch him, shouting, "Bâtard!"

Andreas instinctively jumped between them to prevent the altercation. Tomas was a second late but rushed to pull Philippe' away. Chevalier was completely stunned by his reaction, realizing Philippe' was very angry.

"What? I read it. Philippe' … were you … going to strike me … over … over a woman?! What the hell is going on?!" Chevalier asked totally confused and demanded some answers.

It was silent for a few minutes. Philippe's face was red, and he began yelling, "I have not had her! I still can't stop thinking about her! It is not because I want to bed her! That is not what I think about!"

The three men were quiet, as Philippe' paced around the deck in his shorts blowing out heavily.

"Yes! Yes, I want to sleep with her! I have since … I don't know but that is not it! … It is … The scent of her. I see the brightness of the moon in her eyes. Her smile warms my heart. Her soft skin is like beautiful, polished mahogany … She is exciting. Intelligent but wants more, to know so much more. Like me she is a sponge. She questions just about everything. It makes me laugh. I do the research to find answers just to see her face glow with knowing. She challenges me. She has a view and knows things I don't know. Yes, even me. Ha! When we debate even when we don't agree, I understand her complex logic. She is like a complicated maze that I have been allowed to find the beautiful end. She is strong, determined, and unmovable but I see the sweet, kind, delicate. No, I feel it when I am near her. She lets me lead yet wants nothing I have, and I want to give her all of it. When I kiss her, it feels as if nuclear shock waves are traveling through me. I care about her. I worry about her. I want her too always be alright. She is my very special friend. Delphine is an amazing woman inside and out … I don't know if I can forget her."

Blank stares are what he saw in their eyes as he stopped pacing and looked at them. Finally, Philippe' confessed, "I … I love her."

33 Men Named Delacroix

Two weeks later, Philippe' was having dinner with his brother, Jean-Pierre who had recently returned from a combat tour in Iraq. At the time, he didn't know his older brother was suffering from internal stresses from his military service. It was assumed as an officer he wouldn't see much combat but that was not something he shared with his family.

Philippe' confided in his brother about his turmoil in loving someone but having the responsibility to marry someone else. When he told his older brother it was Delphine Murry, from Christmas, Jean-Pierre became furious.

"No! You can play with her all you want but no! Philippe' you have obligations, arrangements are made! The Dubois's and Delacroix's are to be a family! You don't get to choose! I couldn't choose! She is not one you can have on your arm, Philippe'. If you must keep her then have her in your bed in the dark. If arrière grand-père were alive, what would both of them say? My God! It's as I said to you about Elke, you can indulge but that will be all. There is no more to be had with women like them. You cannot! An American and a Negro, what are you thinking? She is even lower than Elke!"

Philippe' rose to challenge his brother. Jean-Pierre pulled out his concealed handgun and pointed it at his younger brother causing him to stop his angry charge toward him. Jean-Pierre gave him a clear warning, "Don't, I am not going to stop if you come at me. Are we going to fight, Philippe'? That woman's honor is not being challenged. Philippe' your anger doesn't change the facts I am saying, and you know I am telling the truth of who we are, where we come from. Never in our family has it been the case to have a woman other than arranged and expected, unless she was hidden. Are we going to fight little brother? Shall I shoot you in the foot or the arm?"

Philippe' stood in his older brother's dining room trembling from anger, his words of truth and the loaded handgun being pointed at him. A few small tears eased down his face from the overwhelming emotions he was feeling. Jean-Pierre put his gun down and slowly walked to his brother.

He hugged him and said, "You must care for her deeply. I don't doubt she is a good woman to have captured your heart. But you cannot have her, Philippe'. I could not have my choice. Just like Papa could not have the girl he wanted, and she hated him for it. This is who we are. We are Delacroix men. Our family name, property, wealth is fi rst. Family is second. Country is third. Love … Love is not on the list."

⁂

By September 22, Philippe' was in Lyon meeting with his father in his study. The lack of sleep and constant worry was evident from his unkempt beard and tired eyes surrounded by puffy dark circles.

Jean listened to his son's emotional despair and confusion. They had been in the study for over an hour and only Philippe' had been talking. Pouring up two glasses of brandy and handing one to his son was when he began to speak on things.

"Philippe', the marriage arrangements are contracted. It has been so for years between Andre' and I. It was you and Angelique that chose to wait until you were older, and we granted both of you that freedom. Now you say you don't know if you can fulfill it. How do you think that will be received? She is almost thirty-one as are you. Many other men could have had her long ago, but she was bound to you, to us. Andre' will not accept that and it will create a breach not only in our lifelong friendship but with our business partnerships that we have had over the years." He said to his son, trying to lay before him the truth of the matter and the impacts of his decisions.

"What do I do, père? Pierre said over and over it is wrong to love her, but I do. She is beautiful to me because of what she is inside a diamond, rare and cut to dazzle the eyes of only those that can see her."

Chuckling he said, "Philippe' you have loved many women. There is no difference. You have been a romantic since your younger years. Perhaps there is some truth to you being filled with lust for her more than love, my son."

"No. It is different. I have not felt this way before. No, Père … I … I did not want her at first. I did not find her attractive even— simply not packaged in a way for me. I did not see her in any sexual way. She was just my student. I liked her exceptional intelligence but no more. But the more I got to know her, talk to her, she lowered her guarded walls, and we are alike in many ways and opposites in others. Papa, I did not have a desire to bed her until it had been well over a year. I am not being romantic, but there is a hole in me without her. I cannot describe it." His father stopped sipping his drink and stared at him as he emotionally spoke his heart's words out loud for the first time.

"I could have taken her to bed. It would have been easy to seduce her. But I didn't want to do that. To give her pleasure and then abandon her. I cared for her. I could not hurt her that way. I was an honorable gentleman. She is my complement, Père. I am tormented by the thought of living a life without her. How can I be with anyone else feeling this way? I only want to discover and explore the world with her. In my dreams, I … I see her having my children. We have grown old together and built a life that only the two of us can live. What do I do papa? It's wrong for me to love and need someone I am not meant to have! I can live without all of this. She doesn't want any of it. It would hurt you, but I could. But even if I did. Even if I could be with her, her family will never approve. It is forbidden to even think about. I am not even an American but all…all they see is a White person to fear and hate.

I am to be hated because of the evil cruelties her family has suffered by the hands of people that look like me. We both will be torn apart from our family ... I have to leave everything behind for her ... but what if she does not do the same for me? What if she hates me like, the girl Pierre said you could not have? I am lost. Forever lost! ... Père, I am trapped and cannot escape!"

He fell to his knees at his father's feet sobbing. Jean-Pierre Philippe' Delacroix affectionately stroked his son's head for a few minutes before forcing him to rise to his feet. Trembling from his release of pinned up emotions bound within him, Philippe' ran his fingers through his sweat dampened curls and cleaned his face with his side pocket handkerchief. Jean being only 5'10 looked up at his son standing at almost 6'4 and tenderly tapped his bearded cheek with a smile. Then he said, "Let us go for a stroll. Bring the Holy Bible there on the shelf and mon attaché caisse. Allez!"

As the two walked on a paved pathway along the grassy open acreage, Philippe' listened to his father retell a story of a girl he could not have. A subject he had only found out earlier at his brother's home. "I was young and in my military service station in India. We French were mostly together and didn't much mix with local people as a protection you see. But a few of us came across a local man and his wife with their two daughters, whose transport buggy had been stuck on a watery road that had broken away from the rising river and they were quickly being washed away. Helping them to safety was the right thing to do. Days later his wife and daughters came to the base and brought us dishes of amazing foods they had prepared for the four of us. That was how they showed their gratitude. Navya was lovely at sixteen. When she looked up at me her eyes shot right into my heart. Black pearl I called her privately because of her eyes. She had learned English, and we passed notes to one another weekly through a place in the local market. It was easier to write in English as many people around did not read it well. It was strictly prohibited for a young Indian girl or woman to be alone with a foreign man. We had to be very careful you see. Like you, I too was a gentleman and showed her the utmost respect and honor. Although it had already been arranged that I was to marry your mother, I asked Navya to be my...

my wife, and she agreed. In disguise, I met with her father, and he reluctantly agreed. He made it clear his agreement was only because his family's lives had been saved six months earlier. Weeks after his approval, Viraj was killed in a bike collision. Since Viraj had no sons, his brother Veer, a very violent man, took over the responsibility for his family. One day as we met in the market, two of Veer's sons saw her talking to me as I handed her a yellow scarf from the merchant as a gift. They dragged her out into the street and publicly beat her. I had to be restrained by my friends and military police to not intervene. I begged them to stop. I wanted to take her with me, I was returning to France. They carried her away bloody and screaming. I retrieved the scarf from the street covered in her blood and prayed to just make her be alright. No one would tell me anything. I worried not knowing if she was even alive. The day I was returning home, a message came to meet someone at the front gate. I rushed with my friends, knowing it was her. I would have taken her away right then but when I saw her my heart shattered. Not because of the violence she had suffered temporarily disfiguring her, but it was the hatred and contempt I saw in her eyes that left me broken."

The two had walked to a small pond that frequently the family fished in. Philippe' and his father sat under a nearby tree, and he finished telling his son about his past.

"Philippe' although my story is not like yours, I do know a bit about how you are feeling. There are many things I have learned from that and thereafter. I married your mother and grew to love her very much before any of you children were born. Open the Holy Bible and read 1 Corinthians 13:4 through part of verse 8. Then tell me what you think it means." Philippe' did as instructed by his father.

"Love is patient and kind. Love is not jealous, it does not brag, does not get puffed up does not behave indecently does not look for its own interest, does not become provoked. It does not keep an account of the injury. It does not rejoice over unrighteousness but rejoices with truth. It bears all things, believes all things hopes all things, endures all things.

Love never fails."

Taking several minutes to ponder what he read, Philippe' said, "Love is real. Something tender and adjusting to the needs of the other person. It is selfless and honest, not jealous, or arrogant."

Jean nodded and added, "Truest love is not obtained by many in this world. Philippe', it is very rare, and will easily slip through the fingers if not held tightly. The love spoken here in the Lord's word is not a feeling but overflowing in actions. This love will never separate people but holds them together. It is the unequivocal knowledge that no matter how different or even flawed this person is, they are the rib that fits inside your body. This kind of love requires both to have the same understanding and commitment to every word written. God in his wisdom is telling us here what love truly is and no matter what trials come, this must remain unbreakable, a solid foundation holding your life together."

He paused to give himself a moment to take in the warm air and gaze upon the pond. Philippe' continued to hang upon every word from his father's lips with eager anticipation of the wisdom he was giving him. Then Jean continued his thoughts as he looked out at the water.

"Philippe', a young man, or woman cannot know the deep things of real love mentioned here. A person with honest knowledge of themselves is also necessary to even begin to understand it. Fools or foolish are what most people are. Being moved to act based on what excites the eye, how they feel in a moment or what they may see as a future but with a very narrow view of the world. It is typical that your brother was quick to mention this forbidden love of mine. Since he only knows what I have told you his mentioning it was not for the right reasons. He wanted to prove that we Delacroix men cannot have what we want. He did not understand my story, when I told him that day, he came to me about wanting to marry Elke many years ago."

Philippe' looked over at his father in surprise saying, "He, what? I did not know that he wanted to marry Elke. He told me that he couldn't have someone, but I didn't know it was her. If he loved her why … But why would he tell me to bed her?"

Jean smiled at his son and explained further, "Your brother is not like you, Philippe'. Pierre does not search for answers beyond what he feels. When I told him some of the story of Navya and I, Pierre only took away that her family hurt her because she wanted to be with me, and I couldn't marry her. He reasoned her hatred for me was because of what they had done to her because I could not take her away. He did not understand at all. When I shared this scripture with your brother, he did not try to comprehend anything of what I was telling him."

Philippe's voice was elevated, still reeling that he had slept with Elke when he was a teenager not knowing his brother loved her. "Papa, I wouldn't have if I had known. What … what did I do?"

"Do not have guilt about that. Philippe', you were young and did not know your brother had planned things the way they happened. You see, the day he told me he wanted to marry her, and I made him read this scripture, I asked him two questions. Do you love her like these words? If you do, then you would be willing to give up your birthright as the Delacroix heir, is that so? Your brother immediately said no and there was no more said about Elke. But he behaved indecently, and his actions were despicable, never telling Elke he had no intention of marrying her, but he continued sleeping with her until he married Carmen, as arranged. Then he convinced you to indulge with Elke as his replacement. He did not care for her, only for himself. He didn't even value her as the daughter of trusted friends. He despised her as a lost prize. He was jealous and wanted to humiliate her by having us go to the wine cellar after telling you to take her there for your second rendezvous."

Philippe' hearing this for the first time was speechless.

A few minutes later, his father touched his arm, and continued speaking his secret truth. "I loved sweet and beautiful Navya Jha and I know she loved me. I would have brought her here to be my wife, but your grandfather would never have allowed it. I was to marry your mother. If I had thought on it carefully and honestly, if I had brought her here, Navya would have been loved only as my mistress. In my heart I knew that. You see my love was not like the words of that scripture. How could it have been? I did not spend time with her, or learn about her more than those secret notes we passed in the market. I carried guilt about what she suffered because my foolishness put her life at risk. I did find her many years later and she was still beautiful with just a few faded scars. Your mother and I met her and her husband when we took a trip for me to apologize to her."

"You did? Wouaaaa!" Philippe' was dumbfounded by the revelations of his father's history.

"Oui. I felt it my duty to do so. I wrote to her husband, Mr. Rana and asked permission. He granted it very quickly. The four of us sat in their home drinking tea and I apologized. Imagine what she said."

Philippe' eagerly waiting for more of the story, watched his father chuckle to himself.

"Navya said do not apologize. You have saved me twice in one lifetime and I am forever grateful. I was surprised, looking at your mother, I didn't understand. I said, you came to the gate, and you hated me. It was my fault what they had done to you. But she was shaking her head. I let her explain. She told me that she cared for me and would have left with me as agreed. But after I had gone, she realized she could not have left her mother and sister to suffer, and she would have asked to return. A week before seeing her in the market that day, her uncle had arranged for her to marry an older widowed man, who was as violent as her uncle. The public beating was because it was believed she was now soiled and unclean. The man no longer wanted to marry her, nor would he take her sister instead. Once she healed, she was sent away to an English school. This is where she met and married her husband Oliver Rana, who is half Indian and half British. She works as an elementary school teacher, there in Southampton. Her mother had passed away, but her sister happily lives in Surat with her Indian husband, who is a data scientist. She would never have been allowed to work in India nor would she have found love there, she said. Then she called out their children for us to meet them. She introduced their two children, a daughter Diya Elizabeth, and their son Oliver Pierre. When she said his name … I gasped as she smiled at me, and her husband shook my hand. Philippe' she had named her son Pierre after me. I could not control my tears. Your mother had to hold my hand."

Jean wiped his tears and smiled while glancing back at his son. Philippe' began to cry seeing his father's emotions. After several minutes of tears, he took a few deep breaths and continued.

"Philippe' your brother never got to hear any of this because he was not, as I said, a seeker of answers, he only got and held on to what he needed to serve his purpose. When we sent Elke away to England to give her a fresh start and an education because we love her like our family, she stayed with our good friends the Rana family for a long time. She met her husband Kurt who happened to be one of the personal bankers that worked with Mr. Oliver Rana. The two are happy. So, you see, having the complete story of my lost love, so to speak, is more telling than what your brother chooses to carry. Wouldn't you say?"

Philippe' nodded with unknown words to say, while wiping his slow rolling tears. Jean blew his nose and cleared his throat before holding his son's hands.

Then he said, "Things are made right even when they do not seem so if your intentions are lined with this scripture. Philippe', you are a man of your word. I know you would live without us like you say, but you are unsure if she would do the same. Hmmm. Like with Navya, she would have left me for her family. Never underestimate the power of one's family and the hold or bond they have between them. A person cannot abandon a part of themselves unless they are willing to take a leap and evolve into someone new. Philippe' you would be content with the arrangements made for your life. You and Angelique are compatible and have had the good fortune to have known each other for a very long time. The both of you have genuine affection for one another, which we have clearly seen. But you must have courage and decide one way or the other for your own life. Now, read this scripture every night. Think of the words I have said to you today. In time, you will know what you should do. Then later write this passage down and give it to the woman you choose to marry on your wedding day. Live by these words and your life will be perfect even when it is imperfect."

Philippe' took in every word from his father's wisdom and guidance, nodding and moaning at everything he said on the sunny afternoon at the pond. Th en helping him up from the ground, he glanced at his father and asked, "Papa, did you write down this scripture and give it to mama?"

Jean grinned and said, "Philippe', that is private and only between your mother and me! You really can be very impetuous, sometimes."

The two chuckled walking back to the house.

Philippe' wrote down the scripture and read it every night. He prayed and meditated on what his father had said. He didn't discuss anything but wrote in his journal and read more of the Bible each day. Eight days later, he had written two letters to Delphine Murry and sent them to Claudine's home for her to receive them. He had much more to say and wrote her two more just twenty-four hours after sending off the first two.

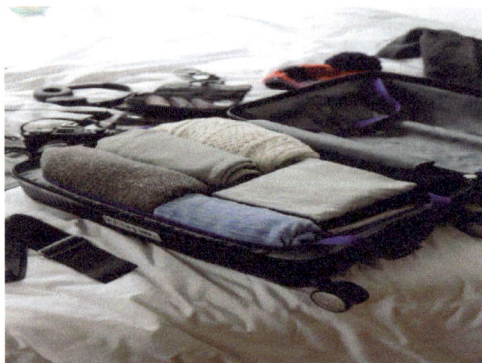

When days passed with no reply, he didn't feel right about calling her sister, Claudine, or her home. Philippe' decided to say everything in person.

34 My People

At the start of an early Louisiana cold and flu season, Philippe' gave no advance notice of his return to New Orleans. He arrived on a chilly Wednesday late morning in mid-October 1985.

After checking into his hotel, he drove to the Tulane University campus. Having no knowledge of her class schedule, he rushed first to the medical buildings to find her. But to no avail. Walking briskly across the large campus, he went to the library and then checked in with Professor Allen hoping he might finally see her. But no. It had been about an hour and still no sign of her. He knew she wouldn't be at home but if he had too, he would just go there and face the drama.

Breathing deeply, he scanned over the area, standing erect at the north end of the quad. The unusually bitter icy wind seemed to slice at his face causing him to flinch as his skin turned red. He thought his face was likely frozen as he heard the crunch of his facial hair when he blew out from his mouth. Bundled in a large gray parka, knit cap and gloves, the air he released immediately turned white as he searched through the moving students actively walking through the quad.

Then it happened …

About fifty feet away, he saw her walking alone. The brown twill straight skirt, long past her knees and the high black boots were her favorite style when it was cold. With an inner smile, he thought … *(I bet she has on a sweater or turtleneck under that coat. Oh, I'm going to marry her.)* Lost in his thoughts he forgot to stop her, and she had almost disappeared.

"Ms. Murray!"

She stopped and turned to find who was calling her. There were so many people moving about initially she didn't see him or recognize his voice.

Walking toward her he spoke again. "Delphine." Turning to her left, her eyes grew wide, and she let out a gasp before shockingly smiling. In front of her, he leaned down, so she heard his gentle words.

"I want to build a life with you, ma chérie. Trust me. Trust in us. I promise I will be all you need. You are my Eve, come back with me."

Stunned, she only blinked at his heart's confession and pledge.

Noticing her shivering, he took hold of her arm.

"It's cold, I'll take you some place warm." Nodding in agreement she followed as they walked to his rental car. She was still in shock, and he was anxious. Without much conversation, only coy smiles and hand squeezes over knitted gloves, they settled in the lounge of his Waldorf suite at the Roosevelt New Orleans. He made coffee mixed with a little hot chocolate from the bar. Silently he let her take a few sips before sitting close to her on the couch. Removing his hat, he touched her knee so she would look at him.

"Dell, come back with me to Paris. We will start our life together and be very happy. I promise."

Sensing her reluctance to respond to him, he took in a large amount of air to relax. Then he confessed, "I have never done this before. Perhaps, I need to do it differently for you to understand what I am saying."

She finally broke her silence. "I … I understand."

Looking away from his bright and happy eyes, she took another sip of her coffee. Removing the fine China cup from her hand, he adjusted his head to reconnect with her dark brown eyes that had filled his dreams. He reached up to palm her round cheek which had now softened from the warmth in the room and the hot coffee. As he began inching to kiss her silky lips that were protected by cherry flavor ChapStick, she turned her head away.

It had been three months since she had left Paris. During that time, Philippe' had written to her. Earlier on he sent some cards and she replied with a friendly letter. Then he sent four letters to which she did not respond. Although they were close, Philippe' was White. In addition, it was mutually understood that like his brother, Philippe' had his future pre-arranged. He was set to marry a French woman from a very wealthy family, like his. He told her that in Canada. Even when reminded by his mother, she never forgot.

To Delphine, it was an experience in Paris, nothing more for either of them. Philippe' had truly opened her to so many new and glorious things, never in her life would she have discovered if not for him. A moment in time for an adventure. That was what he was. Delphine was going to become a doctor. Her senior year at Sorbonne and in Paris was for her education. Their association stopped when he drove away, and she got on the plane back to New Orleans.

(Why did he keep writing?) Is what she thought when his letters arrived at Claudine's apartment for her, and she placed them in a locked box unopened. They both had different lives, cultures, and outlined future paths.

(Is he crazy? What on earth is he doing right now?) She thought while taking in the air of the room around her and purposefully stared into her cup to avoid being sucked into the depths of his ocean. Yes, those eyes that snatched at her heart like an undercurrent pulling her in and drowning her from reality. Her mind thought about the end of the movie "An Officer and a Gentlemen," when Richard Gere showed up being all dashing in those crisp Navy whites and took Debra Winger away from her drab life. The side of her lip crinkled knowing how much Philippe' was a real romantic gentleman.

But her face stiffened seconds later as the truth flooded her mind. She didn't need saving and this was not a movie. Philippe' being a White man was the plain and obvious fact that kept everything in its place with nothing more between them. But she was now aware of facts that made her despise him. She would never be with someone like Philippe' Delacroix.

Delphine began to feel a growing hot hatred in her gut that rose to her hair follicles. That whispering little voice in her head was now shouting from an invisible bullhorn and could not be silenced. Delphine didn't want anything more to do with him and this was the God given opportunity to let him know it.

Scooting back on the couch with her strong business tone and unemotional face, she let it be known where she stood.

"You … know … what …? When I saw that old painting of a large colonial home on what looked like a sugar plantation tucked away in the corner of your family's library, I asked. You said it was just a painting. Out of the six hanging on the wall only that particular one had no story because it was just a painting. Like a fool, I … I believed you. I was so stupid. If I had found out, right then, maybe you thought I might've walked back to Paris in the snow or something. Was it a prepared canned response to lie or was it one from Delacroix spontaneity? No telling what was in your head, but you lied, Philippe'. You lied to me. Nothing … nothing in your family's chateau is just for decoration."

The unexpected words from her mouth took him completely by surprise. Philippe' swallowed hard, licked his lips, and adjusted his body before he attempted to explain.

"Delphine, let me—"

She silenced him to continue talking by raising her hand between them close to his mouth.

"When my suspicious mother figured out, I had been seeing you in Paris, she said nothing. She went snooping and found some of the photos you sent of us together and concocted a plan. She made a point to make her awareness known in a grand way. It was just about a month after I had been home. Imagine my horror coming into the house and she confronts me yelling about secretly dating you. Furiously hitting me and screaming because I went to France to go to school, and I had lied and snuck around being used by some nasty white man. That's what she said. When she stopped hitting me, I tried to explain we were only friends. But she slapped me and said I was stupid because no White man is ever just friends with a colored woman, she said. And do you know what she did? Huh? Do you? She sat me down in the kitchen and pulled out all her detailed research about the Delacroix's of Lyon, France. She was so … so very excited to show me the vile, disgusting, and horrible history that she had dug up about your family. The truth you hid and didn't want me to know because you were just pretending to be someone you're not."

She stood up and stepped to the window feeling her anger bubbling like hot lava inside her. Delphine didn't pause to give him a chance to speak and began yelling.

"Your family money just about half of it was all from the backs of African slaves, Philippe'! I know … I know just how many plantations they owned! Oh, how many African people … human beings … they counted as their goddammed property! How many lives they stole; people they beat, tortured, sold like pounds of meat in a market, and bred like animals! Oh my god!"

He rose to approach her, but she backed up waving her fists at him. Philippe' felt as if he was standing in quicksand and couldn't move. While her gestures of anger became even more erratic as she moved about the room, her voice that used to be so sweet to him grew louder and more venomous.

"Your … your grandparent's marriage was some sort of merger … Ha … Yes, a money deal from one of the richest sugar plantation owners in the Caribbean. . . and a military commander. Oh, did he transport the stolen Africans for his future in-laws? Is that why they gave him their lily-white daughter to marry? Like a reward. Is that why people said he was some sort of damn hero?! Probably a descendant of a slave captain!"

She took in some air as her skin felt like it was crawling with ants. Brushing her hands over her shoulders she continued, "How stupid am I? Studying and excelling in advanced French history and I never thought to look up who you really were. Oh, but my mother did. She let me know how disgusting your colonizing human owning family was. How stupid—not knowing that you enslaved men, women, and children kidnapped from their homeland and forced them to work and die for your family's greed. Now you want me to be indebted to you so that you can own me too. Getting me to trust you with your pretty words! Putting your disgusting filthy mouth on me so tenderly. Yeah, wasn't it just your game … to break me down to screw me … like … like your whorish raping ancestors did to girls just like me on their horrible human breeding plantations!"

Not getting closer, he tried to reason with her. Philippe's voice was a little higher when he said, "Delphine, that isn't who I am. You know that is not who I am. I didn't do any of those things. How could you even suggest that I just wanted to have sex with you? I've treated you like no other woman; never … never have I crossed the line. I've held my promise to you. Because I love you."

She walked further away from him shaking her head and pounding her fist in her hand. He was unable to find her eyes to connect to her while he kept speaking with a hint of pleading.

"Ma chère, slavery the entire business of it, in every country during any period of the world was terribly wrong. I don't deny that. Yes, it … it was my mother's family history. It is something I can't change, nor do I broadcast because it isn't important to how we live our lives. It's just what was. Most Europeans had dealings in that terrible business. Unfortunately, that was considered normal at that time. I didn't tell you not for reasons you are thinking. We have talked about the cruelty of many people in the American South and those connections to your family history. You told me about the injustices, lynching, and your great aunt. You even told me about the mistreatment you felt being darker skinned than others in your own community. These are some of the main reasons why you are so guarded, hard on the exterior, determined to overachieve, and why you have those emotional scars. I knew that. But I don't want to own you; I want to build a life with you. Leave all that Black and White behind and just be us. Make our own traditions. Have our own life, just you and me. That is not owning you. I don't care what your parents say about me or even what they think. I don't want to live my life with them but with you. I didn't let you enter my heart and care for you because you are a Negro woman, Delphine. I did it because underneath all those rough edges of hard coal, you let me inside. We are alike. They won't approve … Never will they approve … I know but you must take this leap of faith and trust me … I will take care of you, support you, love you and you will do that for me. You don't need their approval. You are an independent strong and intelligent woman and I love you. Trust me. You are not like them. The way they think is from a different time. Their scars are too deep to heal. It isn't the way you feel. I know it isn't. Don't let their hatred blind you and put walls between us."

She blurted out, "Oh, so now you're blind. You don't see color?!"

He spoke quickly, "Of course I do. But I look beyond it. You know we both do; how could we have even gotten to be so close all this time if we didn't. We see the inside of each other. The strong pull of us, the connecting tissue of you and me. We are the pieces for each other. I know you feel it. Why would I long for anyone else now that I found you? Why would I care what anyone thinks now that I know what I want?"

She stopped moving around the room and peered at him. She was cold and firm in her statements.

"You can't possibly know what it would mean for me even to associate with you, knowing the truth. Betray everything my family has stood for and fought for to be with a slave master's great grandson. What would that make me, Philippe'? A traitor to my family, and my ancestors that sacrificed even died for me. How could I live a life as a traitor just to be your whore?! All you want is for me to be your whore!"

Philippe' bent himself down on to one knee resting on the lush cream carpet, and said softly, "Delphine, I am asking you to be my wife. Live with me in France and we won't look back at things we cannot change. We will make our own life."

Before his last words of that sentence, he held his arms out to her to come to him. She didn't move. Only their heavy breathing could be heard for a few seconds before she told him what she was thinking.

"Your wife? Are you kidding? Forget who I am? Who my people are? Forget my family, Philippe'? Could you forget yours?"

"Oui!"

"Liar! You are a liar! Nothing is more valuable to you than your superior all-knowing whiteness. All that pride in your family history. You couldn't leave your status, or your damn slave plantation money! You damn two bob-honkies just want us to give up everything! While you just take from everyone else. That's all you do is take what isn't yours, devour and destroy lives while you get richer and richer. Like a fat hog. It's been hundreds of years of the same and I knew better. I was taught never ever trust you people. Get what you need and run. Don't show them who you are, never let them know what you're thinking because they will lure you in, distort reality and betray. They plot to deceive like ... Judas's kiss just to crush the unity and our black power. These were the rules, and I broke them. Letting you weaken me with your fake kindness and lies. Damn it!"

Philippe' slowly retracted his extended hands back down to his side but stayed on bended knee as he listened to her. Controlling his breathing and emotions, he periodically clenched his teeth, and his jaw would tighten while concentrating on remaining calm. She was like a raging bull, and he forced himself not to get angry. He wanted to reason with her. He loved her. They got in her head. He knows she is proud and hurting but ... But each word from her mouth seemed to hit his flesh like a flaming arrow killing his joy with every syllable and consonant she annunciated.

"Do you know what you're asking? You want me to live a life being constantly reminded of who you people are and what you did! ... Whites who profited from the labor and lives of my people!"

"Your people?!" He inhaled and exhaled deeply before saying, "Delphine, this is your parents talking. It's not you. They have twisted things. Dearest, you are confused—"

Waving her fists, she cut him off with a sharp burst of anger. "My people, Philippe'! I am a child of stolen Africans. Did you think it was a coincidence that we have African names. They didn't just make those up! It is the blood that runs in my body. African blood! Africans kidnapped and transported on floating graves to be slaves in America! Rounded up like animals. Treated like dung only to be used for the profit and pleasure of those evil people that lorded over them. Stripped of our history, not having any rights, no language, no freedom, no voice. Hunted, tortured, beaten, hung for the sport of it. Women worth more only to breed more property for inhumane greedy people. Bred in farms like animals. Cities built on the backs of men unable to protect their own women from the evil white's violating her over and over. Broken people not knowing they were mating with their kin folks because they were torn away from their families and sold as children. Those innocent infants in fields on the backs of their mothers. Then when they barely learn to walk, they are right alongside their momma picking cotton, rice, tobacco, and sugar. In the mud, rain, cold, dying from fever, snakes, gators. Babies being ripped from their mother's arms to be placed on the block just so some little privileged white girl can get a new dress for her tenth birthday. People …people with value only good enough to be bartered for the disgusting wealth of those so-called white owners! Oh my god! I'm confused?! Now, I don't know my own mind! I can't make decisions that are best for my own damn life, it must be my parents talking. Is that what you said? Really!? I don't know how to think for myself, right? I can't despise what you did and loath who you all are?! That's so very white of you, Philippe'! Spoken like a true slave owner! Shall I call you, Massah, now?!"

He lowered his head, closed his eyes, and exhaled out a long sigh. "… Delphine …"

She grunted folding her arms across her chest. Then she coldly made it clear. "Get up off the damn floor. I won't be going anywhere with you, or anyone in your disgusting colonizing, rapist, slaving family, you lying son of a …" Delphine abruptly stopped talking and closed her eyes for a few minutes.

Philippe' moaned, opened his eyes, and stood up. He cleared his throat and spoke calmly as he watched her pace in front of the window with folded arms, mumbling to herself and scowling at him.

"These … these must be the reasons you did not answer my letters."

She cut her eyes from him huffing but said nothing. He squeezed his hands into tight fists to stop them from reacting. It was silent. Then he sniffled and smacked his lips right before he spoke slowly and calmly but with distinct clarity.

"Not even as a boy, did I ask a girl to be with me. Certainly, not ever begged one. There are just too many women in the world. You have already decided. Really there isn't much more to say. Go on, Delphine and find yourself a Negro man. I am sure your so-called friend, Lucian Clement, would fit the role nicely. Then all the Blacks will jump for joy since they've won you over so easily with their hatred. I hope you will be happy in that small belligerent Black world you so desperately want to stay in with your damn parents. I pity you for being so narrow-minded to only look behind and not ahead. Delphine, is that really what you want? Is it? You know, if I leave here without you, right now, I won't return, nor will I look back—there will be nothing. Everything will be as if we were two ships sailing past each other on the open sea. You … you realize that don't you?"

Standing proud, with light perspiration dripping from his forehead and his fists shaking by his side, he waited. Hoping. *(Dell?)*

She turned glaring at him with disgusted eyes of heat. Then with sarcastic emphasis she said, "You know what … At least, mine isn't a damn slave ship!"

He exhaled with a sharp burst of air from his nostrils.

"Adieu … Adieu Delphine."

Without another word spoken between them, she watched him slowly retrieve his small travel bag from the bedroom and walk out the suite door.

The end.

35 *Confessions of a Black Woman*

Life was normal for the Murry family and on December 27, 1985, Delphine, Eleanor, Hellene, and Lorelle went out for a Murry women weekend like they had done over the years. Staying at the International House Hotel, having formal afternoon tea, dressing up for Sunday brunch were some of the highlights of their regular lady's weekend.

But this year, they arranged their fun around the premiere of a new movie they all were dying to see called, "The Color Purple." They all agreed to read Alice Walker's book before the scheduled weekend. It was so moving that they went to the film two days in a row.

"That Whoopie Goldberg, she deserves an Oscar." Eleanor said prior to going back to refill her bucket of popcorn before leaving the crowded movie theater on the Saturday afternoon. Hellene and Lorelle chimed in a moan of agreement as Delphine was staring off into space.

Getting her attention, Hellene nudged her and said, "Twin, what's going on wit chu?"

Startled, she answered, "Huh? Nothing. I was just thinking about the movie."

Hellene studied her face and could tell she was lying. But she didn't say anymore because they were with their mother. Anything could set Eleanor Murry off to fuss and be negative the entire weekend.

Eleanor had picked up the conversation right where she left it when she stepped away to fill up on free refill popcorn. "This even better da second time ya see it. Sum-tings I missed da first time. Mister hid that money all 'round da house like granddaddy used ta do. Oh, and I'd be done shaved Mister all right let me tell ya' that bastard had a shavin' comin' to him for sure. Back in Franklinton, ya' cousin Weechie's first husband was like him. One day, he just come up missin'." The other three Murry women chuckled knowing exactly what she meant.

Making their way and getting their early dinner at the fine creole restaurant in the Royal Sonesta New Orleans, Delphine was pleasant but less engaged to chat. Her mind wandered every few minutes thinking about the life path she was on. It felt like a maze of thoughts periodically clouding her mind with flashes of a future that felt just like where she was in this moment with her sisters and mother eating fine Creole food; trapped in a box, routine and stagnant.

She asked herself, *(Will I be alone like Miss Celie? She was happy but she waited a lifetime and ... There is more in the world ... more to explore ... to be and to know ... Being with a good man who ... kind, intelligent, self-sacrificing, supportive, loving ... He'll constantly search behind my eyes to find what's truly there ... Is there a real gentleman ... knowing the depths of me ... and ...)*

Delphine exhaled then excused herself from the table. In a corner bathroom stall, she sat on the toilet and started to cry. Then she couldn't stop. While her sisters and mother were enjoying their dinner and superficial conversation, she was bawling her eyes out as ladies' footsteps shuffled in and out and toilets occasionally flushed. "What am I doing?" she said in a low voice, blowing her nose in the balled-up toilet paper. She stayed in the stall until Hellene came into the lady's room, calling for her.

"Twin! Twin!"

Coming out of the stall she quickly walked over to the porcelain sinks to wash her hands and freshen her face.

"Dell, are ya alright?" she asked with a tone of concern.

Nodding but not looking at her, Delphine continued to freshen up and then walked to the exit. But Hellene pulled her arm and turned her around. Once she looked in her older sisters' eyes it came out.

"I think I may be going crazy. Really crazy. I … I think I made a mistake Hellene."

"What cha talkin 'bout? Is dis 'bout dat professor?"

Delphine nodded sitting down in a parlor chair at the entrance end of the bathroom, while a few more ladies came in and out.

Hellene stood in front of her real close and lifted her head up by her chin to see her face and said, "Ya told me, ya didn't want that man. Not cuz what momma or diddy said 'bout him or them pressin' ya cuz he white. That's what cha said. Now, fess up—tell me, what part did ya lie 'bout?"

Her eyes filled with liquid before uttering the words, "All. . .All of it."

"Oh, no, Delphine!" sighing heavily, Hellene sat down next to Delphine. She thought about telling her off, but she didn't want to cause a scene in the bathroom of a nice restaurant.

"I should smack ya silly for being scared to live ya own life. Ain't I always in ya corner? From what ya say, he's good for ya but ya let 'um talk ya out of it, didn't ya?"

She just nodded and grabbed some tissue from the counter to dry her eyes. Then after a few moments she told her sister the truth.

"Sis, I … I love him but I never said it. Diddy always say I'm a train going straight. It's on me to make him proud to be a doctor in our family. He put all his cards on me, Sis. When I come back from Paris … Momma … went snoopin'… Then she made me watch "Mandingo" and "Roots" with her. The whole time she say it's in his blood to conquer and own Black people. She say he lied 'cuz that's what they do to trick us. They can't be trusted no matter how nice they bein'. 'Cuz they turn they back on ya in a minute. Can't never trust what they say. They taught to be deceitful and break us down. Remember how they done Ellen and Kizzy she say. When I told her we was just friends … She slapped me, said ain't no cracker devil gonna be friends with a colored woman … He only tryin' to make me his bed whore. Everythin' is ta make me his whore, she say … I tried ta tell her that he be kind, good … He respect me and … and I … safe, stronger, smarter… and I … loved … him. She slapped me so hard, my lip started bleeding. She start hittin' me wit da strap. Just wildly swinging it. Then she was walking 'round da kitchen and yellin' I'm stupid!"

Hellene was patting her back to ease her little sister's stress. Tears just continued to fall as she kept talking but she began to gasp and stutter finally telling things she never told anyone.

"She was yellin', if ya' wanna be with dat sugar plantation owner's kin, da spirits of them killed, tortured, raped, and sold … be lost in hell forever… She say if I want Philippe'… I be like da slaves in da big house … Laying up with da massah … havin' him babies … Cursed by my own people … it be just like auntie Paula… Why she kill herself from shame … My kids gonna be white and demon crazed like Kendrick, she say … She kept hittin' me, shouting, crying dat it be my fault her LaRoyce … went ta prison … for nothin' … 'cuz if I say I love dat white man … it be 'cuz Kay put sum-tin wicked on me … and …I must've liked what he done … No daughter of hers would ever be … wit a white man after what he done… not less she liked it… That's … That's … What she said to me, Hellene! … She said I liked what Kendrick done! … If I love Philippe' … she say, I … I liked it! … Not her child no more 'cuz … I be a filthy, trifling, whorish girl, liked what Kay …"

Delphine trembled all over as the tears soaked the cluster of tissue crumbling in her hands. She couldn't catch her breath. Hellene tried to comfort and calm her; even though she too was sobbing.

"Dell, hush now … Ssshhh … we in a—"

But the walls of her dormant secret had crumbled and she continued to spew out the never before spoken truth.

"I never told what he done … I never told it … but I didn't like it! … Hellene, I swear … I didn't … I didn't like it! … I was so … so scared … He … He said I be oldest, gotta help him… I strongest... He ain't got what they askin' 'bout. He said he White, just be like his slave, do what he say… I yellin'… No! I don't wanta… Don't touch me… He say, Twin… them men gots guns… and they… gonna come in and … kill us… if … if I didn't let… Oh, God!"

Delphine was hysterical and mentally shattered. She collapsed in her sister's arms and wailed from the hurt, shame, pain, and confusion of her mind and heart.

36 Sooner Than Later

Many days had passed since that night in December. Delphine was conflicted and depressed, the entire time. She wouldn't go anywhere but to school, the library and home. Often, she would cry over nothing. Just weep from some commercials playing on the television, to the rain falling from the sky. She was in so much pain feeling guilt and shame wanting to break free but afraid of what that would mean. Delphine wanted to talk to him. She had gone to Claudine's apartment to call Philippe', but his home and the library numbers had all been disconnected.

(He won't never talk to me again.) She thought. "Write him and say how ya feelin'."

Is what Hellene had told her, a few days after she couldn't get him by telephone. She didn't know how to say what she was feeling but she sent a couple of I'm sorry cards, apologizing for how things had gone when he came. Inside each one she wrote asking if they could talk.

But by the middle of February 1986, Delphine had received all three back, unopened, and internationally stamped returned to sender. Knowing him as she did; she had hoped he would've open them but in the back of her mind she figured he wouldn't. There was nothing left for her to grab on to. The realization of that fact made her even more heartbroken.

Cleaning out a box in her closet, she found the unopened letters he had written to her back in the fall. Holding them in her hands, she began biting her thumbnail nervously hesitating to read what he said before he came to find her on campus that day. Delphine felt buried alive in the claustrophobic atmosphere with no one to talk to at her parent's house. She needed to get away.

She packed the four letters in her suitcase and went to visit Hellene in Lafayette for the long Presidents' Day weekend. Hellene understood Delphine and could help her make sense of the things scattered in her brain. She also knew she'd be a strong shoulder to cry on when she read his letters.

On her weekend visit, little Sam was at his father's, and it was just the girls. There were no heavy discussions, but they did the sister time routine. Cooked, watched old movies, and danced to music videos on BET. This time they watched "GiGi, "The Way We Were," "Sparkle," and "Lady Sings the Blues". Just being there Delphine felt like she could breathe and truly relax. She, Hellene, and Tamera's little hands made sour cream cookies and batches of banana bread and zucchini bread for the freezer.

On Sunday, while listening to Luther Vandross and making lasagna the Murry way, the two had private time to talk. Delphine shared more things that happened in Paris and Lyon. She told Hellene most of the details from what had happened in the Roosevelt suite when he came to confess his love. Delphine expressed her heartache being tortured by her feelings knowing where he comes from. She really had begun to believe what her mother said about subconsciously liking what happened to her. Delphine felt like a dirty unrighteous woman because she wanted to be with him and that meant something horrible. Finally, she stopped stirring the sauce and sat down at the kitchen table, sobbing, and blowing her nose.

Handing her a box of tissue, Hellene said, "Ya better had sat down with all that blubberin', we'd have ta toss out da sauce if ya done got snot in it."

Delphine snickered and began playing with the baby doll Tamera left in a chair at the table before her nap. After a long sigh, Delphine said, "Sis, Philippe' is a lovin' kind man. He not the way momma say. He pushed me to learn more and see the world like it should be. He didn't act like most people thinkin' I is ugly and unwanted 'cuz I not thin and pretty like them light-skin girls from da quarter. He liked I'm smart. He laughs hearin' me switch back and forth speakin' proper. He made me feel I had no limit to what I can know, where I can go, and who I could be. I was so free and could relax with him. I wasn't scared of havin' affection. He wasn't gonna let me fail or hurt myself. He watched over me, not like no child but like a giant net to catch me if I need. He always was building me up and giving me more just ta fill my cup to know things and ... be excellent."

Hellene turned down the sauce and gave her a glass of sherry. Then she sat down at the table, moaning in agreement. Delphine kept pouring out her thoughts as they came to her.

"Philippe' was like no man I ever don read about. At first, I thought, what kind of man is he ta be so strong? He didn't beg or try ta be slick and touch me. He just wanted to kiss me. He would ask to kiss me. I loved the way he kissed me. He respected and valued me as a woman with the limits I set. He never crossed them not once. He never asked me why ... he just kept bein' a gentleman without knowing. I felt safe, secure, comfortable wit him, dat I liked when he smiled at me, when he touched me. We fit like a hand inside a Winter glove. He's magnificent no matter what color he be. But I can't be feelin' this way 'bout him. It ain't right. His money be from slaves. Our people and da awful part of American history we are branded with on our soul... How can I love him? What's wrong wit me? Maybe what momma say be true. I must be a sinful vile woman, 'cuz Hellene, I can't help it. I love him. I miss him."

Tears overflowed over the skin on her face again as she pulled more tissue from the box to wipe them away.

"Dell, look a here. Stop wit all dat foolish talk. Stop lettin' momma confuse ya ta make ya do what she say. What Kay done, whatever it was, it be wrong. Ya knows that too. Even bein' twelve ya know'd it. Lettin' him don't mean ya' liked it, neither. Ya was a terrified child,

Dell. Stop thinkin' like momma. Kay was on drugs, and LaRoyce fixed it. What happen back then ain't got nothin' ta do with adult Dell and da Professor. Enough of dat past shit. Ya love Philippe' 'cause he done touch ya heart, ya soul, and ya mind. Touchin' a woman's body don't mean it come close ta any one of them three things. Read them letters he wrote ya and see if I ain't tellin' ya da truth."

Hellene gestured for her to go get the letters from her suitcase, and she did. She opened one at a time and moaned with a hint of a giggle, when she pulled out the cream monogrammed stationery, she remembered was from his personal desk in his bedroom. Then glancing over them, she quickly realized they were not letters at all but one page poems Philippe' had written in calligraphy. They were words she had never heard him say or read before.

The first poem was called Music of Heart, and it started:

You are the special warmth of a heavenly star that surrounds my heart and brightens my life. There is no sound more glorious than your voice hitting my inner ear like a wind chime welcoming the gentle breeze …

The second poem was titled My Vision, and it began:

Solid you formed under intense heat and pressure. A treasure I have found; Rare and beautiful. You are my black diamond …

The third poem was called Never-Ending, and it started:

The earth around us rumbles and quakes, fire from hell beneath our feet opens the ground to swallow us whole but I will never release my embrace, even as ash I will forever hold you tightly …

The fourth poem was titled You and Me, and it started:

Sweet lady of moon light. Gentle goddess of sunrise, you are my one. Come and we will discover all the hidden stars of the galaxy, explore the wonders of our world, and love one another for eternity…

Delphine sobbed and smiled simultaneously as she read each one out loud. Hellene had tissue dabbing her eyes. During the reading of his love poems, Hellene got up and poured herself a glass of whiskey to calm her flow of tears. The two sat in the kitchen quietly for a while, just exhaling slowly and looking at the four papers on the table, until Hellene finally broke the silence clutching at her neck. "Damn, he had some words to say."

Delphine looked over at her sister nodding. Thenshe said, "Yeah. Beautiful words. Just like him. I was special to him. Not like momma say, not filthy and not no whore. Why didn't I read these before. I'm so stupid. Hellene, he can't be blamed for what his great-great grandparents done. He can't choose his kin. We wasn't even born. Ya right, my lovin' him ain't got nothin' ta do with da past like momma say. They just both is White but only one loved me the right way. A Godly way like a maiden in the Song of Solomon. That … that how Philippe' loved me."

Hellene tapped Delphine's hands on the table and gave her clear advice. "Ya must live ya own life, Delphine. I do, ya sista do. Maybe ya just bigger than Louisiana. It makes no sense for da Lord ta give ya all them brains for ya not to fill it up and use it. Ha! Look, we ain't in da Color Purple, and ya ain't Ms. Ceilie, trapped. It 1986, ya can love anyone and live anywhere ya want. I always support ya, Dell."

"I … I was so confused, Hellene. I didn't know what to feel. I felt so dirty. Momma had my mind messed up. He doesn't even know I love him. I never told him that I loved him. I … I need to tell him."

"Yeah, ya do. Best be sooner rather than later." Hellene said, before sipping more of her special brand of whiskey.

Delphine read the poems several more times while in Lafayette. After doing a little research, she found out when Philippe' came in October, France had changed their entire telephone system.

"Sis, maybe he wasn't tryin' ta stop me from callin', reachin' him like I thought. Da whole country—every number done been changed. Philippe', could still . . . I got ta go there."

Rejuvenated with hope, Delphine and her older sister discussed a plan to go back to Paris without her parents being suspicious. It had been several months that she had cut off all contact with him and they had no knowledge about his being there in October. Since she had received scholarship awards to Sorbonne it would have been easy to have discussions about their medical school program. However, they agreed that the less she told them the better. So, all she said was she was taking a two-week vacation with Claudine, somewhere warm. They didn't ask where and she didn't tell them anything more. Delphine was glad she didn't have to lie, even though she had one written out to tell them just in case.

Convincing Claudine to go with her was easy. She had been seeing a nice guy who lived in Los Angeles, but the long-distance romance was a challenge for her. Tony Jefferies had asked her to move in with him. Claudine was going to take this opportunity to see if she really wanted to be that serious. She let Delphine know she was going to reconnect with Pierre Clement again, if he was still single with the intention of helping her decide about shacking up in California.

"Girl, I'm not judgin'. You are grown, Dene. But you know what they say. Why buy the cow if the milk is free. Uh, is Tony lactose intolerant?" Delphine said laughing.

Claudine punched her in the shoulder shouting, "You stupid! I held out a long time, heifer. But when I went there for New Years, I gave him some. I think dat started da problem. He's flying here in May. He's super sweet but well, I just don't know."

"Dene, stop trippin' ya know ya goin' ta live with him but ya want ta have one last fling before ya do." Delphine said giving her the stink-eye.

"Okay, ya right. I hate ya know me so well. Dell, what if Pierre asks 'bout ya? Uh, really, what if Lucian does? What ya what me ta say?"

"Dene, I'm sure he won't. I didn't answer his calls or letters last year. But if he do, ya can tell Pierre, I am no longer inclined to entertain such an acquaintance."

Snickering, Claudine said, "Alrighty than, Miss Black Jane Austin!"

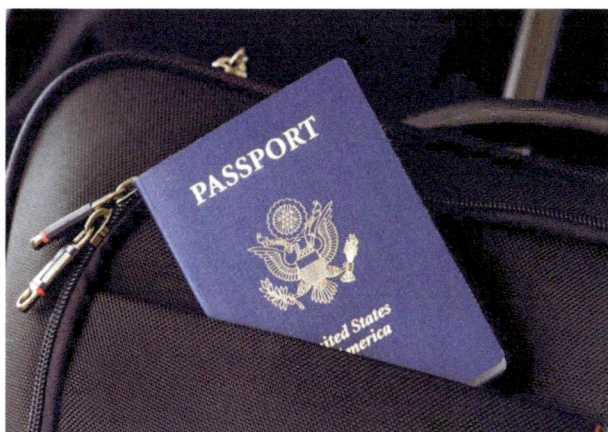

Three days before their trip, Delphine went to visit Lorelle for back up just in case her mother got nosey. Once Cedric had left with the kids for a while, she shared her real plans to tell Philippe', she loved him and then see what happens. Lorelle easily agreed to cover for her, if needed. She was ecstatic about Delphine breaking free and doing what was best for her own life.

She said smugly, "I told ya' he be ya crush!"

"Shut up!" Delphine shouted as the two laughed while giving cheers with their drinks.

Not long after the amusement faded, Lorelle began acting a little antsy. She wanted to say something but was stalling trying to figure out if she should, not knowing how her sister would react. Delphine picked up on it.

"What's wrong wit chu?" She said finishing the last swallow of her homemade hurricane.

Being put on the spot she gathered the courage to talk. "Dell, I need to tell ya sum-tin, I didn't think it was important back then but maybe I should tell ya."

Delphine looked over at her sister waiting as Lorelle sat on her large tan sectional couch biting the inside of her bottom lip.

"Well tell it." Delphine said bugging out her eyes at her.

"Okay, well, when da professor come 'round that time to Momma and Diddy house, he come here later ta help fix it with Cedric. But when I told him it could been bad him going to the house he said, ya told him they don't much like White folk's for the lynching and what happen to auntie Paula. I say yeah but also uh, 'cause what Kendrick done."

"What?!" Delphine sat up with the rapid increase in her blood pressure.

"Dell, I didn't know ya ain't told him 'bout that. He knew 'bout other stuff. But he says what did he do? I tried sayin' nothin', but he kept on pressin'. He said, if it helps him know why they don't like White people; he wanna understand … need ta know it. So, uh … I told da story. I left nothin' out … Even dat Kendrick be auntie Paula's son and 'bout LaRoyce goin' to prison for killin' him for what he done."

Delphine started yelling, "Why? Why in the hell would ya ever tell anyone that! What's wrong with you! What did ya say about me? What did ya tell him? What? Lorelle, what?!"

"Uh, I … I talk mostly 'bout me but I said nobody know what all happened in dat room, and we never ask. I told him Kendrick was white like him wit straight hair and green eyes. He was on drugs and not in his right mind. When he told ya he not our brother, he tell ya ta be like a slave. Momma and Diddy have what he done to never trust no white people. I say, it could've been me in dat room wit him, but … but it wasn't. That all." Lorelle burst out crying, "I'm sorry, Dell. I thought he knew already. I did. I mean, I told Cedric after we was married. I thought he knew 'cause you say he ain't never try to do nothin'. I didn't mean ta … I'm sorry. Please don't be mad. Please … I'm sorry."

"That was last year! He … he knew this before I graduated … before he said he loved me … Oh, God!"

Delphine wanted to hit her sister. Hit her hard right in her face! But she blew out heavy, pacing and counting out loud to twenty. Just when she got to twelve, Lorelle fell to her knees pulling at Delphine's green stirrup pants tearfully pleading for forgiveness.

Closing her eyes and not looking down at her sister, Delphine's voice went from loud and then soft as she tried to contain her rage as she spoke.

"Damn you! Lorelle, ya always runnin' ya mouth! Talkin' too damn much! I can't be 'round ya right now or ... or... I'ma hit ya til ya bleed...Tellin' ya husband 'bout ya-self is one thing. But ya had no right ... No right! Tellin' anybody 'bout me! I don't want ta see or talk ta ya, not for a long time. How dare ya talk 'bout what ya don't know and ya never supposed ta tell. Never!"

Delphine broke free from Lorelle's holding her knees and left her house while she fell crying on the floor of her living room.

37 Springtime Action

In mid-March, the two-week school research in Paris with Claudine plan was in full execution mode and going as expected. They rented a secure one-bedroom loft near the Champs-Elysées.

Pierre took Claudine to London with him for ten days, a day after they had landed in France. How convenient. With no one to explain her actions too, Delphine did some investigative sleuthing and located Professor Philippe' Delacroix's lecture and class rotation schedule. It was easy for her to get, since she knew the network of the school, library and her fluent French speaking was very close to sounding like a native.

On her third day in Paris, she snuck into his fine arts and history lecture at Théâtre du Ranelagh unnoticed. Hidden by the darkness of the crowded auditorium, she watched and listened to his lecture quietly. It made her frequently smile, hearing the slight inflections in his voice when he wanted to make a point. How dashing he was in his gray corduroy sport jacket, white shirt, and creased pressed gray trousers. His oxfords were polished, and they shined when he adjusted his stance. He was so smart and charismatic. She had been completely in love with him, and he ignited sparks of a life she knew could only be possible with him.

A slight shiver ran down her spine with each sound of his baritone voice hitting her like a loud symphony drum. But she wasn't sure of what would happen. He had returned her attempts to talk. Now, fear kept her hesitating to act. She just wasn't ready to face him yet. She needed to plan.

For several hours Delphine talked to herself and listened to new music she brought with her to keep her mind relaxed. While biting her nails and chewing on the end of pen caps, she planned and scripted dialog in her journal. Seriously strategizing and mapping out what to do and how to say what she needed to without being afraid of what he would say back. Then she outlined countermoves to how he might respond or what he might do when she saw him. When the low sounds of Luther Vandross's "The Night That I Fell In Love" song hit her ear, Delphine took a pause and thought back to times they had spent together. She redirected her thoughts to determining when she knew she loved him. It came to her without much pondering that it was that unforgettable New Year's Eve.

"My heart knew it right then. Watching him play the piano. How he bought all the seats to be alone with me on the boat. Oh, my lord the champagne. His jokes! The way he held me. Even how he asked to kiss me at midnight. Philippe' cherished me, even later knowing …"

Delphine made the decision to visit some of the cafés he had taken her to during her year in Paris. While sipping tea she periodically laughed out loud to herself remembering being with him there. A few hours passed, and Delphine felt tranquil as she watched the people of Paris walking around. It no longer mattered when she knew she felt this way, but she loved him, and somehow, not matter what, Philippe' needed to know it.

Saturday, two days later, after a late morning of writing in her journal, she checked on her research notes listing where he would be with a group of other important people. She arrived early in an inconspicuous disguise, then waited for his party to arrive at the Goumard restaurant. A bit later, Philippe' came in with a couple of men and women and seemed to enjoy his meal and conversation with the group. He paid particular attention to the thin tall woman with flowing blonde curls he sat next to.

Pretending to sip her French onion soup under shades and a large floppy hat, Delphine analyzed his every move, while a growing feeling of sadness came over her. When he began to leave, she observed his finger loosely latched to the woman's finger, while the two walked through the restaurant. Holding back the urge to call out his name, she was unable to stop herself from trembling as salty liquid welled up in her eyes. A few drops fell when she witnessed him kiss the woman's forehead and hold her lower back before she got into his car brought up by the valet and he drove away.

That night at 10:15 p.m. she couldn't stop thinking of him. Lying under the soft duvet she stroked it remembering how his long creamy fingers had felt on her skin. She pondered on the affection and tenderness he had shown to her and how he had offered to always give them to her, but she rejected him. Wiping the now fallen tears, she sat up and decided to do it right at that moment.

Delphine traveled by cab in the middle of the night determined to say what she needed. Once she arrived at his luxury penthouse, she rang him through security at the front of the building. She took a big risk, since she had no way to know for sure if he was alone. But she didn't care.

"Delphine?"

She heard his startled voice through the security system video.

Slowly, she lifted her head for the lights to shine over her face and answered, "Oui."

He didn't immediately buzz her in. *(Delphine?)* After a few seconds, he responded in a surprised higher pitch to his normal deep voice, "Qu'est-ce que tu fais ici?" (What are you doing here?)

"Philippe', please, may I come up? I need to speak to you."

There was silence.

38 Eve

The security access buzzed, and the door clicked allowing her inside. Philippe' opened his door wearing striped, burgundy pajama pants, a long matching robe, and leather slippers. It was late about 11:30 p.m. but he had been up reading. It was evident from the book in his hand and his glasses resting on the curls on top of his head. Startled by her presence, he asked again. "What … What are you doing here?"

Looking up at him she answered, "I came to speak to you. It's important. Are you alone?" He nodded and closed the door.

Then he motioned for her to come in. "Entrez."

He said coldly while rubbing his chin and walking into the large living room next to warm heat coming from the corner fireplace. Placing his book and his glasses on a table he walked to a small bar and poured up a dark liquor in a short glass.

"Would you like a drink?" He asked glancing back and saw her shake her head in refusal.

Exhaling before taking a large gulp of his drink, he then turned to face her standing straight and clenching her pocketbook.

"What is it you want to say?" Were the next words that chilled the air around him. His frostiness made her tremble inside. But she came to say it and no matter what happens she had to tell him how she felt. It was something she should have said to him six months ago.

"Philippe'… I'm sorry. I said some terrible things that hurt you and …" He waived his hand smirking as if he had been unfazed. Then confessed, "You didn't hurt me. I needed to know it. Your vitriolic attacks about my family, well it was how you felt. It was honest even with the acrimonious way in which it was delivered."

Taking a step toward him she shook her head rapidly as she said, "No. No, it's not. I'm sorry. I couldn't see past your family history and that was wrong. You are not those people neither is your sister or your parents. Everyone, everyone is genuine and kind. I didn't think about what I had experienced with you. If I had … maybe my brain could have counteracted what my mother was saying and showing me. I could have thought things through logically. I was emotional and confused about a lot of things."

Philippe'was like a stone casually sipping his drink but Delphine was determined and kept saying the things she had held inside.

"I'm sorry I didn't say this before now. I should have but I was afraid to tell you that I love you. I do. I have for a long time." She paused a second then continued as he watched her from across the room.

"I never said it because I was afraid, I would make the wrong decision. If I said it that it meant something bad. Because I was taught, I wasn't supposed to feel this way. I was made to believe that something was terribly wrong with me if I loved you and wanted to be with you. But that isn't true. It's not. I'm not afraid anymore."

He shook his head and huffed before pouring himself another drink and taking a sip.

"Did you honestly come all this way to tell me these words?" He huffed again then continued. "As I recall it, there was never a question of if you loved me. It was the fact that you didn't trust me or love me enough. You had no faith in what you didn't believe in. That's all over now. I have no interest in digging up something dead and buried. Why are you even here doing this?"

Delphine took two steps forward, then said it. "Philippe', tu me manques. (I miss you.) J'ai besoin de vous. (I need you.) Je veux avoir ma propre vie avec toi." (I want my own life with you.)

Shaking his head and chuckling under his breath, he glanced back at her with an expression of slight irritation and arrogance. Then he took another sip from his glass. Delphine watched his smug reactions to her confession as she gripped her purse tighter.

Without warning, he blurted out, "I'm with someone. I will be marrying Angelique as arranged. So, you saying these things is very unnecessary. As I said, it is dead and in the past. Even your being here is highly inappropriate—"

She cut him off with a desperate elevation in the tone of her voice. "You said, I was special and like no other! You said, the rays of sunlight only shine bright when you look upon the glow of my face. Touching my skin was like heavenly dew nourishing the hills covered in blades of grass around your home. There was no other moment in time that gave your hearts truest joy except with me."

He stared at her as she continued to recite parts of stanzas from the poems he had written to her last fall.

"Philippe', you said I was your black diamond. An uncut treasure that only sparkled nuzzled perfectly in the carved placement setting of your heart."

He pressed his lips tightly and closed his eyes inhaling and exhaling heavily from his nose. Then he opened them fixed on hers as a few small tears trickled down her cheeks.

"You said, you loved me, Philippe'. You said that my true self dug its way into your soul and planted seeds with deep roots that grow as wild lavender never to be harvested. You said, I am your warmth, your complement, your desire … a rare jewel meant to discover, cherish, protect, and shower with love always."

Philippe' inhaled and exhaled slowly from his nose as his heart hammered inside the walls of his chest hearing his written words again. But he stood emotionless, unmoved by her reciting them. It was then just silent.

Finishing his second drink, Philippe' walked to place his empty glass back onto the bar while saying under his breath.

"A man will say just about anything to get laid." He snickered to himself before glancing back at her. He realized she must have heard what he said because he could see the hurt in her slow watering eyes.

For just a couple of seconds they stood several feet apart with pride and stubbornness holding them in place. Delphine slowly wiped the tracks of tears from her cheeks as the burning wood crackled from the fireplace. He decided to speak first. This time his natural thunderous tone was purposefully softer, and he spoke more gentlemanly.

"I know what I said. At the time, I meant the words I sent to you. You are special, Delphine. I know you will find a nice Black man to be happy. I am sure of it. But now, it is very late. Let me call you a car to take you back to where you are staying."

His slippers made a shuffle sound along the hard wood as he slowly moved to the phone on the other side of the room. As he was walking further away from her, Delphine spoke again.

"Are you saying you don't love me, Jean-Philippe' Henri?"

He stopped, quickly his head turned. He glared at her hearing her say his given name.

She waited only a moment, then said, "Is this what you expect me to believe, Professor Delacroix? That … that you would simply toss away your black diamond. Are you trying to convince me that you don't care about me or want me anymore?"

He replied in a tone still very soft speaking to her. "Delphine all of that is in the past. It is over. There are no more feelings to be had. It is dead and buried. I have moved on with someone else and you should do the same. As I said, it is very late; I am going to call a car for you."

Turning his back to her, he took a few steps and then grabbed the phone next to a high table and low chair. A minute later, he started to say a greeting in French. Then he turned to ask her where the car would be taking her, and he immediately stopped speaking.

With wide eyes and his mouth hung open he froze until the voice on the other end of the line broke his trance. He slowly sat down in the low chair and hung up the phone never breaking his intense stare.

In those few moments with his back turned, Delphine had quickly removed her clothes and was standing in front of him in her navy-blue lace bra and lace trim panties. Her smooth dark mahogany skin glistened in front of the low fire, while her voluptuous size 18 frame filled out every centimeter of her snug underwear. She wasn't scared but confident in what she wanted him to be certain in this moment. Her family was important, but they were not going to make her loose the happiness she wanted with him. There was no questioning her motive. Delphine made it unequivocally transparent, before he could formulate words, by saying, "Take me to bed, then I'll leave."

Philippe' blinked quickly for his brain to jolt and register what she said. His mouth formed the word "what," but no sound came out of his throat.

Knowing she had his complete attention, she stepped out of the bundle of clothes gathered at her feet then reached behind her back to unfasten the five hooks of her 40 DD cup size bra.

He raised his hands motioning to her, and he stuttered, "S-S-STOP!!" Finally, he had made a sound that matched his frantic head and hand movements. She paused but before he could come out of his shock, she spoke in a tone that was very matter of fact.

"You don't care or love me anymore, it's apparent by your coldness that you've really moved on. I'm offering my body to you. You said you wrote those things to get laid. It's what you wanted that night in your wine cellar, isn't it? Now's your chance. Since you have made it crystal clear to me that I mean nothing to you, just do it and I'll call my own damn car to go."

With a tight face and squinting eyes, his head shook slightly, while a slow release of "Whaaat?" came from his mouth right before Philippe' covered it with his hand rapidly blinking. Within seconds he gazed up at the vaulted ceilings for a couple of minutes. As his eyes roved about to avoid gawking at her and control his thoughts trying to calm his body's awakening, Delphine removed her bra. When he turned his head back to glance at her, he gasped. A slow gurgle came from his throat. She watched him carefully without speaking. Then she moved her hands down to the waistband of her brief panties.

She paused when he shouted at her, "DELL! NO DON'T!" and sprung to his feet fumbling off his robe rushing toward her. She stood there as he rapidly approached and their eyes locked. His hands trembled rustling with the robe to cover her. A tingling sensation was felt on her skin from his light touch as he moved to conceal her partial nakedness. He constantly shook his head with a creased forehead expressing his total disbelief in her actions.

"Wah … What is wrong with you?" He paused a moment to collect his garbled thoughts and say just the right thing. He was always saying the right words, but not tonight. She had confused him. He didn't get what was happening. Philippe' had so many conflicting thoughts and it was what came out of his mouth when he spoke.

"I don't … You … you … Why? … Delphine, are you drunk?... Why are … Why are you offering yourself to me like this? … You're acting crazy! … Showing me your body … This isn't you! … What is wrong with you?!"

Staring up at him with fierce boldness in her eyes, she didn't answer his questions but taunted him. "Don't you want to know me, Philippe'?"

He slowed his rapid breathing and bit his lip. Then he ran the back of his long fingers over her plump warm cheek and nodded. Seconds later, he whispered, "Oui, j'aimerais beaucoup." (Yes, I would love too very much.

Blinking leisurely, she told him, "Since it will mean nothing, you can finally have me, Philippe'. Like you wanted. Won't you just take me to bed?" Her words came out like an airy whisper as she fell deeper into the powerful undertow from his romantic stare.

Standing so close, underneath his silky robe her body pressed against his bare skin. She had that distinctive smell of sweetness like he remembered.

He chuckled to himself knowing it was her skin care ritual that included a mixture of Jafra's Almond Oil and Avon's Skin So Soft.

Philippe' licked the bottom corner of his lip before answering with a nod sounding out every syllable to his low breathy answer of "Oui."

Thenhe lowered his hand so that his long creamy manicured index finger began stroking over the firm roundness hidden just below the silk. He watched her carefully try to control her subtle twitch from his delicate touching. Her body warmed hearing his eyes whisper her name through his intimate gaze. Her heartbeat loudly as if it were coming out from behind the walls of her chest, feeling the alluring heat from his naked torso. She swallowed hard, followed by rapid waves from her natural long lashes to keep her composure.

Philippe' smirked reading the elusive hint of her body language, he had come to know too well. Next with sweet tenderness, he elevated his opposite hand to cradle the left side of her face and began stroking her cheek with his thumb. Within seconds he displayed a broad smile before licking his lips and speaking again.

"Mais je suis un homme de parole. Je ne le ferai qu'après m'être marié avec toi." (But I'm a man of my word. I will, only after I marry you.)

Delphine tried to muffle her chuckle, but it grew into a giant smile, and she covered her mouth with her fingers. Tears quickly formed and fell. In a breathy response, she said long and slowly, "Philippe' … You … love … me."

In this masterful game of chicken, Philippe' realized that Delphine had successfully called his bluff that everything was over, and he no longer loved or wanted a life with her. *(Liar!)*

It was in this very moment, Philippe' knew with all certainty that she did love him enough and trusted him to give her a newlife. A life he had wanted with her when he confessed his love on the Tulane University quad that cold day in October. He grinned and confirmed it so.

"Oui, je t'aime, ma une Eve. Tu es le doux joyau de mon cœur." (Yes, I love you, my one Eve. You are the sweet jewel of my heart.)

She hugged his tall muscular body and exhaled in relief and peaceful joy as the side of her face playfully moved over the fluffiness of his chest hair. Lifting her head with her face a little twisted she said, "Wait, Eve—Eve like from the Bible?"

Within his firm hold, he moaned a yes stroking her partially covered back from the opening of his robe he had placed over her backward. Leaning back to see his eyes, her voice grew higher when she spoke.

"Why are you calling me Eve? Because I'm disobedient? Are you sayin' I … I'm eating the forbidden fruit and cursing the world with sin for all mankind? Is that … that why I am Eve? That isn't very romantic Philippe'."

He kissed her forehead releasing an airy chuckle, then he gazed at her with a smile, and said, "You are my Eve because no matter how foolish, believing the lying words from a wicked angel posing as a damn talking snake, I still love you. I love you so much, I willingly take any hardship of a new life just to be with you forever. You are an irreplaceable bone from my body that's placement is the one that makes me whole. That is why, Delphine Murry, you are my Eve."

His sweet words sizzled over her body like Crisco dropped in a hot cast iron skillet. While the tips of his fingers slid over her naked spine like liquified butter on top of freshly baked pastry dough.

"Awww," floated from her parted lips as Philippe' pulled her body up to meet his yearning mouth. The slow-moving collide grew into a long and passionate kiss. His tongue opened her mouth to venture inside. She firmly pressed her body against his with a delightful moan. His body felt strong, and his mouth was warm with a delicious hint of a spicy rum that he must have been sipping. She had desperately missed him. Delphine began caressing the smoothness of his wide muscular back while melting away in his loving arms and feeling charges from their intense and electrifying kiss.

Consumed by the taste of her, Philippe' felt the peace of being whole once again. His tongue stroked hers as they remained connected in love's rhapsody. After several long minutes of kissing, Philippe' abruptly ripped his mouth away, breaking their kiss.

"Dearest love every curve of your dark chocolate body is more beautiful than I had imagined."

She grinned as he kept talking. "But if you don't put your clothes back on, it will be difficult for me to keep my promise. I … I am only human."

Both chuckled as he released her. She grabbed her clothes in the bundle on the floor. Quickly she rushed to the nearest bathroom, which was beyond the kitchen across from the back set of stairs and next to Andreas's guestroom.

Standing in the large bathroom and glancing over the lush green meadow décor, Delphine giggled, removing the robe from her body. An electric tingle came over her skin as happiness thoughts confirmed she had not lost him after all. She knew in her heart he loved her, and he had waited for her to come to her senses.

"Thankyou, Lord." She whispered in the full large mirror over the dual sinks. Realizing she was just standing in her panties, she paused to really examine her nakedness in the mirror. Her giddiness slowly faded as she thought back to his brief touch over the robe moments earlier. Delphine placed her fingers over her neck and caressed her skin as she eased her hand down to where Philippe' had stroked her so tenderly. She exhaled and took a couple of minutes just staring at herself. Delphine thought about what she wanted in this moment. In silence, she slipped out of the bathroom and crept up the back stairs.

Philippe' was tending to the fire that was no longer blazing but only the hot remnants were left from the burned logs. Not hearing anything for what seemed too long, he called out to her, but she didn't answer. Confused he went to the bathroom, calling her name softly. The door was cracked open, and her clothes were on the floor along with his robe. His heart jumped. He immediately glanced up the stairs blowing heavily from his mouth. Philippe' loved her and he wanted her. But he didn't move for several minutes and just stared at the back stairs going up to his second floor leading right to his bedroom.

Philippe' began to talk to himself, "I know, she's in my room; Dell wants me to make love to her. I don't have to wait anymore. It won't matter because I'm going to marry her as soon as possible. I'll be very slow and gentle with her. I can be. I love her."

He went up the stairs but stopped in the hallway, rubbing his beard as his conscience started to prick his brain. *(Will she be scared? What if she has thoughts of the past and then refuses to be my wife? I promised her I wouldn't touch her. I should keep my word. But do I have to keep it if she is telling me she wants me to break it? How will she feel after? Will this be a stain on our marriage we won't ever be able to wash away?)*

Philippe' swallowed hard before he opened his bedroom door. Delphine was sitting up against his headboard waiting for him. He smiled at her. She looked heavenly under the white ruffled canopy with her naked body snuggly wrapped and strategically covered in his white sheets.

Delphine smiled, then said, "You don't have to keep your promise. I don't want to wait anymore. I'm going to be your wife; give you children and make you very happy—"

Walking toward the bed, he cut her off but spoke tenderly, "Dell, I ... I need to tell you something first."

She was attentive watching him sit next to her on the other side of the bed. He reached and held her hand before licking his lips and speaking.

"Do you remember when I told you that I cared for you without having sex?"

She moaned with a nod, and interjected, "But I want to."

He stroked her hand and squeezed before continuing, "I know, and I am going to marry you as soon as we can. I am not perfect or some kind of machine. Dell this ... this ... is very difficult for me. I want you. Dell, I want to be the one to show you the magnificence of physical love. I do. But baby, I promised you, Dell. . . I . . . I promised myself, I would respect you. I have been reading the bible see and there is this scripture ... I mean ..."

He took a pause to organize his thoughts. Then he spoke again, "Chérie, how can God bless our marriage if we do this before we are meant to? How could you ever trust me or even my word, in the future if we do this now? I wouldn't be any different from what your mother had said about me, if I break this first promise of honor. As much as I want to be with you right now, I don't want our life to start off that way. I don't want to feel guilty or ashamed about touching you and I don't want to wonder and worry, if you do, either."

Tenderly he stroked the softness of her hand and watched her eyes slowly gloss over as they filled with water. As she spoke a few tears fell and her body slightly quivered.

"Did you say blessed? Honor? But … but you know. I know you do. Since last April … Lorelle just told me, when you came to her house … You know I'm not a virgin … You never let on but just kept treating me the same … as if I had been saving myself for marriage … And now you're sayin' words like our marriage needs to be an honored blessing before God … How? Why would you say that Philippe'? Why? Knowing what happened to me … It … it can't be. Not after what he did… I'm not …" She stopped speaking as her body began to shake. Her voice had elevated saying these never spoken things.

He held her hands tightly, stroking softly to calm her. Philippe' watched her with loving eyes and whispered, "First, if we ask God, he will help us build a strong family. We need him because our life together will not be perfect. Second, my love, you … you were never a conquest. Delphine, you have always been precious to me. Tu es le joyau de mon cœur. (You are the jewel of my heart.) A rare diamond. Knowing that didn't change anything." He smiled at her. Then he said something he had felt in the back of his mind after Lorelle had told him about Kendrick. "Honestly, when she told me, I thought perhaps I unknowingly might have reminded you—"

She cut him off shaking her head squeezing his hand tighter, "No. Not in any way. No." Delphine paused only a moment, then said, "You love me the right way. You didn't treat me like I was stained, and I never felt I was. How was I so lucky to have found you? You make me feel like at any moment I will burst into a thousand stars and fill the sky. I love you so much, Jean-Philippe'. I trust you completely, my beautiful best friend. You are my balance, and you have my whole heart, mind, and soul. On our wedding night, I will give you my body and then you will have all of me. I can't wait to wake up with you next to me every day for the rest of my life. I am your Eve, and you … you sweet prince are my Adam."

She displayed a soft smile, while he wiped her tears with his bent index finger. Moments later, he delicately kissed her forehead, and whispered, "My sweet Delphine."

Philippe' got up and went into his closet and gathered an oversized shirt. When he moved to place it on the bed next to her, Delphine asked a burning question.

"Earlier today at Goumard, the woman you left with … Was that … Angelique Dubois?"

His head darted up. Philippe' began to study her face searching for answers for a couple of seconds before he responded. "What? How did you know I was at that restaurant?"

"I … I was there. Was that her?"

He sat back down on the bed moving the clothes closer to her, and answered, "Oui. Yes, it was."

Feeling a little insecure she kept probing, "Oh. She looks like a model. How … I mean … What will happen now?"

Philippe' ran his fingers through his hair and took a deep breath. "I will talk to her in the morning. Don't worry."

"But isn't it bad for you and your family, if you don't marry her?" She was worried and couldn't stop thinking about how this was going to impact things.

He smiled. "Perhaps but don't worry about that. I am marrying Delphine Asha and no one else."

She pulled his hands toward her closer, saying, "But breaching the contract, it is gonna—"

He silenced her by stroking her lips with his fingers. "Hush. It will be alright. Angelique and I have been very close for many years."

"Yeah, I'm sure you are … I mean, when I came tonight, I thought she would be here. It wasn't going to stop me if she was, but I really was expecting to see her."

"Why …? Why would you think she would be here?"

"Philippe', when I saw you today … The way you were touching her … Well, it seemed as if … she would be spending the night."

Smirking, he whispered, "We are friends Delphine."

"Yeah, well, I know men need physical things. Even your mother said once you love women, but she was the only one you had brought to your family home. Well except for me those two times."

"Delphine …"

She kept talking, "I never really thought about it before but when I saw you touching her—"

He cut her off, "Our relationship is not what you think."

"Huh?" She looked at him confused and got no clues to what he meant from his facial expression. Philippe'exhaled and said, "Delphine, you see, Angelique … Well, she doesn't particularly care for men."

She busted out laughing, startling him upright in the process. She managed to get the words, "She's gay?!" between her cackling and hand clapping.

"Uh, why is that funny?" He said a little taken back by her reaction.

Lowering her head and waving her hands as if she was feeling the spirit, she slowed her laughter. Holding her chest, she admitted, "I … I thought you … you might love her. Oh, oh my god! I was jealous but … She's gay! Ha-ha-ha!"

Chuckling, he pulled her hands down from now covering her eyes as she continued laughing, and said, "I do but like a sister. She is a good friend. Her family planned this early thinking maybe she would grow out of it, but she didn't."

Exhaling hard, Delphine calmed down and grabbed his cheeks squeezing them together for his lips to poke out and gave him a quick peck. Then she released his face, and said, "Oh lord! I thought you had been sleeping with her. Oh, I'm stupid! So stupid being jealous for nothing!"

Philippe' turned his head. For a few seconds only the air moved in the room as she stopped laughing and saw him looking away.

Delphine forcefully grabbed his bearded chin back toward her and moved her head to connect with his squinting eyes.

"Look at me, Philippe'! You said she's gay. She is gay, right?!"

He licked his lips before he confessed, "Yes. But … Well, … I never said I hadn't slept with her."

"What?! Oh, you nasty French freak!" Delphine let out a disgusted groan, folded her arms, and rolled her eyes at him.

Smirking, he reached over to unfold her arms, then moved his head to reconnect with her eyes. Contact. Philippe' quickly clarified.

"Listen, I was in the military, we were maybe eighteen. I mean we were going to be married and she was curious. It is cute that you are jealous. But don't be. A bit later, we discussed it, agreeing to keep things private and marry when we were much older. That way she could live her life the way she wanted, and I could live mine."

Philippe' ran his thumb over her jawline then across to her plump bottom lip. She grinned slightly with the feeling she knew enough not to be jealous. He got off the bed and walked to the door.

"I'll be downstairs in the guestroom since someone I love has claimed my room for the night. Goodnight, Delphine."

Grinning, she began spreading out over his king size bed, announcing, "I always wanted to know what it felt like to sleep in the Count of Monte Cristo's bed. I'm so excited to find out. Oh, I love you too. Goodnight."

Laughing, he left closing the door behind him.

39 *June 7th*

The suite phone wake-up call rang, and she woke up at 6:15 a.m. on the dot. After a quick nude plunge in the small private pool outside, she took a shower then the butler served breakfast at 7:30 a.m. With just a few sips of aromatic coffee down she was about to dig in and enjoy. But the disruption of Hellene, Lorelle, Claudine, Lolli, and Nannette shouting that they came to enjoy the freshly prepared delicious omelets, exotic fruits, and buttery breads with her, made her pause. Since they had the temporary code for the day to enter her suite, their barging in was expected. She shook her head and said to the butler, "Antoine, I'm sorry but can you prepare a bit more, please?" Who replied with a quick, "Oui, Madame."

Playfully glaring at her wedding party, she said, "You heifers are messing up the flow and timeline. We need to be done soon. Philippe' made a point to say no CP time."

Giggling followed since that was known to be slang for color people time being late. Initially, Nannette didn't get it so Lolli explained and then stressed only Black people should say it. Then more giggles resulted when Nannette said, "Wait a minute. You mean, I'm not Black?" Everyone laughed.

Delphine winked at her very fair-skinned, long sandy-blonde curly-haired, green-eyed friend and soon to be sister-in-law, then said, "Oui, Nannette you are to me!" Nannette snickered.

At 8:45 a.m., they were in the lavish treatment rooms for the five-hour Delacroix wedding spa package. It was a water skin hydration flush, full-body scrub and polish, mineral milk bath. Then an executive chef prepared lunch, two-hour full body relaxation massage, eyebrow arching, herbal facial with cold stone treatment, pedicure, and manicure that continued the luxurious time all six ladies spent together. The hours of gossiping, laughing, sharing stories and hugging was necessary pampering for them to not only bond, but to prepare for Delphine and Philippe's special day.

⸎

Hellene and Claudine noticed that Delphine and Nannette were drinking lots of herbal infused waters and teas, but no alcohol. At lunch they both had fresh vegetable salads, grilled fish and chicken, the healthy options, not the red meat and heavy sauces.

Claudine couldn't hold back her thoughts. She just shouted. "Uhm, which one of you is pregnant?!"

Everyone froze in mid-chew or sip looking at Delphine, whose eyes were now a little wide and afraid. Then they glanced over at Nannette, who tried not connecting with their peering eyes. Hellene then added, "You two are not drinking. I did have a dream 'bout fi sh days ago. So, tell it."

Lorelle stared at her sister to try and read her nonverbal communication but got no clues as she too avoided her eyes. Motionless and silent they remained until Lolli said, "No secrets. Tell us! We all in here half-naked together. Come on now. Spill." Still there was silence, no movements except slightly roving eyes.

Moving to exit the spa, Claudine shouted, "If ya don't say right now, I'ma go ask your men!"

Coughing came from Delphine as she reached for her water. Hellene and Lolli chuckled and Lorelle pinched her face tight looking at her sister.

Then it happened…

A light voice said almost in a whisper, "It's … it's me. Please don't say anything. Andreas doesn't know yet. I didn't think it would happen again so soon. But he is like a wild sex animal when flowers start blooming." Nannette had a pitiful sad look on her face.

Hellene, Lolli, Claudine and Lorelle started laughing and cheering with their champagne and wine glasses. While sitting next to her, Delphine squeezed her hand resting on the table and smiled. Nannette had a few drizzling tears when she mumbled to her, "I work so hard to get my figure back, Dell."

Delphine nodded in agreement, then said, "I know. But that's probably why he couldn't keep his hands off you. You know, stretch marks are natures tattoos for hot and sexy mommas."

Nannette giggled and they both joined in the cheers with the others.

After lunch, Hellene happened to be in a mineral bath pool along with Delphine. It seemed she had arranged it that way, to specifically strike up a serious conversation.

"Dell, I want to tell ya sum-tin."

"Hellene, is ya pregnant again, too?"

She flung water at her, shouting, "Shut up! Twin, ya know Momma and Diddy love ya."

"Do they?"

"I know ya thinkin' they don't but they just from a time when mixin' was horrible, tragic, and shunned. No matter what they say before, you is their beautiful daughter and they do love ya. They can't see past havin' a good life with someone that is white. You so much like LaRoyce. Dell, you a strong woman, smart and determined. Once you set ya mind to sum-tin you don't bend. Just like he was. He been so happy ta give ya away today."

Delphine smiled, feeling the approach of misty eyes imagining her older brother doing just that.

"I know diddy say, if ya have a baby, and if it got sum color like a real Murry, it'll be easier ta maybe welcome ya back in da family. But no matter what them babies look like, ya always be family with me and Rell. Don't forget. Nothin, changin' with us. Ya' hear? We proud of ya, Dell, and we love ya."

She kissed her cheek as the two embraced, tears slowly dropped into the water from both of their eyes. A tranquil feeling came over Delphine from the loving words of her always supportive older sister. She took nothing for granted and was very blessed to have Hellene and Lorelle with her on her wedding day.

By 2:00 p.m. everyone was in a shuttle van with their bags and on the move to arrive at the Hotel Hermitage around the corner. Delphine thought, *(This is crazy and it is so much fun playing musical hotels.)*

They had two connecting suites with seaside views to get ready. Nannette checked them in, and focused on her other job making sure they did not dilly dally. Inside were a variety of fruits, hard and soft cheeses, pastries, mini desserts, teas, juices, and champagne on ice.

Walking around in her body sculpting girdle and long white slip, everyone was mostly concentrating on getting the bride ready while nibbling on the food. Delphine had her hair in a larger braided bun at the back of her head for her wide tulle, pearl, and lace hat to attach snuggly. Her Fashion Fair styled face was light and fresh in earth tones with soft ruby lips. Her white A-line style wedding gown was covered in lace embroidery strategically placed up the puffed shoulder and sleeves down to a snug lace fit down to her wrists. The conservative sweetheart neckline connected to beautiful white sheer material to her mid-neck, traced with white pearls around the trim. She wore 2-caret diamond and pearl earrings; her nails were naturally round, and painted the color of soft taupe, wearing an unseen low heel white pumps with pearls gathered at the slightly pointed toe.

Saturday, June 7, 1986, was a sunny day in Monaco. The occasional breeze from the direction of the sea was warm and had a light sweet aroma of citrus as it passed through the large white columns and open windows of the decorative room, overlooking the ocean marina from Hôtel Hermitage Monte-Carlo.

As concert musicians played symphony instruments, the soft melody of Pachelbel's "Canon in D" signaled Philippe' who was stylish in his custom Stefano Ricci seven-piece all-white tuxedo with silk trim, with his groomsmen, Chevalier, Tomas, and Andreas to travel down the aisle toward the Gustave Eiffel-designed glass dome. The four handsome gentlemen took their positions between the surrounding high pillars of white roses and greenery in front of the large windows viewing the aqua waters of the ocean.

Jean-Pierre Philippe' like men in the family wore a classic Louis Vuitton black tuxedo. He escorted his grinning wife, Marie wearing a flowing soft lavender gown with small eggplant color crystals around the collar and down the sleeves designed by Oscar de la Renta. The two sat next to their eldest daughter, Josephine, in a Coco Chanel style eggplant chiffon gown and her handsome fiancé' Hassan Lazar also wore a Louis Vuitton black tuxedo. The Delacroix heir, Jean-Pierre in his tux sat next to his date Lady Sophia von Strauss, who wore a light canary yellow draped Donna Karan gown, behind his parents. The Delacroix family members were all on the right-side of the white aisle path lined with white floor vases featuring giant white rose flower arrangements at both ends of every other row of seating.

The Murry family were at the front on the left. Behind both families were the other guests.

Next walked nephews, Francois, and Tomas, in matching groomsmen tuxedos. The two carried lace pillows with wedding rings. Next in a single file came her bridal party, Nanette, Lolli, Lorelle and her maid of honor, Claudine.

Followed by a groomsmen suit wearing LaRoyce, looking handsome and ringing a large gold bell saying, "Da bride is comin' … Da bride is comin' … Everybody rise now, 'cuz my auntie Dell is the bride, and yep she be a comin'!" Guests laughed at that.

Seconds later he grabbed his little cousin's hand to help her walk down the long path in front of stranger's eyes with grinning faces. Tamera wore a yellow floral tulle dress and carried a large basket of white, yellow, and lavender fresh rose pedals. Confidently holding her bigger cousin's hand, she slowly dropped them along the way walking. Midway she focused her attention on the front left side and her mother, Hellene's proud and grinning face.

Guests then stood for the bride's timed entrance. Photographers took quick snapshots before she started her count to step forward on the down beat of the first song she chose, Louis Armstrong's "La Vie En Rose." Delphine hummed it walking towards Philippe'.

When he heard the trumpet playing, he smiled briefly looking down at his feet.

Moments later when he finally saw her walking toward him alone on the rose covered path, she was glowing like the moon on a clear night in winter. His heart fluttered. Philippe' thought her beautiful dark smooth skin reminded him of melting chocolate now surrounded by pure white clouds made of whipped marshmallows sprinkled with clear rock candy. He thought, *(She's exquisite and delicious. How … How on earth did I find such a precious jewel?)*

Suddenly, he felt nervous, and his mind rattled a bit with uncertainty. *(Will I be able to make her happy? Forever? What if she wants to go back to the States? We can't live in Louisiana. Is she still hurting because of her parents? How do I help her forget the past? Putain!)*

Although he never took his eyes off her unhurried walk toward him, Philippe' slowly covered his mouth with his left hand. Then he quickly rubbed his hands together at first as though he was starting a fire and then like he was smoothing them with lotion. To those closest to him, it was one of the few indicators that the always even-tempered Philippe' Delacroix was nervous. He felt as though he had puddles of perspiration about to drip from his temples. Grabbing his monogrammed handkerchief from his side pocket, he quickly dabbed his forehead. Then Philippe' looked down at the floor.

It was then that his meilleurs ami at his right standing wearing white jacket black tuxedos, Andreas, Chevalier, and Tomas, each quietly stepped forward and squeezed his shoulder or nudged his arm for reassurance. Giving him a boost of musketeer strength and courage. Philippe' grunted low then glanced over at Claudine, Lorelle, Lolli and Nannette holding floral clusters matching their knee length dresses in different shades of purple. He noticed each one when they smiled at him.

As he turned to refocus on his bride down the aisle, she now stood next to him. He exhaled and the fast beating of his heart significantly slowed. Philippe' held out his hand for her to rest her sheer gloved one and then he squeezed. She giggled, squeezing his hand back, and then winked at him. He smiled wide showing his straight white teeth.

Delphine's eyes widened underneath her large, tilted hat covered in lace and tulle realizing that Philippe' had shaved away his facial hair. No beard. No mustache. He had a square chin, a chiseled jawline, and his skin was milky smooth.

Whispering the words, "Philippe' you …" Delphine momentarily forgot where she was and reached up cupping his creamy bare cheek.

Smirking, he removed her hand from his face kissing her gloved palm before holding it tightly.

Everyone was asked to be seated except for the wedding party.

Nannette		Tomas
Lorelle		Chevalier
Claudine		Andreas
Delphine Asha		Jean-Philippe' Henri

The wedding officiant dressed in a white and gold robe adjusted his microphone and began speaking in French and then again in English. He welcomed guests to this special holy occasion blending the lives of Jean-Philippe' Henri and Delphine Asha as one. He gave more words emphasizing God's foundational guidance as the third part of their union, which binds them together for strength, and blessings.

Delphine started to slightly tremble as he spoke. Philippe' still holding her gloved hand began an inconspicuous gentle stroking of his index finger and then delivered a light squeeze. It seemed to be in a constant sequence of stroke-stroke squeeze, stroke-stroke-squeeze for several minutes. She exhaled slowly from her nose and no longer trembled from nervousness. The ecumenical ceremony had a few modifications because no one was there to give Delphine away. However, no one seemed to pay much attention to the omittance.

In silence as the two prepared their ring exchange, Delphine giggled a bit feeling the gentle caress from his fingers after she removed her gloves. As he slowly slid a vintage two carat eternity band featuring an intricate open pattern crafted from the finest gold shimmering with diamonds delicately set in the design, on her wedding ring finger, Delphine's mind floated into a moment of blissfulness.

Smiling she gazed at her very tall, muscular blonde Frenchman with no ass, creamy white skin, a narrow nose, thin pink lips, and mesmerizing deep blue eyes. In quick flashes, she saw the coming joys of their future and smiled. He was a distinguished and educated gentleman, proper in every way. A charismatic, well-bred aristocrat, with a hunger for knowledge, slow to anger and a total swashbuckler. Yes, Jean-Philippe' Henri Delacroix was indeed her professor prince charming. Her new life was way beyond the confines she felt in the State of Louisiana. He would make diligent efforts to bring her ultimate happiness and she would do the same. Delphine was confident that they would succeed at doing just so. While her mind wandered, imagining life with him, she didn't realize Philippe' had grabbed her opposite hand. As all eyes were on them, Delphine blinked back into reality and thought he was nervously making a mistake. *(He gave it to me already.)*

In a quick reaction, she snatched her hand back away from him. Mumbles from the guests could be heard. Philippe' stepped toward her then whispered, "Wife, give me that hand." The microphone was on, and everyone heard him tell her to give up the hand and were now in full blown snickering. Although confused, she complied.

Chuckling, Philippe' leaned back as Andreas pulled out another ring from his upper pocket. Things had happened so quickly; Delphine had not gotten an engagement ring. Philippe' knew she wouldn't want anything outrageous or flashy, but she adored the color of his eyes. Delphine gasped seeing her engagement ring for the first time, while he eased the two-carat floating blue sapphire and diamond band on her other ring finger. Her eyes drifted up to his smiling face. In surprise she shouted, "No, you didn't!" He winked at her, and guests laughed hearing her expression. She caught herself, a little too late but whispered, "Oh, Philippe'."

Finally, it was her turn to quickly place the wide band with centralized black diamonds and engraved with their names inside on his ring finger. Holding hands and smiling with their eyes fixed only on each other, the entire room seemed to be sparkling from their love and joy.

Philippe' and Delphine had previously decided not to have personal vows. So, she thought. Expecting the officiant to instruct them to kiss, she turned her head wondering why he wasn't saying anything. In the next second, Philippe' nudged her hands slightly for her to refocus on him. Immediately, he began to recite his poetic words in front of everyone, with his ocean eyes reeling her into his gaze like a fish caught on a line.

"Aujourd'hui, ce n'est qu'une étape vers la construction de notre propre famille. Vous êtes le soleil, et je suis la lune, vous êtes les cieux, et je suis la terre. Des compagnons constants puissants ensemble, et une seule force pour créer la vie et l'énergie. Enrichi de nourriture pour fortifier l'équilibre ultime, pour accomplir notre plus grand bonheur. Une grappe trouvée parmi le charbon des mineurs; un trésor rare que j'ai découvert votre magnifique splendeur. Delphine, mon amour, tu es le diamant de mon cœur."

(Today is just one step to building our own family. You are the sun, and I am the moon, you are the heavens, and I am the earth. Constant companions, powerful together and only one force to create life and energy. Enriched with nourishment to fortify ultimate balance, to fulfill our greatest happiness. A cluster found among miners' coal, the rarest of treasures I have discovered your magnificent splendor. Delphine, my love, you are the diamond of my heart.)

A flurry of goosebumps rose underneath the layers of her gown and her eyes fluttered as he spoke each word. He observed that soft shimmer behind her eyes that signaled to his heart to pump a bit faster for his cherished diamond that was now Delphine Asha Delacroix. Before tears fell from her perfect make up face, he gave her a simple lip kiss that sealed their vow of love from the forty-five-minute ceremony in front of approximately two hundred and forty-six guests.

"Mesdames et Messieurs, permettez-moi de vous présenter M. et Mme Jean-Philippe' Henri Delacroix. (Ladies and gentlemen, may I present to you Mr. and Mrs. Jean-Philippe' Henri Delacroix.)"

Everyone stood and the room rang with the clapping from joyful faces showing bright smiles. Smiling and standing together in front of their guests, the two tilted their heads slightly as a visual gesture of gratitude. When the music from the second song Delphine chose began, Nat King Cole's "Let There Be Love" Philippe' kissed the back of her hand he was holding. The two walked up the long rose pedal covered aisle and exited the opened ornate doors to take several more steps and enter a private side room at the right.

Once they entered the floral room that Delphine and her bridal party had been waiting in before the ceremony, Philippe' grabbed her cheeks leaned her back and kissed her long and passionately.

As the wedding party entered the room, Andreas was shouting, "That is how we musketeers kiss! Now, get a room!"

Claudine took a quick snapshot of this private moment between Philippe' and Delphine before they broke off their kiss and started laughing. Lorelle ran to hug her sister with Nannette and Claudine giggling to be next. Tomas, Andreas, and Chevalier were a bit misty-eyed while bear hugging their musketeer brother, but they quickly began teasing him about sweating during the ceremony.

Photographers were setting up for official formal shots of the bride and groom, their wedding party and family, while the reception guests were engaging in conversations over cocktails and prepared hors d'oeuvres outside of the crystal bar and on the terrace under the sun.

Guests were mostly Philippe's family, friends, classmates, colleagues, and a network of families from European social, artist, political, and business circles. All were in luxurious formal attire in decorated spaces overflowing with white roses, white stephanotis flowers, lush greenery, and glittering candelabras.

Although the wedding happened within a couple of months after that night of her Springtime confession, Philippe' would have given Delphine whatever she asked for to make it just right. But having all her dorm mates and friends from Sorbonne, Lolli, Claudine, and their families, her closes cousins from Louisiana, Professor Alfonso Allen, and his wife Tracey, both her sisters and their families was all she wanted. Philippe' made it all happen. It was the most luxurious and extravagant evening that the Murry women and their friends had ever seen, let alone participated in. The feeling was of a perfect fairytale for a happy ever after love.

Even a few photographers and reporters from Elle and L'officiel magazines were in attendance. They all seemed very interested in Delphine's custom wedding gown. She didn't think it was nearly as amazing as Princess Diana's in 1981 and thought it probably wouldn't be as grand as Sarah Ferguson's gown when she and Britain's Prince Andrew marry in a month but to Delphine it was absolutely perfect. A few social reporters took a great deal of photographs of the ceremony and her gown for upcoming issues of their magazines.

While Philippe' was having photos taken with his parents and family, Hellene made a point to whisper to the girls as they all huddled around her. "Them photographers not caring ' bout ya dress. They takin' pictures 'cuz a big sista-girl done married da rich handsome blonde professor who looks like a blend of men in movies we like ta watch. Yep, he lookin' like Paul Newman in "Cat on a Hot Tin Roof " Marlon Brando in "Sayonara" and Ryan O'Neal in "Love Story". They steady tryin' ta figure out if ya pregnant. Y'all know, my dreamin' of fish don't count for Nannette."

Lorelle choked a little on her champagne. Delphine's eyes got big sipping her wine. Claudine started to rapidly shake her head no. Then Lolli smugly announced, "Must be one of y'all. It's been over a year and I ain't no damn elephant."

The four busted out laughing but observed Lorelle put her glass down and slip off to stand quietly next to Cedric and their kids. She appeared to be upset as she was inconspicuously punching him in his chest whispering in his ear. Cedric seemed to be sweating and rubbing his forehead. Hellene shook her head and glanced over at Delphine, then said, "Well, now, we know who it be." The three nodded giggling.

Under the beauty of the decorated grand room, the reception was a lavish affair with professional musicians playing classical music during dinner. There were candles flickering atop pristine white lace tablecloths with large bouquets of fragrant fresh white flowers, multiple champagne towers and servers with white jackets and gloves floating between guests like a choreographed ballet. They were holding trays of colorful cocktails and guiding guests to their assigned tables.

After the thankful blessing, everyone was excited to dig into the executive chef at Payvllon's special plated dinner served on exquisite Royal Crown white and gold tableware and Sequoia gold flatware.

Course: Hors d'oeuvres

- Caviar on mini pancakes

- Brie Raspberry En Croute

- Lobster tails in butter sauce

- Assorted cheese and fruits

Course: Salad

- Waldorf with walnuts

- Caesar

- Spinach

- Beet

Course: Entree

- Beef Wellington with rosemary potatoes

- Roasted Lamb Chop with garlic potatoes

- Cornish Hen stuffed with herb wild rice

- Crab Stuffed Tiger Prawns with pineapple cilantro rice

There was so much excitement, toasts came somewhat out of order, Philippe's parents were the first to deliver a toast of well wishes to the couple. Quickly followed by, Tomas, Claudine, Chevalier, Andreas, and several other guests.

Around 7:30 p.m. just as the dessert course was being served the reception was lively with joyful chatter and soft classical music. Philippe' leaned over and whispered in Delphine's ear, "Dell, I need you to come with me right now."

Laughing at something Claudine had said to her, she looked over at him rise from his seat, and said, "Honey, dessert?"

Philippe' tilted his head and pulled her chair out for her to rise. Then whispered again. "It's time to dance with my wife." She giggled rising slowly.

Although she had prepared for it with the removal of her hat and one of the layers from under her full skirt before the reception, Delphine didn't know what the dance or music would be. Philippe' handled all that. She had only one request that it wasn't the waltz since she didn't feel confident enough with her one week of practice. She didn't want to embarrass herself or him. Holding her hand as he escorted her to the grand ballroom floor that sparkled with soft lights, guests started clapping as they looked forward to the dance visually representing love and unity between the newly married couple. In the middle of the floor, Philippe' glided her around in a circle for everyone to see his beautiful wife, cheers grew louder, and Delphine laughed as his free hand pointed to her as if to say, "See what I got."

Chuckling he positioned himself formally to waltz. Delphine stopped smiling and spoke with minimal movement from her lips. "Philippe' not the waltz." He tilted his upper body forward to her, then said, "Look up. Dell, trust me." He repositioned himself. With all eyes on them, she exhaled easing one hand on his shoulder and the other in his extended hand. He placed his hand on her back firmly holding her with proper and elegant form. The musicians were on hold to be ready, while staff paused serving dessert and guests got quiet, waiting. Charles Trenet's "La Mer" began to play and Delphine looked into his eyes ready to trust him to lead. But Philippe' didn't move. Guests murmured looking around not really understanding what was going on.

Delphine nervously prepared to say something to her husband but before she could open her mouth the music changed to a recorded mellow tune. Philippe' let go of her hands transitioning his body into a slow spin before a foot side tap and slide on the beat. Delphine stood looking at him in shock, saying, "What?"

Hellene shouted, "That's right!" while she snapped her fingers and swayed. Some guests began to move to the groovy tempo of the O'Jay's "Forever Mine." Philippe' launched into singing the lyrics to her as she stood giggling and shaking her head. Feeling amused by his antics, she still didn't move.

Philippe' playfully asked, "You're not going to dance with me? What if I …" He immediately broke out performing his John Travolta in "Saturday Night Fever" hip thrusting moves. Delphine shouted, "Oh Lord! No-no!"

Guests' laughter rang through the room as she frantically grabbed his hands just before he started his water wave hands. Chuckling, he placed her arms around his neck, and he wrapped his around her waist as they slow-danced. They sang to each other the words of the song. Philippe' winked at her. She couldn't stop grinning, and said, "I love you baby; you are so cool. But you have to stay in this decade. No more disco moves."

He smirked before pulling her closer for a tender lip kiss. Tenderly he brushed her nose with his finger and sang The O'Jay's "Darlin' Darlin' Baby," as it was mixed in.

Delphine smiled thinking, (*I love him. My French White man with Black man rhythm and no butt. Ha!*)

At the end of the romantic couple dance, everyone clapped, and cheered. Philippe' obtained the microphone and formally thanked friends and family for coming and wishing them a happy life, while the staff served dessert.

Course: Dessert

- Opulence Sundae with edible gold shavings

- Strawberry Romanoff

- Crème Brûlée

A few minutes after the dessert service, the wedding party coupled up to dance, as Delphine danced with her father-in-law, and Philippe' danced with his mother on one of her favorite songs by Gloria Lasso called, "Etrangère au Paradis."

Quickly followed by the Deejay spinning up-tempo French and English mixed genre music while the musicians enjoyed eating their dinner. The party was now underway, and more guests moved to the dance floor.

The bride and groom periodically stopped dancing to receive congratulations and hugs from guests. Delphine needed help for a few restroom breaks, which gave her time to chat with her sisters and girlfriends. At one point while making a bathroom trip, Claudine noticed Philippe' was dancing with Angelique Dubois.

"Wait … Why is she here? Girl, we need ta jump her in da bathroom. I'ma get Lolli and we goin' get it straight."

Snickering Delphine calmed her maid of honor who had started to remove her earrings. "Dene, ya so crazy. Nah, no beat downs. Her family was invited. See they over there." Delphine whispered while nodding her head to the right toward a table of guests.

"Her family ain't mad?" She whispered no longer preparing to fight.

"After a couple weeks, Andre and Pilar Dubois were not as upset. Especially once she told them she met me and was happy for us because she never wanted to get married in the first place. She told us her parents finally agreed to stop tryin' to make her straight. She said it helped that her married siblings all supported her."

Stunned, Claudine's mouth dropped, "Wait… she's gay?"

Smacking her hand to keep it down, Delphine whispered, "Hush. She keeps all that private. Don't say nothing to no one. I shouldn't have told ya but I didn't want ya thinking she was trying to be messy at my wedding and ya try ta snatch her up somewhere."

"Girl, did he know'd it?" Claudine looked at Delphine for a re-sponse. She nodded, then added, "Only her family and Delacroix's know. Well, now me and you do. She is nice. She gave me this beautiful black and gold nightgown set from a luxury Egyptian designer … that happens to be her very special lady friend. I'ma get ya da hook up when you marry Tony. Ha!"

Claudine rolled her eyes and said, "I ain't getting married, we just gonna shack up."

"Whatever. Lorelle is pregnant so ya next to get married, cow." Delphine said snickering.

"No. Lolli is not me. Don't ya curse me." Claudine said firmly while waving her hands and shaking her head in disagreement. Laughing, the two made their way to the bathroom.

Closer to 9:00 p.m. the announcement was made they would be cutting their wedding cake. Their towering seven-tier white wedding cake was covered in edible mini white roses and small sugar pearls that swirled like a staircase trimmed in yellow and lavender lace ribbons. More photos were taken as they made the ceremonial cut into each tier. During the evening, Philippe' and Delphine tasted each of the delicious custom cake flavors he had ordered special for her.

Course: Wedding Cake

- Pink Champagne with vanilla custard

- Louisiana Red Velvet with sweet cream cheese crème

- Chocolate with chocolate ganache, and caramel

- Southern Butter Pecan with rum crème and toasted coconut

After having the last sample of all flavors, he asked, "Dearest, which one did you like the best?"

Taking a pose as if she were thinking very hard, her eyes were circling the ceiling and she displayed tightly pressed lips. He chuckled waiting for her climactic reveal. She leaned closely to whisper in his ear, "The one that I got to taste off your lips was my favorite."

Philippe' stretched his brows and grinned before whispering back in her ear the romantic words that meant he wanted to give into temptation in French. "Je veux croquer ta pomme."

Although the party continued in full swing, shortly after those words, the two slipped away about 10:00. After taking their secure Rolls Royce limousine around the corner, within minutes they were back in her beautiful princess suite now overflowing with fresh flowers, cards, chilled wines, fruits, and chocolates.

"Merci d'avoir amené mes amis et ma sœur ici. You make me so happy, Philippe'. It's all like out of a dream— a fairytale." She said pulling him by his suspenders and planting a giant kiss on his cheek.

He held her firmly by her hips covered by several layers of fine material and asked, "Didn't you say I was your prince? I believe I delivered but is that little kiss all I get?"

His deep pools of blue locked her to captive stillness, and she praised him with a promise. "My intellectually gifted prince charming, you'll have so much more for the rest of your life."

His smile was so wide it seemingly touched the corners of his eyes. Seconds later, his mouth smothered over her lips with erupting passion from within him. Strategically multi-tasking with sensual kissing, unfastening the pearl buttons of her gown and then slowly lowering her long back zipper, Philippe' refused to release her from his hold or his lips.

Delphine, feeling herself being swept away, pulled back pressing his chest with her flattened hands. His facial expression was in a playful mid-lip pucker when she stepped out of her dress, skipping to the large bathroom to wash away her makeup. She was gone just a minute too long, resulting in Philippe' rushing in and tackling her mouth again with long wet kisses. While she chuckled with his lips overtaking hers, he backed her up against the shower gripping and tugging at her white-lace undergarments.

Sliding her hands over his smooth hairless face, she leaned back to break his passion and said, "I can't believe you did this. I have never seen you without a beard. Philippe' it's a very young and handsome face you have my husband."

Quickly dropping down his suspenders and unbuttoning his shirt, he confessed, "Chérie, a fairytale prince does not have a beard. Well, I'm sure Viking ones do but I am French. Besides, as your husband, I'm going to be doing many things to you that require me to be smooth and slippery."

Standing in her long half-slip and bra, she let out a cackling howl, then said, "You're such a nasty freak, Philippe'." Covering her cheeks with her hands her laughing continued even louder as he pulled down her slip then licked his lips wildly. Not pausing but still removing the rest of his tuxedo, he gazed at her with a look of bewilderment. Then questioned her, "Nasty freak? Am I? No, no ma chérie. I am French. Madame Delphine Delacroix in due time my sweet love, you too will become a French citizen. Ha-ha-ha!"

With an outburst of laughter, he turned on the shower and gently maneuvered her inside under the hot jetting sprays of water that pulsated onto their bodies. She snorted releasing the word, "Nasty!" with a constant giggle.

Just moments later, their lips gently merged with a heat surge that could melt wax. Strokes from loving hands teasing slowly with erotic tenderness. Scratches from clawing fingernails over moistened skin create arousing sensations. Their exploring tongues form delicate tasting expeditions in erogenous zones erupting in blazing wildfires.

Jean-Philippe' and Delphine Delacroix indulged in their very first all-night lover's play and erotic expedition. Over the next few hours, the creaminess of his skin, the color of steamed milk folded into the rich dark-chocolate smoothness of hers. The air in the room had a hit of sweetness encapsulated within its warmth of other union. Perhaps it was the cascades of fruits and flowers throughout the suite or the gentle breeze of ocean air from the open doors of the terrace over-looking the vast waters. The beautiful fragrance flowed over the soft symphony of harmonious love language among disheveled sheets. And then it was quiet.

Philippe' watched her trace along the definition lines with the fineness of delicate brushes over his bare chest. Periodically, she bit her bottom lip and lightly moaned. It made him smirk with a leisure tilt of his head to see her every expression. His mind wondered, *(My love is awe-inspiring. Why do I feel like I'm revived and floating, like that song by Billy Preston and Syreeta "With You I'm Born Again. Wow! My heart is racing. When should I teach her to… Stop!)*

Before tonight, Philippe' had sampled nothing more than her kisses. He fought within himself, often writing down a list of reasons he could not have more until after she was his wife. He honored her, himself, and God. They had discussed how tonight would be, so it would be at the right pace for her. He planned out everything for her comfort. But he didn't consider himself or a love such as this. In the past, he never had given all of himself to any woman nor had he ever been with a woman of color. It was not until he listened, searched beyond, and found the true person of heart in Delphine, that he became awakened. At first it had not been difficult but later there came a point, where Philippe' had become overtaken by his exaltation and lost control. His passion for her took over.

After clearing his throat, he spoke in an airy whisper, "You are the most exquisite, my love." Grinning, she maintained her focused touching around the smooth pigmented areas of his pectoral muscle.

Leaning a tad bit forward to catch her eyes, he asked, wondering if she would tell the truth. "Did I hurt you?"

Silently, she shook her head no.

His mind wondered again. *(Sweet liar.)* "Surely, you know I am aware."

Not making eye contact, she whispered, "It's supposed to."

Philippe' inhaled her essence, and then whispered again, "Only until your body adjusts. Thank you, my love, for giving yourself to me. We will have a lifetime to stumble upon our very own physical love language. But for now, I want you to close your eyes. This time will be just for you."

She finally looked up at him suspiciously. She raised her eyebrows as he took hold of her hands and caressed them. Curious and excited about what was going to come next, Delphine said nothing, only closed her eyes and began to giggle uncontrollably.

40 No Longer Living

When Delphine had returned to New Orleans after that Paris visit in March, she waited one week before confiding in Hellene, Lorelle, and Lolli about her wedding on June 7th. Then she simply packed her things, told her parents she was marrying Philippe' Delacroix and walked out of their house. She lived with Lorelle before leaving for Paris on May 10th to stay with Nannette and Andreas before her wedding day.

Once Delphine made her announcement to her parents and left New Orleans, everyone was made aware of the Murry rule that Delphine was no longer living. Her parents stubbornly demanded that no one ever speak of their disgraced daughter in their presence because to them she was dead.

Before and even after those few members of her family returned from her wedding in Monte-Carlo no one said a word about Delphine around them.

⁕

Over time, Lolli DeRuen had long moved to Washington State working for a growing company there called Microsoft. Claudine Saint-Claire, now Jefferies, lived in Los Angeles with her handsome civil rights attorney husband, Tony Jefferies. They both complied with the rule whenever visiting their families in New Orleans, which included the Murry's. No one liked it but it was understood this was Charlie and Eleanor's way, and no one wanted to be thrown out or be unwelcome, so they said nothing about Delphine around them.

Charlie and Eleanor knew full well that their daughters, and even their play ones regularly kept up with Delphine and her new life in France. Privately that information was sufficient to indicate to them that she was alright.

However, the random announcement from Hellene during the November holiday dinner caused some change.

When she conveniently said she, "had a flashback dream about catching two catfish with LaRoyce one summer." She took note of her parents' reaction. While everyone enjoyed their meal, chatting about the weekend shopping, and fussing with the children at the kid's table, Eleanor gasped dropping her fork into her pile of dressing and looked up at her husband. Charlie froze in mid-speak just staring at his half-eaten plate of Thanksgiving southern fixings. Several minutes passed as the two locked eyes before slowly resuming their dinner.

Two days later, Charlie Murry took his eldest daughter with him to pick up the fresh seafood required for the Sunday brunch. It was on the way home that he looked over at her in the car passenger seat and said, "Sis, tell it."

Inconspicuously smirking, Hellene knew that was the best her proud father could muster, and she simply gave him the information both her parents were desperate to hear.

"Diddy, they don got a surprise after getting back from them long honeymoon trips. She say in September, she collapsed at school and the ambulance rushed her to da hospital there in Paris. She say, he come runnin' in with his doctor friend, Chevalier. Diddy, she was scared after they done run lots a test for sum-tin maybe she done caught in Kenya, Egypt, or the Holy Lands they was visitin'. But she say when Chevalier come in ta her room laughing and sayin' she ain't sick, she be expectin', they both surprised. But sum-tin 'bout them hormone levels bein' too high. They check her with ultrasound and diddy, when she seen dem two lights flashin' for da heart beats she passed out again from dah shock."

Charlie Murry lowly chuckled at the end of the story, and he continued doing so for days thereafter. However, nothing more had been asked or shared after that ride in November. Except for the periodic private tabs Charlie kept on her, by pulling Hellene aside giving her the look or clearing his throat repeatedly, when the two talked on phone calls. It was enough that he knew she was well.

Although, there was the rule that if she had a child that looked like a Murry, having the mark of black excellence; she could possibly come back to the family. Everyone knew the rule.

But what they didn't know was that Charlie and Eleanor were thinking much deeper than just Black family pride, wanting only to accept brown grandchildren. Between the two of them, they felt it was necessary to look, be and know who you were, where you come from to know your value. Without that, a person would be broken, lost, and tormented. If Delphine's children looked like her, they would be more grounded, with a purpose in life, and it would be easier to be loved and supported by others that looked like them. Having less of a chance for lifelong heartache and pain, like they experienced with Kendrick. He suffered terribly and caused so much devastation all because he looked white- not like his family, who loved and raised him.

Secretly, it was these private thoughts about their son, knowing what he had done; LaRoyce's life giving sacrificed to eradicate it, and comfort, vindicate, and uplift his sister were some of the unspoken things that haunted Charlie and Eleanor Murry.

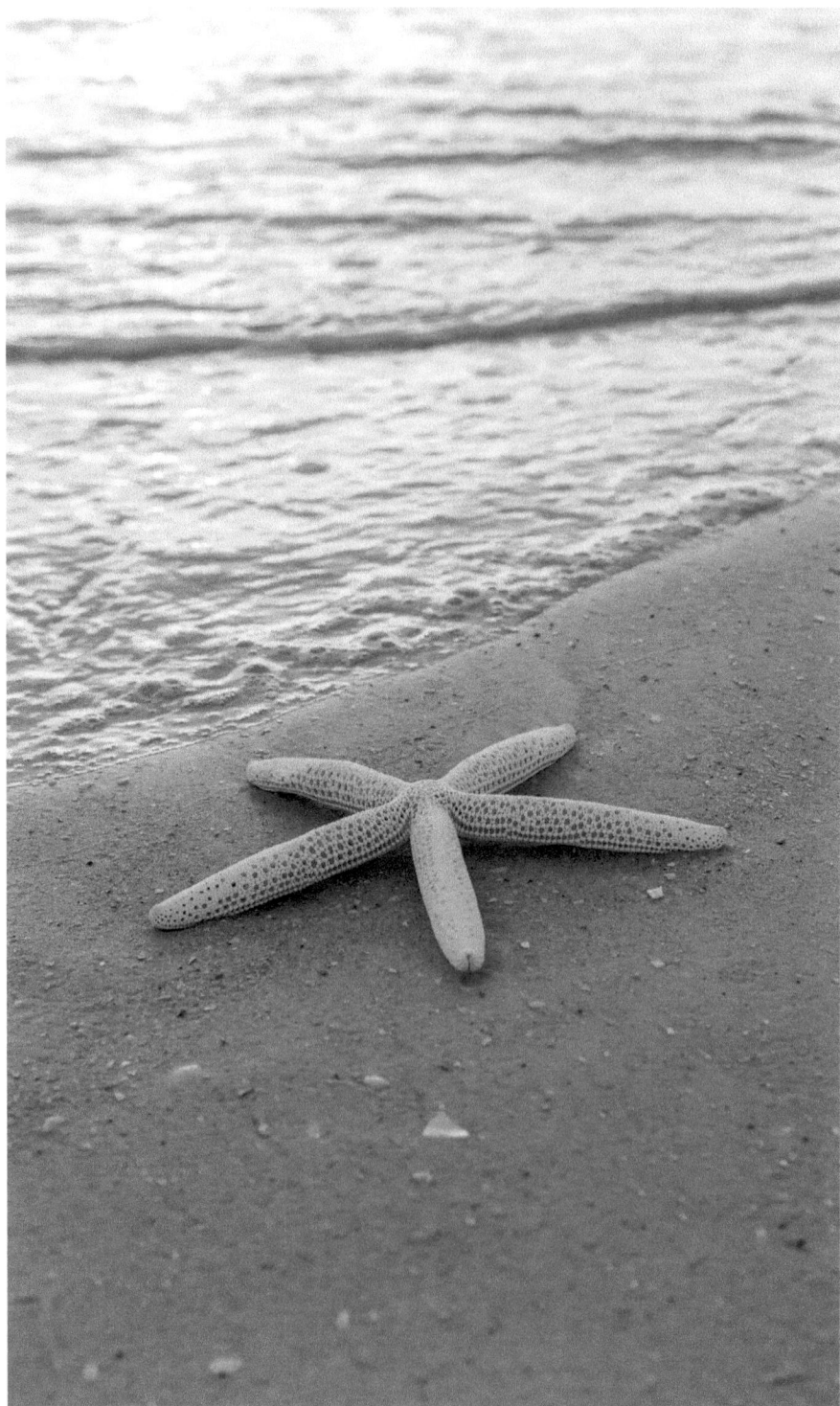

41 Happiness Deferred

Unfortunately, happiness did not lay out the way Philippe' and Delphine had planned. It seemed to come in small increments like the occasional starfish coming in from the ocean tide resting on the shore.

Although early on Philippe' and his entire family were excited and making plans for the coming additions, it was soon overshadowed by devastating heartbreak and grief. Philippe' remained somewhat attentive and constant with his affection but Delphine had never witnessed her husband so emotionally broken. Everyone around her was experiencing the same pain and it snuffed out the expected joy of becoming a mother.

Jean-Pierre François had not been overly supportive of their union from the beginning. Perhaps it was because of his regrets, his own family troubles or maybe his battle with his suppressed psychological disorder. His erratic and occasional violent behavior increased each time he returned from being away from home for months at a time for his military duty.

Long before the wedding, while he was away, Carmen's affair with a Spanish man from her hometown became known after she left France to be with him and she took their son with her.

Although the two quickly and quietly divorced, they shared custody of their son. Jean-Pierre had quickly been sought after by many prominent European families. The list of acceptable heiresses was long but after a few months, Jean-Pierre had gotten engaged to the beautiful Lady Sophia von Strauss of Vienna. He officially announced her as his fiancée and their future marriage plans in the coming year during Philippe' and Delphine's wedding reception.

The last time Jean-Pierre had spent time with his son was during and after Philippe' and Delphine's wedding, in which young François stayed with his grandparents for the entire summer before returning to Spain to begin school.

But in early October, the Delacroix family received word that Jean-Pierre François's ex-wife, Carmen, and their son François-Philippe, along with her husband and twelve other people drowned after being trapped inside a sinking ferry in Spain.

Within a few days of hearing the tragic news about their beloved grandson, the Delacroix family were hit with another devastating blow. Their oldest son, Jean-Pierre François had been listed as one of the casualties in a military base explosion in the Middle East. Being private about their losses, it was requested there were no public reports about the family. But in no time, several high-ranking officials, longtime friends and business associates, and numerous military personnel came to Jean-Pierre Philippe' and Marie Delacroix's home in Lyon to pay their respects for their terrible losses.

Philippe' functioned daily simply out of routine but he was depressed and withdrawn as he grieved the loss of his only brother and eldest nephew. He wanted to be engaged but he just couldn't make himself. He took on more at work so when he returned home, he was so exhausted that he would eat a little and go to bed. He didn't really talk to her nor did he touch her other than the routine morning kiss goodbye and the nightly peck on the cheek. No holding her hand, no poems, no trips, no cuddling, no private music concerts, no talking to her belly. It was nothing like before. Delphine was worried but kept it to herself. She stayed busy with medical school, eating right, exercising, and making plans to change the sister guest room to her new baby's room.

In addition to journaling her experiences, she shared most of her unknown feelings and new emotions about the changes in her body with Lorelle and Hellene. Philippe' often asked but she decided to simply tell him everything was wonderful, in order to give him time she felt he needed. He didn't want to talk to her about his grief and she stopped occasionally opening the dialog for him to lean on her.

Delphine took the initiative to follow up with her doctor alone when she felt something wasn't right or for her twice a month routine checkup. She stopped reminding Philippe' of the scheduled appointment dates and times. He had them circled in red on his desk calendar, but he never remembered.

She stayed positive and didn't get angry or tell him how she felt and little by little he did get better. He started to read to her a few times a week. When he played the piano or his saxophone the music wasn't always sad. They took long walks and discussed trivial things like what to eat and where to spend a Saturday night. But that was far from the Philippe' she had known and how their life had been. Although it was hard, Delphine did what needed to be done to make sure she took care of the house, cooked, kept her grades high, and their babies were growing healthy.

On Wednesday, January 28, 1987, at 2:10 p.m., Delphine was slightly reclined and getting warm slime smeared on her belly by a jolly technician named Victoria. The scheduled ultrasound appointment came to a pause after Victoria was interrupted by a doctor's emergency call. Excusing herself, she left the room but kept the lights off. Minutes after exiting, she returned to the dark room with two masked physicians who stood behind a barrier next to the ultrasound machine. They did not speak because Victoria announced, "Madame Delacroix, these specialists are here to observe the process is done correctly. They will read the ultrasound as it is being done and after I obtain the images. They are here only to observe me not you, alright?"

Unsure of the protocol, Delphine simply moaned in agreement. Reapplying fresh warm goop to her very round belly, she said, "Madame Delacroix, earlier you mentioned you are a twin, is that right?"

Smiling Delphine answered, "Oui, I have an identical twin sister." As the men stood behind her, Victoria adjusted the monitor more for them to see, and said, "So do multiple pregnancies run in your family?"

"Oui, my father is an identical twin. His older sisters Melva and Mattie are identical twins too. My aunt Mattie has a set of identical twin girls older than me, and one of them has a set of identical twin boys that are about eight years old, I think now. It's been sort of a Murry family pattern; I suppose."

Smiling Victoria placed the attached probe mechanism onto areas of Delphine's belly and began to press, measure, and take still shots. Their heartbeats were strong, and it was a pleasant sound that Delphine would grin every time she heard them during her appointments. One of the physicians behind her seemed to softly grunt a few times which made Delphine look over at them. It was then she could almost make out that they seemed to be fully covered from head to toe in surgical wear. She thought to ask but because they weren't saying anything, she assumed nothing was wrong.

"Madame Delacroix, each set of measurements are in line with the 95 percentiles for the gestation. Very good. Do you have a preference according to that twin family pattern, you mentioned?" Victoria asked softly with a slight grin.

"Mmm, I'd like girls. It was fun being a twin but … well, my husband lost his brother and nephew recently. So, for him, I hope that they are boys. I believe it will be healing for him and his family if they were. Boys are what I wish for." Delphine started to release a few tears as she talked. "I miss his laugh … I really want them to be boys. I'm sorry. I don't know why I'm crying." She wiped her face slightly embarrassed.

"Madame you are pregnant with twins you don't need a reason to have emotions." Victoria said, handing her some tissue and adding more goop to another area of her belly. Smiling she said, "Well, I hope you get what you wish for. Shall we find out if we can see if it's boys or girls?"

"Yes, they better have penises!" She said and Victoria and the two physicians snickered softly. Delphine exhaled and looked up at the dark ceiling for a second and then at the monitor as Victoria pressed into her belly again and slid the probe around.

"Madame Delacroix, it seems twin A is not cooperating. Let me check twin B … Oh … Let me try one more time and take photos."

Nervously, Delphine closed her eyes and rubbed her hands together. She didn't notice the two physicians whispering to each other and to Victoria. Minutes later, Victoria moved from the stool next to the bed and Delphine opened her eyes. As the three were moving to the door, Victoria touched her hand and said, "Excuse me Madame, I need to get the images to be sure. Just rest for a moment."

Delphine smiled with a slight moan.

Moments later, the door opened. Only one of the physicians entered, closed the door and turned on the lights. Feeling alarmed, she said, "Is … is something wrong?" As her eyes were adjusting to the lights.

His voice was very low walking toward her as he said, "No Madame." She didn't recognize it as being familiar because she was more interested in why he was there and not the technician. Then he kept talking and she started giggling, "But you can give this 50 Francs to your damn husband because I lost the bet." Hearing him speak more as he removed his mask, she realized it was Chevalier.

"Oh, you … You are always around to shock me, Chevalier!" Smiling, he handed her the 50 Francs and kissed her cheeks twice.

"Delphine Delacroix, the African American goddess who stole my musketeer's heart … you are my favorite person to shock, dear lady. You're making me an uncle again; I adore you even more. My colleague is in training, so I had him wait outside. When I saw you come in, I had to ask a favor and sit in on your appointment. You don't mind, do you?"

Still giggling she shook her head no. Then he asked her, "You really want boys?"

"I do. For Philippe'— we can have a girl next time. He is better but … well …"

He squeezed her hand and smiled at her. "All will be well, Lady Delphine. Alright back to business. I'm going to bring in the other two. One to do her job and the other to observe."

"Wait, Chevalier Ratliff, you … you are not going to tell me?" Her voice was slightly elevated and demanding.

"Officially, she must tell you but between you and I, you will get your wish." He whispered with a sly wink then kissed her hand.

While he moved toward the door, he pointed at her and said, "Act surprised." She nodded. Delphine was beaming with joy. She was having two boys, and it was just what the doctor ordered. She thought, *(He … He will be so happy. Thank you, Lord!)*

Victoria and the other physician came into the room. Victoria had images in her hands but didn't sit down. Chevalier was steady rolling his eyes and shuffling his feet. A moment later, he reached over and quickly snatched the money from Delphine's hand, shouting, "Just give me this!" He forcefully shoved it into a hand of the physician by the door. Delphine screamed when Philippe' came from behind the barrier pulling away his mask and head covering rushing toward her.

"Oh! Philippe'! You're here! It was you the whole time!"

His eyes were watering as he kissed her holding the cheeks of her plump face tenderly. She began laughing and crying from her surprise and happiness.

"Oui, ma douce. Oui. I'm sorry, I wasn't supposed to break character, but I had to kiss you." He said before kissing her slowly and then kissing her belly in several places. Next, he spoke directly to it. "Papa is here, my little ones. Grow well in there. Share the food! Your mother and I love you very much!"

Victoria grabbed some tissue to dab her eyes before clearing her throat to get their attention.

Holding hands, they heard her say, "Madame et Monsieur Delacroix, vos jumeaux sont une fille et un garçon. "

(Mrs. and Mr. Delacroix, your twins are a girl and a boy.)

"Quoi?! Je ne comprends pas! Non, mais..." (What?! I don't understand! No, but... Delphine shouted looking over at Chevalier, who was holding up his hands.

Quickly the notorious prankster said, "What do I know. I am not a damn technician. I'm a doctor!" Before hitting Philippe' on the back laughing and motioning for Victoria to exit with him.

Clearly the joke was on Delphine because Philippe' was not surprised at all. He chuckled, planting quick lip kisses that seemed strategic to catch the rolling tears on her face. She was stunned and paused in silence.

"Dell, we have one of each. I pray they both are as strong and beautiful as you."

His words touched her heart, and she blinked back into the moment. Stroking his full low beard, she smiled soaking in his romantic gaze, and said, "No, that would not be fair. I will pray for a perfect blend of both."

He gave a soft moan in agreement. As he helped her sit up, she asked, "50 Francs ... What was this bet?"

Rubbing his chin with a sly smirk, Philippe' said, "I told him, you would want whatever would make me happy, even if it wasn't what you would prefer. He didn't believe me. I said, I know my wife, Chevalier, she will. He was not convinced, and he foolishly bet money to prove me wrong."

She giggled as he slipped on her shoes. "I love seeing you smile. I know you are still hurting and sad Philippe' but I've missed you."

"I'm sorry." He sat down in the chair next to her.

"No. I don't want you to apologize. You should be ... uh ... I don't mean it that way. I just ... I feel alone sometimes. Like I'm having these babies by myself. I know you're trying. But you must be stronger and help me, while you are grieving. No more shutting me out. It was alright before but it's going to be harder the bigger they grow. I've never had a baby before and I'm a little scared. I need you to help me because I ... I may not be as strong later on."

"I will. Dell, I will. I promise."

Removing the rest of the hospital surgical gear, he said, "What should my handsome son and beautiful daughter have to eat? I am taking them out for something exquisite and delicious, right now. Oh, and you can come too."

She gasped and punched him in the arm as he winked and chuckled, helping her to the door.

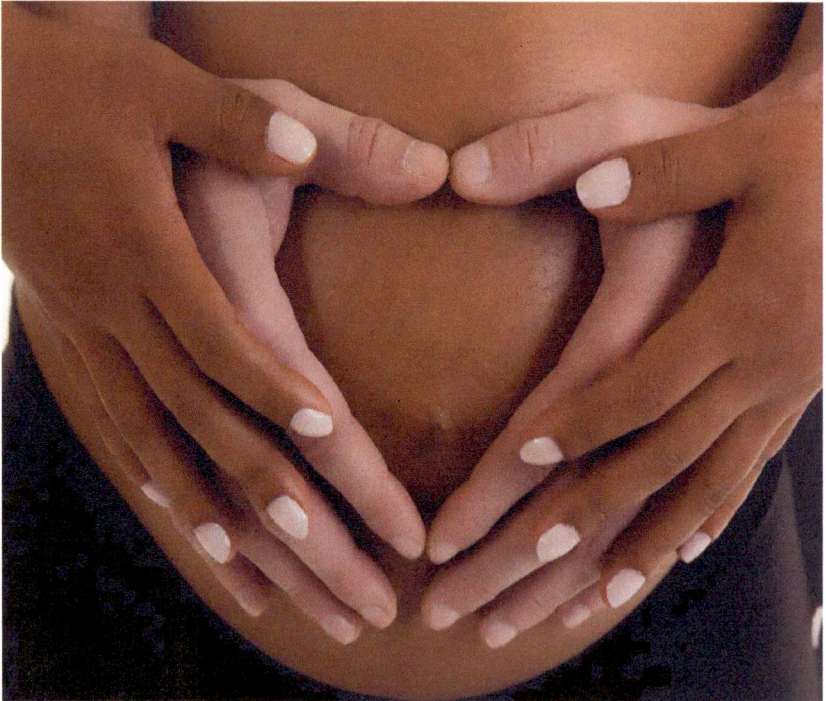

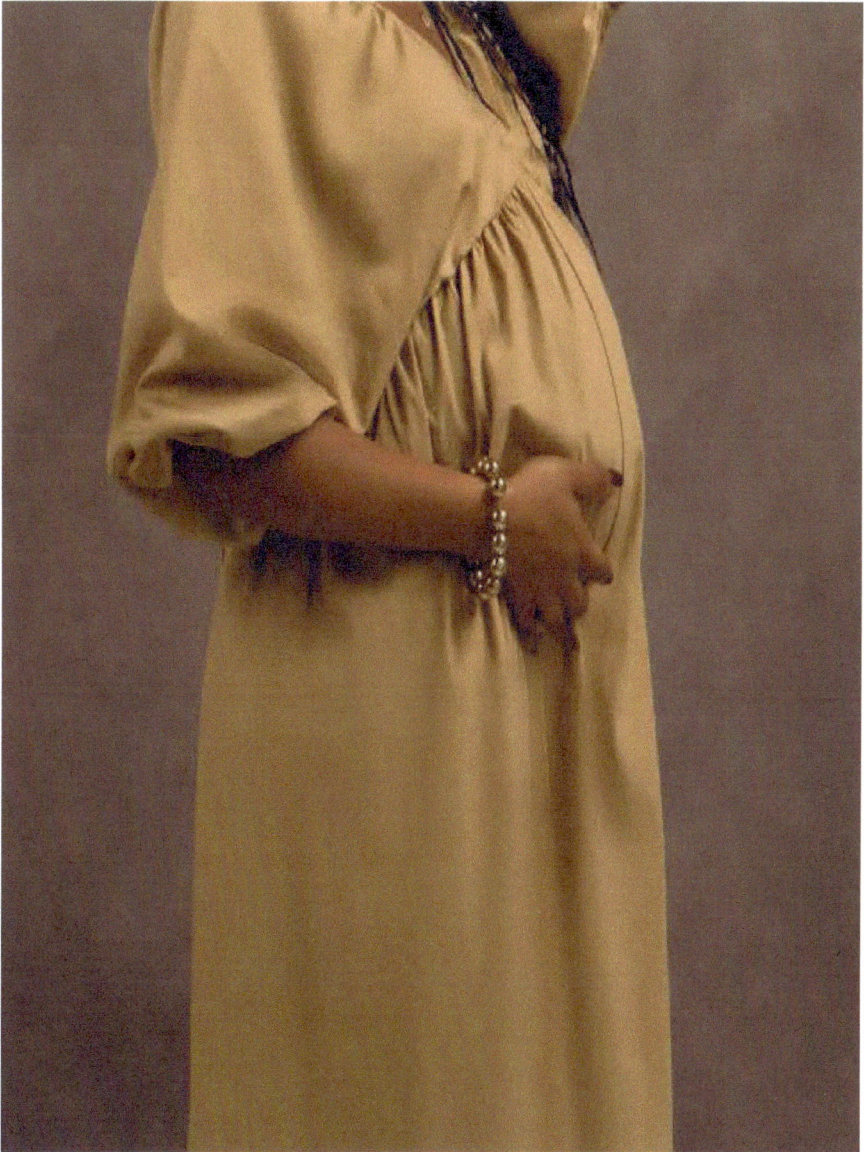

42 Chocolat Chaud

When Hellene and Lorelle received word that their sister was miserable, surprisingly Eleanor volunteered to take time off work to care for all five of their grandchildren, including the newest one born in October, while they take a trip together. It was unspoken yet obvious that Charlie and Eleanor Murry were concerned about their daughter, even after they had abruptly removed her from their lives.

As soon as Hellene and Lorelle arrived in Lyon in the midday of Saturday, April 23, 1987, they dropped their bags at the door and Gert immediately took them to her. The last ten weeks had been horrible for Delphine due to having gestational diabetes, and hypertension. She was so stressed, and it showed. Delphine had gone from a voluptuous size 18 on her wedding day to a very round size 26 gaining about seventy pounds so far. She knew it was going to happen, but she was still upset that she had to withdraw from school and move to Lyon. After she had almost fallen four weeks prior, Philippe' wasn't taking any chances and forbid her from walking around.

Hellene and Lorelle were greeted with a wheelchair bound, snot dripping and teary faced Delphine Delacroix.

"Oh, you're here, Sis … and Rell." Her words came out as she sobbed.

"Damn girl, that be the ugly cry!" Lorelle said laughing as she rushed to kiss Delphine's outstretched swollen hands and cheeks.

"We here, now twin. It be alright." Hellene said patting her head and pressing it onto her round and fluffy body for sisterly comfort.

"Twin, ya almost done. Stop all dis crying, ya gonna make dim babies get da hiccups. Stop now!" Hellene's harsh tone was demanding but she continued to stroke Delphine's long French braided hair lovingly.

"I'ma … a giant whale. I hurt all over. Sis, I don't wanna do dis no more." Delphine told them looking up at Hellene while wiping her face.

Lorelle sat down next to her in an armless chair, laughing, and said, "Dell, it ain't like ya can turn it off. Nobody told ya to be doin' it all the time. Damn ya ain't finish with school and ya got two babies coming. Ya copy-catter!" Lorelle leaned back laughing harder.

Scowling Delphine reached over and smacked her in the back of the head. "Shut up, cow! Ain't no body tryin' to be like no Lorelle Murry Ricard. That be for damn sure. It … it just happened." Delphine announced while still looking pitiful.

Hellene got comfortable sitting on the other side of Delphine. She took a few sips of her sweetened iced tea, before saying, "Dell, stop it now. It done happen 'cuz ya was doin' it with no damn raincoat! What ya expectin'? Ya done married a young blue eyed, freaky French man. Hell, I'd be knocked up too."

The three women cackled with laughter under the warmth of the glass enclosed sunroom on the south side of the Delacroix chateau.

<hr>

Having her sisters with her during the last weeks of her pregnancy was the best thoughtful gift Philippe' could have arranged for his wife. Although she didn't believe the old folk's tale that deaths occur in a succession of common connection by three, for some reason Delphine became increasingly nervous about dying during child-birth. So much that she had told Hellene months before their arrival, what she wanted her to do for her when she died. Hellene didn't take her too seriously but realized she probably needed to talk to Philippe' about visiting. She was glad she did and Lorelle came with her. Philippe' arrived the next day and wasn't returning to Paris until several weeks after his children's due date on May 10th.

The residence of the Delacroix estate had just as much fun with Hellene and Lorelle's visit as Delphine did. The Gauthier family especially. Since Elke and Kurt had long returned to their home in England and Hans stayed in Canada after marrying Tess, only Gert, her sister Heidi, her brother Wolfgang and his wife Lylah, and their parents Alexandre and Ava lived on the estate.

"This why ya ass so big, all this bread and cheese!" Hellene grumbled in the kitchen making her sister some good old-fashioned grits and eggs.

"What else did you bring?" Grinning and tapping her feet, Delphine was excited to know what was in the second suitcase of stash she had brought from New Orleans.

"Just ya wait. Ya can't have no gumbo ya pressure too high. No pork neither but I brought some special stuff and seasonings, jellies, ya skin and hair stuff, lil bit for ya from Lane Bryant. I got sum cute things from Penny's for da babies. I'm gonna braid up dat hair better when ya done." She said handing her the large bowl of hot grits with a little salt and butter under three fried eggs. Hellene started chuckling as she watched Delphine mix it all together like she did when she was young. Next, she placed out the rest for the others all around watching her cook.

Marie, Ava, and Heidi were curious but not sure if they were going to like grits, eggs, maple bacon, salmon cakes, creamed beef on biscuits and wheat toast with watermelon or apple jalapeno jelly that she had prepared.

Philippe', Jean-Pierre, Gert and Alexandre didn't wait but grabbed their portions and began digging in moaning. Lorelle got hers and encouraged the hesitating ladies to go on and try. There was a split decision on which jelly was better, but everyone enjoyed saying breakfast was delicious.

After that the Delacroix and Gauthier families let the Murry girls show them some New Orleans food love. Over the next few days there was a smorgasbord of Murry family fixings. Delphine and even Philippe' were in hog heaven. From southern fried chicken, greens, corn bread, fried green tomatoes, red beans and rice, black eyed peas, shrimp and grits, crowder peas, fried potatoes, étouffée, jambalaya, beef sauterne, and Murry lasagna to homemade strawberry ice cream, coconut cake, pecan pie, 7-up pound cake, and walnut balls.

Every time the families came to eat there was moaning and laughter just like Delphine was used to and she was glowing with happiness. There was so much joyful laughter, sharing conversations that echoed through the rooms of the Delacroix home that one night at the dinner table, no one even heard Delphine say, "I think my water broke."

Pausing in terror, she just sat there looking at the water in her wine glass slightly move. Philippe' was laughing and turned to see his wife not moving. He said, "Are you all—?" She screamed in horror, "My water broke!"

Everyone stopped moving and speaking for three seconds. Then Lorelle looked into her eyes and said, "Damn Dell, ya' so dramatic. Why da hell ya' screamin'? Okay, ya pee'd. We heard ya, dodo bird!"

Instantly, Delphine and Lorelle howled with laughter, and they didn't stop. Ava was helping Marie try to wake up her son who had fainted.

"Philippe'… Philippe'… Philippe'… Philippe'…" Marie decided to splash water on Philippe's face. That did it.

Gert swiftly and quietly went to get Delphine's pre-packed bag, but Heidi stood up panicking saying, "Coat? … I can't find her coat! … Does she have a coat? … She needs a coat! … I've got to buy her a coat! … Where's her damn coat?!"

Alexandre was toasting and repeatedly shouting "felicitations!" While Jean-Pierre was stumbling to a phone, trying to recall how to call for an ambulance.

Wolfgang and Lylah were shouting at each other over which keys went to which car, so they could get one from the garage. "This one!

No, it's this one!" "Stop, that is to the truck not the car!" "You don't even drive! Give me this." "I know which key it is, so what if I don't drive. No, it this one. The blue one." "White. Listen to me!" "You are sleeping on the couch." "Good I won't hear you snore." "I hate you!"

Hellene just sat calmly eating her chicken and greens, snickering at the chaos all around her.

Philippe' drove his wife to the hospital approximately fifty minutes away and a procession of cars followed. Delphine arrived at Hospital Saint Joseph Saint Luc around 8:22 p.m. It took about thirty minutes for emergency personnel to get her IV started, fetal monitors around her belly and check her cervix which they said she was dilated to 2cm.

"It is going to be a long night." Marie said and Hellene agreed, saying "Yes, ma'am, it is."

By 12:30 a.m., she was still the same and Philippe' told the family to go home and get some rest, but Delphine wanted her sisters to stay, and they did. Tomas and his mother had also come to the hospital, but Mrs. Durand went home with the Delacroix and Gauthier families while Tomas stayed with Philippe'.

It happened when everyone was asleep, including Delphine. That is when it hit her. A sharp pain in her back that woke her right up grabbing Philippe's hand.

"Umm …" Her throat was dry, and she said it low, but he heard "Dell?" She didn't answer but he sat up telling her softly, "I am here."

She smiled at him and held his cheek. He kissed the palm of her hand before covering his hand over hers. It wasn't a long or unbearable pain. It startled her more than anything.

That was at 6:40 a. m. Not long after, Delphine told him, "Yes, go please." He didn't want to leave her alone.

"I will just take a shower, clean up a little, and then come right back." Philippe' said going only because she was insisting, saying, "You smell like a wine drinking sweaty polecat and your breath smells like Doritos."

The Murry sisters, Tomas, and Philippe' went back to the estate, freshened up and gave updates. Andreas and Nannette with their son and newborn daughter, Odette, as well as Chevalier had all arrived from Paris. Josephine, Hassan, and her boys were in Greece on holiday but called for a status.

Grabbing a quick bite to eat and returning to the hospital, he had been gone roughly three hours. When Philippe' and everyone came in close behind him, except for Nannette and her children, Delphine had dilated to 5cm and was having sixty-second contractions just about every ten minutes.

"Dell … What can I do? Tell me. What can I do?" He was a little excited but wanted to do whatever she needed.

She said calmly, "Can you rub my feet they hurt. My shoulders too. Laying here I hurt."

Nodding he did as she asked, even getting warm towels to help with circulation. Then he helped her pull herself up more to massage her back. He fed her ice chips because she couldn't eat any food. He read to her and played music. When he needed to take a break, his mother came in and gave her affectionate kisses and talks of encouragement.

Later, alone with their sister, Hellene and Lorelle held her hand for her to squeeze during contractions. Delphine was covered in sweat and already tired from intensive pain in her back and her lower body that now came in five-minute intervals. It was hard to breathe in enough oxygen before she tried to do the Lamaze breathing, they had learned. She couldn't concentrate and only panted through each contraction.

She started crying, "Sis, I'm gonna die … I'm gonna die … I know it. What if what momma said come true … Oh no, another one."

Hellene put a cool towel over her head and waited for the contraction to pass. Then she snatched her chin to focus on her and said, "Ya not gonna die, Delphine. Da babies need ya ta stop givin in ta da devil thinkin'. Babies need ta come ta da world happy, with love. Not fear or pain. Ya' stronger than us. Da Lord done give ya two babies. That how strong ya be. Ya' hear me?"

She kissed her forehead, and Dr. Blanchet came to check her again. She was 7.5cm and it was time for Philippe' to come back and be the only one with her from here on out.

Philippe' had been in a hospital bathroom throwing up whatever he had eaten an hour earlier.

"I told you I didn't think eating an egg salad sandwich was a good idea." Tomas said handing him a wet towel for his neck.

Andreas gave him something fizzy to settle the nasty taste in his mouth. He drank it and exhaled. "Merci." He said as Andreas forcefully hugged him with the complete understanding of his rollercoaster feelings, he was having right at this moment. Philippe' gave him a smile back. The two stared at each other in silence.

"Are you two going to French kiss now or what?" Chevalier said with his hands up looking at their overly affectionate bonding. Then he said, "The goddess is in there trying to squeeze a cantaloupe size human through a hole the size of a kiwi, twice! Philippe' get in there!"

Pep talk given and he was off. While Andreas looking confused said, "Uh, fruit?" Tomas and Chevalier laughed leaving him standing in the bathroom waiting for clarification.

Hellene and Lorelle left when Philippe' came back in and it was just the two of them with the medical team.

"I am here, now. You are doing so well, my beautiful diamond. Trust me." He whispered to her moments before she grabbed his hand and squeezed with a grunting sound that came from within her marrow. Philippe' locked on her eyes and demonstrated the pain relief breathing they had learned. She followed his lead and it passed. This continued for a long time.

Nurses adjusted the birthing bed and put her legs up for Dr. Blanchet to check her cervix. She was now dilated at 10cm. Philippe' was given surgical wear just in case things changed and he quickly put it on.

"Philippe'!" Her weary arm searched for his hand as there were no more breaks between the horrible pressure, she now felt ripping through her body.

"I am here." He pushed through to get to her, and she squeezed with all her might. "Delphine, look at me!" He shouted for her to find his eyes. Contact. The rhythmic breathing began.

Words came from the masked Dr. Christopher Blanchet, "Delphine, your cervix is very high so there is more way to travel for this little one. I need you to do exactly as I say, and we will get you through this as quickly as possible. When I say and not before, I want you to bare down like you are having a bowel movement but ne chie pas sur moi."

Philippe' glared at him, thinking, *(Jokes?)*

She started laughing but her mouth was sealed shut. It turned to whimpering quickly as tears fell and she started trembling.

"Delphine, give me a small push on trois … ready, Un, Deux, Trois push … stop …stop."

"Ahh!" She was in mid-contraction.

"Dell, stop!" Philippe' turned her head to face him and she paused her breathing to stop pushing.

"Madame, we need you to breathe, please." A masked nurse said.

Dr. Blanchet spoke again, "That was very good. Papa, would you like to come to see, your baby's head is about to crown."

A nurse moved for Philippe' to have the experience, and another held Delphine's hand right when another contraction hit her.

"Aww! Auugh! Ughhh!"

Philippe's eyes widened seeing the hair of the baby's head pushing through. He gasped and felt a rush of exhilaration. His eyes welled up with liquid and he blew out heavy rubbing his covered chin.

"Philippe'! Auh!" she shouted, shocking him back to her side. "Dell, she … she has an afro!" He smiled at her as she chuckled for two seconds before another contraction came more severe than the one before. "Ooooo, Aaahhhh!"

Breathing techniques continued and she was instructed to push during the next contraction without stopping until told.

"Good. Let's do that again." Dr. Blanchet said calmly.

It seemed like there was a chant of voices all around her.

"Push!" "Push!"

"Yes, keep pushing."

"Keep pushing!"

"Good. Rest."

"You are doing wonderful, Delphine. Let's do that again."

This had gone on for almost an hour and she was done. Her head flopped around on the bed, she was exhausted, thirsty, drenched, and wanted to stop. Philippe' put ice chips over her lips and mouth, kissed her tenderly then said, "Allez, almost done. Don't quit. We don't quit." Philippe' then lifted her shoulders off the bed to push again.

"Push! Push, Dell!"

"Mmmm! Aahhhh! Ooohhh!"

"Great job! If you can give me one more big one, I think this little person is going to be out. Can you do that?"

"Baby please, you can do this, one more big one, okay." Philippe' said pleading and kissed her hand that was bolted to his.

She nodded sobbing, and the contraction came. Delphine gave it all she had for fifteen whole seconds, which seemed like forever.

"Gahmm! Auughhh!"

"Voilà! You have a girl!"

It was 4:40 p.m. and she collapsed back onto the bed, sobbing, gasping for air and smiling, as Philippe' wept kissing her.

"Papa, would you like to cut the cord?"

"Oui!" Philippe' said as he felt like he was floating in an alternate universe of wonder.

Delphine was given some oxygen and her blood pressure was taken. It was a little high but nothing like it had been weeks before. She had some continued discomfort but wanted to see her daughter.

"Is she alright? Is she?" She mumbled from behind the mask. A nurse nodded patting her shoulder to ease her concerns.

Nurses were performing their duties and Philippe' was right next to them inspecting everything they did and staring in amazement at their baby. He thought, *(My pretty ... pretty little lizard.)* As they cleaned her off, he saw beyond the goo, and he was instantly in love. Philippe' stared at his beautiful daughter as she hollered fiercely.

Contractions came hard and fast again. "What the hell is this? Don't I get a break?!" She said behind her oxygen mask before the nurse removed it. Philippe' had come back to her side, as Dr. Blanchet was checking for twin B.

"Alright, Delphine the hard one is over. This one will not be as bad. Twin A, she opened the door for the second baby, but you will have to push a bit to help the little traveler. When I tell you to push, do it and don't stop but wait until I tell you. Alright?"

She nodded, grunting through the contractions, and squeezing the blood from Philippe's hand.

"Can I push now?!"

"No. Not yet. I will tell you when. Not yet."

"Watch me, breathe, my love." Philippe' got her to focus on him and imitate his breathing again.

Her body tightened and she let out, "Augh!"

"Not yet, Delphine." Dr. Blanchet was motioning for a nurse. "I may need the forceps." A nurse gathered some equipment rolling a tray close to him.

"Alright Delphine it is time to push on the next contraction. You give a push."

"Awww! Gahhmm!"

"Well done. I want you to do that again."

"Mmmmm! Ahhhh!"

"Keep pushing Dell!"

"Good. Let's do that again but next time put more behind it, like you are going to poop all over the floor. Ready. Push. Push. Keep pushing!"

"Auah! Rrrrahh!"

"Voilà, you have a son! Excellent! I told you the second one would be easier."

The time was 4:52 p.m. Exhaling deeply Philippe'embraced his wife, shouting, "You did it! Dell, my love. You did it!"

Laughing and kissing each other was all they did until Dr. Blanchet asked, "Papa. Do you want to do the honor again?"

"Oui!" Philippe shouted, while rushing to cut the umbilical cord of his son.

Philippe'watched the nurses handle him, as he cried hearing his initial sounds and mumbled, "I love you, my beautiful boy!"

Another doctor gave Delphine some medication in her IV and nurses praised her for all her hard work. She had some additional discomfort, but it didn't really register. She was exhausted and happy.

Dr. Blanchet announced, "Delphine, you did not tear at all, so no stitches. Good job. The two placentas look very good. Which means you made a wonderful healthy home for your twins. I am going to monitor you for a few days because your pressure and blood sugar levels are a little high. Your babies are a little early. Two weeks is common for twins but still they will be in the specialist unit to make sure all is good. But they look great. The nurses will continue to clear things up and I will check on you in a few hours. They will take you to recovery. Then in time to your room. I am ordering you stay at least three days. We have given you medication to reduce infection, help you sleep, to get that pressure down and a kick to rehydrate your body. Congratulations, Madame and Monsieur Delacroix."

He shook Philippe's hand and then he kissed Delphine on her cheeks.

As he left the room, a specialist from the neonatal intensive care unit came rolling twin A over to see her momma. Delphine was able to touch her little hand just a minute before they took her away for monitoring. She covered her hands over her mouth and began bawling uncontrollably. Philippe' rushed back to her side and held her in his arms gently rocking back and forth.

"Don't cry, my sweet. Delphine, please don't cry. Tell me what is wrong?"

She only shook her head no and tried to hide her face inside his chest. A few minutes later, another specialist rolled over twin B, who never cried after that first yelp. They were able to touch his little hand before he was whisked away like his sister.

Delphine continued to cry but not as deeply as before, the medication began to relax her.

"Dell, what an amazing woman you are, I love you so very much my darling." Philippe' continued to breathe rapidly and kiss her from his high doses of adrenaline running through his body. The oxygen mask was finally removed for good, and her cascade of tears lessened while she gave a constant sound of simultaneous moaning and chuckling.

After he kissed her lips firmly expressing his excitement and love, she said, "Philippe' they are beautiful."

"Oui, beautiful like their mother." He whispered as the nurse replaced some of the coverings from her body and removed the monitors.

"We made little people. God helped us make little people, Philippe'." Her voice was soft with a tone of gratitude and amusement. He nodded wiping the water from his cheeks and beard.

A few seconds later, Delphine got a sudden burst of energy and pulled his hand clutching it toward her chest. He moved closer to her. Then she said rather loudly, "Jean-Philippe' you are the most beautiful, magnificent sexy man in da whole world. I love … I love..." He smiled at her as she spoke, looking into his eyes as her lids were heavy. She spoke more of her thoughts out loud, "I love ... I love... licking your delicious body."

Gasping he shouted, "Delphine!"

Nurses around were giggling.

"De-Dell…"

Trying to connect with her eyes, he stopped speaking when she squeezed his hand harder and spoke a little slurred.

"No. I ain't gonna be no French citizen no more. I mean it. Act like ya know. Keep your big thingy ta yourself. Grease lightning! I'm not doin' dis again… Don't catch these hands, nope! . . . I've one of each. Cool beans! Xanadu . . . Elvis, done left da building … Where's da beef? Jitterbug … Wake me up, before ya go-go. Wham! …Get ya sum business boy and ease on down - down da road . . . Like Prince say, dis be what it sounds like when horses fly!"

Laughing along with everyone else in the delivery room, Philippe' glanced over at the anesthesiologist around a few machines and her IV and curiously asked, "What in heaven did you give her?"

She looked up, smiled, and answered. "A sedative for her body to rest and recover. She won't remember what she's saying. But you very well might."

Low and high laughter filled the room from the three medical staff and Philippe'. When he turned back to Delphine, she was knocked out with her mouth hanging open on the pillow still holding his hand.

Kissing her forehead, he whispered, "Dearest I will be here when you wake up. I love you."

While Delphine was being transferred to the recovery room for monitoring, Philippe' gave a lengthy silent prayer of thanks before entering the waiting room to tell the nervous, pacing and chatting family members the news of twin A, his daughter and twin B, his son.

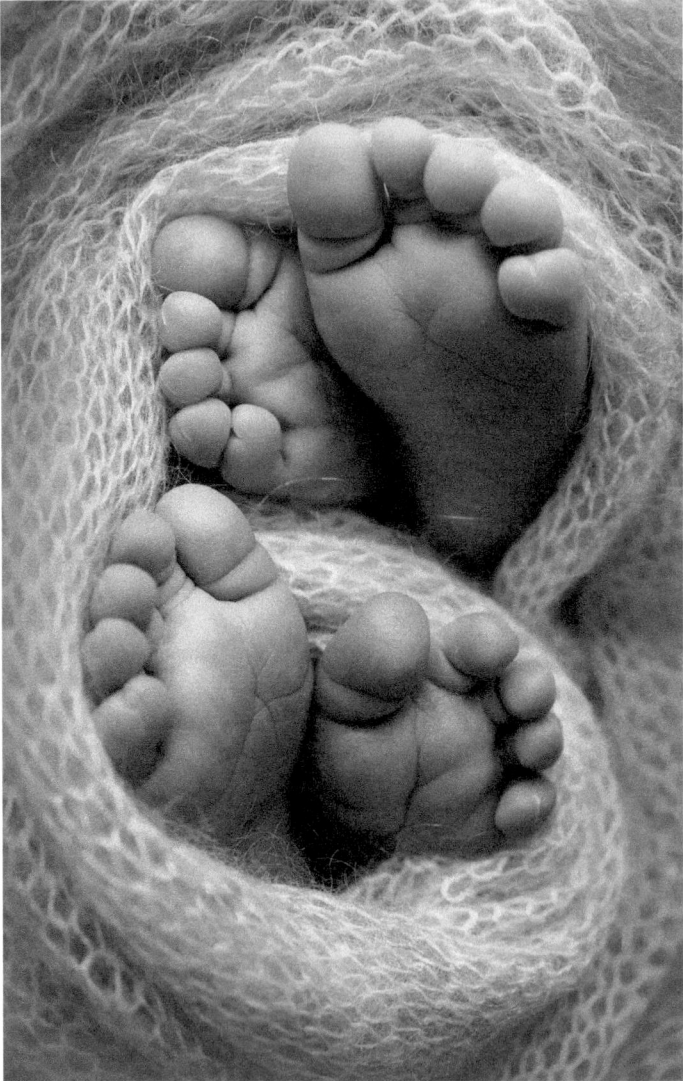

43 The Letter is …

During her recovery, everyone returned to the Delacroix chateau to celebrate because Delphine could not have visitors.

The Delacroix twins were determined to be about a week older than originally estimated in utero. Both were cleared and brought to stay with their mother in her room thirty-six hours later. There is where Delphine and Philippe' snickered and moaned, really inspecting every detail of each little one in their arms.

Teaching her daughter to latch on to her breast, she removed her hat to see her full head of seemingly dark brown hair with a hint of golden shimmer. Then she said without removing her eyes from her daughter, "Philippe' her hair is straight. Just like yours. She does not have an afro like you said."

Sitting holding his sleeping son in his arms, he chuckled and said, "She doesn't? No? My mistake that must have been you."

She snorted, startling her infant. Then she whispered, "You make me sick. Nasty…" trying not to laugh too hard. He looked up at her and puckered an air kiss to her grinning.

"Did you decide on your name?" He asked holding his son like a delicate rugby ball. She moaned a yes but didn't share but asked, "How about you? What are you going to name her from your list?"

They were both hesitating to share because the two had agreed to pick one baby and name them. They each had a list and were not to share it until after they were born.

"You go first." She said anxious to know what he chose.

"Me?" He was stalling. But after a few minutes, he announced, "I need to hold her to the moon like in Roots."

She snickered *(Silly.)* "Uh, no. They will put you in jail if you try that. Let's switch."

Removing twin A from her breast, they traded. She put her son on the other side. Trying to get him to latch on was more difficult but he got a little before going back to sleep.

The discussion then continued, "Alright Philippe' now you have her. What is the name you picked." She pressed him to share a name for their daughter.

"Okay Delphine, remember the rules. We each pick a letter and a name that starts with it. No matter what that will be their first or middle name. We each must pick another name to match the letter of what the other had picked. Got it?" Nodding in agreement, she smashed her face at him to tell it.

"Alright. My letter is M. I chose Marie. She will be a Marie after my mother." He said it smiling and waited for her reaction.

"Hmmm. Marie. Okay. My letter was C. Now don't be upset but C for Chevalier."

Shocked and frowning with her reveal, he blurted out, "What? No. Why? He is not even the coolest musketeer; I am and then it is Tomas. No change your letter, Delphine. How about D for D'Artagnan or T for Thaddeus?"

Shaking her head and standing firm in her decision, she said, "No. Don't change the rules. I want Chevalier."

Still attempting to change her mind, his voice was a little pleading, "He will be more unbelievably arrogant, if my son has his name, Delphine. He will imply you secretly love him. You know he likes to joke. He … I love him but … he is a bit of a scoundrel. Let's pick something else."

Amused by his whining tone, she wasn't changing her mind. "Philippe' the letter is C, and his name will be Chevalier. I don't care what he thinks. But my reasons are simply, the first movie I saw that made me fall in love with France was "Gigi," and I loved the way Maurice Chevalier sang, "Thank Heaven for little Girls." In my French studies, I learned Joseph Bologne, Chevalier de Saint-Georges, was a famous Black Frenchman who was known for being a virtuoso violinist and master composer. I loved that part of history. Now regarding Chevalier Ratliff, he was the first person to tell us, we were having a baby. Thenhe pranked me with them being both boys. He wins as the bringer of good news. So, these are the reasons why I picked it. I want Chevalier to be our son's name."

He couldn't argue with her, since she had no comment about naming their daughter after his mother.

"My father may be a little disappointed but that is your choice, and I agree. Now, what C name will you have for Marie?"

Flipping through the pages of her notebook to the letter C for her list of girl's names, she said, "Chantal."

"Aww. That is lovely. I like that. Marie Chantal Delacroix. Chantal Marie Delacroix. That is better. Chantal first."

Delphine smiled in agreement.

"So, Chevalier must be first then. What will his M name be?"

He gazed at her and confessed. "It was not on my list at all. I never thought you would pick his name. But it was what I would want. Maximus. What do you think?"

She turned her nose up, "I don't like it as much as the M one I had on my list, Maximilian. It's close but I like that better. Chevalier Maximus or Chevalier Maximilian. You decide."

"You are so wise my sweet wife. Maximilian it shall be." He said winking at her. "I love you, Dell."

"I love you too."

When Delphine and her children were released, the celebration was still going on with lots of food, wine, music, dessert and gifts. Everyone was there to welcome the twins, except Josephine, who came with her family a week later. None had been told their names until they had finally arrived at the Delacroix Chateau that Saturday mid-morning on May 2.

Both the Delacroix and Gauthier families along with the musketeers gave more joyful rowdy cheers and toasts after finding out the twin's names. Chevalier without a second thought, very loudly told Philippe' in th presence of everyone, "Je savais que c'etait vrai. Tu sais que ta femme m'aime en secret. (I knew it was true. Your wife secretly loves me.) In which, Philippe' promptly challenged him to a duel for being an arrogant scoundrel. Then he looked at Delphine with big eyes as if to say, "see I told you." She only grinned at him.

Over the next couple of weeks, the newest members of the Delacroix family stayed at their maison des grands parents with their very proud parents and over-the-moon grand-pere and grand-mere. They got to meet les cousins who couldn't hold them but gave each giant smiles and mini fist-pumps.

The Delacroix twins were the first ever in family history and were both smothered with love and gifts from all of their overjoyed tantes et oncles (aunts and uncles), including the sassy ones from Louisiana who couldn't stop kissing Philippe' and Delphine.

Hellene and Lorelle extended their trip three extra days and seemed to laugh-cry up until the day they left.

Two months after the birth, an official announcement was published.

The Delacroix Twins Arrived on April 28, 1987

Our Daughter

Chantal-Marie Delacroix at 4:40 p. m. 20 inch, 6 pounds 3oz

Our Son

Chevalier-Maximilian Delacroix at 4:52 p. m. 22 inch 6 pounds 6oz

We are overjoyed that our blessings reflect the
culmination of our faith and love.

Both have their father's narrow nose and ears, and their
mother's plump cheeks and lips. They have wavy
hair, a light complexion, and remarkable eyes.

Her unique beauty. . .

His distinctive handsomeness. . .

Are our perfect blend of French Chocolate.

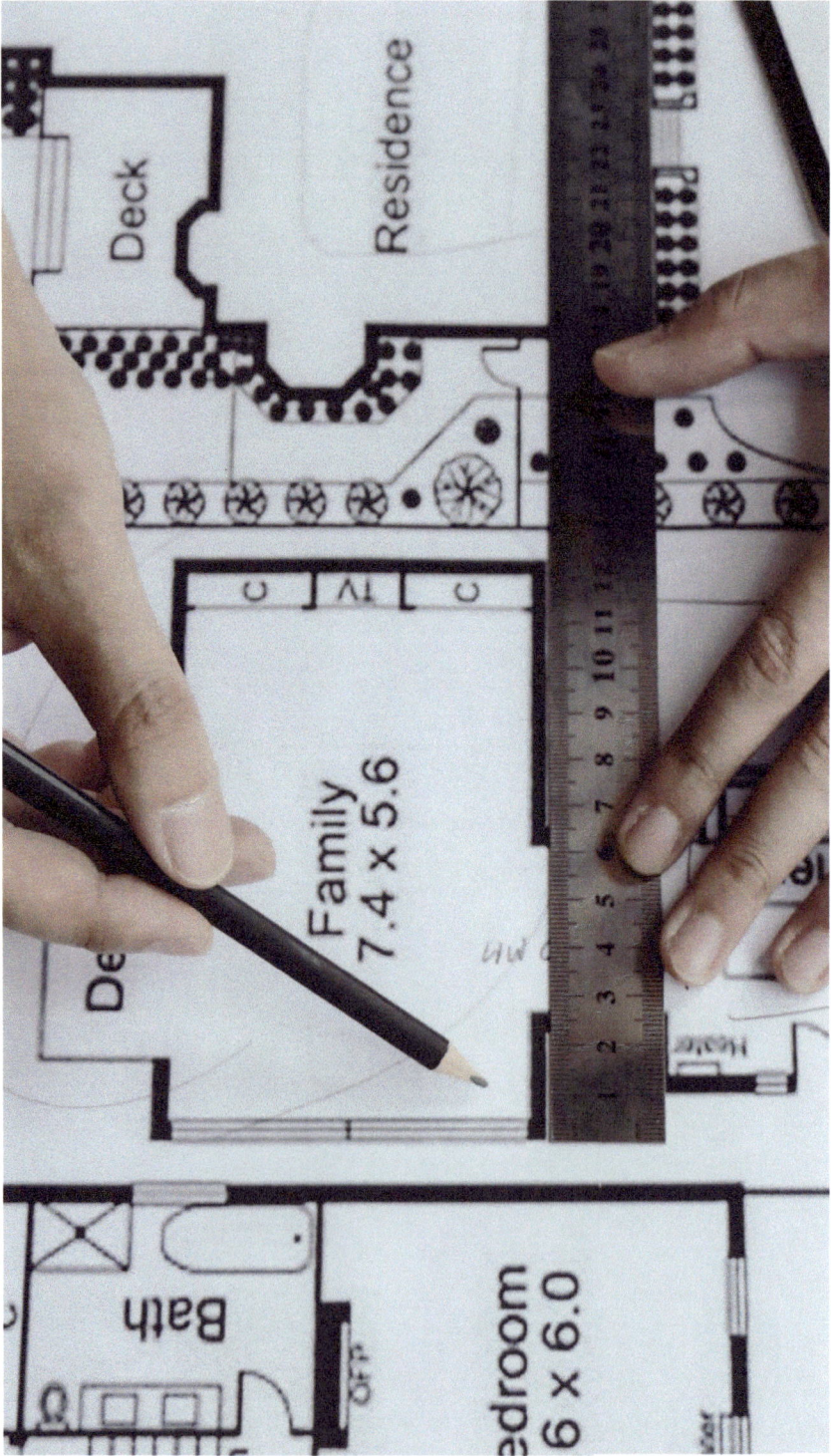

44 Hard and Soft

It had been very difficult while Philippe' lived in Virginia. He managed the construction of their new home and the international curriculum in the business program at Washington and Lee University.

The university board was extremely flexible allowing him to be in Paris for seven months that first year. But the last two years, he could only see his family once every three months for just two weeks.

In the meantime, Delphine was in Paris raising their twins, finishing medical school, and finalizing the contracts for their Paris penthouse to be managed and subleased by executive board members from La Bibliothèque Nationale de France.

Delphine could only have juggled medical school and growing twin babies with the live-in help of Gert and Heidi. The once-a-month sleepovers with Marie, Mrs. Durand, Ava, and even Nannette's support gave her the ability to keep her grades high, and her babies happy. Delphine was no longer at the top of her class, but she was satisfied with being within the top fifty passing her exams and certification. Next was her residency, but they were moving to America. European requirements were similar, but she would have some additional classes, a residency and board exams again to practice medicine in Virginia.

Delphine knew that would take her even more away from raising her children and they were her priority now. She researched and talked it over with Philippe' and decided to adjust her medical career path to a nurse practitioner, specializing in pediatric care. Delphine discovered this route would require less commitment time and only a few courses and exams versus the longer journey of becoming a practicing physician in the United States. They agreed she would go back to school and complete her requirements when their twins begin elementary school. Everything was going as planned.

One early December morning, Delphine was slowly awakened by a mellow song "Baby Come to Me," by Regina Belle and light kisses traveling up her arm to her neck and then to her chin. She smiled before opening her eyes because she knew it was her husband. She felt him lying on top of the bed next to her. He spoke with a sultry whisper, "Good morning."

Opening her eyes leisurely, she said with a slight growl and stretch, "Good morning, you're a day early. I was supposed—" In mid-sentence his lips smashed over hers for a firm long lip kiss. She chuckled with a long slow moan. It had been almost ninety days since he had been home.

"I made you breakfast." He whispered tenderly, kissing her left jaw and then below her ear.

"You did? Aww. That's so sweet, thank you. I missed you baby."

Nibbling on her ear, he removed her head scarf that wrapped up her straight permed black hair. He loosened the swirl mold with his long fingers to let her mid-length inverted bob fall. She bit her bottom lip before grinning as her eyes followed her hand stroking his low sandy-blonde beard. Free falling into the ocean maze of his rich blue eyes, she smiled with the joy of his returning touch, while humming the soulful melodies playing that he had started to set a romantic mood.

"I missed you too, beautiful brown eyes." He said, before collapsing over her lips as she giggled. Philippe' moved over her body that was nuzzled underneath the covers. His soft lips parted and locked a few times to her plump ones before he attempted to open her lips with his wide tongue. Delphine shook her head and moaned no. She began pushing him up away from her by his warm cheeks.

"What?" He frowned with his quick question. "Philippe' I need to brush my teeth first."

"Why? So, what if you have stinky breath? Mine is flavored with peppermint; it will mix nicely." He said smirking as he leaned to kiss her again.

Moving her head giggling. "Eeuwa. Nasty. No! I need—" He cut her off with his mouth, capturing hers again as his prisoner to a passionate kiss. This time he forced her mouth open with his powerful tongue. He would not be denied, and Delphine wrapped her arms around his neck as he plunged deep into the exquisite taste of her. As his hands moved to shift the covers away, she stopped him again. Breaking free from his mouth that followed her for several minutes as Anita Baker's "Angel" played, she mumbled with some undertone of amusement.

"No. No, Philippe'." She held his shoulders back to give her space, as he growled to get to those lips once more. Chuckling from his playfulness, she pushed her lips inward so he could not get a kiss until she got her way.

"Hey, you said you missed me. Don't say it's that time. I know it's not, Dell. It's on my calendar. I always count the days and plan my flights around it!" He said, raising his eyebrows and then licking over the crease where her lips would be if she didn't have them sucked in.

"Count? Oh, lord! I need to take a shower." She told him quickly before pushing her lips back in as he continued to try to kiss her.

"Dell, we are going to be very sweaty in about fifty-five minutes. Let me free you from these blankets you're wrapped up in." Philippe' tugged at the blankets covering her, but she snatched them back over her body. Groaning, he attacked her neck and face with frantic kisses as she began laughing from the tickling sensation. His strategy worked and her hands released the blankets. Now, his wife would soon be available for the taking after he removed her blue flannel pajamas.

Laughing softly, she tried to compromise causing him to pause his frisky actions. Delphine sat up, and said, "J.P. why don't you shower with me?"

He sat back on the bed facing her grinning like a devious villain rubbing his beard as if he were contemplating all the things he could do in the shower, which made her laugh.

"Alright, but first I need to tell you something important."

Delphine got serious focusing on him. Philippe' exhaled and then told her, "The plan has changed a bit. Uh, you see, Dell, the final inspections on the house will be done in about sixty days. Then, our shipments from here and the new things we purchased will be delivered after that. So, love, we won't see each other again until you all come to Virginia. That is in five months."

Instantly, she felt a wave of sadness. "Philippe', five months? When are you going to see your parents—your sisters? The twins miss you. I miss you." She was disheartened but knew there was nothing that could change things. It had been three years since he had gotten that new position and for the last eighteen months, they had been building this home for their family.

Delphine couldn't count the numerous times she had to convince him not to resign and finish the house, when he wanted to just return to his old job because he desperately missed them. She thought, *(I can do this, it's only five months and then we will all be together … Right!)*

She changed her facial expression to one of acceptance and gave him a grin with a gentle, "Okay. We're in the home stretch. Almost over."

Philippe' knew she was disappointed and grabbed both her hands. He delivered a sweet "I love you" before kissing the back of both of them. Then he found her loving brown eyes and told her something he had been thinking about for a while. "Dell, let's make another baby, right now."

Shocked, she squished up her face. "Huh? Max and Marie are not even five yet. No. We have one of each. Philippe', it was too hard at the end. We can get some fish and a dog." She tried to make her face and voice extra happy with the last sentence, but he wasn't smiling.

He licked his lips, and told her in a serious tone, "Delphine, I want more babies. We talked about having several more. Don't do this to me, please. You know I'm the Delacroix heir and after me is only Max. We need five or six more. I want a lot of beautiful brown babies with you." He gave her sad eyes and a pouty mouth.

Shaking her head, she let him know her thoughts. "Five? I worked too hard to regularly exercise and get all that extra weight off. I'm a size twelve and feel so much better. I was huge. I couldn't walk. I don't want those complications again. Wait, is that why your ass is counting the days of my period? Oh, brother. Let's talk about it when the twins are … hmmm, say thirteen."

Lying over her lap and looking up at her eyes quickly blinking, he said, "Dell, how about we try to have another one before they turn six, then we will have another one when they are thirteen. This way there isn't so much time between them. We have this big house in Virginia, we need to fill it up! Ooh, if we are blessed with twins again, we need four more, then we can stop. Agreed?"

Chuckling at his silliness, she said sternly, "No! That's too many… I can agree to one more after Marie and Max are ten but not before. That gets them settled in school and my career firmly established to take extended time off. Whatever we get, we'll get. We can talk about maybe another one after that baby is three or so, only if I don't have complications like before. Does that work?"

"Oui!" He sat up and gave her a quick peck on the lips. Then he jumped off the bed saying, "We should practice making one, now!" as he pulled her laughing softly into the bathroom.

While the distant sounds of Miki Howard's "Imagination" played from the bedroom sound system, they embarked on the slow enjoyment of watery passion play. Philippe' and Delphine had mastered the art of their lovemaking, and it took them to profound pinnacles of ecstasy.

Philippe's two weeks went by quickly. He spent time with his children but also his musketeer brothers, his sister's families, and his parents in Lyon. It was his goodbye to them, and it was also very emotional. The reality was that they were moving to America and life would not be the same as it had for anyone.

45 America

Finally, the construction of their seven-bedroom, five and a half bath home located on three lush green acres off Hidden Woods Drive in Roanoke, Virginia was completed. Delphine and Philippe' had collaborated for over a year on the furnishings of their new modern home with high ceilings and stylish white and black décor.

Packing in Paris took over six months. International shipments had arrived and were unpacked by their professional movers. New items were selected, purchased, and delivered. Philippe' made sure the entire home was ready for his family's arrival and he was so excited.

***

Marie Delacroix had been deeply depressed for over a year but the last several months were the worse, as it came closer to the time her twin grandchildren would leave. Marie adored all her grandchildren. She felt it was her duty to have them around her, to teach and enjoy their company. But knowing she could no longer see them with a quick flight to Paris or a drive down to Lyon to spend weeks on the estate, have garden tea parties, read to them, teach them how to ride a horse, have them all together at the same time, was simply breaking her heart. Jean-Pierre felt the same deep sadness, especially as his only son being so far away, but he kept a positive attitude to help his sweet wife cope with the coming changes. She cried daily until the time arrived for Delphine, Max, and Marie to board their international flight to America.

Josephine and Delphine had become very close over the years. Josephine promised that she, Hassan, and her boys would visit as soon as they came back from a long trip to Africa and after they finally had their small wedding in Casablanca.

At the airport, Henri-François and Tomas gave Chevalier games and toys to play with on the plane ride. They were brave older cousins giving big strong hugs and they didn't shed any tears. But Kristoff tearfully refused to let go of the twin's hands as Josephine tried to leave the boarding area. Little Odette and Chantal-Marie were inseparable like they were close sisters. Odette brought two baby dolls to the airport. She gave one to Chantal and kept the one she had colored the face with a brown marker. Then she said, "I will sleep with my pretend Marie until my cousin Marie comes back."

The adults teared up knowing they couldn't possibly realize; they wouldn't see each other every day and it might be a long time before they returned.

So many tearful goodbyes caused Delphine to weep, which made her children and Gert cry too, while traveling down the passenger jetway. Once onboard, Delphine and Gert settled her matching outfit preschoolers for the long flight from Paris to New York. Although they were in first class, they had never been on an airplane. The twins were both very excited and scared at the same time. It was a wonder-ful adventure, with them asking lots of curious questions. They even got to meet the captains and sit in the cockpit and take photos. But at one point, Delphine did slip both some children's Tylenol because they had some pain in their ears from the cabin pressure.

Philippe' couldn't wait a second longer to be with his family. He flew to meet them in New York. A surprised Delphine screamed seeing him standing at the gate when they arrived, startling passersby in the airport terminal. "Papa! Papa!" Came from his overjoyed little ones. Embraces with kisses resulted as he picked son in the other and carried them through the airport. Philippe' had changed their overnight stay into an adventure spending five days in New York exploring. It was spectacular to see the twin's eyes light up, at some points even Gert and Delphine were just like little kids too.

After the visit, the group traveled by Amtrak train, in which most of the way Gert and Delphine slept, while Philippe' played history and visual discovery games with his excited twins in the family suites on their way to Roanoke, Virginia.

At long last, the members of the Delacroix family were together under the same roof. It was a happiness overload! Delphine first called the family in France to let them know, they made it safely.

After unpacking, her next three-way call, Delphine quickly informed Lolli in Seattle and Claudine in Santa Monica, that she was finally in Roanoke getting settled. Extending a visit invitation to Lolli and her future husband, Marcellus, a Tacoma Firefighter she had met on a blind date a year earlier. Then one to Claudine and Tony with instruction to hurry up and bring their son, Toryono, who had recently turned two-years old and needed to meet his play cousins in person. Delphine really missed her girlfriends living in Paris and was so happy to be somewhat closer.

She called Lorelle and got caught up with her family. She found out how long Lorelle was going to keep working as a para-legal before taking off for maternity leave.

"Ya feelin' okay, Rell? Ya got three months to go." She said, after talking for a while and hearing a bit of exhaustion in her sister's voice.

"Yeah. The more ya have da easier da incubation, it be after these jokers come out than be da hard work. Cedric said dis enough. We not tryin' ta have our own basketball team no more. I'm thinkin' of gettin' my tubes tied after this." Lorelle said during her lunch break at work munching on a sandwich.

Laughing between words, Delphine said, "Well, ya got more babies ta love. If ya kept goin' I'm sure ya would have had twins. Ain't no secret, everybody knows it why ya two been tryin' just ta be like me. Copycat!"

"Shut up, dodo bird! Don't nobody wanna be no Delphine Delacroix. Girl please!" she said chuckling on the line.

Later, she checked in with Hellene in Lafayette and got to hear those sweet voices of Sam, Tamera, and her one-year-old niece Tonja whom she had only seen in pictures.

While Delphine was on the quick calls, Philippe' was running around with his twins. He was so delighted to show them how he decorated their very own rooms.

"Pawpaw! Merci! Merci!" Spinning around in the middle of her room, Chantal-Marie loved the star lights around her ceiling and all the colorful flowers and butterflies to mirror her favorite nighttime story her parents would read to her, "The Secret Garden" by Frances Hodgson Burnett.

"No, wait come see mine!" Chevalier shouted, grabbing hold of her little hand and taking her down the large hallway to see his amazing jungle room that looked like something from "Robinson Crusoe" by Daniel Defoe, which was his favorite story.

Since they couldn't agree, the two made little people arrangements to sleep one night in his room and then, one night in hers to see which one was the best.

Having pizza delivered for dinner made things easy. Across the table, Philippe' could not keep his eyes off his wife. Delphine would just smirk trying to avoid his intense gaze. Noticing the need for some private time, Gert announced, "Maxie and Marie, how would you like to play a game with me on my side of the new house all night long?"

"Yes!" "Oui, oui!"

"Okay, finish up. We will get you a bath and into your jammies. Then we will have popcorn and watch a movie then play the spy game." Gert said to grinning fat face, glistening from pizza sauce.

As the excited little ones munched on their pizza, Gert said chuckling, "Hopefully, they won't hear things that will make them think their new house is …" She mouthed the words "haunted."

Giggling, Delphine smacked her arm and Philippe' laughed before taking a large gulp of his wine. Delphine could no longer stop herself from imagining her husband without his shirt and seductively winked back at him.

In their new home, beginning the next phase of their life, that first night was going to be a series of romantic activities. As Philippe' shaved away his beard and mustache, Delphine set up all the R&B slow jams to auto-play throughout the night. The array of fruits, cheeses, and bread on crystal trays sat next to several bottles of wine and Delacroix engraved crystal glasses. Candles were lit and scented steam filled the bathroom from the deep bubbling jacuzzi made for two.

Philippe' and Delphine had been planning this night for a year as the best way to reinvigorate all the spectacular elements of their French citizenship.

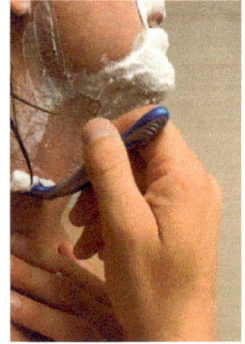

A harnessed moonlight captured in eyes from love's purest gaze, intensifies the delicate manner in which he touches her. Desires interchange immerge from selfless movements of calming winds. Timeless pause as stars perform a slow dance across the clear night sky. Gradually she consumes the essence of him through ravenous pores within her skin. Ripples merge into a crescendo of intimate wonder. Powerful waters sway as gentle waves colliding upon waiting shores seemingly set to echo these moments of euphoria.

46 Heal Thy Self

Hellene called Delphine to chat during the daytime when she knew the twins would be in pre-school. The bi-weekly calls gave updates and the scoop on how she was adjusting to living back in the United States.

"It's gettin' better. Ain't Louisiana dat be fa sho. It be real pretty wit da Fall colors. I got two more classes ta take. Then exams and after dat, I be certified as a nurse practitioner next year. It ain't a doctor but I'm satisfied 'cuz I will focus on specializing in pediatrics." Delphine shared honestly.

They talked for a bit more. Hellene learned it was still an adjustment for her but not Philippe'. He had become well accustomed over the years, but it wasn't as bad as she thought. However, the twins, missed their French family more than she and Philippe' realized.

Chantal-Marie and Chevalier-Maximilian cried a lot when they got the repeated answer that their grandparents and cousins would not be coming to see them today. It had been very hard for them going from having the family around all the time to not seeing them at all. Gert being there helped but it wasn't the same. Everything was so new for them. Because they had been home schooled and in the education system in France, the twins were very advanced for their age. Philippe' and Delphine talked about the twins skipping a grade after they got used to the school system next year. Delphine shared that the hope was when they began school full-time, it would be easier. They would make more friends and not be constantly reminded that Tomas, Kristoff, Odette, Henri, and little Brigette, were not coming over to play. As far as school went, because they were fluent in French and English, the twins being in an American school wasn't as much of a challenge for them. Philippe' had even been teaching everyone Japanese but she put a pause on that until they were older.

Hellene told Delphine about her stresses of being older and having another young one. It was not as easy this time around.

"Tonja don't like no sitter. I can't go out like I wanna no more. Pissed 'bout dat. Ya know I likes to get me a drink and do sum dancin'." She said with a tone of annoyance.

Delphine chuckled saying, "Ain't that how ya got her in da first place?"

"Shut up!" She snapped back, snickering.

"Who her daddy? Ya knows but ain't telling like Tamera? He ain't married to, is he? Ooh, maybe ya get married again." Delphine asked her big sister because she was curious, but she had a backup plan to quickly change the subject if it hit a nerve and she was going to get cussed out.

"Uh, I know who he be, Dell. Don't make me slap ya when I see ya." Delphine began to chuckle, as she continued. "He ain't married neither but not gonna give my life ta no man again. Nope. Sam Dupree be da first and da last husband."

A few silent seconds passed, and then Hellene cleared her throat to say, "Dell, we been talkin' for 'bout thirty minutes. I'ma ask, again. Do ya want me ta tell ya?"

Delphine switched to the cordless phone and walked over to close the door to the library. She didn't answer but moved to sit down with her legs curled up on Philippe's leather couch and started picking her teeth with her thumbnail.

Hellene probed again, "Twin. . . Ya ready ta know it now?"

Delphine knew what she was going to say. Since moving from Paris, Hellene had been giving not so subtle hints in conversations over the last few months.

Leaning her neck back, closing her eyes she inhaled and exhaled as if she could let go of the past by releasing hot air from her body. It was still there, buried deep but always there. How could her parents be so cruel all this time treating her like she was dead? Those horrible things her mother said to her were still in the back of her mind.

It made her angry, so much so that she had three whole journals dedicated to that part of her life, expressing her feelings about all of it. Now they have the nerve to want to welcome her back. To see her and her twins, just because they have a little color. It was appalling. She wished Lorelle hadn't shown them any pictures of her children, then they never would have known.

Delphine and Philippe' had no secrets. Their relationship was founded on the principles outlined in that Bible scripture from their wedding day. They strived to uphold and apply every word each day with regular honest communication, selflessness, and devotion to one another. He knew how she felt, and she knew his mind. She remembered Philippe's exact words.

"Dell, if their attitude is as before, vile, and hateful, intending to divide us, they can't see you or our children. Toxicity, racism, and hatred have no place in our lives. I will not tolerate it, not from anyone. My love, we have peace… peace in our home. We have researched many things and have made our own traditions for our family. We do not act without knowledge and agreement. This may be difficult for others to understand but this is how we are united in everything we do. No matter what, I will never allow anyone to harm you or our children. Do you understand me? No one. There is no compromise with your physical and mental safety. I will fight anyone for our happiness. I mean it. I don't care if they are on their death bed, my answer will always be no!" He paused then added.

"But … if … if they have changed even a little and can genuinely demonstrate to you that they respect you, your life, and what we have built as our family … then … Dell, there can always be room for forgiveness."

Philippe' was right. He usually was. That was one of the great things about him. Thoughts of her childhood flashed before her mind, the good memories.

Glancing up at a huge Delacroix family photo of the four of them dressed in formal wear framed on the wall, Delphine saw the beauty of her mixed-race children. They were part of her and therefore her parents. Max and Marie's hair, and light honey complexion would no doubt cause challenges as they grow up being Black in America.

A need for strength from both cultures was very important to both Philippe' and her. Charlie and Eleanor were not perfect people. Delphine knew that no matter how they had treated her, her parents could give Max and Marie a sense of pride and tools for the courage they would need throughout their life. Just like their history of bravery, a focus on education to succeed, and their example of faith and love for each other had taught her.

Saying a silent prayer for a peaceful heart with a small opening ready to forgive, Delphine answered her sister's persistent inquiry.

"Oui, Hellene, ya can tell me, now."

Hellene, exhaled. "Diddy say to tell ya he not gone miss ya no more. Ya need ta come home so he can touch his Dell. He say, bring dem babies wit cha. Dell, he don't have long. Doctor say maybe two years. Momma don't know how long and we not ta tell her neither. He say, don't matter what she say. Ya his Dell and ya welcome home. Ya husband too."

"Wait, Diddy said Philippe' can come? Did he really?" She said in surprise.

"Yea. He told Momma his Dell can come home and dat be final. He gone send her back to Franklinton wit her people, 'cuz she mad and don't want ta be here if he come too."

Delphine laughed so hard; she started coughing. Then she asked, "Hellene is this because Marie and Max have some color to them like they said or is it because he … he is …?"

Hellene didn't answer right away. Delphine could hear her sobbing. The phone line was quiet for a few minutes until Hellene spoke again.

"Do it matter? Listen, I ain't gone lie, Diddy been askin' me 'bout ya for a long time. Way before they say he got lung cancer. Ya know ta keep da peace, he not told it to momma. She holdin' out and he sendin' her away for ya to come. Can I give him ya number, Dell? He wanna talk to ya. Can I? Please, twin, can I?"

She agreed.

Within the hour, Charlie Murry called his daughter.

"Delphine Asha … Dis be ya father."

"Hello Diddy." She started to tremble hearing his voice after years of silence. Her eyes instantly filled with water.

"Twin, it been long time and I miss ya. I pray you been good and ya family too. I know I don't have much time and I wanna see ya before I go. Ya momma comin' 'round but I ain't gonna let her stop me no more. Ya my joy, Twin. Ya momma named ya after her daddy, but it be me, I named ya Asha 'cuz in African it mean … What it mean?"

Tears fell nonstop from her eyes. She was choked up and cleared her throat before answering, "Life. It means life, Diddy."

"Life. Ya to live ya life. Ya done that. I is proud of ya, Dell for havin' a good life. That all I ever wanted for ya. Sis say ya don't havin' no holiday cuz ya library studin' say none them be holy no ways. But I got things to say ta ya Dell, and ya sistas. Uh, then can ya come, uh, maybe for my birthday, child? Maybe bring ya family?" He paused.

Delphine was crying and unable to speak.

"Delphine don't cry, honey. I don't wanna miss no more time wit cha. Please come. But don't cry, baby girl. Don't cry." Charlie was emotional on the other end of the line as well.

"Diddy I'ma come before ya birthday. Just me, alright? Then we all come for ya birthday."

"I can't wait ta hold ya."

"Oh, Diddy. I missed ya. I really missed ya."

"I missed ya too, my good baby girl. Ya come real soon ya hear."

"Yes'um."

"Let me go fur ya momma gets back from da store. I love ya."

"Oh, Diddy, I love ya too." She hung up the phone in what seemed like slow motion.

Delphine wept uncontrollably. Flashes of memories clouded in hurt, love, and pain flooded her mind like a hurricane hitting the Delta. Fast. Hard. Strong. She couldn't stop the tears, heart-wrenching outcrying moans or those few words of gibberish she made while wailing over the arm of the couch.

What did she need? Her anchor, that peaceful calm of the one person in the whole world that knew every corner of her heart, soul, and body. The only person she entrusted completely with all three. Delphine called Philippe' and he immediately left work to return home quickly. Upon arrival he found his dearest love was curled up in a fetal position on the couch, soaked from salty water. Philippe' tenderly scooped her up and held her in his arms without words for a long time.

Later, Philippe' made his wife some of her favorite French chocolate tea and the two began discussing travel plans for her to visit her father, heal her heart, and forgive him in person.

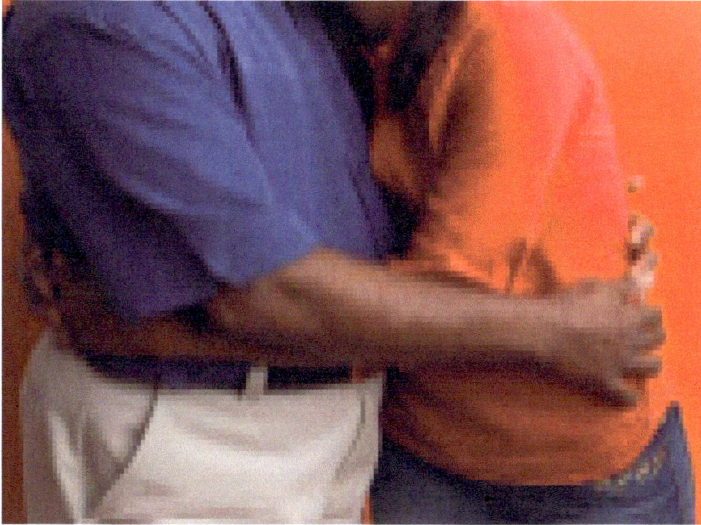

47 Epilogue

A nnually, the Virginia Delacroix's traveled to Lyon, France. It was usually for the entire summer just to be with their family. This became a necessity after moving to America and two years later, their family suffered a tragic loss. On their way to their wedding destination in Casablanca, Josephine Delacroix, and her fiancé Hassan Lazar were killed in a major car collision along with four other people.

Josephine's sons Tomas Delacroix-Winthrop, whose father had died before his birth of a heart attack during a military exercise, and Kristoff Delacroix-Lazar were now being raised by their grandparents, Jean-Pierre, and Marie Delacroix. At Josephine's resting service at the Delacroix mausoleum, Philippe' and his sister Nannette committed to bringing their families together in Lyon, without exception at least once a year. This began to comfort the hearts of the young boys and their grandparents.

Marie and Odette are inseparable. When they see each other, it is as if they never parted. It is a bit remarkable. Kristoff is older but he never leaves Max. Those two are attached at the hip. He teaches him how to fence, play rugby and chess. Kristoff seems to be extremely protective of both Marie and Max. He sometimes even steps in to take their side when either one gets into trouble, and he is around.

Marie, Delphine, and Nannette find it chivalrous and charming but Jean-Pierre, Philippe' and Andreas don't like it at all.

Although Chantal-Marie, who preferred to be called Marie and Chevalier-Maximillian, who was known as Maxie love being in France just about every Summer, but they do enjoy being in New Orleans too.

Marie spends a lot of time with her Gram T, which is what they call Eleanor because before he died, Charlie Murry called her Teence. Mostly, she would be in the kitchen watching her with her older cousins Lorelle-Latrice, and great auntie Melva's granddaughters, Nahmeeko, Hazel-Ann, Kimie, and Shayla. Whereas Maxie hangs out with his uncle Cedric and his son Edwin, and cousin Velamina's twins, Parker, and Perry, boxing in great-uncle Verl's gym, fishing, and playing basketball.

Living in the United States allowed for frequent visits from friends and family which made the life balance Delphine and Philippe' wanted most of all for their children.

The Summer of 1996 was an unforgettable one because Philippe' and Delphine had a full house and then some. When Lolli, her husband Marcellus and son Marcel came for a quick trip at the same time as Claudine, her husband Tony and their children, son Toryono and daughter Rhilynn on their way to New York.

This all happened as Andreas, Nannette, Odette, Brigette, Jean-Pierre, and Geneviève were on the last week of their three-week stay when they arrived. It was unfortunate that Henri stayed in Lyon with his grandparents to be with Tomas and Kristoff.

However, more family came when Hellene and Lorelle brought their families to stay this same week in Virginia. The caravan trip of over 850 miles traveling through Mississippi, Alabama, and Tennessee was part of the once in a lifetime Murry family vacation.

Eleanor "Teence" Murry was not only making this road trip at her age, but this was going to be the first time she had ever been to Virginia.

Although Delphine and her family had visited family and friends in Louisiana, Eleanor had refused to be around if ever Philippe' came. She had not seen or spoken to Philippe' Delacroix since that day many years ago, when he had come to her home looking for Delphine.

As she admired the green acreages and trees, landscaped yard, and beautiful home from outside, thoughts crept into Eleanor's mind, *(Dis be like a plantation, but my Delphine be owning it. Hee hee.)*

Guided by Delphine, she came in slowly using her purple walking cane. Eleanor stopped inside the foyer glancing around at the modern furnishings and walls covered in all sorts of family photos in pristine frames.

When she noticed a silver frame housing an old photograph of herself with her late husband Charlie, their late son LaRoyce, and Hellene, holding three-year-old Delphine and Lorelle on their laps, her eyes instantly released tears.

Rushing to greet her shouting, "Gram-T! Gram-T!" was her growing twin grandchildren with rare, amber-colored eyes, whom she hugged with grandma love and giggles. Maxie and Marie quickly gave a side hug to Hellene and Lorelle, then briskly ran out the door to welcome their uncle Cedric, Hellene's man-friend deputy Carter O'Neil and their cousins.

Walking to the door behind his children's excited greeting and fast exit, Philippe' approached the plump 5'4, silver-headed, expresso color complexion elderly woman with a soft smile. When his ocean blue eyes caught sight of her watering eyes of black onyx, he was standing a few feet in front of her. Philippe' was just about a foot taller than Eleanor, which made her stretch herself up to really see him. He spoke first, "Welcome to our home, Mrs. Murry."

What Eleanor said surprised the three Murry sisters and Philippe'.

"Did my child make ya put up dis here picture for my comin'?" She said pointing to her family photo from the 70s on the wall.

It took a few seconds for what she said to register.

But then Philippe' motioned to the wall and answered, "Uh, no ma'am. That has been in the same spot from the day we unpacked it."

Immediately, she responded. "Ya' mean dat been there all dis time?"

"Yes, momma." Delphine whispered as Philippe' nodded.

Eleanor gasped, quickly covering her mouth with her hand and begin to sob. Helping her into a chair, panic set in. Lorelle, Delphine and Hellene gathered around her very alarmed by her behavior, asking questions. While Philippe' darted across the room to a bar refrigerator grabbing a cold bottled water and a glass.

"Momma, what's wrong? Tell me, please …"

"Is ya asthma, acting up?"

"Don't cry momma. What's wrong?"

Handing her tissue, she wiped her eyes and slowly began to calm herself. Philippe' returned pouring up the water and was preparing to hand the glass to Delphine to give to her. But she spoke and the four of them paused.

Looking lovingly at Delphine who was bending down at her side, Eleanor touched her daughter's cheek saying, "Ya diddy always say ya was a good child, Delphine. Ya is." Eleanor grinned at her, then quickly focused her attention up to speak directly to Philippe'. "I'ma old woman. In all my life, I ain't never felt so shamed as ya done show'd me, how wrong I be 'bout one white man. Thank ya' for invitin' me ta visit ya home, Frenchman. No more Mrs. Murry, ya hear. I'm Momma T. If ya feelin' dat be alright wit cha."

Shocked, everyone remained motionless for a few seconds.

Finally, Philippe' cleared his throat handing her the glass of cold water. Eleanor smiled at him taking the glass from his hand. As she sipped a little water, Philippe' glanced down at Delphine, whose eyes were just running with salty tears. Hellene was squeezing Delphine's shoulder and biting her bottom lip. Lorelle swiftly turned her body around to cover her teary eyes.

Philippe' nodded at his mother-in-law of almost ten years, saying, "Yes, ma'am. I'd like that, just fine. Momma T it is."

After four days of family fun, food, stories, sleeping under the stars, laughter, and card games and music, an afternoon barbecue set up a trajectory that would change the planned future.

Relaxing from lunch, everyone seemed to be spread around waiting for dessert. Some of the kids were dancing to MC Hammer's "Can't Touch This" that was being projected on the outdoor theater screen from BET's Video Soul. Other older ones had just beat Andreas and Tony in basketball and slowly coming back from the court to snack on the food tables Cedric was churning the ice cream. Carter, Marcellus, and Philippe' were chatting and nibbling on the meat they had grilled. Periodically they would refresh their drinks, trade off with Cedric or just laugh at the dance craziness. When New Edition's "If It Isn't Love" came on, the men sat back and watch Maxie, and Marie show everybody they knew all the dance moves to the entire video. Odette, Tonja, Philippe' and Andreas jumped in because they knew a few of the moves too.

All the women went into the kitchen beginning to prep the homemade desserts to take outside. Jokes and laughter continued as they sipped iced tea and fruity water refreshers sing and dancing to Michael Jackson's "Remember the Times" video that could be heard playing from outside.

Then it happened. Hellene looked over at her mother sitting next to her at the breakfast table. Then she loudly announced, "Momma, I forgot ta tell ya, when we was on da road, I had me a dream 'bout a big ole catfish ready ta jump in my fishin' boat."

Lorelle, Delphine, Lolli, Claudine, and Nannette instantly stopped speaking and moving. Eleanor quickly chimed in, "Sis, last night I done dreamed 'bout one too but dis one was talkin' ta some red snappers. Ain't dat funny."

Eleanor and Hellene began chuckling, as the look of confusion, panic, and horror covered the faces of the five frozen women. It was obvious they were all thinking, *(When was my last period?)* Eleanor and her eldest daughter tapped their glasses of iced tea together, then waited. Seconds later, the five other women either had large roving eyes, hands clasping their chest, nervous twitching, or heavy panting. They all spoke without looking at each other.

The ladies spoke all at once.

"Oh no. Why didn't I get my damn tubes tied like I said!"

"Aww hell. Please, don't let it be me."

"You …You guys said those fish dreams don't work on me! I'm not Black. So, it doesn't, right?! Say it doesn't!!"

"Maybe y'all just had gas."

"It's … It's not possible."

Hellene pulled out the drug store bag smirking. After she emptied several home tests onto the table, a mad dash to snatch one resulted. The five frantic ladies fumbled to guzzle down any liquid within arm's reach.

Eleanor laughed louder as they rushed out of the kitchen mumbling to the nearest bathroom to pee.

Hellene got up and got her mother a piece of coconut cake and took a piece of devil's food cake for herself. Then before she put a bite in her mouth, Hellene said, "I love ya momma."

Eleanor replied, "I love ya too. Sis, now, how long we got ta wait ta know who it be?"

Hellene answered, "Well if they done pee quick, five minutes or so. But they may need time ta let it sink in. None look as if they expectin'it."

Twenty minutes later, slowly Claudine, Lolli, Delphine, Nannette and Lorelle returned back into the kitchen.

While Hellene came into the house after setting out a couple of desserts, Eleanor demanded, "Alright, girls. Ya needs ta tell it."

"It's … it's me. I'm still Black inside. He is just a wild sex animal in the damn Spring! Horny toad! I —" Nannette stopped speaking and exhaled heavily shedding a few tears.

"I need a drink. Wait, is there such thing as medicinal wine? I don't believe this." Claudine spoke clearly frustrated as she dropped her head.

"Me … I told him to get off me that night. Damn it!" Lolli said before she rolled her eyes thinking of ways to make her husband pay.

"Tell me why ya just can't sleep? Why ya gotta dream? Why?!" Lorelle said before mumbling a few bad words hitting her fist on the counter.

After a few minutes everyone noticed Delphine hadn't said a word. Grabbing a Haagen-Dazs vanilla chocolate bar from her freezer, she turned to see bugged-out eyes fixed on her and waiting.

"What?" She said unwrapping her ice cream and popping it in her mouth.

Claudine tugged her by the arm and told her forcefully, "You got us here and we all caught in the damn fishing net. You jinxed us, cow."

"Delphine Asha, what dat test say?" Lorelle demanded. Delphine said nothing, just continued smacking on her ice cream.

Lolli got in her face and ordered her to talk, saying, "Heifer don't make me, cut you. Momma T is sitting here waiting. You better tell it."

Delphine said, "Oh, my bad. My test was defective."

"Huh? What cha mean, defective?" Hellene shouted at her from across the kitchen.

Casually enjoying every bite of her ice cream bar, she looked at the confused and twisted faces of the women in the kitchen. Delphine said with all seriousness, "It says I'm pregnant but I'm not. So, it's defective."

Nannette gave her an evil stare and started yelling, "Get my brother in here! This is not fair. Have sex right now, I mean it! Don't leave that room until you're pregnant!"

Lolli slammed her hand down on the counter in disgust. Claudine started walking around with her hand on her hips, huffing and puffing.

"Wait, wait, how ya know ya not?" Lorelle got up and walked closer to her twin to hear her clearly.

Delphine rolled her eyes and explained, "I know I ain't 'cuz it is not the plan. I have a couple more years and then we were gonna try.

Philippe' promised and he never breaks his promises to me. So, it's wrong. I ain't."

The room was still for three whole seconds right before loud cackling, hand clapping, and howling laughter came from everyone in the kitchen, except Delphine.

"I'm tellin' y'all it's wrong! I am not pregnant!"

While the tears and laughter continued from their reality and what she had said, Eleanor got up, walked over to her daughter, and said, "Child, that there talkin' fish I dreamed 'bout must've been ya tryin' to convince ya self ya ain't because ya is."

A wave of dizziness came over her. Quickly she sat down rubbing her forehead, saying, "But Momma, see we … we have a plan. It ain't da plan. It's not."

Snickering, Eleanor said, "Plans change, girl. Plans change."

A scheme was crafted by the women in the kitchen to seek revenge on the unsuspecting men. Recruiting the children to unknowingly execute their plan was the first phase. Pretending to prepare and play a water balloon toss, the children filled up a few buckets of water balloons.

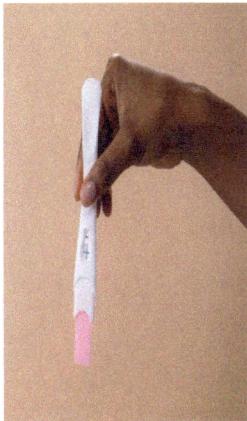

- ✓ Delphine stuck her pregnancy test inside a bottle of water.
- ✓ Lorelle set her test on a plate with a large sharp knife and covered it with a towel.
- ✓ Lolli put her pee stick test in a slice of chocolate cake instead of a fork.
- ✓ Claudine had her test in her pocket and carried a raw egg in her hand.
- ✓ Nannette put her test inside a hotdog bun on a plate with chips.

Hellene called for Carter to come help her with her mother. The three eased outside with the children as they placed the buckets of water balloons close enough to grab when the mothers gave them the signal. The women motioned and the children approached the seated chatting men. Seconds later Marcellus, Andreas, Philippe', Tony and

Cedric were blasted with several water balloons simultaneously. Lolli, Claudine, Delphine, Lorelle and Nannette, chuckled and snickered as their husbands were being soaked with water. Hellene, Carter, and Eleanor couldn't stop laughing as they sat a distance away to watch the show.

Laughter and screams resulted as the children ran away after soaking their unsuspecting fathers. The wives brought each of their husbands a towel and their hidden pregnancy tests.

Lorelle couldn't wait and stood in front of Cedric as he fussed about being wet, she handed him the plate. While he was lifting the towel off the plate, she broke a balloon filled with ice cold water over his head.

He yelled, "Rell!!" Waving the large knife around, she began shouting, "I told you we needed it done. Now look! How 'bout we fix you!" Cedric shot up wet and looked at the plate and said, "Aww, hell naw."

Drying off from the kids balloon spraying, Philippe', Tony, Andreas, and Marcellus, began chuckling at the yelling exchange between Cedric and Lorelle Ricard.

Marcellus got his surprise when he went to eat the piece of cake Lolli handed him. "Babe, I need a fork." He said inspecting the white and pink stick stuck in the frosting. "Lolli is … is this a joke?"

"Am I laughing? Are we on In Living Color? Marcellus, I told you to get off me! I told you not to fall asleep up in there! Damn it!" She yelled, peering at him. Lolli stomped away from the group, and he ran after her.

Although they could not be heard, Andreas shouted, "They look like two mimes having a serious dispute. Ha ha."

Nannette laughed, handing him the bread wrapped in a napkin. When Andreas saw his wife's test in the hotdog bun, he shouted, ""Oui! Oui! Notra numéro six!" Andreas jumped up cheering and kissed her. Nannette slugged him in the gut. As he groaned, holding his abdomen bending over, she kissed him laughing.

After holding the positive test handed to him by his wife, Tony paused glancing over at Claudine. With uncertainty in his tone, Tony stood up and asked, "Dene, uh, are you happy or upset?" Claudine leered at him saying, "What you think?" Tony sat back down and then mumbled, "I'm going to keep my excitement to myself. Andreas got punched." Claudine cracked the raw egg on top of his head. As the yoke oozed down his face, she stood smirking until he jumped up smearing his face over hers delivering soft kisses. "Stop Tony. I wanna be mad don't make me laugh." She said snickering.

Philippe' being surprised by the last fifteen minutes said, "Is everyone pregnant?" Smirking in disbelief he was still vigorously drying his hair. Delphine stood next to him and answered, "Not everyone. We … we have a plan." He winked at her putting the water bottle she handed him down on the table.

A drenched Philippe' didn't understand why all the men had gotten hit but laughing he asked, "Was this game to soak us after lunch? You ladies turned our children against us. Ha-ha!" Drying his face, he noticed she wasn't talking or laughing. Her face was like stone. "Why are you looking at me like that?" There was only silence with a cold stare from her. "Delphine, what?"

"I don't believe this!" She stormed off into the grass away from everyone and their private conversations and laughter.

Philippe' quickly caught up to her, slightly pulling her arm to stop. She snatched her arm away from him and kept walking. He cut in front of her and held her arms to stop.

"Hey. What is going on? Why are you upset, chérie?"

She exhaled. "Why do we have a plan? It is crazy, but they are all pregnant, Philippe'. I'm the one left out."

He embraced her for a few minutes then tenderly kissed her forehead. Philippe' cleared his throat and said, "What are the odds? This is a great moment to remember. I have got to write this down. Delphine, we have a while yet. Then we will try. I love you, sweetheart, please don't be upset. We will have a baby when we planned. Alright?"

She nodded. He said, "It doesn't seem everyone is happy." He clasped her hand, and they began walking back toward the lounge and extended deck by the house.

Philippe' kept talking, "It's obvious your sister isn't. That knife scared Cedric. Did you see his face. Lolli might beat Marcellus in the middle of the night, she has that look of don't go to sleep. Wait he did, that is how she got pregnant. Ha-ha-ha."

Delphine sat down next to Philippe' as he returned to his cushioned lounge chair. He reached over and grabbed the bottled water he had left on the table.

"Let me open that, you missed some wet spots." She said opening the bottle while he brushed the towel over his arms. Delphine handed him the bottle. As he prepared to take a sip, he lifted it to his lips. She stopped him when she placed her hand on his arm.

"Philippe' don't drink that."

"Huh? Why?" He paused confused.

"Because it has pee in it."

"What?!" His face scrunched inspecting the bottle. Holding it up closer, he saw the white pregnancy test stick inside with a giant blue plus sign. Philippe's eyes grew larger, and his head snapped toward her.

"Dell... is this one of theirs?"

Calmly, she answered, "It's mine."

"But we... I mean how? ... We take precautions."

She stood up and said sternly, "That was not my area of responsibility Philippe'! We agreed it was yours!" Huffing, Delphine walked across the lawn and back into the house from the deck. Philippe' followed his wife into the house, upstairs, past several rooms and finally into their bedroom closing the large French doors behind him. He took off his soaked polo shirt and moved to get a dry shirt from his dresser while thinking of something to say. But he had self-talking thoughts, *(Don't laugh ...Philippe' be serious. Ha-Ha! Okay, serious...ready, set, go!)*

With folded arms and a serious tone, Delphine confronted him before he could speak, "You … You wanted more sooner. Did you … Philippe' did you … did you do this on purpose?"

Dropping the dry shirt on a chair, he walked over to connect with her eyes and answer her, "Dell … I always. No … We agreed. When the twins were ten, we would try. That was our plan. I wouldn't change things. Not intentionally. You know I wouldn't." He tried not to laugh at the situation and her scrunched up face.

She slowly exhaled, while he held her hand and told her honestly, "Baby, I'm completely surprised. But … it's a good thing. It is." He smiled trying to coax her to happiness thinking, *(Aww, baby smile! How amazing is this! Everybody . . . Unbelievable. I gotta write this down! What a great blessing. She's not to upset. Surprised more than anything. She got me alone to talk it out. I know my wife. She won't laugh so don't crack a smile first or she'll be pissed.)*

"Philippe' we don't even know when this happened. This is so wrong. I don't want our child to be some fluke or a mistake." Her voice trembled when she spoke. His hands performed that calming sequence touch of stroke-stroke squeeze as he moved his head to lock onto her eyes. Contact.

"Uh … We … we could be very intentional right now."

She huffed with a "What?" Shaking her head, she continued, "Philippe' it doesn't count. I'm already pregnant."

"Well, I mean … I'm not going to tell the baby, are you?"

Snorting from amusement, Delphine began to giggle while he displayed his stretched-up eyebrows and fish lips. He darted to the wall and turned on the sound system to play the paused disc. Seconds later, the middle of a song from Jodeci's "Diary of a Mad Band" filled the air of their bedroom. Before she could say anything, he began unbuttoning her top. She shook her head exhaling when he got it off and began softly kissing her neck.

"Love … If we do this real slow, maybe we can make two. That would be awesome!" He gestured with excitement before continuing his focused task to remove her bra.

Shaking her head from his silliness, Delphine relaxed and didn't resist his undressing her further. But when she caught his eyes, she told him plainly, "Philippe' we … we have company. Family is here."

"Dell, did you forget? I have told you before, I don't like to share. So, no they cannot join us." He said while he freed her from her pretty peach bra.

Pushing his body away, she let out a boisterous laugh with the word, "Nasty!"

Smirking flirtatiously and admiring her partial nakedness, he said, "Mmmh, we're about to make a baby. I love you, my sweet wife."

"Yeah … I love you, too." Humming the beat of the next song that auto started, she pulled off her jean skirt. Then she opened a side low drawer next to her side of the bed and pulled out the leopard print locked box. Stating it sternly, Delphine commanded, "Philippe', hurry up and take your clothes off. You need to be punished for getting my pregnant!"

Chuckling, Philippe' shouted, "Wua, I love that you're French! Oui … Oui … Madame Delacroix. Hit me. Take my money … My house and my car …"

With quivering lips, Delphine desperately tried to hold in her giggles watching her husband frantically do as he was told, while performing those "Saturday Night Fever," hip thrusts dance moves and singing Jodeci's "Feenin" that had started playing.

Getting in the bed, she mumbled, "Freaky Frenchman," while entering numbers for the code protected lock box. Glancing up, he was walking toward her, singing like he was a member of the group.

A thought, *(Which ones?)* "Hmm..." Deciding quickly, she took out two small items. Then she instantly started snickering because of his puckered fish-lips and overly excited nodding for the punishment he would soon be receiving.

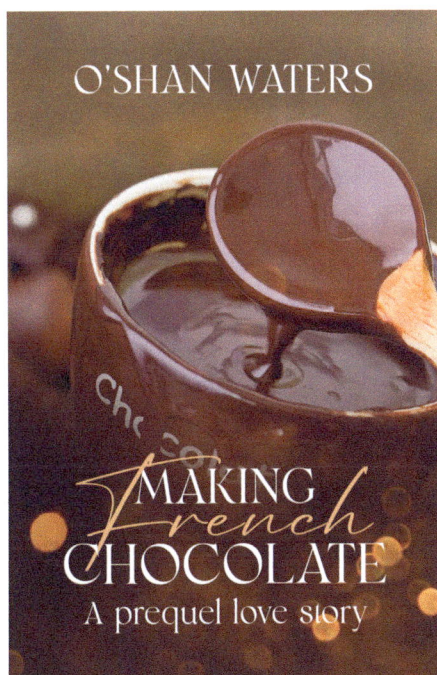

O'SHAN WATERS

MAKING
French
CHOCOLATE
A prequel love story

O'Shan Waters

O'Shan Waters is a Pacific Northwest native. She listened to some good friends and completed her first novel in the winter of 2021. It took only four months.

Her mega novel **Moments With You** was originally intended to be a standalone story. However, the compelling love story of Philippe' and Delphine grew like a wild fire in her mind, and she completed book two, **Making French Chocolate** a few months later.

All four books in **The Moments Collection series** came from O'Shan following the inspirational quote from Toni Morrison, *"If there's a book that you want to read, but it hasn't been written than you must write it."*

There is a gift to writing something in which the reader falls into the words like a deep plunge into clean warm ocean waters. Oh, look at that. Perhaps a little background for her pen name.

This amazing prequel is another story of true love that will shed new light on the complex beauty of the first story and open a reader's heart for the next.

www.oshanwaters.com